Praise for *M*

"I know of few other auth⸍   the
complicated relationship   and
domestic dysfunction. No matter   ⸍cial
context she's built, however, Walton's true strength lies in
creating characters you come to know intimately—and whose
lives you care about intensely, especially when they fall apart.
You may find yourself in tears by the end of *My Real Children,*
but you won't regret a single second you spend engrossed in
its pages."   —Annalee Newitz, *io9*

"Has as much in common with an Alice Munro story as it does
with, say, Philip K. Dick. Good novels show us a character's
destiny as an expression of who they fundamentally are. What
most novels do only once, *My Real Children* does twice."
                    —Lev Grossman, author of *The Magicians*

"Rendered with Walton's usual power and beauty, establish-
ing firmly that both Patricias are valid, fully realized women
with stories worth knowing . . . It's this haunting character
complexity that ultimately holds the reader captive to the
tale."   —N. K. Jemisin,
                            The New York Times Book Review

"Utterly brilliant. Superbly observed and incredibly moving,
this is the story of a split-second decision that literally splits
the seconds. . . . An astonishing novel that will stay with you
long after you close the covers."   —*The Independent* (U.K.)

BOOKS BY JO WALTON

My Real Children

JO WALTON

A Tom Doherty Associates Book

New York

MY REAL CHILDREN

Copyright © 2014 by Jo Walton

"Sonnet Against Entropy" copyright © 2003 by Patrick and Teresa Nielsen Hayden

Edited by Patrick Nielsen Hayden

A Tor Book
Published by Tom Doherty Associates, LLC
175 Fifth Avenue
New York, NY 10010

www.tor-forge.com

Tor® is a registered trademark of Tom Doherty Associates, LLC.

The Library of Congress has cataloged the hardcover edition as follows:

Walton, Jo.
    My real children / Jo Walton. — First edition.
        p. cm.
    "A Tom Doherty Associates book."
    ISBN 978-0-7653-3265-3 (hardcover)
    ISBN 978-1-4668-0079-3 (e-book)
    1. Women—Fiction.   I. Title.
    PR6073.A448M9 2014
    823'.914—dc23
                            2013029673

ISBN 978-0-7653-3268-4 (trade paperback)

Tor books may be purchased for educational, business, or promotional use. For information on bulk purchases, please contact the Macmillan Corporate and Premium Sales Department at 1-800-221-7945, extension 5442, or write to specialmarkets@macmillan.com.

First Edition: May 2014
First Trade Paperback Edition: May 2015

Printed in the United States of America

0 9 8 7 6 5 4 3 2 1

*This is for my friend Gill Goodridge,
who told me stories of her life
and kindly allowed me to use
some incidents in my story.*

Sonnet Against Entropy

The worm drives helically through the wood
And does not know the dust left in the bore
Once made the table integral and good;
And suddenly the crystal hits the floor.
Electrons find their paths in subtle ways,
A massless eddy in a trail of smoke;
The names of lovers, light of other days—
Perhaps you will not miss them. That's the joke.
The universe winds down. That's how it's made.
But memory is everything to lose;
Although some of the colors have to fade,
Do not believe you'll get the chance to choose.
Regret, by definition, comes too late;
Say what you mean. Bear witness. Iterate.

John M. Ford, October 13, 2003

1

VC: 2015

"Confused today," they wrote on her notes. "Confused. Less confused. Very confused." That last was written frequently, sometimes abbreviated by the nurses to just "VC," which made her smile, as if she were sufficiently confused to be given a medal for it. Her name was on the notes too—just her first name, Patricia, as if in old age she were demoted to childhood, and denied both the dignity of surname and title and the familiarity of the form of her name she preferred. The notes reminded her of a school report with the little boxes and fixed categories into which it was so difficult to express the real complexity of any situation. "Spelling atrocious." "Needs to pay attention." "Confused today." They seemed remote and Olympian and impossible to appeal. "But Miss!" the kids would say in more recent years. She would never have dared when she was in school, and neither would the obedient girls of her first years of teaching. "But Miss!" was a product of their growing confidence, trickle-down feminism, and she welcomed it even as it made her daily work harder. She wanted to say it now herself to the nurses who added to her notes: "But Miss! I'm only a little confused today!"

The notes hung clipped to the end of her bed. They listed her medication, the stuff for her heart she had been taking for years since the first attack. She was grateful that they remembered it for her now, the abrupt Latin syllables. She liked to check the notes from time to time, even though the staff discouraged it if they caught her at it. The notes had the date, which otherwise was hard to remember, and even the day of the week, which she so easily lost track of here, where all days were alike. She could even forget what time of year it was, going out so seldom, which she would have thought impossible. Not knowing the season really was a sign of severe confusion.

Sometimes, especially at first, she looked at the notes to see how confused she appeared to them, but often lately she forgot, and then forgot what she had forgotten to do among the constant morass of things she needed to keep track of and the endless muddle of notes reminding herself of what she had meant to do. She had found a list once that began "Make list." VC, the attendants would have written if they had seen it; but that was long before the dementia began, when she had been still quite young, although she had not thought so at the time. She had never felt older than those years when the children were small and so demanding of her attention. She had felt it a new lease on youth when they were grown and gone, and the constant drain on her time and caring was relieved. Not that she had ever stopped caring. Even now when she saw their faces, impossibly middle-aged, she felt that same burden of unconditional loving tugging at her, their needs and problems, and her inability to keep them safe and give them what they wanted.

It was when she thought of her children that she was most truly confused. Sometimes she knew with solid certainty that she had four children, and five more stillbirths: nine times giving birth in floods of blood and pain, and of those, four surviving. At other times she knew equally well that she had two children, both born by caesarean section late in her life after she had given up hope. Two children of her body, and another, a stepchild, dearest of them all. When any of them visited she knew them, knew how many of them there were, and the other knowledge felt like a dream. She couldn't understand how she could be so muddled. If she saw Philip she knew he was one of her three children, yet if she saw Cathy she knew she was one of her four children. She recognized them and felt that mother's ache. She was not yet as confused as her own mother had been at last when she had not known her, had wept and fled from her and accused her of terrible crimes. She knew that time would come, when her children and grandchildren would be strangers. She had watched her mother's decline and knew what lay ahead. In her constant struggle to keep track of her glasses and her hearing aid and her book it was this that she dreaded, the day when they came and she did not know them, when she would respond to Sammy politely as to a stranger, or worse, in horror as to an enemy.

She was glad for their sake that they didn't have to witness it every day, as she had done. She was glad they had found her this nursing home, even if it seemed to shift around her from day to day, abruptly thrusting out new wings or folding up on itself to make a wall where yesterday there had been a corridor. She knew there was a lift, and yet when the nurses told her that was nonsense she took the stairlift as docilely as she could. She remembered her mother struggling and fighting and insisting, and let it go. When the lift was there again she wanted to tell the nurse in triumph that she had been right, but it was a different nurse. And what was more likely, after all—that it was the dementia ("VC"), or that place kept changing? They were gentle and well-meaning, she wasn't going to ascribe their actions to malice as her mother had so easily ascribed everything. Still, if she was going to forget some things and remember others, why couldn't she forget the anguish of her mother's long degeneration and remember where she had put down her hearing aids?

Two of the nurses were taking her down to the podiatrist one day—she was so frail now that she needed one on each side to help her shuffle down the corridor. They stood waiting for the elusive lift, which appeared to be back in existence today. The wall by the lift was painted an institutional green, like many of the schools where she had taught. It was a color nobody chose for their home, but which any committee thought appropriate for a school or a hospital or a nursing home. Hanging on the wall was a reproduction of a painting, a field of poppies. It wasn't Monet as she had thought on earlier casual glances; it was one of the Second Impressionist school of the Seventies. "Pamela Corey," she said, remembering.

"No," the male nurse said, patronizing as ever. "It's David Hockney. Corey painted the picture of the ruins of Miami we have in the little day room."

"I taught her," she said.

"No, did you?" the female nurse asked. "Fancy having taught somebody famous like that, helped somebody become a real artist."

"I taught her English, not art," Pat said, as the lift came and they all three went in. "I do remember encouraging her to go on to the Royal Academy." Pamela Corey had been thin and passionate in the sixth form, and torn between Oxford and painting. She remembered talking to her about safe and unsafe choices, and what one might regret.

"Somebody famous," the female nurse repeated, breaking her train of thought.

"She wasn't famous then," Pat said. "Nobody is. You never know until too late. They're just people like everyone else. Anyone you know might become famous. Or not. You don't know which ones will make a difference or if any of them will. You might become famous yourself. You might change the world."

"Bit late for that now," the nurse said, laughing that little deprecating laugh that Pat always hated to hear other women use, the laugh that diminished possibilities.

"It's not too late. You'd be amazed how much I've done since I was your age, how much difference I've made. You can do whatever you want to, make yourself whatever you want to be."

The nurse recoiled a little from her vehemence. "Calm down now, Patricia," the male nurse said on her other side. "You're scaring poor Nasreen."

She grimaced. Men always diminished her that way, and what she had been saying had been important. She turned back to the female nurse, but they were out of the lift and in a corridor she'd never seen before, a corridor with heather-twill carpet, and though she had been sure they were going to the podiatrist it was an opthalmologist who was waiting in the sunny little room. *Confused,* she thought. Confused again, and maybe she really was scaring the nurses. Her mother had scared her. She hated to close herself back in the box of being a good girl, to appease, to smile, to let go of the fierce caring that had been so much a part of who she was. But she didn't want to terrify people either.

Later, back in her bedroom with a prescription for new reading glasses that the nurse had taken away safely, she tried to remember what she had been thinking about Pamela. Follow your heart, she had said, or perhaps follow your art. Of course Pamela hadn't been famous then, and there had been nothing to mark her as destined for fame. She'd been just another girl, one of the hundreds or thousands of girls she had taught. Towards the end there had been boys too, after they went comprehensive, but it was the girls she especially remembered.

Men had enough already; women were socialized not to put themselves first. She certainly had been. It was women who needed more of a hand making choices.

She had made choices. Thinking about that she felt the strange doubling, the contradictory memories, as if she had two histories that both led her to this point, this nursing home. She was confused, there was no question about that. She had lived a long life. They asked her how old she was and she said she was nearly ninety, because she couldn't remember whether she was eighty-eight or eighty-nine, and she couldn't remember if it was 2014 or 2015 either. She kept finding out and it kept slipping away. She was born in 1926, the year of the General Strike; she held on to that. That wasn't doubled. Her memories of childhood were solitary and fixed, clear and single as slides thrown on a screen. It must have happened later, whatever it was that caused it. At Oxford? After? There were no slides any more. Her grandchildren showed her photographs on their phones. They lived in a different world from the world where she had grown up.

A different world. She considered that for a moment. She had never cared for science fiction, though she had friends who did. She had read a children's book to the class once, Penelope Farmer's *Charlotte Sometimes,* about a girl in boarding school who woke up each day in a different time, forty years behind, changing places with another girl. She remembered they did each other's homework, which worked well enough except when it came to memorizing poetry. She had been forced to memorize just such reams of poetry by her mother, which had come in handy later. She was never at a loss for a quotation. She had probably been accepted into Oxford on her ability to quote, though of course it was the war, and the lack of young men had made it easier for women.

She had been to Oxford. Her memories there were not confusingly doubled. Tolkien had taught her Old English. She remembered him declaiming *Beowulf* at nine o'clock on a Monday morning, coming into the room and putting the book down with a bang and turning to them all: "Hwaet!" He hadn't been famous then, either. It was years before *The Lord of the Rings* and all the fuss. Later people had been so excited when she told them she had known him. You can never tell who's going to be famous. And at Oxford, as Margaret Drabble had written, everyone had the excitement of thinking they might be going to be someone famous. She had never imagined that she would be. But she had wondered about her friends, and certainly Mark. Poor Mark.

The indisputable fact was: she was confused. She lost track of her thoughts. She had difficulty remembering things. People told her things and she heard them and reacted and then forgot all about them. She had forgotten that Bethany had been signed by a record label. That she was just as delighted the second time Bethany told her didn't matter. Bethany had been crushed that she had forgotten. Worse, she had forgotten, unforgivably, that Jamie had been killed. She knew that Cathy was wounded that she could have forgotten, even though she had said that she wished she could forget herself. Cathy was so easily hurt, and she wouldn't have hurt her for anything, especially after such a loss, but she had, unthinkingly, because her brain wouldn't hold the memory. How much else had she forgotten and then not even remembered that she had forgotten?

Her brain couldn't be trusted. Now she imagined that she was living in two different realities, drifting between them; but it must be her brain that was at fault, like a computer with a virus that made some sectors inaccessible and others impossible to write to. That had been Rhodri's metaphor. Rhodri was one of the few people who would talk to her about her dementia as a problem, a problem with potential fixes and workarounds. She hadn't seen him for too long. Perhaps he was busy. Or perhaps she had been in the other world, the world where he didn't exist.

She picked up a book. She had given up on trying to read new books, though it broke her heart. She couldn't find where she had put them down and she couldn't remember what she had read so far. She could still re-read old books like old friends, though she knew that too would go; before the end her mother had forgotten how to read. For now, while she could, she read a lot of poetry, a lot of classics. Elizabeth Gaskell's *Cranford* came to her hand now, and she opened it at random to read about Miss Matty and her financial difficulties back in the time of King William. "The last gigot in England had been seen in Cranford, and seen without a smile."

After a while she let the book drop. It had grown dark outside, and she got up and tottered over to draw the curtains. She made her way carefully, hanging onto the bed and then the wall. They didn't like her to do it without the quad cane but she was safe enough, there wasn't room to fall. Though she had fallen once on her way to the toilet and forgotten that she had a button to call for help. The curtains were navy blue, although she was quite sure there had been a pale green blind the last time. She leaned on the window sill, looking out at the bare branches of a sycamore moving in the breeze. The moon was half-obscured by a thin veil of cloud. Where was this place? Up on the moor? Or was it somewhere along the canal? There might be birds in the branches in the morning. She must remember to come and look. She had her binoculars somewhere. She remembered insisting on holding on to them and Philip saying gently that she wouldn't have any use for them in the nursing home and Jinny saying in her gruff way that she might as well bring them if she wanted them. They must be here somewhere, unless that was in the other world. It would be very unfair if the binoculars were in one world and the tree were in the other.

If there were two worlds.

If there were two worlds, then what caused her to slide between them? They weren't two times as they were for Charlotte. It was the same year, whichever year it was. It was just that things were different, things that shouldn't have been different. She had four children, or three. There was a lift in the nursing home, or there was only a stairlift. She could remember things that couldn't simultaneously be true. She remembered Kennedy being assassinated and she remembered him declining to run again after the Cuban missile exchange. They couldn't both have happened, yet she remembered them both happening. Had she made a choice that could have gone two ways and thereafter had two lives? Two lives that both began in Twickenham in 1926 and both ended here in this nursing home in 2014 or 2015, whichever it was?

She shuffled back and looked at her notes, clipped to the end of the bed. It was February 5th 2015, and she was VC. That was definite, and good to know. She sat down but did not take up the book. It would be suppertime soon, she could hear the trolley moving down the corridor. They'd feed her and then it would be time for bed. This was the same whatever world she was in.

If she had made a choice—well, she knew she had. She could remember as clearly as she could remember anything. She had been in that little phone box in the corridor in The Pines and Mark had said that if she was going to marry him it would have to be now or never. And she had been startled and confused and had stood there in the smell of chalk and disinfectant and girls, and hesitated, and made the decision that changed everything in her life.

2

Adam: 1933

It was July 1933 and Patsy Cowan was seven years old and they were in Weymouth for two glorious weeks. There was a band in the bandstand, and sculptures of animals made of sand, and donkeys to ride and the sea to swim in, and they were building a sand pulpit for Mr. Price to preach from in the evening. She was wearing a brown cotton bathing suit, though most of the younger children and some of the other seven-year-olds still went bare. She could remember running bare when she had been a mere child, but she liked the bathing suit. Her fine brown hair was tied into bunches on both sides of her head, and when she shook her head hard she could make them slap her cheeks. She didn't do it though, because Oswald said it made her look stupid, shaking her head for nothing. Oswald was just ten, she envied his summer birthdays. He wore long striped swimming shorts, down to his knees, and he was beginning to tan already.

They had come down by the late train on Friday night and today was Sunday, only the second whole day of the holiday, with twelve more whole days to go. They wouldn't all twelve be this glorious, Patsy knew that. The sun couldn't shine all day every day even on holiday, there was bound to be at least one rainy day. But on a rainy day Dad would take them to the museum or to an interesting old church or castle, which might not be as wonderful as a day on the beach but it was still fun. There would also be one afternoon when Dad would take Oswald to see football—"Sorry old girl, this is a boys' afternoon out, just us men!" Dad would say, as he said every year. It did no good to argue that she loved football, or that if Oswald was going to have Dad to himself for an afternoon she should have the same. Dad had pointed out last year that she was having an afternoon with just Mum, and of course even then when she'd been only six she had known better than to complain.

They dug the pulpit with spades and with their hands. The spades had wooden handles and metal blades, and they were just like real spades except for the size. Hers was red and Oswald's was blue, and Mum said that if they lost them they needn't think they were getting any more. Mum was sitting reading on a deck chair she had paid for at the top of the beach, but Dad was right there with them, organizing all the church children building the pulpit. Patsy loved the feeling of sand between her toes and the way sand was so easily shaped and manipulated. She loved making a mark and rubbing it out. Sand was hot on top and cool underneath when you dug, and it was clean, it brushed off, or if it didn't you could easily wash it off if you went down to bathe. Sand wasn't like dirt at home. You could get as sandy as you liked and just run into the water and be all clean again.

Best of all was coming down to the beach early in the morning when the tide had washed away all the marks of the day before, and running on the hard-packed sand making footprints. The first morning Dad had brought them down, they had followed the tracks of a man and a dog, the little paw prints running in and out of the edge of the sea, until at last they caught up with them and saw that the dog was a white and black terrier and the man was just a man who said "Good morning" politely to Dad. But this morning coming down before church they had been the very first, and they had run across the great flat sand in the early morning light, "the lone and level sands stretch far away" as it said in the poem, with the waves lapping with little white edges and beyond them the sea stretching out even further away, stretching all the way to America. Dad walked along the edge of the sea looking for shells and seaweed, but the children ran barefoot and free. Patsy could run as fast as Oswald, even though he was two and a half years older. She could run faster than any of the other seven-year-olds. One day later in the week Dad would organize athletics on the beach, he had promised, and she would win, she knew she would. She could do a handstand every time and a cartwheel twice out of three times.

"This is going to be the best pulpit ever!" she said, digging enthusiastically. "Better than last year. And Mr. Price will give the best sermon ever and convert all the heathens!"

"That's right, old girl," Dad said. "But don't throw your sand out behind you without looking, you're getting it on people."

She looked around guiltily, but he was laughing, not angry, although her sand had spattered his legs. It was so nice to spend whole days with Dad like this. It only ever happened in the summer and perhaps for a day or two at Christmas. He worked so hard selling wirelesses and mending them for people. He went off on his bike before she was up in the morning and sometimes didn't come back until after she was in bed. On Sundays he didn't work, but he was usually so tired that Mum made her and Oswald tiptoe around after they came back from church. Sometimes he would rouse himself in the afternoon and take them out for a walk, or organize a ball game in the park. Then she would catch a glimpse of her summer father, the man who loved to play. He had the older children running down to the sea now with buckets, to bring water to wet the sand to shape it. Patsy dug more carefully.

"Why aren't you a minister, Dad, like Mr. Price?" she asked.

"God didn't call me that way," he replied, talking to her the way she liked, as if she were an equal.

"And He did call you to be a wireless installer?"

"Well, I learned about radio in the war, and so when I was demobbed it seemed like a good choice," he said.

That didn't seem as grand as God calling him. "Didn't God—" she began.

"Why do you want me to be a minister anyway, Miss Patsy?" Dad interrupted.

"Ministers only work on Sundays," she said. "You'd be home with us the rest of the time."

For a moment she was afraid from the look on Dad's face that she'd said something naughty, or worse, blasphemous. Her mother shut her in the cupboard when she said anything blasphemous, though she never meant to. She knew thoughts about God and ministers had the potential to get to danger-ous places. Then he threw back his head and laughed so much that all the other children laughed too, even though they hadn't been listening and didn't know what he was laughing about, and other groups on the beach, people they didn't know at all, turned their heads and looked at them. Patsy hadn't meant to be funny, but she was so relieved she had been funny by mis-take and not blasphemous by mistake that she laughed too, but hers wasn't a real laugh or the infectious hilarity of the other children.

"I must tell Mum that," Dad said. "How she'll laugh! I dare say she'd not like it if I was under her feet six days a week instead of only one!"

Oswald was back with a bucket almost full of sea water.

He must have been carrying it very carefully so as to avoid spilling. "Tell Mum what?" he asked.

"Patsy wants me to be a minister so I'll only have to work on Sundays!"

Oswald didn't laugh. "I'm not sure Mum would find that funny," he said.

"No, maybe you're right," Dad agreed.

"Patsy's not a baby any more. She should know that ministers work hard visiting the sick and . . . writing their sermons and . . ." it was clear that Oswald's imagination was at an end.

Dad laughed again. "It's all right old boy. I won't say anything to Mum. You're probably right that she wouldn't see the funny side."

"It's just that she wants us to be like Lady Leverside's children," Oswald said.

Dad pulled Patsy onto his lap and patted the sand for Oswald to sit next to him, which he did, setting down the heavy bucket. "She wants the best for you," he said. "For both of you. That's why she wants you to dress nicely and speak properly and all of that. Your Mum worked for Lady Leverside before we were married, and that's where she learned to take care of children. So that's how she knows how to make bathing costumes and recite poetry and all that. I didn't have the advantages you're getting. Your Gran didn't know any of the things you're having the chance to learn from your Mum."

Patsy smiled at the thought of comfortable old Gran reciting poetry. Gran cooked on the fire and made the best toffee in the world, but she wasn't a poetry sort of person somehow.

"But, while it's good that you have those advantages, this is very important, I want you to know that you're just as good as Lord Leverside's children, as good as any children in the world. You can do as much as they can, more. You can do better than them. You can go far and achieve great things."

"But they're honourable children," Patsy said. "The Honourable Letitia and the Honourable Ralph. We're not like them. Mum says we're not."

"She says she doesn't want us to be common," Oswald said.

"Like when you were playing football with the boys and you came home and said—" Patsy started eagerly, but Oswald punched her arm.

"It's not fair repeating tales," he said.

Dad looked at him reproachfully. "It's better than hitting a girl, and one three years younger than you. That's just the kind of thing I'm talking about, where you have the chance to learn better and you should take it."

"Sorry," Oswald said. "But honestly, Dad, she shouldn't repeat things like that."

"No, Patsy, your brother is right. If he said something he shouldn't and Mum punished him, then that should be the end of it."

"Sorry," Patsy said. "I didn't mean to sneak." She put out her hand to Oswald to shake, which he did.

"But coming back to the other thing," Dad said, "The fact that they're The Honourable and you're just Master and Miss means nothing. You're every bit as good as they are, and you can go as far as they can. When Adam delved and Eve span, who was then the gentleman?"

"Adam!" Patsy said, quickly before Oswald could answer such an easy riddle. "And Eve was the lady!"

Oswald laughed. "She doesn't understand, Dad."

"But you do, don't you? You know what I'm saying. Look at it this way, did Lady Leverside bring up her children herself? No, she chose your mother to do it. You're having the same upbringing they had."

One of the other children came to ask Dad a question about the pulpit and he got up to help. Patsy sat still, crinkling her toes and feeling the sand scrunch up under them. Lady Lever-side's children had seemed as far above her as the sun and the moon. Mum never said Patsy was better than they were at anything, never even as good. It was always "The Honourable Letitia would never have spoken with her mouth open . . ." or "forgotten her cushion . . ." or "come downstairs with her hair unbrushed." Patsy was used to thinking of them as para-gons. She considered Dad's view that she was as good as they were, and potentially even better. Yet she knew they had six of everything, all of the best, and if they grew out of any of their clothes they had more right away, ordered from John Lewis's. She and Oswald only had one set of best clothes at a time, and only two other sets of clothes, and they were forever out-growing them or tearing them. She tore hers climbing trees and Oswald tore his playing football or fighting with boys.

"When I'm thirteen they're going to send me away to school," Oswald said, plopping down on the sand beside her.

"Will they me?" Patsy was alarmed, even though thirteen seemed impossibly far away, almost the whole length of her lifetime.

"I don't think so, because it's really expensive and you're a girl," Oswald said. He wasn't looking at her, he was tracing a complicated design in the sand with his finger. "I think they'll send you to a day school."

"Why will they send you then?"

"Because of what Dad just said about getting on. Dad left school when he was fourteen and he's been sorry ever since. He wants me to be a gentleman, just the same as Mum does." He didn't look up, but he piled up the sand wildly over the pattern he had made.

"Like Adam," Patsy said, and for the second time didn't understand why she had made somebody laugh.

"But it's all such tosh," Oswald said. "I'd a hundred times

rather be brought up by Gran and get a job at fourteen than spend my life trying to ape something I'm not."

"Why don't you tell them so, then?"

"Oh come on Pats, you know there are things you can say and things you can't."

She did know. It seemed she had always known. She wanted to do something to comfort her brother, but there wasn't anything. Gran would have hugged him, but in their house hugging was discouraged. She put her hand out again for him to shake, and he shook it solemnly.

"Come on," he said.

"Where?" she asked, getting up at once expectantly.

"You'd come anywhere with me, wouldn't you, Pats?" Oswald smiled down at her. "I must go down to the sea again!"

"The lonely sea and the sky!" she shouted.

"Anything less lonely than the sea in Weymouth on a hot Sunday morning in July is difficult to imagine," Dad said.

Later, after a bathe where she had swum ten strokes without Dad holding on, she ran on rubbery legs up to Mum's deckchair. Mum was reading the paper and looking very serious, but she put it down when she saw them and got out the towels and their clothes so they could dress nicely for lunch. Mum had sewn brightly striped beach towels into little tents with elastic around their necks so that they could take their wet things off underneath and didn't have to go into the changing huts, which were smelly and besides cost money.

Dad dried his back with a big flat towel. "Patsy's really learning to swim," he said. "You should enroll her for lessons at the baths when we get back to Twickenham. It's easier to swim in the baths," he said over his shoulder to her. "There aren't any waves to smack you in the face."

"All right," Mum said. "If she'd like it. Oswald started going when he was about this age."

"Have you had a nice peaceful morning?"

"Lovely," Mum said, though how it could be lovely sitting still in a deckchair reading Patsy couldn't imagine.

"Is there any news in the paper?" Dad asked.

Mum tutted, which she did when she was going to report on something of which she disapproved. "It seems as if the Nazis in Germany have banned all the other political parties—made them illegal just like that. Theirs is the only party. Goodness knows how they think that's going to work when they have elections."

"I don't suppose they're planning to have elections," Dad said. "It looks to me as if that Herr Hitler intends to be Führer for life."

"And such horrible things," Mum said. Then she changed her tone completely and turned to Patsy. "Aren't you dry yet? They'll be laying out our lunch before we get back if you don't hurry. We don't want to make extra work for Mrs. Bonestell."

Oswald pulled off his towel, revealing his neat shirt and shorts underneath. "I wish we could have a picnic on the beach."

"Not on a Sunday," Mum said, reprovingly.

"We got the pulpit built," Dad said quickly. "Mr. Price will be able to get right up there and preach, and we can all sing hymns as loudly as we can. Patsy was saying he'd convert any heathen on the beach."

"I hope you built it in the right place this time," Mum said.

"We took proper notice of the tide," Dad said. "Don't worry, there won't be any of that King Canute preaching this year. Are you dressed under there yet, Patsy?"

Patsy had got her dress twisted up somehow so she couldn't find the hole for her right arm. Dad held the big towel up and Mum rapidly sorted her out. "Now let's go up and get some Sunday dinner," Dad said. "Lunch, I mean. Come on!"

Twelve and a half more days of holiday, Patsy thought, and

swimming lessons when she got home. Even if Oswald did have to go away to school it wasn't for three years, and even if the Germans were acting peculiar they were a long way away. Mum and Dad were smiling at each other and Oswald was carrying the bucket and both spades, and if they were lucky there might be tinned salmon and tomatoes for lunch.

3

Oystercatchers: 1939–1944

In the end it was the same as if she had been sent away to school, because she was thirteen in 1939 and her day school was evacuated. Patty spent the war years in safe but miserable deprivation in Carlisle. There was never enough of anything, until they grew used to it and did not expect there to be. The days before the war began to seem like a utopian dream. She learned Latin and French and how to do sums in pounds, shillings and pence, she learned long division and A. E. Housman. She did well academically. She made friends but no close friends. The comparative wartime poverty of them all highlighted rather than erased the class differences. She remained athletic but not good at team sports. She excelled in tennis and rowing and swimming, which gained her some popularity as she moved up the school.

In due course Oswald left his minor public school at seventeen, and went straight into the RAF, where he ended up in Bomber Command. He was killed in the autumn of 1943 flying a raid over Germany. Patty went home to Twickenham that Christmas, all heartiness and perpetual appetite, in the middle of a late growth spurt. She found her mother trying to be proud of her heroic son but succeeding only in being desolate. Her father looked ten years older. She knew she was no compensation to them for Oswald's loss, and did not try. Her own loss was constantly with her.

On Boxing Day she dragged her father out for a walk. "Come on, Dad, got to blow off the cobwebs!"

He was almost silent as they walked their familiar circuit, up through the park, where they had collected conkers every year, around the church and back down the hill, past the bushes where they always picked blackberries. The absence of Oswald was almost deafening. "How are you doing, old girl?" her father asked at last.

"Oh, you know," she said. "How about you, Dad?"

"I do miss that boy," he said, and his face crumpled up.

"And how's work?" she asked, embarrassed, desperate to change the subject.

"You know I can't talk about my war work!" he said.

It was the last time she saw him alive. He was killed a few months later by a direct hit from a V-1, on the day she took the Oxford entrance exams. She went up to Oxford for a visit and was awarded an Exhibition to St. Hilda's College, which would provide her with enough money to live on while she studied, without need for parental support. She called to see her mother on her way back to school, spending an uncomfortable night in her old room. There was very little for her to eat, and she had a long complicated train ride ahead of her. Her mother took the triumph of having been accepted and awarded the Exhibition entirely for granted. "They'll be taking more women because so many men are out because of the war," was all she said. After Patty's obligatory words on meeting, her father was not mentioned.

Going upstairs early to bed, clutching a hot water bottle for warmth in the cold spring, she quietly opened the door to Oswald's old room and found it stripped bare even of the furniture and carpets. Only the paler patches on the wallpaper where his photographs had hung showed that he had ever been there at all. In her own cold bed, where there was not enough light to read, she wondered how much of a mark Oswald had left on life. He had broken their parents' hearts, and helped her grow up. (Almost eighteen and newly accepted at St. Hilda's, she felt thoroughly grown up.) He had probably cheered his comrades in the RAF. She wondered if he had had a girlfriend. She had seen so little of him in the last few years, both of them away from home, and the war. And of course, though she didn't like to think of it, he had thoroughly changed the lives of the people whom he had bombed. She thought of factories destroyed that would not make bombs that would not kill people the way her father had been killed. She thought of planes damaged by Oswald's attacks so that raids took place later and killed different people, or didn't take place at all. She tried not to think of houses in Germany falling and crushing their inhabitants like the bombed-out houses she had seen in Twickenham and Oxford. Oswald had done his best, as her father had in two wars now, while she had done nothing. She had been a child, but the war was still on and she was proposing more study, not war work.

The train journey the next day was even more gruelling than she had expected. The main line north had been bombed and not yet mended, so the train crept around by branch lines, last in priority after troop trains and even goods trains. At Rugby an American soldier got on and tried to flirt with Patty, who had no idea how to respond and stood frozen until he apologized and said he had thought she was older than she was. She was about to have her eighteenth birthday. She knew other girls her age flirted and joked and were at ease with men.

At Lancaster, which should have been five hours from London but which had been eleven, the train came to a permanent halt. She stood on the platform of the Victorian station, part of a group of stranded travellers. "There's nothing going north tonight," the guard said. "Not unless you want to go around by the Cumbrian Coast line. There's a train just starting for Barrow, and it'll go on up that way. But you'd do better stopping the night here."

"Does it go to Carlisle?" somebody asked.

"Yes, all the way round the coast to Carlisle. It's slow like, but it gets there in the end."

Patty climbed into the little train which rattled along the rails. It was full of workers in overalls making for the Vickers yards at Barrow-in-Furness. One of them, a gray-haired man with a lined face, prodded his younger companion into giving Patty his seat. "Can't you see the young lady's tuckered out?"

Patty sat gratefully. "I am. I've been travelling all day."

"Where have you come from then?" the man asked.

"London."

"That's a step! What took you there?"

"I had an interview yesterday at an Oxford college, and I spent the night with my mother just outside London."

"Oxford!" The man was gratifyingly impressed. "An Oxford scholar! You must be a brainy one then."

Patty smiled. "They're taking more women because the men are off at the war. I've been wondering whether I should go even so, or whether I should be doing war work."

"If you have the chance to better yourself you should take it," he said, and though his manner was completely different he reminded her of her father. "I'm a fitter, and I've done as well for myself as I can. Now our Col who gave you his seat, he's a fitter too, but he's taking night classes and after the war he means to get on."

"Your son?" she asked.

"My nephew," he replied, and was silent a moment, then

changed the subject. "Now, where are you going tonight? Are you going to school?"

"Yes, back to my school. It's been evacuated to Carlisle."

"Carlisle! You won't get there tonight!" As if to emphasize his words the train slowed to a stop.

"The guard on the platform in Lancaster said this train went around the coast to Carlisle," Patty said.

"Well, so it does, but not until tomorrow. I don't know if we'll be in Barrow before midnight, but whenever we get there the train will stop there until the morning and go on to Carlisle then. Tom, what time does the train go out to Carlisle in the morning?"

The man addressed had a little rabbitty moustache. He pulled a booklet out of his pocket. "Ten oh eight," he said after a moment's perusal. "Why's that, Stan, what do you want with going to Carlisle?"

"It's not me, it's the young lady here. They told her in Lancaster she could get to Carlisle by this train, but it's not so is it?"

All the men looked at Patty, who blushed under their attention.

"Well, whatever they told her she won't get further than Barrow until ten oh eight tomorrow morning. You'd have done better to have stopped in Lancaster, lass," Tom said.

"Don't worry, you can stay with my Flo and me," Stan said reassuringly. "Flo will make you up a bed in no time and find something for your supper too, as I expect you're hungry."

"I'm always hungry," Patty said, sincerely, but all the men laughed.

She slept that night in a worker's cottage in Barrow-in-Furness. She woke early to the sound of seagulls calling. She had not known Barrow was by the sea. She opened the black-out cautiously and saw gray waves by the gray daylight. It was just before seven in the morning. She dressed quickly. The room was a boy's room with a carefully made hanging model of a Spitfire and framed amateur perspective drawings of birds. She wondered where that boy was, dead or away at the war? She remembered Stan's face when he had said that Col was his nephew. She went downstairs. Flo was in the kitchen already, making up the fire. "You're an early bird, Patty," she said. "Would you like a cup of tea?"

"You've been so kind, and I would like a cup of tea, but I just saw from my window that we're by the sea. I haven't seen the sea properly since before the war, and I thought I might just slip out quickly for a walk now, first, before I do anything." As she said it Patty thought she was being silly, but she remembered the clean-swept sand and the sound of the sea.

Flo looked skeptical. "It isn't the proper sea, just the bay, like. You need to go around to Morecambe for the proper sea with a bit of a beach and things to do."

"There wouldn't be anything to do at this time of the morning anyway. I just want to run down and see it."

"Well it's right there at the bottom of the street, for what it's worth," Flo said.

Patty pulled on her coat and went out. The wind was gusting and the sky was brightening a little. The cords of an empty flagpole were clapping repetitively, a solitary empty sound.

As Flo had said, there was no proper beach. The waterfront was just a narrow shelf of stones and broken shells where the waves were breaking. Out across the bay she could see the shadow of the other shore. It couldn't be more different from the blue sky and limitless horizon of Weymouth before the war. Yet still the waves ran in endlessly and comfortingly on the strand. In and back, each a little closer, breaking in a rush of spray, and then the sound of the shingle being sucked back, drowned as the next wave came forward, each wave different and each the same. The sea was as new as the morning, and yet the same sea as when she had been a child and Oswald and her father still alive, and the waves ran in and back as they had been doing all the time since she had last seen them.

Above the seagulls circled and called. Nobody else was down by the water. Patty felt herself taking deeper breaths. There were other birds at the edge of the waves, not seagulls, black and white birds with sharp beaks.

She crouched down. It was too cold to consider sitting on the pebbles. She did not throw a stone because she didn't want to hurt or frighten the birds. She watched them wading in the shallow water at the edge of the sea. It felt like a blessing being there and watching them. She remembered Mr. Price preaching from the pulpit they had built for him one of those summer Sundays, not the King Canute Sunday, and not the day her father had quoted "When Adam delved," some other ordinary holiday Sunday. "You can always bring your troubles to Jesus, and you can bring him your happiness too. Jesus is always there for you. Jesus loves you, loves *you,* in your griefs and your joys. God is your father, everybody's father. He loves you like a father. If you turn to him in your troubles, God can help."

In recent years she had grown away from the simple piety of her childhood. In school many of the girls mocked at the way the teachers hypocritically mouthed religious sentiments, and some of that slopped over into mocking Christianity itself. And the war had lasted such a long time, and taken so much from her. But the sea was still here, and just like it God was still here, waiting patiently, although she hadn't been paying attention. Jesus was there, and loved her, and the sea was there, endlessly going in and out. She had lost her earthly father and brother, but she still had her heavenly father. And of course they were not just gone, they were with God. In a sense she still had Dad and Oswald. She had the hope of seeing them again. Tears came to her eyes and she let them spill down her cheeks. There was nobody there but the sea and the seabirds. She felt as if she had been given a great gift.

Back in Stan and Flo's kitchen they had breakfast just ready: Cumberland sausage and fried bread and strong tea with milk and sugar. "We'd give you an egg if we could," Flo said.

"Sausage is more than enough. I know that's from your ration," Patty said.

"Sausage makes the meat go further," Flo said.

Stan said grace unselfconsciously, as he had the night before. Patty's "Amen" was less automatic and more heartfelt than it had been then, but nobody remarked on it.

"Did you find what you were looking for down by the sea, then?" Flo asked as she started to cut her sausage.

"More than I was looking for," Patty replied as soon as her mouth was empty.

"More?" Stan asked.

Patty couldn't speak.

"She said she hadn't seen the sea since before the war," Flo said.

"Reckon it might be a thing you could miss at that," Stan said.

"What are those black and white birds with pointed beaks that run along the edge of the water?" Patty asked.

"Why, those would be oystercatchers," Stan said after a moment's pause. "Do you like birds then?"

"I don't know much about them."

Stan got up and went to the bookshelves above the big wireless in the corner of the kitchen. He pulled down a big green book and flicked through it to a sketch of the bird she had seen. "One of those, like?"

"Yes, that's it!" she was delighted.

"Our Martin was very fond of birdwatching. It's a nice hobby for a boy. Doesn't cost much."

"I can see this would be a good place for it," she said. "And I'm sure my brother would have loved it, though Twickenham wouldn't be so good."

"You'd be surprised how many birds you can see in a suburb," Stan said.

"That's Martin's room you were sleeping in," Flo said. "He's in a Japanese prisoner-of-war camp. We don't hear from him half as often as we'd like."

"At least he's still alive," Patty said. "My brother—"

"There's no call to upset yourself," Flo said, and put a hand on her shoulder.

"No reason birdwatching wouldn't be a nice hobby for a girl too," Stan said. "I think we have a beginner book here that our Martin grew out of long ago." He pulled out another much slimmer book. "You take this, and that'll be a start."

"You've already been so kind," Patty said.

"Now I have to get off to work, but you'll find your way back to the station all right, won't you?" Stan said, finishing up his breakfast.

"I will. And I can never thank you enough for taking me in, and the book, and . . . and restoring my faith in human nature," Patty said.

"You think of us when you're an Oxford scholar," Stan said. "And we'll think of you. And when Martin comes home we'll tell him he had a girl in his bed when he was far away!"

4

Sculling: 1944–1946

When first Patty went up to Oxford she threw herself into the Christian Union and her newly rediscovered love of God. All her friends were drawn from Christian Union circles, which were happy to include her. Although she remained shy and awkward, for the first time in her life she felt she belonged. It was the autumn of 1944, the Education Act had been passed, and free and equal access to education for everybody was for the first time a reality. The invasion of Europe had begun in June with the Normandy landings, and although she was no longer so entirely riveted to the radio for news updates as things dragged out, it seemed finally possible to imagine that the war might one day be over. There was a spirit of optimism and the sense that a better world was coming. Meanwhile the petty daily inconveniences of the war ground on, with everything in short supply. Oxford was full of women and cripples—men injured in the war. Patty rowed both in the women's eights and alone. She went on outings organized by the Christian Union. She read Milton and struggled with Old English. She worked hard. Her essays got unspectacular but good marks.

VE Day came and Hitler died in his bunker, and although the war with Japan ground on, there was a sense that everyone was more than ready to be done with the whole thing and move on. Then in the summer the Americans dropped the atom bomb on Hiroshima. Patty heard the news on the old humming wireless in her mother's house, and shared the sense of relief everyone initially felt. She went back up to Oxford feeling a burden had been lifted, though rationing was worse than ever and new clothes were impossible to find even if you had the coupons. A few veterans were in that year's intake, and a few young men postponing conscription now that the war was over. There was an election, in which Patty could not vote, being under twenty-one, but in which she took a close interest. The Labour party under Attlee were elected with a massive majority, which she saw as a mandate for social justice and true equality for everyone, and rejoiced. In other ways, her second year was much like her first.

She acquired a boyfriend, an earnest young man called Ian Morris. He was a year younger than she was, one of the men who deferred his conscription to go to Oxford. He had not taken any part in the war, and it was hard to imagine him as a soldier. She found him profoundly unthreatening. The Christian Union might argue passionately over faith versus works or on the precise way to administer charity, but they were united on the subject of sex—they were against it. Rather, they professed to be for sex within marriage for the purposes of procreation, but for all of them that was for a distant future. Patty rarely thought about sex, and when she did she felt a vast apprehension and an equally vast ignorance. She knew almost nothing about it. Some men, and indeed some girls, she found sexually frightening. She felt safe with Ian. He occasionally put his arm around her shoulders when in company, never when they were alone. They agreed that they were "waiting." He did not press her. They danced together at Christian Union dances, and Patty pretended not to notice that she was taller than he was.

She had imperceptibly become aware that neither the Christian Union nor Oxford were as shining and perfect as she had initially thought them, and had become accustomed to making excuses for them in her mind when they fell short of what she felt they should be. She called this "being charitable." She easily began to exercise the same slightly brisk charity with Ian. He never came into her mind when she read the Metaphysical poets.

It was towards the end of the Trinity term of her second year that Patty fell out with the Christian Union.

There were two girls who lived on her staircase in St. Hilda's, Grace and Marjorie. Marjorie was in the Christian Union and as such was a friend of Patty's. Grace she knew mainly for her extreme shyness and nervousness. She was reading chemistry and was reputed to be brilliant, though how brilliance in chemistry manifested itself Patty had no idea. She had long pale hair and large breasts and tended to scuttle, clutching her books to her chest, darting sideways glances if addressed. The first Patty knew of the scandal was when it was whispered to her by Ronald.

"Have you heard about Marjorie?"

"Heard what about her?" Patty had stopped in at Bible tea on her way back from the river. She'd had a ducking and her hair was dripping down the back of her neck, which made her rather impatient. The Bible tea was a regular event held in the house of Mr. Collins, a minister attached to the Christian Union. A group of them would meet in his house for tea and then a Bible reading and discussion—they were working their way through the Acts of the Apostles, and Patty generally enjoyed it very much. She was early today, and nobody was there except Ronald, who had an artificial leg and was reading PPE. PPE, the dreaded Politics, Philosophy and Economics degree, often seemed to attract know-it-alls, in Patty's experience.

Ronald was one of the members of the Christian Union toward whom she found it most difficult to extend charity, though she had prayed to do better.

She cut herself a thick doorstep of bread and buttered it, then ladled on gooseberry jam. The gooseberries had been extremely plentiful that year, and they had all saved their sugar ration for the jam. Patty had put in a great deal of time stirring the jam in Mr. Collins's kitchen, so she felt entitled, as well as hungry. She felt that Ronald was observing her greed and that he would report on it unfavorably to others.

"She's a lesbian!" Ronald said, as if delighted to pass on the intelligence. Patty literally did not understand for a moment until he went on. "She's actually been caught sleeping in the same bed as another girl."

Patty knew about this kind of thing. It went on in girls' schools as it did in boys' schools, however hard the teachers tried to stamp it out. She was more repelled by Ronald's prurient delight in telling her about Marjorie than by what Marjorie was supposed to have done, which she could not clearly imagine.

"Mr. Collins has spoken to her and she refuses to give it up or repent," Ronald went on.

"It's probably all the most ridiculous nonsense," Patty said, stuffing her bread and jam into her mouth and speaking with her mouth full. In Patty's private opinion, Mr. Collins was too ready to be uncharitable and had it in for the women. "I'm going to talk to her."

"You're not!"

"I certainly am."

Patty strode off full of indignation, which carried her back to her residence and to the door of Marjorie's room. She hesitated before knocking, and then the memory of Marjorie's clear voiced declarations of her love of God sustained her. She knew Marjorie wouldn't have done anything wrong. She knocked.

"Who is it?" Marjorie asked.

"It's me, Patty," Patty said.

"What do you want?"

"Just to talk to you." Patty's courage was draining away. "It's not important. But Ronald told me the most frightful nonsense about you and I wanted to tell you I didn't believe it."

Marjorie opened the door. It was apparent that she had been crying. "Oh, it isn't true!"

"I knew it couldn't be."

Marjorie ushered Patty into her room, where she sat on the bed to allow Patty the chair. "Would you like—" Marjorie hesitated. "Well actually I haven't got anything except some cough sweets my sister sent me, but would you like one of those?"

"I'd love one," Patty said politely.

"The thing is, I have been sleeping in Grace's room," Marjorie said, once Patty had the cough sweet in her mouth.

"Grace!" Patty said.

"I know. But she has the room next to mine. And I could hear her crying in the night, and I couldn't just leave her to sob on and on. I went in to her. It turns out that she was blitzed and all her family killed. She was buried in the rubble for a day and a half. She can't bear to be alone in the dark, it brings it all back. Of course she can't keep a light on all the time, because they come around and check we're observing lights out, though she did try for a bit with flashlights except that she couldn't afford the batteries, and with candles she worried she was going to burn the place down. So I started sleeping in there with her, and she can get to sleep, and when she wakes up in the night I hold her hand. And that's really all there is to it."

"But that's just . . . just Christian kindness," Patty said.

"It is!" Marjorie said. "I'm so glad you understand. Mr. Collins didn't believe me. He insinuated the most awful things. And at first I slept on the floor, wrapped in my blankets you know, but in the winter when it was so cold I started to get into bed with her, and I suppose it looks bad, but I shared a bed with my sister at home until I came to Oxford and I didn't see that it was any different."

"Didn't you say that to Mr. Collins?"

"He wanted me to repent and be forgiven, but I haven't done anything wrong! And he wanted me to promise I'd never sleep in there again, and I couldn't, I just couldn't. Grace has the most terrible dreams. And he wanted to know why I hadn't told anybody."

"Why hadn't you? We could have taken turns."

Marjorie sighed. "It was because Grace begged me not to, she doesn't want anyone to know about her dreams and her family. You know what she's like. It was hard enough for her to tell me."

"If she had told the college they might have put her in one of the rooms with two beds so she'd have had somebody there," Patty said.

"She was in one of those last year, but you know how they make a thing of the single rooms. Virginia Woolf and all that. I hate to even have to explain to Mr. Collins and you now, but I have to defend myself. Grace must see that."

"I think you ought to explain to everyone in the Christian Union. Once they know they'll understand." Patty felt sure of it. "They're good people, they love God, they know you do, they'll understand you're doing it in Christian kindness and you need to go on doing it. And they'll keep quiet about Grace, and it's better than what they're thinking about her now!"

"Could we be sent down, do you know? I mean if people really believed Grace and I were lovers? If we really were?"

"Of course you couldn't. Think of the willowy men."

"I think it is illegal, though," Marjorie said, crushing her handkerchief in her fingers.

"It's nonsense for it to be illegal," Patty said briskly. "It may be immoral and unclean because it's outside marriage, but it shouldn't be illegal. That's nonsense."

Marjorie began to cry again.

"Look, come down now. Nobody was there for the Bible tea when I left except Ronald, but they'll all be there by now. Come down and clear it up, and have some tea."

Marjorie was reluctant but Patty persuaded her to come with her. Mr. Collins's house was nearby, and the whole group was gathered when the girls came in. An awkward silence fell. Ian looked at Patty in horror. Patty saw at once that there was no use waiting for somebody else to say anything. She had developed a technique for overcoming shyness where she took a deep breath and then shut her eyes for a second as she began to speak. She did this now.

"Marjorie wants to tell you it's all a mistake," she said.

"There's really nothing wrong at all," Marjorie said. She went on to explain, as she had to Patty.

To Patty's astonishment, although the members of the Christian Union listened they did not immediately see that Marjorie was telling the truth. She was caught wrong-footed because she had been so sure that they would react exactly as she had and see that it had been an act of Christian kindness. Instead they said nothing, until Marjorie stopped talking and then one of the girls said, "If you want to repent we'll take you back into fellowship, but until then it would be better if you left."

Marjorie ran out of the room weeping. Patty began to follow her, but as soon as she was outside Ian put his hand on her arm. She thought at first that he had followed for the same reason she had, to comfort Marjorie, but he paid no attention to her. "Stop, Patty," he said.

Patty stopped and turned to him. "Didn't you see that she's telling the truth?"

"It seems a really unlikely, contrived kind of story. And if it's true, why didn't she tell anyone before?"

"Because Grace didn't want everyone to know and feel sorry for her." This seemed like a very reasonable answer to Patty, but Ian smiled cynically.

"I hardly find it likely. She has done wrong and is lying about it."

"No. I don't believe that, and I can't see how you can."

"You're such an innocent," Ian said. "It's good of you to try to see the best in everyone. But you have to think how it looks."

"How it looks?" Patty was bemused.

"If you defend her people will assume that you're a lesbian too."

Patty felt hot all over as if she was coming down with a fever. She could hardly believe this was Ian saying this to her. He took her stunned silence for acquiescence. "Come on back in," he said. Instead she turned on her heel and walked away from him.

The Christian Union did try to reach out to Marjorie, begging her to repent in a way that strongly resembled bullying. They tried the same thing on Grace, who fled them, and who did not return to college the next year. Patty became lonely again. She worked hard and spent a great deal of time sculling alone on the river, where she still felt close to God.

5

The Epistles of Mark: 1946–1949

Patty's third year at Oxford began in the autumn of 1946 and ended in June of 1947. In that year she engaged in a passionate affair with English literature, falling in love successively with Robert Herrick, her old friend Andrew Marvell, Elizabeth Gaskell, and finally and most spectacularly with T. S. Eliot. She also joined societies for various social causes, feeling that if the churches were falling to petty bullying, the secular world should be doing what it could. Oxford has many churches, and in the Michaelmas term she and Marjorie tried them all out, a different one every Sunday. She discovered a deep love of choral music and auditioned for the Bach choir, where she sang happily for the rest of the year. She continued to row. The war was over, but rationing and deprivation continued and were harder to bear. These were the years when Orwell was writing *Nineteen Eighty-Four* and understanding the value of the two-minute hate. There was a great deal of grumbling, to which Patty tried not to add. The first months of 1947 were the coldest she had ever known, and the shortage of fuel for heating made everything worse. She suffered terribly from chilblains.

This was the year when she worked hard on overcoming her shyness. She made herself talk to people and found that she could. She found it worked best to treat everyone as equals, elderly dons and small children alike, and they mostly responded well. She tried hard to find something interesting about everyone—elderly housekeepers, women in shops, postmen. She usually found it, and began to make friends. Her chilblains were useful, everyone had them or had friends with them and had a suggested remedy. They cut across class barriers in a satisfying way. She tried to become outgoing. She made it a policy that if she was invited anywhere she would go. When the summer finally came, with finals looming, she cut her hair short because she was rowing and swimming every day and was tired of how long it took to dry. People told her she looked boyish in her flannels with short hair, but she knew she had never had any beauty to spoil.

In her last week at Oxford, with finals behind her but results not yet announced, she stopped in on a party in Jesus College. Cledwyn Jones, whose rooms they were, was a serious young man who cared about prison reform. There was beer at his party, which Patty declined; she had been brought up to shun alcohol, and besides she found it revoltingly bitter. She took lemonade and soon joined a conversation discussing the new National Health Service legislation. Wittgenstein was there, holding forth as usual. He was horribly drunk. Patty wondered how he ever had time to do any work at his official job in Cambridge when he seemed to spend all his time at parties in Oxford. She moved on and was introduced to a man called Mark Anston, who was in his first year. He was an inch or two taller than she was, but not especially good-looking. He was reading English, like her, but he seemed to be much more interested in philosophy. He also seemed very interested in her. She grabbed Cledwyn and asked about him. "Mark? Oh, he's brilliant. He's just got the highest marks anyone ever got in Mods or something like that. He's from the

Midlands somewhere. One of the stars." When at last she left, Mark offered to walk her home.

It was a beautiful evening, warm and starlit. They walked together back to St. Hilda's, talking, and then, as they had not finished talking, walked on past the college, on and on, up and down, crossing and criss-crossing Oxford, past the colleges, out along the river and back. His conversation went to her head. She had never heard anyone talk so well. It felt worthy of the architecture of Oxford in the moonlight. She did not always agree with him, but she found him fascinating. He seemed equally fascinated with her, which was in itself intoxicating. She found herself telling him about Stan and Flo and the moment on the beach in Barrow, which she had never told anyone.

"I haven't seen you at the Christian Union though?"

"I've more and more come to the conclusion that I can find God better alone, in nature and in the world. There's so much hypocrisy in organized religion. I was in the Christian Union, but there was this terrible incident last year when I realized that they were just bullying this poor girl because they believed—or wanted to believe—that she was a lesbian. They came and prayed outside her window, prayed that she would repent, when in fact she had done nothing wrong at all. I couldn't bear it."

Mark took her hand, and she felt as if all her nerves concentrated there where he was touching her and spread out through her body. She almost gasped. "They should be pitied and prayed for, not shamed like that," he said.

"Yes, exactly!"

"You've never felt pulled that way?"

She didn't understand what he meant for a minute. "Oh—no. Honestly, I've never felt very much that way for anyone. But neither did Marjorie. She was sharing a bed with the other girl because the other girl was afraid to sleep in the dark. That's all there was to it."

"You're a little innocent," Mark said, looking charmed.

"No, really, that's what happened. And the Christian Union—they're like sheep, and they're not sincere—or individually they may be, but acting all together like that and asserting that they know God's will, they're not."

"Women have a simpler faith," he said. "I've often remarked it. Men need the dogmas, the organization, the clearly marked paths, where women have intuition."

Although she had said that she felt closer to God alone, and although he was praising women, Patty did not feel entirely sure about this. "I sing in the Bach choir, and I certainly feel close to God there," she said.

Mark nodded. "As for the Christian Union, I belong, but I try not to let them stifle me. Wittgenstein says—"

"Are you a friend of his?"

"I have that honor." Mark spoke a little stiffly. Patty was impressed. "My father is a clergyman," Mark said, beginning again. "He always intended that I should follow him. But I believe I will stay here and become a don."

It was a noble ambition, and at that moment, outside the moonlit Bodleian, it seemed the most desirable thing in the world, never to have to leave Oxford. "How lucky you are," she said.

"I don't know how it is I didn't meet you until now," Mark said. "A whole year wasted. And you'll be going down soon. What are you going to do?"

"I'm going to teach at a girls' school near Penzance," Patty said. She had been so pleased and proud when she'd applied for the post and been awarded it.

"Cornwall!" He seemed utterly dismayed. "That's so far."

"We could write," she suggested timidly.

A clock struck eleven, and Patty froze. "I have to get in or I'll be in serious trouble." They walked swiftly towards St. Hilda's. Patty took one step up on the steps, but Mark did not release her hand.

"We must get engaged," he said. "But we can't marry for some considerable time. I have two more years here, and then a fellowship and a doctorate which would be another two or even three years, before I could possibly support you."

Patty stared at him in astonishment. "I want to say 'This is so sudden'!" she said. "We only just met!"

"Yes, but there's no question, is there? Except working things out. This was clearly God's plan for us. You go to Cornwall and we'll write, and we'll see each other when we can, and we'll marry in four or five years."

Mark was like a force of nature, and his belief in Providence swept her away. "All right," she said. She expected him to kiss her, but he did not, he just nodded as if things were as they should be and wished her a good night.

She barely slept at all. The next day he took her to a little jeweller's shop and after having her finger measured bought her an engagement ring. He did not ask her opinion, which she thought romantic. Her ring was a thin hoop of gold with a tiny chip of diamond, and it was clearly the best he could afford. She was moved by this, as she would not have been by a ring bought by a rich man. He did not seem quite so magical by daylight, but she did not regret her decision.

Two days later, she left Oxford with an Upper Second degree. She spent the summer in Twickenham with her mother, who found fault with everything except Mark, when he visited. She even extended a little grudging approval of Patty for attaching him.

Patty saw Mark only twice that summer. The first time was that one occasion where he came to dinner at Twickenham to meet her mother, and the other time was in the buffet at Bristol Temple Meads, when she was on her way to Cornwall and he was on his way back to Oxford from a walking tour with some philosophers in the Scottish Highlands. He was in strange spirits on that occasion and kept talking about resisting temptation. He kept shifting in his seat and couldn't relax, so that she was almost glad when her train was called and the hour was over.

She heard from him every week, however. He sent her long erudite letters, full of quotations from poets, full of passion and philosophy, conversations he had had and thoughts he wanted to share with her. It took her days to answer them, and she never felt she reached his level. Yet he poured out his heart to her on paper. His letters were the best she had ever seen—as good as Browning, she said to him. She had been bowled over by him on that night in Oxford, she truly fell in love with his letters.

She continued to receive them all that winter in Cornwall, another cold winter but not as cold as the year before, the first year of her teaching. Mark had sent her a green silk scarf for Christmas, and she wore it constantly against the Cornish winds. The Pines was a small school, exposed on top of a cliff. It was a fee-paying school, like the one she had attended, although only half the pupils boarded. It felt like regression after Oxford, being back to hockey matches and school reports and the smell of chalk. Oxford had continually stretched her mind; here she felt her horizons visibly shrinking. The girls did not much care for English literature, and she was working to a rigid curriculum set by the head of department. She was overwhelmed by their numbers and found it difficult to remember their names. She tried to keep up with the news and found it hard to care. India became independent, and Israel. They were both hot and far away.

She thought about leaving and taking a post at a grammar school where she would be teaching ordinary children. Mark argued against it, saying it wouldn't be worth it when it would only be for a year or two. She timidly suggested that perhaps she could find a post somewhat nearer. He said the separation was their trial, and was so eloquent about it that she wept. The weekly arrival of his letters was the brightest spot in her routine.

The next summer he took her to Nottingham and introduced her to his parents, who were cold and disapproving and said, separately, that they hoped she realized that Mark had no money and she had to wait. She did not tell them that she was earning money and he was not or that she had saved more than half her salary from that first year teaching. She said to Mark that his parents seemed to be Victorian leftovers. He did not laugh, but assured her that they would warm to her once she gave them grandchildren. She did not tell him how much they seemed to dislike her. She was very relieved when the week was over and she went back to Twickenham.

Marjorie got in touch and suggested that the two of them spend a week in France, camping and seeing the country. Patty counted her money and reluctantly declined, though she had never been out of Britain and longed to go. She did spend a week with her mother by the sea at Hastings, where the beach was made of rocks and roared when the tide came in, and there were concrete blockhouses to prevent invasion. Nobody seemed interested in removing the defenses that had been assembled so rapidly, and Patty wondered if they would be left to crumble. Her father had taken her to see crumbled castles. She wondered if future fathers would take children to see crumbled blockhouses. Bombsites, bright with purple fireweed in summer, were everywhere, modern ruins that she now passed almost without noticing.

Back in Penzance, Patty found her second year of teaching easier. The rest of the staff had relaxed a little and even made overtures of friendship, so she was less lonely. She had made some tactful curriculum suggestions that had been accepted, so she was less immured in Hardy than she had been the previous year. She began to take long walks along the cliffs and discovered accessible bays where she could swim entirely alone. "Smugglers' coves," one of the other mistresses said when she mentioned them. From seeing Cornwall as bleak and friendless she began to like it. She liked it when the sea swept up wildly at the base of the cliffs, and she liked it when the sea was calm and she could go down on the sand. She kept a wary eye on the tide, which she knew could easily cut her off, and made sure one of the other mistresses knew where she had gone and when she should be back. When it grew too cold to swim she continued to walk on the cliff tops, and even to go down to the edge of the sea and watch the waves. By the sea she always felt that God loved her and cared about her. She returned refreshed and ready to see the best in everyone.

She began to develop a brisk classroom manner to which the girls responded. She reminded herself that there was something interesting about everyone and began to find it in her pupils. A company of actors came to the school and put on *A Midsummer Night's Dream,* which was that year's set play for GCE. They were good, and she managed to use the visit to find some real enthusiasm in the girls, especially the girls in the lower forms who hadn't read the play beforehand. She petitioned for some gramophone records of Shakespeare, and the head of department agreed to consider it for the future.

All that year the highlight remained her weekly letters from Mark, the letters in which he felt so close. He was funny, passionate, fascinating—he told her everything and had suggestions about everything. When she told him, awkwardly, about feeling close to God by the sea, he expanded on the Romantic view of nature and then extended that to the created world. In person, when they managed to meet, at Christmas and Easter, he was awkward and seemed a little shy of her, but she told herself that when they were married it would be like the letters all the time. He addressed her as his "second self" and said that she would redeem him. She read them over and over until she knew them almost by heart.

At the end of the year on a day when she had been invigilating examinations all day and had forty-five papers to mark before the next morning, she was unexpectedly called to the telephone.

The telephone at The Pines had been installed in the Thirties, and stood in a corridor in a pine cabinet shaped much like a red post office telephone box. There was a modicum of privacy, but not much more—anyone walking down the corridor could hear you. It was not much used except in cases of emergency, and it had been installed largely for the benefit of anxious parents. Patty had called Mark once to tell him she couldn't meet him in Bristol because the school was under quarantine for mumps. They had not used it for communication. They had their letters. As she hurried along she knew what it must be—his results were due, his long-awaited First, and he must want to tell her in person.

She hardly recognized his voice at first, it sounded so harsh through the long distance line. "I have a Third," he said, in tones of tragedy.

She was astonished. "How could that happen?"

"I've not been working at English, I've been concentrating on philosophy instead. I assumed I'd just walk through. I always have before. My real work was with Wittgenstein, but that wasn't how they saw it."

"Of course it wasn't."

"What? What did you say?"

"I'm sorry. Can you—can Wittgenstein do anything?"

"Nobody can do anything for me now. My life is ruined."

"It's not as bad as that," Patty said.

"I won't get a fellowship. I'll have to become a schoolmaster. I'm calling to say I want to release you from our engagement now that I have no prospects." Hysteria rose in his tones.

"But that's ridiculous. I'll stand by you, you know I will. I'll wait as long as you like."

"I won't let you down, I promised to marry you, but you'll have to marry me now or never!" Mark said.

Patty felt faint, and the smell of chalk and cabbage and girls' sweat rose up around her. She did not want to be a burden to Mark, to marry him when he could not afford to start a family. As a married woman she would not be permitted to teach, and what else did an English degree qualify her to do? Besides, if they married, she'd soon have a baby, and she'd be unable to work. Yet she couldn't bear to give him up, to have his letters stop, for him to go out of her life.

"Oh Mark," she said. "If it's to be now or never then—"

6

What the Poetry Is About: Tricia 1949

". . . now."

It was two weeks before the end of term. At first Mark tried to insist that she come to Oxford right away, that day, that very moment. There wasn't a train, and Patty knew they couldn't be married for three weeks in any case. Mark reluctantly agreed that she could serve out the term while he took out a marriage license. Even as it was, Patty endured the withering scorn of the headmistress when she gave her notice—it sounded so absurd. Yet she couldn't continue teaching. Married women were not permitted to teach. Patty felt very much that she was letting The Pines down. She left the headmistress's room with a strong sense of burned bridges.

She marked her forty-five papers feeling she might as well be generous to the girls and give them marks for good intentions.

The rest of the term passed quickly. The other staff members gave her a leaving party, where she felt awkward and uncomfortable at their jokes. She did not hear from Mark during this time, neither by telephone, which she did not expect, nor by mail. She wrote and told him the train she would be taking but had no reply.

On the day before she left there was an envelope in her

pigeonhole and her heart rose, only to fall when she found it was a letter from Marjorie, inviting her to join her on a trip to Rome. She wrote back at once, explaining and inviting Marjorie to the wedding "which will be in Oxford next week, I'll let you know the details if there's any chance you can come."

It took all day to travel between Penzance and Oxford. There was a fine damp mist as she set off, and as the train rattled its way the length of Cornwall and then through Devon, she came to watery sunshine, and then once past Newton Abbott it unfolded into a beautiful day. She alternated between panic and exhilaration. She was to be married to Mark, and the clatter of the train seemed to sing this as a refrain "married to Mark, married to Mark."

She changed in Bristol Temple Meads and bought a pallid sausage roll at the station buffet which she could hardly eat despite her hunger. She was afraid—of Mark, who had been so strange on the telephone and so silent since, of the new life she was plunging into, of marriage, and most of all of her wedding night. Everything she knew about sex came from literature and now came back to her—Shakespeare's bawdy, *Roderick Random*, D. H. Lawrence, *Brave New World*. She wondered whether Malthusian belts existed in real life and where they could be obtained. Sex seemed to have an aura of the eighteenth century and the nineteen-twenties, of beauty patches and the Charleston. She stared out of the window at hay stooks in meadows as the train drew closer to Oxford, and thought of Andrew Marvell, painfully aware that she didn't know what to do in bed. "A hundred years would go to praise thy lips and on thy forehead gaze. A hundred thousand for each breast . . ." Her own breasts were small. Would Mark be disappointed? "Let us roll all our strength and all our sweetness up into one ball . . ." But what did it mean, literally? She would have shrunk from any conversation with her mother on the subject, but she wished she had a married friend who might have advised her. What would Mark expect? She took one of his old letters from her handbag and re-read it and was comforted. His tone was so confident, so definite, and after all it was to her that he chose to address these intimate reflections.

It was late afternoon by the time she disembarked at Oxford. Mark wasn't on the platform, and her heart sank. She telephoned him in his lodgings. He still sounded strange and distraught. "You came, then," he said. "I wasn't sure."

"You can trust me to do what I say I will do," she said.

He turned up at the station in half an hour, in a car borrowed from friends. He did not kiss her or embrace her as she had half hoped and half feared. He barely seemed to look her in the eye. She wondered if she had made a terrible mistake. "You're going to stay with the Burchells for the next few days until we can be married on Wednesday. It's extremely good of them and I hope you'll be grateful."

For a moment Patty resented his assumption that she needed to be told how to behave. Then she forgave him. He was under a strain, of course.

"Wednesday? I'll write to my mother."

"I suppose you have to."

"What church?"

"St. Thomas the Martyr, in Osney."

Elizabeth Burchell treated the entire thing as a joke. The only thing she took seriously was Mark's Third, which she saw as tragic. "We'll have to try to do something with him," she said briskly. She was several years older than Mark and Patty, a philosopher with published books. Patty knew her only slightly. Her husband, Clifford, was a Classicist at Magdalen. They had a small daughter who seemed perpetually grubby and tearful.

Over gray sausages and watery cabbage she returned to the

theme of Mark's failure and future. Clifford had apparently found Mark a teaching job at a boys' school in Grantham. "Until we can find something better," he said.

"You know how much I appreciate it," Mark said.

Patty would have appreciated being consulted as to where she would live, but she supposed there had hardly been time. The three of them clearly knew each other well and were well into making plans. Patty felt like a child, with her future being decided for her. This feeling intensified when after dinner Elizabeth, who had declined help, served watery coffee and stared at her over the cup. "You're not a bad little thing, but I positively can't call you Patty," she said. "It makes you sound like a little pie."

Patty looked to Mark for help, but he was laughing with the others and did not see it. "My full name is Patricia if you prefer that," Patty said, with what dignity she could manage.

"That sounds like a girl who rides to hounds," Elizabeth said.

Clifford snorted with laughter. "And it means a female member of the Roman upper classes. I can hardly imagine how it came to be a name at all."

"Tricia isn't so bad," Mark said, seeing her distress. "I think I'll call you Tricia. Would you like that?"

"Oh yes, much better," Elizabeth said, cutting off Patty. "And tomorrow we must find you something to wear. Do you have any coupons?"

Patty made herself a dress on Elizabeth's sewing machine, white cotton, short and very simple. She intended to dye it a more serviceable color later and wear it for a summer dress, but she resisted Elizabeth's suggestions of buying colored fabric. If there was white fabric available she intended to get married in white. It was the only part of the whole process where she managed to make her own decision stick. Mark, Clifford and Elizabeth had decided everything else. She spent most of her time in the Burchell house looking after the little girl, Rosemary.

"Children are a bore," Elizabeth said frankly, after she and Patty had bathed Rosemary and put her to bed one night. "You're not in the family way, are you?"

"No," Patty said, indignantly. She gathered her courage together. "I wanted to ask you about that."

"Oh yes, I am, about four months along and due in November if I've counted right," Elizabeth said. "You are a funny girl, making a mystery about that. I hope it's a boy this time."

Then she opened the door to the sitting room, where Clifford was reading, and Patty could not explain what she had really wanted to ask.

On her wedding morning she felt awkward in her wedding dress. She looked at herself critically in Elizabeth's huge Victorian mirror. There was something about the shape of the neck that didn't flatter her. But what did it matter anyway? She carried pink roses from the Burchells' garden bound together with a ribbon Rosemary had given her. She wore her tiny gold confirmation cross and remembered her father giving it to her.

Her mother came up from Twickenham for the occasion, wearing an enormous hat that Patty remembered from before the war. She looked ridiculous, but it made Patty feel terribly fond of her. She looked sharply at Patty's waistline but did not ask, as Elizabeth had, whether she was expecting. Patty tried not to mind the look. What was anyone to think, with them getting married at such speed? Clifford gave Patty away and Cledwyn Jones was best man. Mark's family did not attend. Marjorie, surprisingly, did.

St. Thomas the Martyr was High Church, and there was incense, as well as candles and splendid vestments. Patty did not mind them on that occasion and in the medieval building. She did find herself resenting the words of the marriage service, St. Paul's admonitions and her requirement to obey Mark. She promised meekly, and Mark Timothy Anston took Patricia Anne Cowan and they were pronounced man and wife in the sight of God and of the congregation.

Marjorie was the first to kiss Patty afterwards. "I'm on my way to Rome, but I've waited to wish you joy," she said. "I hope you'll be very happy." She didn't sound confident of it.

"Congratulations, Mrs. Anston," Elizabeth said.

"You congratulate the groom and felicitate the bride," Patty's mother said sharply. "Felicitations, Mrs. Anston, congratulations, Mark."

"Oh, of course, felicitations, Tricia," Elizabeth said.

Mark was looking over her head. Patty had been thinking that everything would be all right once they were actually married, that it would change everything. Once the ring was on her finger, she realized how idiotic that assumption had been, how it was magical thinking, and how Mark would despise her for it.

They had very little money, but the Burchells had insisted they spend their first night in a hotel—and from what Mark said, Patty assumed that they had paid for it. The Oriel Guest House was right in the middle of Oxford but had little else to be said in its favor. It had threadbare carpets and a pervasive smell of overcooked vegetables. They ate dinner together, awkwardly, talking about the wedding. She felt disloyal laughing with Mark at her mother's hat, but it had been so absurd. "Mothers are supposed to dream about their daughters' weddings."

"This one can't have been what she dreamed."

"She would have dreamed my father and my brother there," Patty said.

Mark looked at her for what felt like the first time since she had come to Oxford, and put his hand on hers. "I'm so sorry they couldn't be there for you, Tricia," he said.

She realized he had been calling her Tricia ever since Elizabeth suggested it, and that he really liked it, preferred it to Patty. She thought of protesting, but it seemed such a terrible time, when he was actually paying attention to her and being kind. Anyway, what did it matter, she was changing her surname, she might as well go the whole hog and change her first name too. It was part of her name, anyway, always had been. And maybe Elizabeth was right; perhaps it was a more sophisticated name, more appropriate for her new life. Perhaps as Tricia she would be armored a little against whatever was going to happen upstairs.

Mark ordered two hot baths, first for her and then for him. She had bathed that morning at the Burchells', but did not protest. She took off the wedding dress and bathed again, thinking that when next she bathed she would be a woman. Then she shivered in their room. She owned two nightdresses, one red flannel and one striped blue and white cotton, which she had chosen as being newer and more summery. It was July and should not have been cold. The hotel room seemed to be all drafts.

It was not a large room. It had a double bed with a scratchy brown blanket, a rickety chest of drawers, a table by the window, and one overstuffed horsehair armchair. The blackout had been taken off the windows and replaced with limp chintz curtains. Mark's brown leather suitcase stood open next to her tweed grip, bursting with alien male clothes. On the wall there was a Doré etching of the damned in Dante's *Inferno*. She had brought nothing to read, and had nothing to do while she waited but stare at it, thinking of Sayers's translation of Dante and then of Sayers's *Gaudy Night*, which extolled the virtues of female intellectual work and yet ended with a kiss. Then there was that remark in *Busman's Honeymoon* about shabby tigers . . .

Mark came in from his bath, wearing a brown wool dressing gown with his hairy legs visible beneath it. He was carrying a wine bottle and two glasses.

"I don't drink," Tricia said, shocked. "You know I don't. You don't either."

"Clifford says it's essential," Mark said. "Have a glass of wine. It's medicinal. It will relax you."

She obediently drank down the red wine, which tasted like altar wine and made her feel as if she were blaspheming by drinking it at such a time. She did not feel at all relaxed. She tried to imagine Mark asking Clifford what to do. She had not imagined Mark's previous experience, just assumed that of course men had some. But perhaps he had not? She felt fonder of him and less in awe. Mark drank his wine with an equal grim determination, then gathered up the glasses and set them on the table by the window. He drew the curtains and turned out the lights, making the room gloomy rather than completely dark. "Mark, I—" she began.

"Don't talk," he said, desperately. "Get into bed and don't talk."

It was done in the dark and in silence, as if it were something shameful. She could not relax, and he fumbled and battered away at her, with what she knew must be his male member, but which felt so strange. She had imagined it would be rigid like a truncheon, but it was evidently not. She would have liked to have touched it. She had seen Oswald's and other little children's when they had played on the beach. When she tried to put her hand out to it Mark pushed her away and then turned his back on her and seemed to be furiously whipping away at it, or at something. He had bound her to silence and she dared not inquire. He turned back and lay on top of her again, battering away between her legs again, clearly trying to force a way inside. She tried to keep completely still to help. At last he managed it—she bit her lip to stop herself whimpering, but it was no good, as the battering went on and on she could not stop herself crying or later from begging him to stop. There was no dignity left to her. This couldn't be it, the thing all the poetry was about, this painful bestial thrusting? At last he climbed off her and got out of bed, leaving her to cry alone in the dark.

"Mark?" she asked.

"I'm sorry," he said. "I'm sorry. Be quiet. I'm sorry." She saw by the streetlight through the curtains that he had wrapped himself in the blanket and was settling himself into the chair. She thought she should sleep, but she was burning between her legs and desperately needed to relieve herself. She got up and made her way to the toilet. There was blood on her thighs and in her pubic hair, no worse than she might have from the first day of a period, but stickier. No matter how she wiped herself she couldn't seem to get clean. She ran cold water into the basin and washed as best she could. She wished Mark had ordered her bath for afterwards instead of before. She tried not to think about it, about him. She should have asked Elizabeth, even if Elizabeth would have laughed. But what good would knowing have done her? No wonder they kept it so secret when it was so unpleasant. She washed herself over and over with cold water until the door to the bathroom rattled and an unpleasant male cough came from outside. Then she checked for any signs she might have left, and made her way up the stairs to their room.

Mark was fast asleep in the chair. She got into bed under the thin sheet, bitterly cold. She would have appreciated the blanket, if not her husband's presence. She hugged herself to try to get warm. She feared she had made a terrible mistake, but thought again of Mark's letters, all that love and devotion. He needed her. He really did, however he appeared. He was snoring a little. She would be a good wife to him, and mother to his children. She knew he wanted children, they had talked about it in their letters. Even if she had to go through *that* to get them. Perhaps she would grow accustomed to it, though she couldn't imagine how.

"And tear our pleasures with rough strife, through the iron gates of life," she thought. Plenty of tearing, and plenty of rough strife, but where were the pleasures? Andrew Marvell had a lot to answer for.

7

Heartbreak: Patty 1949–1951

"...Never!"

Patty was sorry the second she had spoken, but Mark seemed almost relieved that she had decided to relinquish him. She stood in the little phone box for a moment after she had put the receiver down, trying to feel noble but wanting to cry. She made it back to her room before the tears spilled out of her eyes. She locked the door and flung herself down on her old patchwork quilt to sob. She wanted to re-read his letters but could remember them quite well enough. For the last two years he had been the focus of her life, and before that she had hardly been more than a child. She could hardly bear to resign herself to a future that had no Mark in it, coloring everything with his beautiful words and ideas. She forced herself with grim determination through her forty-five exam papers, feeling she was being unfair to the girls and pointing out every childish mistake. As soon as they were done she cried herself to sleep and woke to a misty Cornish morning and at once knew herself bereft.

It reminded her of hearing that Oswald had died, and she was immediately furious at the comparison. Mark was lost to her, but not dead. She had given him up because it would be better for him. They could still be friends, perhaps. He had said so on the telephone, but his voice had been falsely hearty. She was shocked at herself for comparing it to losing Oswald. It made her feel cheapened. All the same, she had the same lump in her throat getting dressed and going down to the classroom.

It was two weeks to the end of term. She wrapped up her engagement ring and sent it back to him with a note that took her hours to write. When she took it to the post office she found herself reluctant to let go of the parcel. It felt like her last link with Mark. She flung herself into her work, the examinations and final marking. She volunteered to take the girls for walks, and took long cliff walks alone. She could not help compulsively checking her pigeonhole for mail, even though she knew he would never write again, not even to acknowledge the return of the ring. She had renounced him for his own good, but how could he possibly forgive her? She could hardly forgive herself. On the day before term ended she saw an envelope waiting and felt her heart race, only to be dashed as she saw the handwriting. It was a letter from Marjorie, inviting her to go with her to Rome. She read it twice. This thin future was what she had instead of the rich future with Mark. She would never have love or marriage, never have children. She would take holidays with female friends and live for her work.

She replied to Marjorie and said she would go. She had plenty of savings, after all, now that she was not intending to marry. She had never been out of Britain. She might as well see the world. If she was to live without Mark, it would be good to get away from places where Mark had been. She could be miserable in Rome just as well as in Twickenham. She wrote to her mother telling her of her changed plans, and felt a sense of relief when that letter was posted.

She met Marjorie in London. "I don't know that I have the right clothes for Italy," she said.

"Nobody will care," Marjorie said.

"Italy . . ." she said.

"It's not like going to Germany," Marjorie said decisively.

On the boat from Dover Patty thought the gulls sounded different from the gulls in England, greedier, with a different accent. She wondered if they really were different. For the first time in a long time she remembered her book of birds that Stan and Flo had given her. She wondered if their son Martin had come home from the war, and if he had been very changed.

They took trains down through France and across the Alps. Patty found herself enchanted with everything—the long baguettes, the strong-tasting cheeses and patés, even the citron pressé, so different from English lemonade. Both of them had schoolgirl French, neither of them could make themselves understood, but it didn't seem to matter. Once they were in Italy they could get by with Latin—written Italian was absurdly easy, and Italians seemed happy to go out of their way to try to understand. Of course the men wouldn't leave them alone, but there were two of them, and Marjorie was good at getting rid of them, sometimes by appealing to the old women in black who always seemed to be around.

There was a lot of bomb damage, just like at home, and there was hot sunshine and wonderful simple food, which was very different. Patty ate pasta that was not macaroni, ate porcini mushrooms, ate pancetta and fresh mozzarella and pesto and delicious tiny zucchini. There were few tourists, even in Rome. They stayed in a cheap *pensione*, sharing a room, and saw all the ancient sites. Patty was amazed at how layered Rome was—modern ruins side by side with ancient ruins, a restaurant serving delicious Italian *pizza*, flatbread with toppings and cheese, in the old temple of Pompey, Renaissance and medieval buildings made from Roman bricks and marble. Even when she saw Mussolini's name on a museum on the Palatine

Hill, it was easy to forget that these friendly people had so recently been enemies, had been fascists, trying to kill them all.

In the Pantheon Patty looked up at the circle of blue sky at the center of the dome and saw three birds wheeling left to right across it. She knew that would have meant something to Agrippa and the Romans who had built this building. Augury. She did not know what it augured, but she felt it was something good. The clutter down below, the graves of modern kings and even the artist Raphael, seemed irrelevant to this purity of form, the grave splendor of the dome, the pillars, the circle through which the eye was drawn up to heaven, to God. She wept, and understood that she did not weep for herself. She knelt and prayed for help, opening her heart to Jesus as her father had taught her.

After that she began to heal from her heartbreak over Mark and to reconcile herself to life without him, as she had hoped. On the journey home she told Marjorie that she was no longer engaged, and Marjorie nodded sympathetically and did not ask more. They had a last continental meal in Calais, pooling the last of their francs. Currency controls had prevented them from taking much money out of England. They shared a citron pressé, taking alternate sips. "Let's do this again next year," Marjorie said.

Patty spent the rest of the summer with her mother, and returned to Penzance at the start of the new school year. It was another lonely year in which the absence of letters felt like a physical ache. She wrote to Mark once in care of his parents, asking how he was and saying that she was well, but she received no reply.

The Pines was so remote that it was hard for her to engage with life and avoid brooding. She threw herself into long walks, school activities and teaching, but all the things that had annoyed her about The Pines before seemed harder than ever now. Even the institutional food seemed unbearable now that she had tried something better. She tried to write poetry but was too severe a critic to continue what felt like an indulgence. She began to watch birds and try to identify them and to keep a "life list" as the book suggested, recording each species she saw that was new to her. She joined the RSPB and enjoyed their earnest publications. She bought binoculars and took them with her on her long walks along the cliffs. She decided to leave The Pines and move to somewhere with more life. She gave notice at Easter. She applied for and was given a position for the following year at a girls' grammar school in Cambridge.

That summer, the summer of 1950, she went again to Italy with Marjorie, this time to Florence. There she fell completely in love with Renaissance art. She spent days alone in the Uffizi— one day was enough for Marjorie. Nobody bothered her when she stood in front of Botticelli's *Madonna of the Magnificat*, or Raphael's portraits of popes. There, in the gallery that had named the very concept of galleries, for the first time she saw man-made beauty that was as beautiful as the beauties of the natural world. She was unsophisticated in her tastes. Botticelli's *Primavera* and *Birth of Venus* kept her spellbound for hours. Looking at portraits, she wanted to know the people in them. She bought books on art, on Florentine history. After seeing his *Ganymede* she bought Cellini's autobiography in a cheap paperback translation with black and white photographs. She bought a book on Italian birds. Marjorie went home and she stayed on alone, visiting all the churches mentioned in her guidebook. She began to imagine a possibility of a life where she taught all year and spent her summers in sunlight with beautiful art. It was months since she had taken out Mark's letters to cry over them. She could almost speak Italian, which in Florence was like sung Latin anyway.

She sat alone in restaurants, eating pasta and refusing wine. Men looked at her lecherously and occasionally tried to touch her, but Marjorie's technique of appealing to old black-clad ladies continued to work. She spent her days looking at art and architecture, and eating gelato and drinking granita in a little place she had found near the church of Orsanmichele, called "Perche No!" Gelato was not ice cream but pure essence of frozen fruit, with flavors she could not have imagined—watermelon, lemon, strawberry. She thought she would never eat ice cream again. She sat eating it and staring at Verrocchio's statue of Doubting Thomas poking at Christ's wound in a niche outside the church. That was the Christian way to deal with doubt: open yourself up to being poked at. Not shut it in a cupboard, as her mother had done when her childish inquiries about religion crossed some invisible and unpredictable line.

All her life she had had inferior things, ersatz things, ice cream instead of gelato, prints instead of paintings, rationed tasteless British institutional food instead of delicious Italian food. Only nature and music and poetry had really touched her soul in England in the way that everything did here. They had brought her closer to God, but in Florence everything did, every stone in the narrow streets, every metal sconce on the houses, the golden roof on the Baptistery, the proportions of the church of San Lorenzo, the taste of melon and prosciutto, everything. It was as if she had been lifted up through that circle of sky in the dome of the Pantheon and was in heaven. She found that she was crying into her gelato.

At last, Patty ran out of money and had to go home. She spent the last of her lira on a print of Ghirlandaio's *Last Supper* and went back hungry across Europe on the slow trains, third class. Early one morning, somewhere in France, an old lady shared her coffee and croissants with her. "I don't know why British people don't understand food," she said, knowing nobody would understand her. "I never had food in my life until I came to Europe." An old man in a Panama hat laughed, and translated her remarks to the others.

"At least you have food now," he said, wiping his moustache. He then proceeded to tell her about his adventures in the Resistance until she had to change trains in Paris.

In Cambridge she was much happier than she had been in Cornwall. There was music, which she had always loved, and there was the Fitzwilliam museum, which could not compare to the Uffizi but was better than nothing. There were student plays and orchestras. She joined two choirs, one sacred and one secular, and enjoyed singing challenging music. She also had the opportunity to row regularly, which she discovered to her surprise that she had missed very much. She went rowing alone early every morning that the weather made it remotely possible. Often she had the river to herself, with no sound but her oars and the wind in the trees. She began to watch birds more seriously, continuing to enjoy the RSPB's pamphlets but also attending their meetings. She took the train to Ely one Saturday to see the cathedral and watch birds on the marshes.

The grammar school was excellent and she liked her colleagues. She was no longer the most junior, and the head of department was open to her suggestions for curriculum improvements. The girls were hard-working and keen to improve themselves. She liked the fact that they were from ordinary backgrounds, and that in the new Britain they had every opportunity to go as far as their talent could take them. "As good as any children in the world," she remembered her father saying, and now she understood what he had meant and told them. She taught Shakespeare and poetry and showed

them pictures in her art book, which made her look forward
to visiting Italy again. She read everything she could find on
Florentine history and the Renaissance.

That winter, the winter of 1951, Marjorie wrote to her saying that she was going to a meeting in Cambridge and asking if
she could stay the night. Patty asked her landlady's permission
and then wrote back cheerfully. She liked her digs. Rationing
was finally over, and though food in Britain could still not
compare to food in France or Italy, it was not as bad as it had
been. Her landlady managed to get chicken for Marjorie's visit.

"What's the meeting?" Patty asked her friend.

"Oh, it's a silly thing really. There's a group of people trying to get people to know their rights. Homosexuals, you know."
Marjorie looked embarrassed. "Somebody knew what happened to me and they asked me to speak at the meeting in
Oxford, and I did. What happened to me and Grace—and we
hadn't even done anything! Imagine if we had. People don't
know what's legal and what isn't and what the law can do
and what the colleges can do. Then they asked me to speak at
this meeting in Cambridge. I wouldn't have been able to except for staying with you, so thank you for that."

"I think I'll come too," Patty said.

"Oh really? You wouldn't want people thinking—I mean,
teaching, being with girls?"

"That's exactly the problem, isn't it? But I don't think anyone would think that, or even know. So many people are homosexual, and everyone knows, but it's still illegal and they
can get into trouble for it if anyone wants to make trouble. It
shouldn't be that way."

The meeting was well attended. Marjorie spoke well. The
other speaker was a man who explained that the best policy
was to keep quiet. "We all know what happened to Wilde,
and that is still the law. But as long as we don't give anybody

incontrovertible evidence and keep on denying any allegations, it's very hard for the police to move against us. It's not as if people want to know. If we're quiet, we're safe."

An undergraduate stood up and asked if the meeting thought it would be possible for homosexuality to be legalized in their lifetimes, and there was much debate.

A tall stooping man came up to Patty and Marjorie afterwards. "I liked what you said," he said. "I hadn't really realized before that there was this kind of problem. What happened to your friend was really unfair."

"Thank you," Marjorie said. When he had gone she turned to Patty. "Who was that?"

"Some crazily brilliant mathematician, I think," Patty said. "I've seen him around. He goes to concerts. Turner, or something like that. No, Turing. He's not a don. I'm not sure what he does."

A week or so later, as the pussywillows were just beginning to come out on the banks of the Cam, Patty met one of the girls who had been at the meeting as she was coming back from rowing. The girl had short hair as Patty still did. "Hello," she said. "I recognize you from the meeting."

Patty felt her heart beating unaccountably fast. "Hello. I've been on the river."

"I'm just going on the river," the girl said. "It's such a good way to start the day."

"Even at this time of year," Patty agreed.

"Would you like to row together sometime? Maybe on Saturday?"

Patty hesitated. "I would. But you should know that I'm not a lesbian. Not a . . . a homosexual. I was just at the meeting because I think the way they treat you is wrong."

The girl laughed. "We usually do say lesbian. But it's not a requirement to row with me," she said.

"I just didn't want to be on false pretenses," Patty said, stiffly.

"Understood," the girl said. "Well if you'd care to meet me here this time on Saturday morning, I'd still be happy to row with you. My name's Lorna Matthews."

"Patty Cowan," Patty said, and they shook hands.

Lorna and Patty began to row together weekly, and Lorna would sometimes invite Patty to parties, and she would sometimes go. She felt she was developing a wider circle, a more bohemian circle, and she liked the idea. She began to make other friends too, in school and in choir. Her contract was renewed for the next year and she looked forward to coming back to Cambridge after the long vacation.

That year Marjorie went to the south of France and Patty went back to Florence alone. She stayed in a tiny *pensione* and did all the things she had done the year before. Some of the waiters recognized her, as did the staff at the gelateria "Perche No!" where she felt almost like a regular. As she walked into the Raphael room at the Uffizi she felt a great sense of homecoming, as if this could really be her life and that it could be good, a life without love but with work and friendship and summers in Italy. She still missed Mark, she was sure she would always miss him, but she had passed beyond his horizon and felt capable again of being happy.

8

Blood: Tricia 1950–1952

Nine months and two days after the wedding, on March 15th 1950, Tricia gave birth to a ten pound baby son in Grantham General Hospital. They had previously agreed on a name for a boy, Douglas Oswald—Douglas after Mark's father, not after General MacArthur, who later that summer made headlines in the war in Korea. She looked at the thin threads of pale hair on little Doug's scalp as he lay sleeping in the cot beside her bed, and felt a rush of love so strong that she almost thought she would be physically sick with it. This made everything worthwhile, she thought, putting out a finger to touch his cheek. He opened his dark blue eyes at her touch, then began to cry. She picked him up and he soothed at once, looking at her with what she felt sure was curiosity. "You're like a miracle," she said to him. "You're wonderful. You're amazing. You're mine."

She had been sick a great deal throughout the pregnancy, and she had found keeping house difficult. Before her marriage Tricia had spent ten years living in institutions, schools and colleges, and before that she had been a child. It did not help that they had so little money. Mark's teaching job was not well paid, and her own savings, which had after all been intended for marriage, quickly vanished into furnishing their little house. The house was not in Grantham but in a little village outside it. There was a shop and a church and a post office but nothing else. It was an hour's walk to Grantham, or there was a bus that ran every two hours. Mark had a car, but she could not drive and he used it to go to work every day, leaving her stranded at home. He would drive her to Grantham on a Saturday to use the library and to shop, but he regarded it as a chore and a favor he did for her.

Mark, it turned out, had extremely firm ideas of what to expect in a wife. He wanted her to wash clothes and keep the house clean and provide food, to bear children and not complain. Tricia had very little idea of cooking, even when she was sufficiently well to eat herself. Her mother had given her Mrs. Beeton, which became her bible in keeping house. There were lots of mistakes at first, at which she ceased to laugh once she realized Mark did not find them at all funny.

Coal was delivered, but it was a constant struggle to light fires, essential all year round as they provided hot water as well as heating. Mark would carry in coal from the shed, but otherwise he regarded the whole thing as Tricia's department, raking out the old coals and laying and setting the fire. It was challenging, but he was sarcastic if she could not manage it and he came home to find the fire out. On several occasions in the first months before she got the trick of it she resorted to begging her next-door neighbor for help.

There was a gas stove, on which she cooked, or more often burned, dinner. All washing had to be done by hand, put through the mangle to wring out water, then dried on the line in the garden, or in front of the fire if it rained. It rained a lot in flat Lincolnshire. Tricia could not have afforded domestic help even if there had been any available, but there was not. In 1950 in the newly democratic Britain where there were opportunities for everyone, nobody wanted to be a servant. Tricia struggled with everything and did her best. Mark came in tired mentally and physically from a day's teaching and said he was perplexed at how little she had achieved in the home.

He would not talk to her about teaching, and refused to see that her experience there was in any way parallel. "Spoilt girls in a private school, what do you know about it?" he asked. The boys in Grantham gave him a great deal of disciplinary trouble. He was also trying to write a book, a treatise on philosophy. He shut himself up in his room after dinner on most nights to work on it. He refused to discuss it with her, though he expected her to type his handwritten chapters on his heavy typewriter, though she could type no better than he could. He would tell her what a word was if she couldn't make out his handwriting, even spell it out if it were some obscure German technical term, but he would never tell her what it meant. He laughed at her ignorance, as he would not laugh at the domestic failures where she would have been able to laugh too.

Whenever Mark was especially harsh and sarcastic, or when he seemed to treat her like a bad servant, she would turn to his old letters to remind herself that he did love her really, however he behaved. She did not do it too often, but it unfailingly worked. Even a few lines from one of the letters would reassure her, would fill her with renewed confidence to keep going at her drudgery. He might not seem to appreciate her, but he had written these things to her, had opened his heart. He might do so again one day when things were better, when he was over his disappointment, if she tried hard enough. She tried hard to love him. Sometimes he would accept her love and unfold and be friendly towards her. Other times she felt that he was judging her for not loving him enough.

Mark had not paid her any more conjugal visits after their wedding night. Their house had three bedrooms, and they had arranged without any discussion that they would have one each. Mark's was officially his "study" but he inevitably slept there. She did not enter it except to clean it, change the sheets on his bed, and put away his clean clothes. She never entered it when he was home.

In their first weeks in the house she had quickly discovered that she had become immediately pregnant, and she imagined that this would confirm everyone's prejudices about her hasty wedding. The memory of her wedding night came back as she was giving birth, which also hurt and stretched her and took her to that place without shame where she cried out in pain and anguish and terror.

Her mother came to stay after Doug was born and was immensely helpful in showing Tricia how to care for a new-born. She had also made him many tiny clothes, to supplement those Tricia had made. She brought Tricia her sewing machine. "You'll need it more than I will now." Tricia was touched; she remembered her mother teaching her to sew and how to make clothes when she and Oswald had been children. Caring for small children was her mother's one real skill, and Tricia was glad to be able to learn it from her. They became close for the first time since Tricia was herself a small child, united in their love for Doug, or "Douglas Oswald" as her mother always called him.

There was room in the cottage, as Doug slept in Tricia's room for now. Tricia's mother lived alone and was lonely in Twickenham. There was no reason why she should not have stayed on indefinitely, helping out in their newfound close-ness. But Mark grew impatient with his mother-in-law. Tricia realized that he was jealous of both her mother and the baby. She persuaded her mother to go back to her own house.

Despite the fashion for using formula and bottles, Tricia chose to feed Doug herself. She liked doing it, liked the animal closeness, liked feeling she was providing for him from her own resources. She even liked the tug of his lips on her breast and the feeling of relief as the fullness was drained.

Rationing was finally over, and at last she could buy all the milk and eggs she wanted. She continued to cook chops and vegetables for Mark's dinners, but she ate little herself; mostly milk and eggs and fruit.

When Doug was nine months old, Mark came home with a bottle of wine. "We want more children," he said.

"We do," Tricia agreed, her heart sinking. It was not the birth she dreaded but the conception. She put Doug to bed in the third room and that night, after a bath, she heard Mark tap on her door. The process of their wedding night was repeated—the wine, the jabbing, the awkwardness, the whimpering and pleading, the muttered apology. This time was better because Mark had his own room to go back to and she had hot water to wash herself with. She did not become pregnant, and the process was repeated twice more in the following months before there were results.

Tricia loved being a mother and loved Doug beyond reason, but she had been very unwell in her first pregnancy and now found herself even more unwell and with a toddler to deal with. Doug was a year old, crawling, beginning to talk, totally demanding of his mother's attention. Tricia was constantly queasy and easily exhausted. She miscarried in August 1951, in her fifth month, waking in the night to a tide of blood which terrified her. Mark left Doug with a neighbor and called an ambulance. In the hospital they could not help her until she had expelled the fetus, for fear of being considered accomplices to abortion. She felt sure she was dying, and demanded to see Mark to make him promise to have her mother bring up Doug. Of course Mark was not there. She wrote him an incoherent bloodstained letter, which she destroyed the next morning. She survived, but had to be given a transfusion.

Two days later, back at home, she fainted when alone with Doug, but fortunately he was strapped into his high chair and did not come to any harm.

Two months later, in October, Mark brought home a bottle of wine once more. Nothing was said, but she heard his footsteps approach her door with dread. "Please, no," she said when he came in.

"It is our duty to God," Mark replied. "We don't want too big a gap."

His book was finished and sent off to a press. They heard nothing for some time. Tricia was pregnant again. Doug was eighteen months old and more demanding than ever.

Seven months into this pregnancy, at the end of the academic year of 1952 and with nothing heard about the book, Mark snapped at her when she asked about it. Tricia was nauseated and tired. She had entertained Doug all day and made a meal for Mark. "Why will you never talk to me about it?" she asked. "You used to talk about philosophy in your letters. I'm not stupid, you know."

"Oh, you throw that in my face now, do you?" Mark spluttered.

"What?" Tricia asked, genuinely confused.

"My Third, when you had an Upper Second. It doesn't make you better than me or cleverer than me."

"I never thought it did!" Tricia protested. "The thought never crossed my mind. Mark, you're clearly brilliant and the Third was a fluke. Everyone knows it. Elizabeth said so."

"You shouldn't discuss me with Elizabeth Burchell," he said, but he seemed mollified.

"You're a brilliant original thinker," she said. "I'm nowhere in your league."

"Well as long as you know that," he said, leaning forward to stir the fire.

"I do. And the parts of the book I could understand really showed your brilliance. I wish I could have understood more of it so that we could talk about it. I could help you in more ways than just typing it. You know we used to discuss these things. In your letters—"

"I wish I'd never written you those letters," Mark said. "You constantly bring them up in this way and throw them in my face. I believe you care more about them than you do about me. What did I say in them anyway? I can hardly remember them. Go and get them."

Tricia could not believe that he really couldn't remember them, but she made her ungainly way upstairs to retrieve them from the drawer where she kept them. She took off the ribbon which she used to tie them, a pink ribbon given her by little Rosemary Burchell on her wedding morning. She didn't want him to scoff at her sentimentality. She did feel sentimental about them. They were the best part of Mark, so fluent, so passionate, so beautifully expressed.

Going downstairs with the letters under her arm, two years' worth of letters, in careful chronology, she began to believe that they would melt his heart. They were the real Mark, she knew that. Surely seeing them again he would remember how he loved her, over all the everyday irritations of living together and being married, and Doug crying in the night and the fire smoking and dinner being burned or undercooked again.

He took the bundle from her without remark and drew one letter out from the center of the pile at random. He read a few lines, and she saw his face relax into a half smile. Then he looked up and saw her, there in front of him, her distorted belly making her stand awkwardly. "No, I should never have written these things to you," he said, and thrust the whole bundle of letters into the heart of the fire.

Tricia stood gaping as the papers blackened and then caught

flame and flared up. For a moment she couldn't believe what he'd done, then she was weeping, on her hands and knees scrabbling at the fire with the poker trying to rescue any fragment she could. Mark watched her, bemused.

"They shouldn't have meant that much to you," he said, pulling her away from the fire. "Come on now, you'll hurt yourself. You'll hurt the baby."

"I can never forgive you for this," she said.

She looked at him, this terrible smug man she had bound herself to, Doug's father and the father of her unborn child, her only financial support. He did not love her, he never had. She had loved him, but he had destroyed her love. He had burned her letters and she hated him for it.

9

Delight: Pat 1952–1957

When she came back from Italy after the summer of 1952, Patty moved out of her digs and took a small furnished flat. She delighted in having her own kitchen and bathroom, as well as a sitting room and tiny bedroom. It was the ground floor of a Victorian house on Mill Road, within walking distance of school and the town center. She sent her washing out to a laundry, but she cleaned for herself and began to learn to cook, trying to re-create Italian food with inadequate British ingredients. She had parties, bringing together her friends from the different spheres of her life—boating friends, birding friends, choir friends, fellow teachers, Lorna and her friends from the homosexual community. To her surprise, after initial awkwardness they always seemed to mix well. Her parties were popular and people began to ask when she would have another. One of her work colleagues mentioned that she admired Patty for knowing such an interesting range of people.

She had a party for the Coronation which filled the flat and spilled over onto the stairs. She had bought a television for the occasion, but she was so busy talking to her friends and providing snacks that she hardly watched it. Late at night Lorna and Jim, an old man from the RSPB, helped her clear up. "A new Elizabethan age," Jim said, skeptically.

"At least rationing is over," Patty said, scraping a plate.

"Who knows what we're heading for," Lorna said. "But it's nice to have a queen instead of a king. A young woman instead of an old man."

"He wasn't old," Jim protested. "Middle aged. Young to die. The strain of being king killed him."

"It's still nice to have a new young queen, though," Patty said.

They all murmured assent. The figure of the queen had been tiny in the small screen of the television, but unexpectedly moving when she made her vows and was crowned. "She doesn't make any real difference, but it does seem like moving into a new era," Patty went on.

Over those years Patty imperceptibly became Pat. It began with the birders and spread from there through the parties, eventually coming back to the staff room. It was a more grown-up form of her name, and she had never really cared for Patty, which had been her name at boarding school. Her mother still called her Patsy, her childhood name. She went to her mother's at Twickenham dutifully for Christmas, and occasionally for a day or so at the end of the summer. She and her mother were formal with each other. They had one spat when her mother asked wistfully about her marriage plans. Pat felt she had put all that behind her.

She began to work on a guidebook to Florence, aimed at British people going there for the first time without any background in the history or art, the way she had. She sent it to Constable, who to her astonishment accepted it immediately, and with hardly any revision. It was published in the spring of 1955, and her editor asked her if she would write a similar book about Venice.

She thought about using the advance for the book to buy a flat in Cambridge, a flat like the flat she rented, but which would be her own. It wasn't sufficient, of course, it would have covered perhaps half of what she needed. She approached the bank about a mortgage, and was informed that they did not lend to single women. A building society told her that they did lend to single women over thirty who had had accounts with them for at least five years. She was twenty-seven, so she opened a savings account with them. Then, the next summer, in Venice doing research for her guidebook, she looked at house prices and realized that she had enough to buy a house there. She felt drunk on the idea, even after she remembered currency controls made it impossible. She went around daydreaming about houses she could have afforded if she could have taken her money out of Britain. At that time the maximum that could be taken abroad was twenty-five pounds, which was barely enough to live on for a month.

She worked on the Venice book in Italy and back at home. Pat felt life was going smoothly for her, until she fell unexpectedly in love.

Bee was just finishing a Ph.D. in biology. She was two years younger than Pat. They met in choir, and what first drew Pat was Bee's soaring voice. She befriended her, invited her to parties, and discovered that Bee had original and fascinating ideas. They became close and spent a great deal of time together. It took Pat much longer than it should have to realize that it was something more than simple friendship. It was the summer that made her realize. She was in Italy as usual, in Venice putting the finishing touches on her book, and then in Florence, which increasingly felt as much like home as Cambridge did. But that summer for the first time since she had first seen it, Italy wasn't enough. She missed Bee. She wanted to show everything to her, and know how Bee felt about it. Sitting below Cellini's *Perseus*, watching the sky darken above the Palazzo Vecchio and wanting to share it with Bee, she realized with a shock that this was love.

It was a very different love from the love she had had for Mark. There she had felt Mark was far above her, but also that he had chosen her. She had felt privileged to be the object of his choice. With Bee it was all different; she was the one who had chosen. Pat sat staring at the windows of the Palazzo, one of which had been Machiavelli's office. They reflected the darkening sky and were now a luminous twilight blue against the pale stone. Pat had never considered being a lesbian herself, had never thought about it personally. It was her sense of injustice that had led her to take up Marjorie's cause, and then go to the meeting with her. She wasn't sure if what she felt for Bee was even physical. She was, at thirty, still very naive and entirely lacking in sexual confidence. She had no idea what Bee felt, except that she knew Bee admired her, as she admired Bee. It would probably be best never to say anything about anything else, when she wasn't sure. There was so much else in the world that was so beautiful, and their friendship was a wonderful thing. She felt glad to have identified what she felt, even if she could never talk about it. Perhaps next year Bee would agree to let her show her Florence. Meanwhile the windows and the sky darkened together, and Pat felt happy because the world had Bee in it.

Bee met her on the station platform on her return to Cambridge. "You shouldn't have come all the way out here!" Pat said as they hugged each other.

"I have bought a car," Bee said, proudly. "You don't need to drag all the way into town on the bus when you're tired and I can drive you."

"A car!"

"Yes, and taken lessons and passed my test."

"You told me about that in your letters, but not about buying a car." Pat felt shy with Bee, knowing that she loved her, especially as Bee had taken her heavy bag and was swinging it as they walked along the platform. She looked sideways at Bee's square face and slightly stooped shoulders, unable to suppress a grin.

"What are you smiling at?"

"I'm just so pleased to see you," Pat said, honestly. "It's so lovely to be met."

"It's easy with a car. And I needed one. I've got the fellowship. So I'll be going out to the countryside all the time to research, and a car seemed like a sensible investment. It's second hand, but it runs. And now you can learn to drive too." Bee was bubbling with enthusiasm.

"You've got the fellowship?" Pat's grin spread even wider.

"Yes, it just came through." Bee looked a little self-conscious.

"That's marvellous. After all we've talked about with women in science, it really is a triumph that you should have got it." Bee smiled.

"There's a Botticelli painting in Florence where the Virgin Mary has exactly that smile," Pat said, before she could stop herself.

"I feel just as smug about the fellowship as she did about her baby," Bee said.

Every weekend that autumn Bee took Pat out for a driving lesson. Together they explored the countryside around Cambridge. They watched birds, and Bee showed Pat the patterns of hedgerow growth she was studying. Pat never said anything about what she felt for Bee, though now she was quite sure she did want to touch her. She asked Lorna in strict confidence what it was that women did, and was surprised and enlightened by the answer.

Then, at the end of October, Britain, France and Israel invaded Egypt to take back the Suez Canal. Cambridge was full of anti-war protesters, Bee and Pat among them. There was a march through the town center, with chants and banners. The two of them went back to Pat's flat afterwards, chilled by the wind and the events. "Let's get the news," Pat said. They huddled together on the sofa drinking tea. As the newsreader appeared and tapped his papers together, Bee said, "He knows already. He's read what he's going to read us, and we don't know yet." There wasn't any real new news, except that the Russians had invaded Hungary to crush the protests there. "And what can we say? We're as bad as they are," Pat said.

Then Bee turned and clung to her, and Pat hugged her back, and they were kissing. "Are you sure," she said, when they drew breath. "Are you sure this is what you want?"

"If it's what you want," Bee said.

"It's what I want," Pat said. She had kissed before, had kissed Mark, but it had always been awkward and frightening. This wasn't awkward, and she was dizzy with excitement but not afraid. They kissed while the newsreader told them of deaths in Suez and deaths in Hungary, until Pat got up and turned it off and then they went into the bedroom.

She was glad she had talked to Lorna, but she felt that it wouldn't have been necessary. It was a case of touching and paying attention and asking what felt good. Afterwards she was so proud to have made Bee happy that what she felt herself was secondary to that, and yet what she felt was momentous, was unlike anything else. Later in the dark she felt that Bee was crying. "What's wrong?" she asked.

"I'm so lucky," Bee said.

"No, I'm the one who's lucky," Pat replied.

They paid almost no attention to how the Suez crisis unfolded, nor to the horrible things happening in Hungary. The US intervention and the return of the troops seemed to be happening in counterpoint to the unfolding of their love. All her interests took a back seat to Bee. They told a few friends, but most of them did not make any assumptions at seeing two women constantly together. Pat felt replete, her joy in Bee's existence redoubled by Bee's return of love, and transmuted entirely by the happy glow of sexual satisfaction they shared.

Pat's Venice book came out in the spring. Only in the classroom was she entirely focused on something that was not Bee. When Britain joined France, Germany and Italy in a new European Economic Community, signing the Treaty of Rome, Pat only paid enough attention to realize that now she would be able to buy her house in Italy.

She and Bee drove down the length of Europe in June 1957, stopping to eat and explore wherever they wanted to. In Florence Pat felt she would explode as she showed Bee everything, until Bee protested laughing that she could not take it all in at once. They stayed in Pat's usual *pensione* but had a double room, both saying to the landlady that they didn't mind at all about sharing a bed. Pat introduced Bee to her Florentine friends.

They looked at houses and flats for sale, which in itself would have made an entertaining hobby. Pat would have bought an apartment at the top of a twelfth-century tower near Orsanmichele, but Bee wanted a garden. With the help of Pat's friend Sara, who taught English at the university, they eventually found a house. It was just south of the Arno, outside the old city walls, which Mussolini, the barbarian, had pulled down. It was in walking distance of the Uffizi, and it had running water and a fig tree. They planned to find students to rent it during the academic year, and to live in it themselves in the summers. "We can plant rosemary," Bee said. All their plans were "we," and Pat thrilled to it every time.

"I can probably help you find students," Sara said. "This year I might be interested in living there myself. My lease is about to run out, and it is a lovely house."

"That would be perfect," Pat said.

One day they saw a family walking across the Ponte Vecchio with the father reading aloud from Pat's guidebook. Bee
nudged Pat, and Pat stared hard at the statue of Cellini in the
middle of the bridge, blinking tears out of her eyes. "It's really
helping people," she said, when they had gone on in the direction of the Pitti Palace. "I saw it on the shelves, but I didn't
really believe people would use it."

"Why did you write it then?" Bee teased. "It's real. It's a
real achievement. You can be proud. I'm proud of you."

Pat glowed.

On their last day in Italy Pat went into the Duomo alone
and went down on her knees to thank God for Bee.

"I am bringing you my joy, Jesus, as I was taught as a child.
Thank you for Bee. Thank you for making her, thank you for
letting me find her, thank you for making me worthy of her.
Thank you for our house in Florence, for her fellowship, for
my teaching. Thank you for our lives, our love. And if this is
all there is, if she decides she wants a man later, wants to
marry and have children, then so be it. Thank you for giving
us this time to be together and be happy," she prayed. She felt
God heard her and looked down on her in kindness. When
she stood up again in the perfect harmony of the Duomo she
had tears of joy in her eyes.

10

Babies: Tricia 1952–1961

Tricia's second baby was born dead. The birth was as hard a struggle as Doug's had been, two days of labor with nothing to show for it at the end. The dead child was a girl. Mark had her baptized Hilary. Tricia was too ill herself to have any say in the matter. It took her a long time to recover from that birth. Her mother came down to care for Doug while she was in hospital, and remained for a few months afterwards, during which Tricia felt constantly exhausted. It was the most she could do to eat and talk to Doug. Going to the bathroom left her needing to rest for an hour. Her mother went home in October. Tricia's doctor prescribed exercises and a tonic. She slowly regained her strength. At the time of the Coronation, in June, Mark again brought home a bottle of wine and left it sitting on the sideboard. Tricia saw it as she came in from the kitchen and almost without thinking picked it up and smashed it in the fireplace. The plummy scent of red wine rose immediately into the air, and she stood staring at the green glass shattered all over the grate.

Her rebellion did no good, of course. Mark, coming in, looked at her and the broken bottle patiently. Her violence had put him in the right, made her into the child and him the adult. It bought her one night, for which she had to pay with reduced housekeeping money the following week, for he stopped the price of wine out of it.

This pettiness astounded her. Where was the man she had thought she was marrying? Or forget that, where was normal human decency? She would not do that to a dog. She told Mark she was pregnant almost immediately, before she could possibly have been sure, but he did not question her. She hated lying, but she had come to the end of her resources. She had loved him, and even after she had stopped loving him she had tried to make the marriage work, and this was what it had come to. She made a desperate plan to run away to her mother in Twickenham—a journey requiring a bus and two trains and most of a day, no easy trip with a three-year-old. She reached her mother's house after six at night, to her mother's astonishment. She took them in and put Doug to bed at once. Then she insisted on telephoning the Lincolnshire neighbor who was prepared to take messages for Mark and Tricia.

"He'll be so worried about you," she said, dialling. No matter what Tricia said, her mother insisted on treating it as a temporary problem. "All marriages have these little blips," she said. Mark agreed that Tricia should stay until the weekend and then he would fetch her back. She felt her mother conspired with him to make her again the child, the misbehaving child.

"I want to leave Doug with you and take a teaching post," Tricia said to her mother. "I'll be able to send you money for his keep."

"Married women can't teach!" her mother said.

"They can now," Tricia said. "That law has been changed. Or if I can't teach I'll get secretarial work. Goodness knows typing Mark's book has taught me something."

But her mother wouldn't hear of it. "Your place is with your husband. I know you took losing the baby badly, but the best thing for that is to have another baby as soon as possible. I lost a baby between Oswald and you. It's natural to hate Mark for putting you through all that pain, but it isn't his fault really."

She tried to tell her mother about the way he had burned the letters and his pettiness with the housekeeping but she couldn't make her understand. She made light of everything and kept repeating that all marriages had these problems. When Tricia cried, her mother said she was run down, and made her cups of Bovril.

On the Saturday morning Mark arrived in the car, Doug was delighted to see him. Tricia was too busy being sick to care. She tried to blame the Bovril, but she knew she really was pregnant again.

In the car she tried to make an ultimatum as Doug ran about the back seat pointing out cows and horses excitedly. "We have to move into town. I can't stay there in the village where there's nothing. It's driving me mad. I never talk to an adult. I'm completely trapped. There isn't even a library."

"I'll consider looking for a house in Grantham after the new baby is born," Mark said, with the air of somebody making a huge concession.

The baby was born in January 1954, and it was a girl. They called her Helen Elizabeth, after Tricia's mother and Elizabeth Burchell, and perhaps the new queen. The order of names was at Tricia's insistence. She was again very pulled down after the birth, and her mother again came to stay. Doug was jealous of the new baby and of his mother and grandmother's attention to her. He had been toilet trained for more than a year, but he began to deliberately soil himself. Tricia found this so distressing that she broke down in tears every time it happened. She still had to wash everything by hand herself. Mark dealt with it by spanking Doug, much against Tricia's desires. "He's too little," she insisted. "He doesn't really understand. It's just because of Helen. He'll be fine again soon."

"Haven't you seen the look on his face? It's deviltry and he's doing it on purpose."

"Well, he is, but he doesn't understand." Tricia was furious with Doug herself, but she couldn't condone hitting a child so young. Mark, however, was implacable, and as his methods worked and Doug gave up his rebellion it made it more difficult for her to continue to insist the next time he wanted to punish his son for naughtiness. This seemed to happen more and more frequently. Mark's book had been rejected by the publisher after long deliberation, and while he had sent it to another he was angry about it and took it out on Tricia and Doug. He did not hit Tricia, but he did not need to—sarcasm was always a sufficient weapon to reduce her to misery.

At Easter they visited the Burchells in Oxford. Tricia still didn't care for them, but she welcomed anything like a change in her routine. Mark wanted to talk to them about what to do with his book. Tricia was so delighted to see Oxford again that tears came into her eyes as they drove past Blackwell's. She took the children for walks, pushing Helen in the pram and holding tightly to Doug's hand. It was vacation, but there seemed to be plenty of undergrads around, running and bicycling and laughing in the spring sunshine. They took no notice of Tricia even when she smiled at them, and she realized she was invisible to them. When she had been an undergraduate, a woman with a pram would have been invisible to her, too.

The second evening, Mark went out with the Burchells, leaving Tricia to babysit her own two children and the Burchells' four. The youngest Burchell child, Paul, was a few months older than Helen, and when he woke screaming Tricia could do nothing to calm him. Eventually, feeling almost as if she were committing adultery, she gave him her breast. He quieted at once, as Helen would have. It was a strange intimacy to have with somebody else's child.

The next year Tricia had another stillbirth and they did move, not because of her ultimatum but because Mark had found a better job. They moved to Woking, in London's commuter belt, to a suburban house with a washing machine. It belonged to them, or as Mark said, to the bank. It was a long but possible walk from the library and the shops, and while the house was ugly and identical to its neighbors, and Tricia would never have chosen it, she was happier there than she had been isolated outside Grantham. She made friends with other mothers of small children, and haunted the library with desperation, burying herself in books, the longer the better. She read *Middlemarch* and found it almost too painful, seeing herself in Dorothea and Mark in Casaubon. She read aloud to Doug and Helen and to herself compulsively in every spare moment.

Mark joined the golf club and she joined the Peace Pledge Union and the Labour Party.

That autumn a publisher bought Mark's book, so clearly it was not Causaubon's sterile *Key to All Mythologies* after all. That night Mark visited Tricia's bedroom after a bath but without any wine. The sexual act seemed to be over faster, which she approved, and he did not apologize afterwards. She did not become pregnant, nor did she the month after, but by February she could not keep food down and she knew she was in for it again.

They visited the Burchells again that summer, 1956. All the political talk was about Nasser seizing the Suez Canal. Elizabeth Burchell compared him to Hitler and Tricia felt cold inside. Surely it would not be war again, so soon? She looked at Doug, who was six now, happily playing with the Burchell children, and imagined him marching off at eighteen and never coming back. It was hard enough for her to bear Mark disciplining him; she could not endure the thought of him being killed in battle. The Peace Pledge Union started a letter writing campaign and urged her to write to her MP, begging Britain to keep out of it. She did, and it must have worked, for the whole thing blew over in a solution brokered by the US and the UN. People stopped saying Nasser was as bad as Hitler. Egypt kept control of the canal but let everyone go through, even the Israelis. During this period Tricia became a devotee of the BBC radio news, and even after Mark bought them a small television it was the radio she used in the kitchen that kept her up to date.

On that trip to Oxford Mark and the Burchells decided to "be received," meaning joining the Roman Catholic church, and on their return to Woking Mark began to take instruction. Tricia flat-out refused to join him. She no longer believed in a loving God, and stuck to that, whatever Mark said. She realized one day as he was lecturing her that he not only treated her as if she were stupid, but genuinely believed she was. He treated her as a baby machine, and she felt as if she almost was one. What was her degree for, when all the reading she did now was to escape from her own intolerable life?

In October of 1956 she suffered yet another stillbirth, during the Hungarian Crisis. She had been glued to the radio hearing about the Soviet troops poised to go into Budapest, and the brave Hungarians defying them by massing peacefully in the city squares. She wanted to give the baby a Hungarian name, but Mark named it Matthew while she was still unconscious and undergoing an operation to stitch up her womb. Poor dead Matthew had torn her insides in some way. The doctor was unsure whether she would be able to have more children.

"Surely two is enough," she said tentatively to Mark. "It's not as if either of us enjoys it."

"God will decide," he said, and by that she had no choice but to abide. It was some comfort to her that the Soviets had backed down on Hungary and were allowing a greater measure of democracy, both there and in the rest of the Iron Curtain countries. Both the Soviets and the Americans were pushing ahead into space, in a kind of competition. The BBC was excited to report the first photographs of the dark side of the moon.

Mark was received into the Catholic faith and took it very seriously. He insisted the children be instructed, and although they had been baptized in the Church of England he insisted on having their baptisms repeated, or "conditionally repeated" as nobody was sure whether the first baptisms had counted. Tricia let him take Doug to church with him, but usually kept Helen home with her. "She's too young to sit through the service," she said, and Mark agreed. Doug, who had just started school, said church was boring, but only to Tricia. He was wary of his father, though more likely to be pushed into rage and defiance than fear.

Tricia's life in Woking was just beginning to settle down into something she could endure when Mark again brought home wine. His book had been published and was getting some attention, or so he said. She lay and endured his attentions and naturally she became pregnant again. Her doctor looked grave and told her to rest, but of course rest was impossible. Doug had to be taken to and from school and Helen was a very active three-year-old. She was sure this baby would die like the last two, but to her surprise it survived. They called it George Ludwig. Tricia protested the Ludwig, but only feebly. Her mother again came to stay and help with the baby, but Tricia found her less use than on previous occasions. She seemed vaguer, less sure of herself. She kept forgetting the names of things. When Tricia asked her about it she said that she needed to change the prescription of her blood pressure tablets because they made her forgetful.

"She's only fifty-eight," Tricia said to Mark after her mother had left. "She can't be getting senile already, surely?"

"She never was especially intelligent, she won't miss it," Mark responded. He was busy writing another book, which he expected as a matter of course that Tricia would type for him, chapter by chapter, and then again with corrections. Georgie was a fussy baby, fussier than either of the others. He did not nurse well, and she had to give him bottles to keep up his weight.

Tricia asked the sympathetic doctor about Malthusian belts. He laughed, and explained that there were contraceptives and he could prescribe them for her, but there was nothing she could use without her husband's knowledge. She endured another pregnancy that ended in a stillbirth, and another that resulted in a baby—Catherine Marian, born in November of 1959. When she visited after this birth there was no denying that Tricia's mother was becoming forgetful.

The doctor told Mark that he was endangering Tricia's life by insisting on more children. All the same he persisted, and she had another stillbirth in the autumn of 1960. In the summer of 1961 the doctor prescribed Tricia the new contraceptive pill. She told Mark it was a tonic and he believed her. Childbirth was over.

11

Real: Pat 1957–1964

Pat's editor wanted her to write a guide to Rome. She found the letter on the mat when she came in on a chilly November evening. She turned on both bars of the electric fire and sat down next to it, removing only one glove to open the letter. The brindled cat, Dante, came up and rubbed against her ankles, then flopped down on her feet in the circle of the fire's heat.

Rome was the logical next step after Florence and Venice, the editor said. The books were selling extremely well, and Constable were certainly interested in producing new and updated editions as she had suggested. They saw no reason why the books couldn't remain in print in the long term, being updated from time to time as necessary. They understood that Rome wasn't (ha ha) built in a day, and that the book would take her some time, but they wished she would start planning it with a completion date of September 1958 for publication in spring 1959, or September 1959 for publication in spring 1960. Then came the offer—three times as much as for either of the other books.

Pat was still sitting staring at the letter when Bee came in and snapped the light on, startling her.

"What's wrong?" Bee asked, immediately coming over to the sofa and putting an arm around Pat.

"Nothing's wrong. They want me to write a guide to Rome." Pat relaxed against the rough wool of Bee's coat.

"That sounds like a logical next step," Bee said.

"That's what they say. It's just—Rome. Rome is so immense. I could write three books the length of my Venice one and hardly scratch the surface. And I don't know it well. It would be so much work. And we've just got our house in Florence. But—" she hesitated and looked into Bee's capable, interested face. "The truth is that the one time I went to Rome I was so unhappy. It was right after I broke it off with Mark. Even though that trip was when I discovered Italy, all the Roman sites seem drenched in misery in my memory."

Bee hugged her more tightly. "Then we should go back together and make some new memories."

Pat felt tears pricking behind her eyes. "You're right, of course," she said.

"And you should face up to your fears instead of letting them chase you into corners. It does no good in the end."

"I'm going to tell them it will take two years," she said, turning the letter over in her hands. "The other thing is the advance. It would be enough to buy a house in Cambridge, or out in the country if you prefer that, where we could grow things."

"They don't give mortgages to unmarried women," Bee said.

"Without a mortgage, just buying it outright, the same as we did in Italy." Pat straightened the letter. "The other books are selling well, I'm making royalties. They think they'll do new editions when they sell out."

Bee frowned slightly. "You know, if we owned a house near Cambridge we could both live on what I earn and your royalties. You could write guidebooks more rapidly if you weren't teaching."

"But I love teaching," Pat said.

"Oh well then. It was just a thought. We should get started on dinner if we're going to eat before the concert."

Bee took off her coat and hung it on the hook beside the door, then without looking put out her arm for Pat's coat.

As she chopped leeks, Pat thought about what Bee had said about facing her fears. "There are things I love about teaching, but there are also things that would be good about writing guidebooks full time," she said as she slid the leeks into the pan, where they immediately began to sizzle in the olive oil.

"I don't know if they'll keep me here at the end of this fellowship. I'd like to stay in Cambridge, but with a research career it can be difficult."

"Especially for a woman," Pat said, stirring the leeks. "The water's boiling."

Bee eased the spaghetti into the water. "I'd rather stay here if I can."

Pat stared fixedly down into the leeks. "The thing is that I'm afraid. I'm not afraid of where you'll work or any of that, I'm afraid we'll make plans together and intertwine our lives and then you'll want to have babies and find some man to marry and leave me alone."

Bee slid a big handful of washed mushrooms into the pan with the leeks and rested her head on Pat's shoulder. She hadn't chopped the mushrooms, but Pat didn't say anything. "I do want babies," Bee said after a moment. "But I want you—our life—I'm not going to go off and live with some man."

"I just keep thinking you'll wake up and want something more real," Pat said, not looking around, still stirring.

"This is real," Bee said. "I wish one of us was a man so that we could get married and make it feel real to the rest of the world. Our friends, your mother, my family. But this is real for me. I'm not going to give it up."

"Give me the bacon, or the spaghetti will be boiled to mush," Pat said gruffly, because her throat was thick with tears.

They bought a seventeenth-century cottage in Harston, six miles outside Cambridge. It came with a long thin acre of land, Saxon field pattern, stretching back from the road. There was a little flower garden in the front and then it stretched back and back behind the house. Farthest away from the house was an orchard, where Bee immediately began to graft apples. They lived there in the academic year and in Florence in the summers, paying Bee's students to look after the garden when they were away. "We always miss the best of the fruit," Bee lamented. But she accompanied Pat to Italy and went with her around the sites, seldom complaining.

At Harston they had two cats, chickens, and a hive of bees, from which Bee gathered honey. "They never sting *you*," Pat said, rubbing her hand.

"They recognize a fellow bee," Bee laughed. "But the truth is that you move too quickly and startle them."

They held parties in Harston, but more often than before went into Cambridge for other people's parties, driving home afterwards. They still knew mixed groups of people. There were more Italians in Cambridge now that the Economic Community allowed free access to education in all member countries, and they became another strand of Pat's web of friendships. "I never know who I'll meet at your parties," Pat's head of department said at a party celebrating their first apple harvest.

"I hope that's good," Pat said. She felt more confident about people at school knowing about her and Bee, now that she knew they could be financially independent without her needing to teach. She liked teaching, but she liked it better knowing she was free to stop. She liked the girls, liked seeing them open up to literature in the same way she had herself. She planned the curriculum to encourage this process. Nobody from school ever asked about her relationship with Bee—two friends sharing digs was common enough to need no explanation. They were known as a couple in the homosexual community, and also to some of Pat's more broad-minded birder friends.

Pat began researching for the Rome book immediately after they moved. It took her all of both summers to complete. Going to Rome with Bee did soften her memories of going there brokenhearted with Marjorie, and by the end she felt she loved Rome almost as much as Venice, though never as much as Florence. "Rome has all these layers, all this history folded over almost stratigraphically," she said to Bee. "Florence is all of one piece, and that's what I love about it. It all fits together so perfectly."

Constable launched the Rome book with a wine and cheese party in London in March 1960. Pat agonized about what to wear, and eventually went in a black cocktail dress adorned with a Roman coin pendant that Bee had bought for her in Rome. She had her hair done, but the hairdresser complained that it was too short to do anything with. Bee wore her interview suit. ("Nobody's going to be looking at me!" she insisted.) Few people had known that "P. A. Cowan" was a woman, and the fact drew some attention. Pat was interviewed by the *Times*. "I just wanted there to be better guidebooks, because when I first went to Italy and didn't know about anything I wanted to find out. I wanted there to be guidebooks for ordinary people that would tell them about what they were seeing, and also where to eat," she said.

Her photograph was grainy, but Bee cut out the article and pasted it into a scrapbook. Pat's mother telephoned in great excitement to say that she had seen it.

Two weeks later, at Easter, Pat went down to Twickenham

to see her mother. Bee was busy with some grafting in the lab, so Pat drove down alone. Her mother was pleased to see her. "You should have said you were coming!" she said.

"I did say," Pat protested, but her mother ignored it. Over the course of the weekend there were more and more tiny things that made Pat realize that her mother was losing her memory. She had entirely forgotten about the interview in the *Times*. She kept losing words. Pat's bedroom was deep in dust, her mother had clearly forgotten to clean it. Peeping through the door to Oswald's old room she saw that it was the same. Pat drove home deeply worried and told Bee about it.

"She's all right for now, but what if she gets worse? How is she going to manage?"

"We'll have to have her here," Bee said, and made a face. "Oh I don't want to and you don't want to either, but there'll be nothing else for it if it comes to that."

"What about Italy?" Pat asked.

"Maybe it won't come to that," Bee said. "But you're the only one left and I'm the only girl, and they see us as single women, so we're going to be the ones to have the burdens for all our parents as they get old." Bee's parents were sheep farmers in Penrith. Pat liked them well enough, but found them dull. Their conversation seemed to be exclusively about sheep diseases and new automatic shearing machines, which was naturally more interesting for Bee than Pat.

"My mother isn't old. She'll be sixty this year."

"For the time being, maybe we could get her some help. Somebody to go in and see that she's eating, and maybe clean a bit. Maybe give her a bit of companionship. Being alone so much can't help. We could afford that if she can't. As I remember when my grandfather's second wife went senile, it was a long slow process."

Pat began writing a guide to Pompeii and Naples. That year, 1961, Bee was given a permanent position as a lecturer at the New College. "They have a wonderful computer," she told Pat. "It fills a whole room, but it's terrifically reliable. We're using it to store data and match patterns. It's amazing."

"Good," Pat said.

"And it's so fast," Bee went on. "All the departments want them."

Then one beautiful day in May of 1962, Bee came home from work with an astonishing idea.

"Have you heard of artificial insemination?" she asked Pat.

"Only when you were going on about those rabbits the year I first met you," Pat said. "What, are you back to animals? I thought your heart was given to plants?"

"My heart is given to you," Bee said, kissing her. "In the US they have successfully done artificial insemination with humans, and it has been considered legal there, though the children are considered to be illegitimate. They're doing it in Scotland with infertile couples."

It took Pat a moment. "Then we could have—"

"Lesbians all over the world will be so happy when this becomes generally available," Bee said, nodding. "But you're thirty-four and I'm thirty-two, so we don't have any time to waste."

"Where would we get the sperm?"

"Find a donor. The same one. So our children would be siblings." They hugged each other in excitement.

"How could we possibly ask somebody?" Pat asked, then saw the answer at once. "One of our homosexual friends?"

"Precisely," Bee said. "Alan would do it, or Piers. But from what I can find out, we'd need somebody who knows the procedure, and they're only doing it for infertile couples."

"How about if we went to the US?" Pat asked. "Though of course, even apart from the expense of that the US seems like an awful place." The failed Bay of Pigs invasion was on the news every night, and the strength of the McCarthyist movement was horrifying.

"I think it would be even worse—I mean, there are more people there doing it, but they'd want even more in the way of identity, and apparently they only do it in cases where the husband is provably infertile. I was wondering if I might find somebody professionally who's doing it with animals. It can't be that different."

"I suppose not," Pat said, a little repelled at the thought of being operated on by a vet.

Bee laughed at her expression. "We're all mammals together!" Then she grinned. "We're really going to do this? If we can? You really want to?"

"I'll take a leave of absence from teaching. You'll have to carry on working, of course. It'll be marvellous. Imagine teaching them about the world! Imagine teaching them birding and Shakespeare, and how to graft pears onto apples, and Botticelli and Bach!"

"It's not that easy. As far as the school and the college are concerned we'd have had illegitimate children. They'd be shocked. It might count as gross moral turpitude."

"Minor moral turpitude, at most," Pat murmured, as she always did when she heard that expression.

"I think it would be best if you resigned and I just didn't tell the college. If we timed it right, I could give birth in the long vacation, and they'd never know."

"They're biologists, Bee! They'd be sure to notice!"

Bee laughed and shook her head. "They're plant biologists. They know nothing about mammalian reproduction. And they don't want to know about human reproduction. They like me because I work hard and do good work and keep up with all the teaching they give me, and because I can teach the first years how to graft and don't mind getting my hands stained." Bee's hands were so permanently stained with dyes used for staining cells that Pat had come to think of it as normal. "They won't ask questions if I don't say anything, but if I do say anything they'll be forced to get rid of me. And while you like teaching, you could get a job teaching anywhere. Biological research isn't like that. And we couldn't all four live on your guidebook income and what we make selling eggs and honey."

"All four," Pat said, her eyes moist. "Do you really think we could do it?"

"I'll see what I can find out," Bee said.

It was a month later and they were almost ready to leave for Italy when Bee gave up trying to find a way to do it. The legitimate possibilities were closed off immediately. No doctor would prescribe AI for two single women, either in Britain or the US. The procedure wasn't available at all in Italy, where Bee suggested that outright bribery would probably have worked to get them on the list. Nor would any of the vets she knew who were doing it routinely with cows agree to try it on humans. "I don't want to give up, but it would seem almost easier to do it the old-fashioned way," Bee said as they were sitting down to dinner.

"I've never—" Pat hesitated, looking at her plate. "I mean, with a man."

"Not with Mark when you were engaged?" Bee asked.

"Oh, I was so naive in those days. And Mark was so religious. I really don't think either of us knew what we were doing. We barely kissed. I had no idea really what people did.

I'm still a little hazy on what men and women do. I assume it's pretty much the same only with the man putting his thing inside when he's ready to orgasm?"

Bee looked away. "It's not the same at all," she said. "I had some unpleasant experiences when I was evacuated. The father of the family where I was billeted came into my room. It went on and on."

"Do you think that's why you're a lesbian?" Pat asked.

Bee frowned, then very deliberately ate a carrot, chewing it hard. "I don't think so," she said, putting her fork down. "I mean that was repulsive, and he was a horrible man, making me promise not to say anything to his wife, saying I'd tempted him and it was all my fault. It took me a long time to realize that I hadn't done anything different on the days when he came in than on the days when he didn't. But it wasn't the sex itself that was so awful. The worst thing was the guilt and all of that, not what he actually did. It wasn't all that important. I think it would be giving it too much importance to say that it made me a lesbian. He was just—a thing that happened. As if I'd got caught in the rain and caught a chill. It would be ridiculous to say that's why I love you. I'd have loved you anyway, no matter what happened before."

"I think the same," Pat said. "No matter what happened we'd have found each other." She put her hand on Bee's. "Do you think you could go through with that again, to have a baby?"

"I think so," Bee said, uncertainly. "How about you?"

"I suppose so," Pat said. "Do you think we should try and find somebody in Italy, or wait until we come home in the autumn?"

"Oh, wait until we come home!" Bee said immediately. "Italian men all think they're God's gift to women anyway, and even the nicest of our friends in Florence would behave as if everything he'd ever thought about lesbians really wanting men had been confirmed if we asked him."

Pat shuddered.

"The other thing I thought was maybe you could ask Donald." Bee picked up her fork again.

"Donald? Your brother Donald?"

"I'd really be related to your baby then," Bee said.

"If only Oswald hadn't been killed," Pat said, immediately seeing the advantages. "It really is so unfair of biology to be organized this way so that we can't just have each other's babies the way we want to."

"I sometimes think I should have been a man," Bee agreed.

"I wouldn't want you to be any different. You wouldn't be you if you were a man."

"Would you want to be a man, if you could just change?"

"Well, yes, I suppose so." Pat hesitated. "Being paid more and everything being so easy—getting a mortgage and jobs and being respected without needing to struggle. But I do like being me."

"Yes, me too," Bee said.

12

Feudalism: Tricia 1963–1966

By the autumn of 1963, Tricia had four children, aged from thirteen to three. Although she'd never been away from them except when she was in hospital giving birth, she found it difficult to understand how she had come to be in this position. They were people, and they had become people while she wasn't paying attention, while she was mired in toilet training and morning sickness and bitter resentment of their father.

Doug was thirteen. He attended Woking Grammar School, where he frequently got into trouble for fighting and belligerence. She was afraid he was becoming a bully—certainly she frequently had to stop him bullying the other children. Mark bullied Doug and Doug took it out on the others. He was protective of her against his father, and she frequently had to stop him from making things worse. Tricia worried about him, about what trouble he might get into, and about how he would grow up.

Helen was nine, and her father's favorite. He spoiled her. Tricia found herself using this—using Helen to ask him for favors, for a visit to Grandma's, a new record player, lights for the tree at Christmas. She did not like to see her child wheedling, but wheedling worked on Mark. Helen was pretty. She had Tricia's fair hair, but with the thickness and body of Mark's hair. Her features were regular. From babyhood, strangers had been cooing over her and admiring her. Tricia worried about spoiling her, and about other people spoiling her.

George at six had just started school. He was nervous of everything—he hated being left at the school gate, was afraid of the dark, cried when dogs barked and when his father shouted. Tricia would have given him a night light, but his father forbade it. She compromised by moving the boys' room to the front where there was a streetlight outside, and allowing them to have the curtain open a crack. George was her secret favorite, because he clung to her and was loving.

Cathy was three, an energetic toddler who liked to walk everywhere, no matter how much it slowed her mother down. They spent time in parks and at the library and at meetings. The Peace Pledge Union had been replaced by the Campaign for Nuclear Disarmament. Tricia longed to go on the Aldermaston Marches protesting the American missile sites on British soil, but Mark had forbidden it. However, he knew nothing about what she did in the daytime, and CND daytime meetings generally had other mothers with children and they traded childcare. Cathy seemed truly gregarious, and loved playing with other children while Tricia signed petitions, and even helped to draft petitions for circulation. CND were writing to the Russians, the French, and the Americans as well as the British. Their aim was nothing less than complete nuclear disarmament and a new era of world peace. Tricia's typing ability was welcome. She began to make friends and feel as if she was making a difference.

She had come back from an afternoon typing petitions on November 22nd. The six of them had dinner, all sitting down together and eating as Mark preferred. Tricia's cooking had improved slightly through practice and with the availability of better ingredients, but she was unadventurous. That night they had pork chops with applesauce and mashed potatoes. Mark complained that the chops were overdone, which they usually were. Tricia was terrified of undercooking pork.

There was a bottle of wine sitting on the sideboard. Tricia sighed when she saw it, but no longer feared this as she had. The act itself remained unpleasant, and Mark's apologies remained painful, but as long as she took her pill every day there was no risk of pregnancy.

After dinner she put Cathy to bed at six, George at seven, and Helen at eight. Doug was allowed to stay up until after the nine o'clock news. So the three of them were sitting together on the sofa watching the news, and they discovered together that the American President, John F. Kennedy, had been assassinated in Dallas.

"The bomb is believed to have been hidden in the massed flowers below the banquet table," the announcer read, visibly shaken. "President and Mrs. Kennedy were killed instantly, along with the Governor of Texas and—" Tricia looked at Mark, who was gaping at the screen.

"Who could have done that?" she asked.

"The Russians?" Mark suggested. "The Cubans?"

"I know the CIA engineered a coup in Cuba in May, the way they did in Guatemala a few years ago, but surely they wouldn't have the ability to do something like that?" The screen was showing them the Vice-President, Johnson, taking his oath of office.

"He had Castro killed, why wouldn't they try to kill Kennedy?" Mark asked. "But you'd think they'd have trouble getting a bomb into a reception in Texas. A Cuban would be conspicuous there. Or a Russian."

Bobby Kennedy was insisting vehemently that there would be a full investigation and that whoever was responsible would pay.

"It doesn't seem right having the President's brother be one of the bosses," Doug said.

"He's not one of the bosses. He's Attorney General," Mark said.

"What does an Attorney General do?" Doug asked.

Mark hesitated. "He's in charge of legal decisions," he said, sounding unsure.

"That's being one of the bosses, then," Doug said. "Having the President's brother be one of the bosses makes them seem like feudalism."

"This isn't the moment, when Kennedy has just been killed," Mark said, angrily. "Anyway, it's time you were in bed."

Doug kissed Tricia goodnight and went upstairs. "I'll come up and tuck you in in five minutes," Tricia said.

"You should stop babying him," Mark said, as the scene of carnage played again on the black-and-white screen.

The next day at the CND office everyone was talking about the assassination. Some of the people were quite well-informed. "There are lots of Latino people in Texas," Sylvia said. "A Cuban could disguise himself as a waiter and get the bomb in on a tray, easily."

Tim, a one-legged veteran of the Great War, disagreed. "I think it was an internal thing. If it had been the Russians, or even the Cubans, something else would have happened by now. The President has been killed, but there's been no attack."

"The Americans can't think they can just do whatever they want anywhere in the world without making themselves unpopular," Tricia said. "I mean sometimes it's good, like stopping us from attacking Egypt over Suez, but all this sponsoring coups in countries because you don't like their governments? It had to end in tears."

"I agree!" Sylvia said. "They have that awful Committee

for Un-American Activities and they're interfering in Vietnam. Maybe this will bring it home to them."

"Well, time will tell, when we see what comes of it," Tim said. "Did we get that Vietnam petition out, by the way? Military advisors my foot."

"Yes, I did it Friday," Tricia said. "Do you really think something else will happen?"

"If it was the Russians it will," Tim said. "Surely they'd have an attack ready to take out America while they're all still reeling. They've declared a national day of mourning, all schools and everything closed. If the communists had real support there would be strikes and uprisings. Or if they don't have that kind of thing because their leaders have all been imprisoned or suppressed, you'd expect a military attack."

"War?" Sylvia asked, shuddering.

Tricia glanced at the peace symbol on the wall. "It feels closer than ever. The war that will end everything. I was tucking my little boy in last night and I wondered if we'd even see the morning."

Sylvia hugged her. "That's how I feel every night!"

No attacks followed the assassination. Things continued on, and the big war news was Johnson wanting to site more missiles in Britain, while sending more troops to Vietnam. Then in February, to everyone's astonishment, Bobby Kennedy's investigation into his brother's death found evidence implicating Johnson in the purchase of the explosives. The evidence was by no means conclusive, and people were vehemently divided on the subject. Some thought Bobby Kennedy was trying to smear Johnson, and others were equally sure that Johnson was the real murderer.

"Cui bono," said Mark, as if he had always suspected the Vice-President of luring the President to Dallas so he could kill him and take his place.

Though some called for impeachment, nothing came of it. Johnson, beaten down by the scandal, declined to run again. Bobby Kennedy, flanked by his brother's children, declared his own candidacy for the 1964 election. There seemed little doubt he would be elected.

"Feudalism," muttered Doug under his breath.

"I always thought that Johnson was a piece of work," Sylvia said. "Not a trustworthy person. I'm glad he won't be the one with his finger on the button any more."

"It's as if they weren't content with instigating coups abroad and had to have a coup at home," Tim said, shaking his head. "Do you think Bobby will relent about those missiles that were coming here?"

"My son says it's feudalism," Tricia said. "Bobby being JFK's brother, I mean."

They laughed, uneasily. "It is like feudalism in a way," Sylvia said.

"Nothing wrong with having political families. We think family businesses are good. If you heard about a son inheriting his father's shop, or a doctor whose two sons became doctors, you'd think that was splendid," Tim said.

"It's different with power," Sylvia protested.

Tim threw up his hands. "It is different."

In the autumn of 1964, Cathy got a place at nursery school. Tricia suggested to Mark one night when the children were in bed that she might go back to teaching, part-time or on supply at first.

"I make enough to keep us," Mark protested.

"Of course you do, but a little extra might be nice, so we could afford a new car, or to get your new book professionally typed. But really it would be an interest to me, now that the children are growing up."

Mark grudgingly agreed, and Tricia began to work as a

supply teacher, filling in for teachers who were ill. Sometimes it would just be a day or two, other times it would be for a few weeks. She continued to volunteer at the CND office in between. She also managed to get over to visit her mother every week. It took a little over an hour to get to Twickenham from Woking, depending on connections. Tricia's mother was getting vaguer all the time. Tricia did her shopping and cleaned the house. She sometimes felt the most important thing she did was sitting and talking to her mother. If she asked what she had been doing her mother didn't know, but they could have real conversations about her childhood, or her mother's childhood. Her memories of times long ago were as clear as ever. Sometimes Tricia would really enjoy her mother's stories— hearing how her parents met, or her mother's work as a nurse-maid. Sometimes she took the children, though they got so easily bored, and her mother could no longer remember their names.

Bobby Kennedy was duly elected in his brother's place, and the British election in the spring brought in a progressive Labour government. She and Mark did not discuss their votes. She did not want to confirm her fear that he might have voted Tory. Mark's new book came out and was well received. Mark visited the Burchells, and came home looking very pleased with himself. "There's a possibility I may be offered a lectureship at a new university next year," he told Tricia.

"Where?" Tricia asked, her heart sinking at the thought of relocating all of them, and just before Doug's School Certificates.

"Lancaster," Mark said.

To Tricia it was still no more than a distant station with no trains going in the direction she wanted to go. "That's so far," she said.

"Nonsense. I thought you'd be pleased. You always hated Woking. And far from what? We'll all be there."

"I am pleased," Tricia said. She could not say far from her friends or her volunteer work, because he did not know about that. "But it's a long way from my mother. You know she's been getting—"

"She's nothing but an old nuisance," Mark said. "You baby her. You baby everyone."

"If the time comes when she can't cope on her own, we'll have to have her with us. In Lancaster if that's where we are."

"And what about my parents?"

Mark's parents were well and strong and continued to look down their noses at Tricia. "If they needed it, we'd have them too, obviously," she said.

"Well that's not the case now," Mark snapped. "Lancaster. A real job for me. Try to like it." He stormed out of the room.

Tricia was shaking. She needed to know when they'd be going, and whether he'd thought about schools for the children. She could get Helen to ask him about that. Lancaster. She remembered the station very well, Baronial style, a Victorian castle, and the little train to Barrow-in-Furness, and the kindness she had found there. People in the North were kind. Maybe it would be all right. Maybe she'd be able to find a proper job there.

13

"If the World's Still Here": Pat 1962–1963

They did not have to wait until they came back from Italy to find somebody. Constable planned to do new updated editions of the Florence and Venice books, this time daringly with color photographs. They sent a young photographer out to Italy to take the pictures. His name was Michael Jacobs, and he was just beginning to make a name for himself. He saw this job as an opportunity to become better known and get more magazine work; and also, as he said, to have the chance to take photographs of some beautiful things. It was his first time out of England. He stayed in their house in Florence. He was the first overnight guest they had had, and they had to buy a pillow for him. Pat liked him, liked what he did with the camera, and liked his enthusiasm for Florence, and for Venice when they went there. He lay flat on the cobbles to take a photograph of St. Mark's, heedless of the damage to his clothes. He was also entirely understanding about their relationship—he treated Pat and Bee as a couple, without being either embarrassed about it, or trying, as people so often did, to make one of them into the man and the other into the woman.

In the Pitti Palace, trying to find a good angle to photograph the fresco of Lorenzo de Medici welcoming the exiled muses to Florence, he suddenly turned to Pat with tears in his eyes. "It makes you realize they were just people, people who were excited about art and making things and sharing it with other people who cared about it."

"Yes," Pat said, gesturing at the next fresco, Lorenzo pointing out the young Michelangelo. "I always call that one *'Let's Have a Renaissance'*."

"I wish people felt like that now," Michael said. "I mean it's fashionable to be cynical and jaded about everything, but when I look at the passion those Renaissance people had, that clarity of . . . of caring about things, I envy them."

"That's what I've always felt here," Pat said. "That's what first drew me to Florence in particular. It's why I wanted to write about it, to explain that to other people. I'm not an art historian, or any kind of historian really. My degree is in English. But I came here and I responded to the beauty and I wanted to know more about it."

Near the end of his two-week stay, Pat and Bee sat down together to discuss him. It was early in the morning, and they sat at the wrought iron table on the patio eating terrible Florentine unsalted bread with wonderful fresh mozzarella and some of Bee's honey.

"He seems ideal in many ways," Bee said. "My only hesitation is that he's rather homely looking."

"Neither of us is anything special to look at," Pat protested.

"Exactly," Bee countered. "I was hoping to give the babies a bit of a leg up there. But he's intelligent and creative and he has no genetic issues—his parents are alive, and his grandparents were killed in the Blitz, which is hardly hereditary!"

Pat laughed. "I hope not!"

"He's Jewish of course, but I don't see that making any difference."

"Considering the Holocaust, I think if anything it's a good thing," Pat said.

"So it's just the difficulty of asking him," Bee said.

They did find it very difficult to open the subject. They tried and failed to find good openings all day, and eventually Bee came straight out with it over dinner in Bordino's. "We want to have babies, and we were wondering if you might help?"

Michael choked on his truffle pasta. Pat slapped him on the back. When he was recovered he looked from her to Bee. "I'm terribly flattered of course, but what are you suggesting?"

"Because of the way biology is arranged, we can't give each other babies, but we want to have children," Pat said. "We need a man who will cooperate with that and not make a fuss afterwards. And we'd like it to be one man, so they can be real siblings."

He took a long draft of red wine. "What would my role be? Just a sperm donor?"

"Well, we hope you'll continue to be our friend, which means you could be a kind of uncle to the babies. But we'd be the parents," Bee said firmly.

The waiter came by to take their pasta plates and they were all silent for a moment. "I don't know how to put this," Michael said. "But have you ever—" he trailed off.

"I have, Pat hasn't," Bee said. "Look, it's perfectly all right if you don't want to. We can find somebody. I know we're a lot older than you are, and it's a strange kind of relationship to enter into. But we both like you. If you want to think about it, or if you just want to turn us down, no hard feelings."

"I do want to think about it, it's a lot to take in," Michael said. "Would you be able to manage—I mean, financially?"

"Yes," Pat said. "We've thought that all through, don't worry. We wouldn't be asking anything from you except a bit of time."

"And genetic material," Bee added.

Michael laughed nervously. "This is the strangest proposition anyone has ever put to me."

They finished their dinner, and the bottle of wine Michael and Bee had split between them, and went home, still discussing it.

Back in the house, the three of them went into the bedroom where Pat and Bee always slept, the shutters latched for privacy but the window open to catch the breeze. "It might not work the first time," Bee warned. "Sometimes people try for years."

"I could come down to Cambridge if necessary," Michael offered, taking off his socks.

"We hope you'll come down to visit in any case," Pat said. "We'll want to see all the pictures, not just the ones they end up using in the book."

In bed it was strange and awkward having a third person present. Pat felt shy and uncertain.

"I don't know if I can manage it with both of you tonight," Michael said, embarrassed.

"You should try first," Bee said to Pat, putting her hand on her arm. "I should really wait until November or December so I could have the baby in the Long Vacation."

"You're talking as if it's entirely under control and works every time," Pat said.

"It's strange, but I feel like that even though I know better." Bee laughed. "Well, we're both in the middle of our cycle. There's a good chance."

"Will I bleed?" Pat asked.

"Maybe," Bee said. "But maybe not, you've been stretched slowly over a long time when we've made love."

"This is just so weird! It's the strangest thing I have ever done," Michael said. "It's very nice of you to ask me, but I want you to remember that I find this extremely peculiar."

Michael's hands were rougher than Bee's hands, but Bee was there as well. Michael's penis felt strange, and she would have liked to have examined it better—she hadn't seen one since she had been a small child on the beach and bathing with her brother. It felt like a little animal, damp-nosed and snub. The sensation of having it inside her was peculiar but not unpleasant, but quite different from fingers. Michael's weight on top of her as he rocked to and fro was the least familiar thing. She was so glad that Bee was there too.

She felt wet and sticky afterwards, and did not wash immediately because she was afraid of washing out all the sperm. There was no blood.

The next day Michael went back to London. They had an arrangement for him to come and visit them in Cambridge for a weekend at the end of October.

Within a couple of weeks Pat was feeling queasy in the mornings and feeling a bloating in her breasts. "Some people really do get pregnant the very first time," she said to Bee. She worked hard on the revisions to her books but felt almost breathless with excitement. She counted months in her head. The baby would be born in May, and Easter was late, so she should arrange to stop teaching at Christmas. She ate fresh fruit and vegetables and fish, which she found more digestible than meat. She went down to Naples and did the research for a new guide book which she planned to write in the spring after she stopped teaching but before the baby was born.

On their last day in Florence before returning to England for the new academic year, Pat again went alone to the Duomo and gave thanks. Most of the church was open to visitors, with just one small section reserved for prayer. As she got up from her knees she noticed a memorial on the wall nearby with a familiar sculpted head. It was the tomb of Marsilio Ficino, the translator of Plato, the librarian of the Laurentian Library, the tutor of Lorenzo di Medici, one of the central figures of Renaissance Florence. "If the child is a boy, I will call him after Ficino," she vowed.

They went back to England for the new academic year. Bee had a heavy research and teaching load and was kept busy in her spare time writing papers for journals. Pat saw her doctor, an elderly man, who confirmed her pregnancy. "Do you have plans to marry, Miss Cowan?" he asked.

"No." It took a lot of effort for Pat not to soften that negative, but she did not.

"Are you happy about the pregnancy?" the doctor went on.

Abortion was illegal, but possible, she had always known that. "Yes, I am very happy about it. This was a planned baby."

The doctor looked at her sharply and shook his head. "Then we'll be wanting to make monthly appointments with the midwife and to decide on a hospital for the birth. I recommend the Mill Road Maternity Hospital. May, you say? I'll also give you a diet sheet. And you'll want to start ante-natal classes in a month or so. Meanwhile, try to get enough exercise—swimming is good."

She saw the headmistress and gave her notice for after Christmas. "If you ever want to come back we'd be happy to have you," the headmistress said. "We'd have strongly encouraged you to apply for the Head of Department post next year when Miss Martin retires."

At the end of October, Michael came down as arranged. "I told my mother I was going to photograph Cambridge in the hope of a newspaper assignment, so I've brought my cameras," he said.

"Not the best time of year for the garden," Bee said. There was an icy wind blowing, stripping the leaves from the silver birch and the willow that stood at the sides of their gate.

"Nor politically," he said.

"Politically?" Pat asked. She hadn't been paying any attention to the news. What was going on inside her seemed so absorbing it was the most she could do to keep up with marking. Besides, the copyedits on the new editions had arrived the week before, and she had been swamped.

"The Americans and the Russians, over Cuba," Michael explained, when he saw that she really didn't know what he meant. "I thought the whole world was on the edge of their seats about that."

"It's just saber-rattling," Bee said. "They'll back down, surely."

"It's a dangerous world to be having a baby in," Pat said, hugging her stomach.

Michael looked at her. "You really are having a baby then?"

"I really am."

He insisted on watching the news that night. Everything seemed terrible. It was a relief to go to bed, even to a fraught bed that had Michael making love to Bee. Pat felt unnecessary and uncomfortable, but stayed, because she remembered what a comfort it had been to her to have Bee there. Afterwards, Michael went to sleep in the spare room and Pat and Bee curled up together as they did every night. "Imagine them growing up together," Bee whispered, her hand on Pat's belly where she had just begun to feel the baby moving.

"If the Russians and Americans leave us a world for them to grow up in," Pat said.

The next morning it appeared that they would not. There had been what the BBC called "a limited nuclear exchange" in the night. Kennedy and Khruschev were reported to be talking.

"Oh, *now* they're talking!" Bee said. "What was wrong with talking yesterday before all those people were killed?"

Pat found it hard to take in. The Russians had bombed Miami from their Cuban bases and the Americans had retaliated with a strike on Kiev, from a base in Turkey. "What does it mean?" Pat asked.

"I don't know," Michael said. "Fallout. Radiation poisoning. And maybe it will be the all-out Armageddon we've all been expecting. It can't be over. I should go back to my parents."

"Thank you for coming. If the world's still here, we'll let you know whether we'd like you to come down next month. And of course, you'd be welcome to visit at any time just to visit." Pat hugged him.

Bee drove Michael back to the station and Pat washed dishes in the kitchen, listening to the radio. Hundreds of thousands of people were dead in Miami, but the fallout seemed to be carried out into the Atlantic rather than polluting the rest of the US. She wasn't sure where Miami was, so she looked it up on an old Penguin atlas of Bee's. Florida. On the coast. Quite near Cuba, really. Britain was in a state of preparedness for war, the BBC announced. In the event of a nuclear attack, citizens should take shelter. Where, Pat wondered, in the cellar? She remembered the bomb shelters in the war. The world was so beautiful and so fragile. They really shouldn't risk it this way.

When she thought of bombs falling it wasn't Kiev or Miami she saw, or even Cambridge, but Florence. Sharp hot tears burned in her eyes as she thought of Florence vanished in a flash, or, almost worse, full of deadly radiation and empty of people, all the art crumbling and neglected. Cellini's *Perseus* would last if it was anything but a direct hit, and Michelangelo's *David*. Marble and bronze survived, but would anybody ever look at them again and understand what they were? She so much wanted to show Florence to her baby, and to Bee's baby, and to future generations.

Then suddenly she was afraid for her baby. Was deadly radiation already filtering down through the bright sky? When she came back Bee could dispel that fear at least. "It would be days before it reached us. And depending on the weather it might never reach us. Stop crying, what good does that do?" Bee took her in her arms and rocked her.

"It's the hormones," Pat said, sniffing. "I thought of Florence—"

"I keep thinking of all those people in Miami and Kiev. So many people. Like the Blitz ten times over and all at once. Men! You'd think Hiroshima would have been enough to let anyone know how terrible a weapon it is. How could they have used it? How could they?"

At six o'clock it was announced that Khruschev and Kennedy had bowed to the Secretary General of the United Nations and would make peace. The Russians would withdraw their missiles from Cuba, and the Americans from Turkey. They regretted the loss of life.

"Regretted!" Bee snorted.

Kennedy's recorded image addressed them from the screen, looking tear-stained and broken, ten years older than when she had last seen him. "He looks guilty enough," Pat said.

"For what good that does."

"The world has come to the brink of destruction," Kennedy said. "We have stepped back from the abyss."

"Can the world just go back to normal, after that?" Pat asked. "I mean, is it possible? People always talked about The Bomb, with capital letters, as if dropping one meant dropping them all. Doomsday."

It was surprising how quickly it could go back to normal. The Cuban Exchange was soon just another incident. But Pat never again became completely absorbed in herself and her family. She kept listening to the radio and watching the news on TV. She and Bee began to go again to anti-war demonstrations. She stopped teaching at Christmas, and Michael visited again, as Bee had not become pregnant. This time it worked. Pat began to write her Naples book. Whenever she thought about Pompeii it seemed like a metaphor for the modern world, people unwittingly living their lives next to an active volcano.

In May Pat went into labor. Her mother came to be with her, vague but full of stories about childbirth and babies. She kept asking who the father was and where he was, and forgetting that she had asked, and asking again. Pat wished Bee could be there, but Bee, herself five months pregnant, had no standing to be at the birth. After six hours the doctor insisted that she needed a caesarean section. "Giving birth vaginally could kill you and the baby," he said sternly.

When Pat came around after the anaesthetic wore off, she had a huge incision across her belly. She was in a ward full of women. There was a button on the table beside her. She pressed it, and after a while a nurse came. "Where's my baby?" she asked, her voice cracking. The nurse held a glass of water to her lips, and Pat gulped it gratefully. Then the nurse went to inquire, and at last came back wheeling a bassinet containing a sleeping baby tinier than Pat had ever imagined a baby could be, with a screwed-up face and a shock of black hair. "Isn't she beautiful?" cooed the nurse, lifting her out, still asleep and wrapped in a blanket.

"She's so tiny!"

"Seven pounds, perfectly average," the nurse said, settling her on Pat's breasts. Pat put her arm around her, wincing a little as she felt the stitches pulling. She looked down into the little face, and loved her immediately and without reservation.

"What are you going to call her?" her nurse asked. "We just put Baby Cowan, because your mother didn't know."

"Florence Beatrice," Pat replied, and as she said it her eyes filled with tears. "Can I have visitors in here?"

"Your mother and your friend are waiting. They haven't seen the baby yet."

"Please let them in, if that's all right," Pat said.

"Just for a minute then, and then they can come back at proper visiting time."

Pat lay with the sleeping baby on her chest and her eyes glued on the door, waiting to show Bee their baby.

14

The Feminine Mystique: Tricia 1966–1968

Immediately before she left for Lancaster, Sylvia gave her a copy of Betty Friedan's *The Feminine Mystique*. She took it with a little roll of her eyes at her friend. "Women's Lib?"

"Women need to be liberated just as much as slaves did," Sylvia replied.

"Liberated from what?"

"Low pay and our children and the kitchen and our husbands' demands. Don't you want to actually use your degree for something?"

Tricia took the book because she did like Sylvia, but although she read all the time it really wasn't the kind of book she liked.

They moved. Mark wanted a house in the country outside Lancaster, but she insisted that the children had to be able to walk to school. Doug was sixteen, and would be beginning A levels at the Boys' Grammar. Helen, at twelve, would be going to the Girls' Grammar. Both of these schools were in the city. The younger ones would need a primary school, which could have been managed in a village.

"The older ones can take buses," Mark protested.

"If we live in the country I need to learn to drive. I'm not being stuck in the middle of nowhere the way I was outside Grantham."

"I don't want to take a bus," Helen said.

Mark walked away from the argument, but a few days later he announced that he had bought a Victorian house on the southern edge of the city.

At fifty thousand people, Lancaster barely qualified as a city in Tricia's opinion. Even if you counted Morecambe, the decayed seaside town to the west, it didn't add up. Lancaster itself was largely an eighteenth-century town, like a decayed northern version of Bath. Some of the best buildings were in a very sad state. It did have a thriving indoor market, with farm cheeses, fresh meat and vegetables, a Finefare supermarket, a Marks and Spencer, and several excellent shops selling fresh bread. The new university was built on a greenfield site three miles out of town to the south, and there was some apprehension in the town as to what the university would mean.

The house Mark bought was positioned to make it easy for him to drive on to campus. It had four floors, though the "garden floor" was barely habitable as yet. Making the house nice was a huge job, which Tricia threw herself into. Doug enjoyed painting and carpentry, and to her own surprise so did Tricia. For once she felt close to her difficult older son as they worked together to paint and furnish the rooms. Nine-year-old George involved himself too, taking instruction from his brother and looking up to him. Helen declared that the whole thing made her sick, and took long exploratory walks around the town. Six-year-old Cathy mixed paints and sanded edges. She and Doug argued about colors—both of them had strong feelings about them.

Tricia let each of the children choose the colors of their own room, and otherwise let Doug choose. Mark, who was settling in to his new office at the university, didn't seem to care. When he first saw the terracotta walls of the kitchen he started to speak, then clearly thought better of it. Tricia had seldom seen him back away from a battle, and she smiled as he walked away in silence. She loved her big terracotta kitchen. She arranged all the china on open shelves, leaving room for her mother's things. That was a battle for another day. And perhaps, like this one, she could win it by acting first without asking permission.

She was unpacking books onto the shelves in the sitting room when she found *The Feminine Mystique* again. She glanced through it and found herself unable to put it down. It was difficult not to castigate herself as she read. How had she been so accepting of so much for so long?

She went into town to find the library to seek out more books on the subject. She found the library easily, a charming dark Victorian building next to the original Town Hall, now a museum. They both faced onto Market Square, a depressing space with smelly public toilets in the center. The library had a little entrance hall, with a noticeboard covered in little notices. She saw signs for *The Mikado* and an art exhibition, for piano and guitar lessons, for help with home computers, for meetings of the CND and the Socialist Workers Party. She wrote down the times of the CND meetings and the numbers for the guitar and piano lessons. Maybe Helen would like to play an instrument.

The library was comfortably old-fashioned inside. She joined it immediately and was welcomed to the town by the young librarian. It was well stocked with fiction but low on the kind of thing she was looking for. She settled for Simone de Beauvoir's *The Second Sex* and Virginia Woolf's *A Room of One's Own*, along with her usual stack of fiction.

Helen wasn't interested in piano lessons, but George was. Doug jumped on the idea of learning the guitar. He was also letting his hair grow, to his father's loudly voiced disgust. Tricia quite liked it.

It was late to be planting a garden, and Tricia knew nothing about it. She took a book out of the library and tried to enlist the children. Helen took it up with enthusiasm and they planted bulbs. George took on the task of mowing the lawn. They had lots of picnics in the garden that summer, but not when Mark was home, as he hated eating outside, declaring it barbarous.

The children all started in their new schools in September. Mark started lecturing, and Tricia began again supply teaching, filling in here and there. She also began to take driving lessons, without mentioning it to anyone. Doug had problems with the school—they demanded he cut his hair, and she had to insist that he do so. He kept it at the maximum length the school would allow, just touching his collar. In October Tricia took her driving test and failed by forgetting to signal before turning onto a roundabout. She took it again in early December and passed—which she announced to the whole family at Sunday dinner. Doug congratulated her enthusiastically. Mark was clearly taken aback, but he choked out a "Well done" after all the children had.

She and Doug went down to Twickenham on the train the next weekend and fetched her mother up for Christmas. They had been working on the garden floor and had a bedroom and bathroom there ready for her mother, painted in lilac and dove gray. "Do you like it, Grandma?" Cathy asked. Her mother stood looking at it in confusion.

"It's very nice, thank you, darling," she said. Tricia woke in the night to hear her mother moving around downstairs. When she went down she found her standing by the sink.

"What's wrong, Mum?" she asked.

"Oh, there you are, Patsy. I got up to use the loo and I just wasn't sure where I was," her mother said. "I think I'll go home now."

It wrung her heart. "You're in my house in Lancaster, and I think it would be a good idea if you stayed here tonight. Let me show you where your bedroom is, and your little bathroom."

All the children were old enough now to understand that their grandmother wasn't remembering things. George found it funny. The others tried their best to help. Doug wasn't patient enough with her, Tricia thought, but he was ideal at getting her turned around and back to her room. He had a way of putting a gentle arm around her shoulders that always worked. Tricia wondered if it reminded her mother of her father. She always seemed to relax when she saw Doug. "Do you remember when Doug was born?" she asked one evening.

"Patsy, you speak as if you thought there was something wrong with my memory," her mother said. "I remember perfectly. You were living in that horrid little cottage in Lincolnshire."

"Hard to believe he'll be seventeen in March," Tricia said.

He had a girlfriend, Sue, who back-combed her hair. They were starting a band with another friend, Joe Pole, always known as Poley. They practiced in one of the unfinished rooms on the garden floor at times when Mark was on campus. One day Mark came home earlier than expected and heard them.

"What is that row?" he asked, bursting into the kitchen where Tricia and her mother were polishing the cutlery. Tricia had discovered that if she got her mother started on some domestic task she would remember how to do it and get on with it happily, often while talking about the old days. Tricia had heard a lot of the stories of the old days, but she didn't mind hearing them again if it kept her mother happy.

"It's just Doug and his friends practicing some folk music," Tricia said. "You won't hear them if you're in your study."

Mark's study, also his bedroom, was at the very top of the house. "I could hear it half way down the road," Mark protested. "I'm going to tell them to stop."

Mark stormed off down the stairs, and the sound of music stopped shortly afterwards.

Tricia saw Doug before dinner. "Was everything all right?" she asked.

Doug grinned and pushed a lock of hair back off his forehead. "Yes—we have a new band name."

"I meant with your father?"

"I know, so did I. He called us Philistines. So we were thinking that might make a good name, but it was too soft for what we're doing. So we're going for the biggest Philistine of them all and calling the band Goliath."

"Lovely," Tricia said. "Try not to fight with your father over Christmas?"

"I won't fight with him if he doesn't pick fights with me."

Tricia sighed. "I suppose that'll have to be good enough."

Christmas went well—the turkey was neither raw nor burned. Her mother had been a real help in the kitchen and taught Cathy how to make gingerbread. Mark gave Tricia a scarf, as he usually did. There were a few little squabbles but no big fights.

On Boxing Day, Mark asked when Tricia's mother was going home. "She can't manage at home," Tricia said. "She'll be all right here. I think she should sell her house in Twickenham and stay with us. You've hardly noticed her being here, really. She won't be in the way. It's our Christian duty to take her in. And you've seen what she's like."

Mark drew breath to protest, and let it go again. "Maybe she should be in an old folks' home," he said, reasonably gently.

"Maybe she'll get that bad later, but she's not that bad now.

I can look after her here. And she had too much money for a NHS home, and when you have to pay for them those homes are very expensive. Better for her to be here."

"What about when you're teaching and the kids are in school?" Mark asked.

"She's not so bad that she can't be on her own for a few hours like that. She just can't really look after herself properly. She won't remember to buy food or eat it or do the cleaning. But she'll be all right with us."

"If you think so," Mark said, and shrugged. "I'm working on a new book on Wittgenstein. When will you have time to type the first chapter?"

"I'll do it tonight," Tricia said, delighted that he had agreed so easily.

Tricia had difficulty making her mother understand about selling her house. She drove down alone one weekend in February and cleared it out, bringing back with her what she thought her mother would want. It was the first long drive Tricia had ever made, and she had been apprehensive beforehand. In the event she thoroughly enjoyed it, going south into the spring, able to stop whenever she wanted. Her mother was pleased to see her things, and enjoyed arranging her china on Tricia's kitchen shelves. She signed papers for the sale, and her house went on the market.

That spring, 1967, Doug's band Goliath started to play in local venues—upstairs at the Yorkshire House, in the King's Arms, and once on campus. Tricia bought Doug a new guitar for his birthday, one he had chosen from a music shop on King Street.

"Waste of money," Mark growled.

"I like to see him really caring about something," Tricia said.

"Be better if he cared about his school work," Mark said.

"By the way, I'll be late tonight. I'll eat on campus, don't save dinner for me."

"All right," Tricia said. Mark often worked late now, and she appreciated it when he warned her. She stood a moment looking after him as he walked away, wondering how they had come to this. They were familiar sarcastic strangers, dealing with each other unkindly, working around each other. She had loved him once, she knew she had. Now she loved the children and her mother, and Mark was an obstacle she knew how to get around.

During the Easter holidays her mother's house sold, and she had to go down to Twickenham to do the final clear-out. She considered taking her mother, but in the end she took Helen. Helen was thirteen and just on the edge of puberty. Her periods had started, and she was beginning to grow breasts. A spot on her nose had recently so blighted her that she demanded to be allowed to miss school on its account. On other days she lapsed back into babyhood and played with Cathy's dolls. Tricia thought it would do them good for the two of them to have some time together.

Seeing her old family house finally sold made Tricia sad, but Helen was indifferent. Helen didn't seem to care about anything except her looks. "Did you notice how the estate agent looked at me?" she asked her mother.

The money was safely banked and they drove home. "I liked my friends in Woking, but I like our house in Lancaster better," Helen said, as they got back into the car after stopping for lunch in Evesham. Tricia realized how much her daughter's conversation was focused on herself, all "I". Had she been like that at thirteen? She tried to remember.

"I was your age the year the war started," Tricia said.

"Mum! That's ancient history!"

"Recent history," Tricia said, and drove on northwards.

She had made some local friends by now, mostly through CND and teaching and the parents of other children. She joined a society to preserve and restore Lancaster, and was soon elected secretary. They campaigned for a one-way system with a ring road, with the whole town center to be pedestrianized. "It's the latest thing," the chairman said. Tricia wanted the toilets in the square replaced with a fountain.

Goliath got more local gigs that summer and autumn, and became locally popular. Tricia went to hear them play several times and noticed the crowds increasing, and the size of the venues. They began to sing more of their own songs, written by the three of them. Just after the New Year of 1968, they were, astonishingly, offered a record contract. Tricia had to sign, as Doug wouldn't be eighteen until March. "And there's no use asking Dad," Doug said. Once she had signed, he told her he was going to be dropping out of school.

"I think you'll be sorry if you don't finish your A Levels and go on to university," Tricia said. "I've told you what fun I had at Oxford."

"But music is what I want to do, and this opportunity might never come again. Goliath could be big. We could be the next Beatles."

The fight with Mark was spectacular and never seemed to stop—it smouldered away constantly whenever Mark and Doug were in the house together. She was glad Mark was working so hard and absent so often. Goliath put out a single immediately, which went to number 36 in the charts. In March, the moment Doug was eighteen, he moved to London with his girlfriend, to work on recording Goliath's first album.

Tricia's CND friends were excited about events in Czechoslovakia, the "Prague Spring" movement. "It's happening everywhere," Tricia said. "Young people want different things from what we wanted when we were young. They're not going to put up with what we put up with."

"But what if the Russians send the tanks in?" David asked.

"They didn't in Hungary, they won't do it now. We should start a letter writing campaign in support of Czech freedom."

"It's not nuclear," David said. David was an Aldermaston veteran, and he credited himself with getting US missiles out of Britain, practically single-handedly to hear him talk about it. He didn't want to widen the peace mission.

"Having peace in Europe is the best way to avoid nuclear war," Tricia said firmly.

In May, Paris erupted in student riots. In July, Doug's album was released, and a single from it went into the top ten. The Americans landed a man on the moon, fulfilling President Kennedy's brother's dream. In September there were elections in France and a communist government was elected. Mark was disapproving, but Tricia couldn't see why it mattered. There had been several communist governments in Italy, and Britain had a socialist government. The Czechs had a liberal government. Tricia's mother slowly became vaguer and started forgetting the names of everyday items.

15

Journeys: Pat 1963–1967

They did not go to Italy that summer. It was the first time since 1949 that Pat had spent a whole summer in England. They let the Florentine house through an agency. They had wanted to go, despite everything, but Pat had to acknowledge that she just wasn't well enough. She spent most of June hardly moving from bed, doing nothing but caring for the baby. They called her Flossie, or the Little Tyrant, and joked that she had been born knowing only the imperative mood.

They worried about fallout. Milk from hill regions was condemned after checking for radioactivity. "At least they're checking," Bee said. "Some of my friends are buying home Geiger counters, but I think that's paranoid. But maybe we could think about getting a cow. It would be nice to be self-sufficient. In case."

Pat fed Flossie herself. Her breasts, which she had always felt were embarrassingly small, were still smaller than Bee's even when swollen, but she had no shortage of milk. Pictures of evacuated children from the Ukraine were on television— both women wept when they saw them. "Damn hormones," Bee said, wiping her eyes. "I'd have been upset, but I'd never have cried, before."

"Me too," Pat agreed, and they laughed at themselves.

"Mind you, I hated being evacuated," Bee said.

"I just went with the school. It wasn't too bad," Pat said. "But we didn't have to go to new countries. Those poor kids, going away to East Germany and Hungary and Russia."

Bee's baby was born in September. She was a girl. Pat could not be with her for the birth, and she waited at home with baby Flossie. They had already discussed names.

"If it's a girl, Marie Patricia," Bee said. "After Marie Curie, of course."

"And if it's a boy?" Pat asked. She was lying in bed, with Flossie sucking hard at her breast and clenching and unclenching her fists as she did it, which always made both her mothers smile.

"I don't know. Patrick sounds so Irish."

"Not Patrick," Pat agreed. "If Floss had been a boy I was thinking of Marsilio."

"Marsilio!" Bee hesitated. "It would do in Italy, and of course Ficino, but in England? Maybe as his second name?"

"It's up to you," Pat said.

"Philip Marsilio?" Bee tried. "Philip Marsilio Dickinson. What do you think?"

"Lovely," Pat said. "Why Philip?"

"After Dr. Harrington," Bee said. "He got me that fellowship and took a chance on me, and not just me. He believes women should be in science. And he loves plants. And he has arranged the calendar so that I get the sabbatical to write the plant disease book this autumn, without ever saying a word about why."

"I thought you said plant people took no notice of mammalian biology?" Pat teased, moving Flossie to the other nipple.

"That's his way of taking no notice in a quietly supportive way," Bee said.

So Pat was expecting Marie, and was astonished when Bee

told her instead that the baby, nine pounds two ounces, was Jennifer Patricia. "What happened to Marie Curie?" she asked.

"Jennifer, after the midwife," Bee said. "She was amazing. She held my hand while I was pushing. If only you could have been there to hold my other hand! Jennifer is a good name, look at her. Doesn't she look like a Jenny to you?"

"Of course she does," Pat said, again overwhelmed with tenderness and love.

Bee and Jenny came home from the hospital. Pat drove and Bee sat in the passenger seat, with both babies in carry cots wedged into the back seat. "We may need a bigger car," Pat said when they got home and levered the carry cots out. Her incision barely hurt now, though at first she had been almost incapacitated by it.

It was hard having two babies on different schedules. They both fed both babies indiscriminately—their plan to each feed their own didn't outlast Jenny's first day at home when Pat automatically put her to her breast while Bee was sleeping exhaustedly. Neither of them ever had enough sleep. "We should have scheduled this better," Bee said, getting out of bed in the middle of the night as one crying baby woke the other.

"It's terrible," Pat agreed. "But it's also wonderful."

Bee laughed and padded off, coming back with a baby under each arm. "Flossie's getting heavy," she said.

"And Jenny always was heavy," Pat agreed.

Bee finished her book on plant viruses, and Pat corrected the copyedits and proofs of her Naples book. Their house grew messy around the edges. Washing piled up and floors went unswept. Bee arranged for the summer gardeners to come every week and save the garden from neglect. Denmark and Greece joined the European Economic Community. A computer beat a man at chess, and they saw their friend Alan Turing sounding shyly confident about it on the BBC.

Bee began lecturing again after Christmas. Pat found it terribly hard at first to be home with both babies. They worked out a routine where when Bee came in she spent an hour and a half with the babies upstairs while Pat had a rest and made dinner uninterrupted. She loved the babies, but she looked forward desperately to this break, in which she often just read quietly. That and the very early mornings with Bee were her favorite times of day. The babies always woke when the cock crowed and were fed, but they both readily went back to sleep after that dawn feed. Pat and Bee would lie awake and talk, or make love, or just cuddle together quietly until it was time for Bee to go to work.

Cambridge was not a town friendly to babies. There were few parks and no indoor playgrounds. Besides, Harston was six miles outside the city, and Bee needed the car to go to work. If Pat and the babies went in with her they were stuck there for the whole day, or they had to take a long slow bus ride home. This was exacerbated by how difficult it was to do anything with the babies—cafes and restaurants frowned on them, and even the librarians looked disapproving when Pat wheeled the double pram in. Most of their friends had no children, and while they were delighted to fuss over the babies when they had time, they worked during the day. More and more she stayed at home, looking after the babies and working whenever naps coincided. They dropped out of choir, and she made only a few birding expeditions that spring. They could seldom make parties, and Pat felt her horizons shrinking. At the same time she was overwhelmed with things that needed doing. She made endless lists and checked things off on them. One day Bee picked up a list and started laughing. "The first item on this list is 'Make list'!"

Pat's editor at Constable wanted her to write about Athens, but she turned him down and counter-proposed doing three new books about Rome—one on visiting ancient Rome, one on Renaissance Rome, and one on modern Rome. He agreed enthusiastically, and suggested color photographs. She told him how happy she had been with Michael's work, and he arranged for Michael to go out to Italy again that summer.

At the end of term Pat and Bee packed up their new larger car for the long trip across Europe with the babies. They had not been further with them before than Pat's mother's house at Twickenham. They had to stop frequently, and the nights in *pensiones* on the way were appalling, as neither child would settle to sleep. What surprised them was how once they crossed into Mediterranean France, suddenly everyone was tolerant and delighted, nothing was too much trouble. A waiter at a cafe in Dijon carried their thermos and blankets to the car for them. A maid at the *pensione* sang to the babies in French, and soothed them into amazed peace. As soon as they were over the Alps the proprietor of a restaurant where they had stopped before made some special baby pasta for Flossie, which she ate with more enthusiasm than she had ever yet shown for anything but breast milk. "Bella piccola Firenza," he said, enthusiastically, when she threw some on the stone floor. After Cambridge, where nothing and nobody catered for babies, this stunned both women.

"We should live here year round," Pat said, after a neighbor they had never seen before came around with eggs "for the babies" and cooed over Jenny.

"If I didn't have to work," Bee said.

"There's a university here . . ."

"I don't speak Italian well enough, and they probably don't have anything in my field. Still, it wouldn't hurt to look." She looked around at the garden. "We really could get a cow. If we needed to be self-sufficient, if civilization collapsed, we'd be better off here."

"Do you think it might?" Pat asked. "I mean with the new European alliance everything seems a bit more stable?"

"It doesn't stop the Americans and the Russians glaring at each other above our heads," Bee said. "No, Flossie, don't eat that!"

The children were much too young to appreciate Florence, apart from the food, which they appreciated with gusto. "I was the same when I first went to Italy," Pat said, watching Jenny guzzling zucchini flowers.

When Michael came, he stayed in Florence for a few days, then despite the inconvenience and the expense, every day for a week he and Pat went to and fro to Rome on the train and worked hard at photographing what she wanted for all three new books. "I'll do the Ancient and Renaissance books first, and then the modern one after next summer, because that's the one that'll need most checking."

"I don't know how you manage at home on your own," Bee said when they came back on the third day. "Even here, where we can walk into town and everyone fusses over them, it's driving me mad."

"Do you want me to take a day off and stay tomorrow?" Pat asked.

"No, get it done and out of the way while Michael's here."

Michael was shy with the babies, in a way they had already seen with some of their Cambridge friends. Flossie was already saying words, and Jenny was babbling syllables. It took Michael a week to join in and behave naturally with them. "Do you think they look like him?" Bee asked in one of their early morning conversations.

"Jenny's ears are just like his. And Flossie has his feet and hands."

"I've noticed that too," Bee said. "It's strange how it does and doesn't matter."

"Because they're ours," Pat said, and kissed her.

Sometime that summer as Flossie's words grew more distinct, "Jenny" became "Jinny" to all of them. As Flossie was sometimes Florrie-Bee, Jenny was Jinny-Pat. These were their special in-family-only nicknames.

Pat took them into the Baptistery and held them up to see the gold ceiling, which they pointed at excitedly. She wished she could have them baptized there, but she wasn't going to make any promises to bring them up in the faith. Nevertheless, she thanked God for them, there, and in the Duomo, and in San Lorenzo, and indeed several times every day whenever she thought of it. She went alone to the Uffizi—churches were different, but they really were too young for an art gallery—and stood before Botticelli's *Madonna of the Magnificat* and thought about Mary, the Annunciation, and how differently she felt about all that now that she had a baby. Before, her attention had mostly been on Botticelli's angels. Now she concentrated on the mother and baby. The smile really did remind her of Bee. She bought a good copy of it in the gift shop.

Bee talked to Sara about the prospects of teaching and researching in Florence, and reluctantly gave up the idea. "The whole way academia is organized here is crazy," Sara said.

The drive back home through Europe felt even more epic an adventure than driving down had been. As they went north Pat felt sad, as she always did leaving Italy. "It's not just the food and the art and that it has given me a way of making a living," she said. She was sitting on the back seat with the babies while Bee drove. "And it's not just that everyone loves children, which English people really don't. There really is something about it."

The epic car journeys became a feature of their lives, and at length they all blurred together—the one where Jinny nearly fell off the cross-Channel ferry, the one where Pat nearly fell asleep on an Alpine road and forgot what side to drive on and almost hit a lorry, the one where Flossie refused to stop speaking Italian, the one where Bee went off to pee on an Alp and found a gentian, the one where Pat was pregnant and kept having to stop to be sick and the children found it hilarious. Pat wrote the three Roman books, then a guide to Siena and the small towns of Tuscany. Bee's book on plant diseases was republished in America. Spain and Portugal joined the European Economic Community, and elections were held for the new European parliament. President Rockefeller visited China and was given a panda. Bee and the children shared a great longing to see the panda and Pat teased them all about it. They bought toy pandas for both girls for Christmas.

In November of 1966 there was a flood in Florence, killing six people and damaging some property. Fortunately the weather computers had predicted it well in advance, so most people had evacuated and most works of art were moved to safety. Some frescos were damaged. Pat wrote articles about their restoration and sat on a committee to raise money for it.

In January of 1967, when the girls were four and three and a half and Pat was seven months pregnant, she had to go to London to meet her editor for a meeting about the Tuscany book. It all went well, and the editor agreed to use a picture of her that Michael had taken, with her head and shoulders against the stairs of the Bargello. (Pat's favorite of Michael's photographs was one of Bee sitting in the garden with both babies on their first summer in Florence. She had an enlargement of that in a silver frame on the mantelpiece in Cambridge. She had the *Madonna of the Magnificat* in a matching frame next to it.) As she made her way out of the lift into the lobby of the Constable offices, she was astonished to run into Mark.

Mark looked older and a little less prosperous than Pat remembered him. His hair was receding and graying, and while his clothing style was still academic dinginess, it suited him less. To her astonishment he didn't seem to notice her at all. He just walked past towards the lift.

"Mark!" she said. "How are you?"

He paused, looked at her, and blinked. She realized that he really hadn't recognized her. "Patty!" he said. "My goodness."

"Are Constable your publishers too?" she asked.

"They're bringing out a book of mine on philosophy, yes," he said. "Too? They're publishing you?"

"Oh, just a series of guide books to Italy I write," she said, and was instantly furious with herself for deprecating her work before Mark, of all people.

"You're P. A. Cowan?" Mark asked. "I wondered if it could be some relation. I didn't know you knew anything about Italy."

"I didn't when I knew you," Pat said. "What are you doing now?"

"Oh, lecturing. I'm at Keele. Are you still teaching? Or—I see you've married." He gestured vaguely at the obvious bulge under her good wool coat.

"I gave up teaching four years ago when I was having a baby," Pat said, sidestepping the question. "Fortunately I could carry on with the writing."

"Yes, very nice," Mark said. "I have to go, I have a meeting in five minutes. Are you free afterwards? We could have some lunch or something, catch up on old times."

Pat looked at her watch. "I have to get back to Cambridge," she said. "I—my—it's complicated, but I have to get back for my children."

"Well it was nice to see you, and I'm glad you've found happiness." Mark hesitated for a moment and then leaned forward and kissed her cheek before going in to the lift.

She thought about him all the way back on the train, and

when Bee met her at the station she told her about it immediately. They couldn't talk about it then, because the children were in the back seat and Bee needed to get into college before her class. Pat dropped her off and then took the children home. After they were in bed, stories read and songs sung and the light turned emphatically off, she went down to pour it all out to Bee over a cup of tea.

"Once, my heart turned over whenever I saw him, and there wasn't a shred of that left. I felt sorry for him. He had a neglected air. He didn't say, but I'm sure he wasn't married."

"Chalk dust," Bee said. "It must be horrid being at Keele when he wanted to be at Oxford. I'm bending over backwards to be fair to him, when really I hate him for abandoning you and making you sad."

"It was me who abandoned him. He gave me the choice. And I'm sure I made the right choice. But it was so strange. I wanted to tell him about you, about us, about my life. But on the other hand I was glad I was wearing gloves so he couldn't see that I wasn't married even though I'm so very visibly pregnant."

"Did you give him our address or phone number or anything?"

"No." Pat put her free arm around Bee and snuggled close. "I didn't think of it. And even if time hadn't been so short with getting back before your class, I don't think I would have had lunch with him. I don't really want him back in my life. It was just so strange running into him like that."

Pat's baby was born in April, again by caesarean section, this time planned in advance. He was a boy, and she called him Philip Marsilio, as they had agreed.

16

Liberation: Tricia 1968–1972

To Tricia's complete surprise, Doug became a minor but significant figure in the pop world. Goliath released albums and toured, and Doug, Sue and Poley were names people knew. Mark tried to ignore it, and kept saying that Doug would soon have enough of it and go to university. With the proceeds from one of his hit records, Doug bought his mother a car, a green Volkswagen Beetle, for Christmas 1968. Mark said nothing. He had given her a scarf, as usual.

Tricia saw a poster in the library asking for volunteers for adult education. "I think I'll apply," she said. "I could teach literature to adults."

"It's the most you can do to teach it to children part time," Mark sneered. "Why do you think adults would want to listen to you? What do you have to bring them?"

She gave up the idea.

Mark was home less and less, leaving for work immediately after breakfast and seldom returning before the late evening. On weekends he was usually on campus. Now that Tricia had her own car she could accept supply teaching further away, and was working almost all the time. It was a good way to get to know the schools and the county. If she was driving past a bus stop with a mother and small child waiting, she would stop and offer them a lift. She sometimes did it when she saw a mother and child walking slowly along. She remembered all too well what it was like being stuck like that. The mothers received her offers with mixed feelings. Some accepted, some refused. Of the ones who accepted, almost all of them asked her why she was doing it, and many seemed skeptical of her answers. She became aware that her voice was a severe disadvantage to her, as it was in the classroom. She sounded Southern, posh, stuck up. She tried to change her voice, but then it just sounded unnatural.

"I sound stuck up," she lamented to her mother.

"You sound very nice, Patsy," her mother said. "Refined."

"No, Gran, Mum's right. She does sound stuck up," Cathy said. Cathy was ten now, in her last year of junior school.

"It's ridiculous for people to think I'm stuck up. My father mended wirelesses and my mother was a nursemaid."

"But you went to Oxford and married Dad," George said. "Try to talk more Lancashire. I do in school, and people like me better."

But Tricia couldn't deliberately change the way her voice came out of her mouth. Instead she tried to find things to talk about to them that cut across barriers. Childcare, illness and her mother's senility worked for this, as her chilblains had long ago in Oxford.

In 1969 homosexuality and marijuana were legalized by the Labour government, and the death penalty was abolished. Mark saw the first of these as signs of the forthcoming apocalypse, but Tricia was delighted about all three. The Americans broke ground on a moonbase. Tricia watched the men walking on the lunar surface and wondered what use it was to anyone. George went briefly astronaut mad and spent his pocket money on magazines and books about space and trips to the moon.

In January of 1970 Helen turned sixteen. She took her O Levels in June and did well. Nevertheless she insisted that she was not returning to school. "I'll get a job," she said. When her father raved at her she threatened to move to London and stay with Doug. Helen had always been her father's favorite, and he seemed devastated that she was abandoning his ideals, as he put it. He blamed Tricia, although she disapproved of Helen's decision as much as he did, if more quietly.

Helen got a job in a coffee bar in town. She back-combed her hair and bought tie-dyed clothes. She looked like a hippie princess. She found boyfriends and spent a lot of time out with them. Tricia wasn't sure whether to be relieved or horrified that she went through them so fast, and always had two or three of them ready to take her out. Tricia took her to the doctor and begged her to prescribe the pill for Helen. Tricia still took her own pill every night, though it had been a long time since Mark had brought home a bottle of wine. She thought about that as she walked back from the surgery with Helen. Perhaps Mark believed she was too old for more children? Perhaps he would leave her alone now?

Tricia worried about Doug, worried about drugs and the price of early success. She went to London, or somewhere he was playing, every few months and saw him, and he always came home for Christmas. He and Sue were as settled as a married couple, although they were not married and there was no suggestion of marriage. Mark refused to countenance the relationship, but Tricia saw no point in closing her eyes to it. Sue wasn't what she'd have chosen for her son, but she was clearly his choice. She wrote the music for their songs and Doug wrote the lyrics.

Back at home, Tricia was working at Morecambe Grammar School for a few months as the English teacher was on maternity leave. She enjoyed teaching the same girls over a period of time, and they seemed to like her. She liked More-cambe out of season, the deserted sea front with the clacking flagpoles, the distant water, even the way the sea came in side-ways over the sands. She had always loved the sea. She didn't like the way the place was decaying. She suggested that the Lancaster Preservation Society take an interest in it, and found herself alone. You could walk from Lancaster to Morecambe in an hour, but they were worlds apart emotionally, and the people of Lancaster wanted nothing to do with it. Undeterred, Tricia started a Morecambe Preservation Society by putting up a notice in Morecambe Library announcing the first meet-ing and then seeing who showed up. She served as secretary for that society too.

The teacher was supposed to return from maternity leave in September, but the headmistress took Tricia aside one day and told her that she wouldn't be coming back. "We're going to advertise the post, of course. We have to. But if you applied we'd look very favorably on your application." Tricia could take a hint; when the post was advertised she applied for it and was duly taken on permanently for the new academic year of 1971. At the same time she found a woman called Marge who lived nearby to come in and care for her mother in the daytime, as now she really couldn't be left. She felt she was underpaying Marge, who was endlessly patient with the old woman.

One Saturday that autumn when she and George were at the library returning and collecting books, she spotted a new notice on the noticeboard: "Women's Consciousness Raising Group, Thursday evening 7:30 pm, upstairs, Ring O' Bells." It was the same pub where CND met. Tricia showed up, uncer-tainly, not sure if she wanted her consciousness raised or what that really meant. What she found was a group of women like her, mostly housewives or women returned to work after children, women who had read *The Feminine Mystique* and *The Female Eunuch,* and wanted something better than the lives they were offered. Tricia tried to persuade Helen to go to the next meeting, but she rolled her eyes and said she was meeting a boyfriend that night.

Tricia's attitude to Women's Liberation was that it had come too late for her. It could have made a huge difference to her life if it had come along ten years before, but as it was she had mostly freed herself. She had a job and a car and the children were older. Mark had stopped bothering her for sex. But listening to these women talk she did feel that they were, as they said, sisters. They had shared experiences she had never been able to talk about with anyone before. It meant so much to be able to talk about these things. And she wanted things to be better for the next generation, for Helen and Cathy to have the chances she had not had.

At Easter 1972, Tricia, George and Cathy came back from a visit to Doug in London to find a note from Helen: "Gran in Infirmary. Please come." Tricia rushed around to the Infirmary, which was just around the corner, close enough that they heard ambulances so often that they didn't look up at a siren any more. "My mother," Tricia said. "Helen Cowan?"

They directed her through the Victorian building to a newly built ward where her mother was strapped into a bed and unconscious. Helen was there looking exhausted, her hair a mess. "She fell," Helen said. "I came home and found her. Well, I didn't find her at once. She was downstairs. I came in late and was going to bed, but I heard something. I thought a cat had got in. I went down and she was on the floor outside her room, in a pool of pee. I didn't know what to do. I called the doctor and they sent an ambulance. They say she's broken her hip."

"Have you been here since last night?" Tricia asked, hugging Helen. "How marvellous of you. I'm here now, and I'll stay with her. You go home and get some sleep, and see that the little ones eat something if you don't mind. Where's Dad?"

"I don't know. He wasn't there. Last night. It was gone eleven." Helen flushed a little. Eleven was her curfew, which Mark had insisted on while she lived at home. "It was closer to midnight. And of course I thought he must be in bed and went to wake him. I thought he'd know what to do. I wasn't sure whether to try to move her. She was whimpering, oh it was horrible, Mum. But Dad wasn't there. No sign of him. I knocked, and then I opened the door, and the bed was made and empty. I looked in your room too, in case, but of course he wasn't there."

"No, he wouldn't have been," Tricia said, absently. "I wonder where he was? Had you seen him in the morning?"

"No, nor the night before. I hadn't seen him since Friday morning, when after you left he asked me if I was going to church with him and then stormed off when I said no, I was working."

"I hope he's all right," Tricia said. "If he'd collapsed or anything they'd have telephoned, and nobody would have answered." Just then her mother moaned from the bed, and Tricia went over and took her hand. "I'm here, Mum, you're in hospital, but everything is all right."

"Patsy?" her mother said.

"It's all right. It's all right, Helen. You go home. We'll sort out the mystery of where your father is later. I'm sure there's some perfectly sensible explanation." She wondered what on earth it could be.

The doctors had set her mother's broken hip, but they wouldn't let her go home. "She shouldn't have been left alone," one of them said, a young Pakistani man.

"She wasn't. A woman comes in to be with her when I'm in work, and the rest of the time I'm there. She can only have been alone for a few hours. And I thought my husband would be there." Tricia felt guilty, and yet she seldom left her mother. "I took the younger children to London to see my oldest son, who lives there." Now she felt she was explaining too much, and that the doctor was judging her.

"Well she can't return yet in any case," he said.

"Mammy! Mammy!" Tricia's mother called from the ward. "Where are you?"

"She's calling for her mother," the doctor said. "Everyone does that in the end."

"Her mother died in 1930," Tricia said. "Wait. Do you mean that she's dying?"

"Oh no. There's nothing organically wrong with her, except the broken hip. People can live a long time with dementia."

Tricia left her mother in the hospital for the night and went home. Helen had fed the younger children fish and chips and put them to bed. The papers were all over the kitchen table. Tricia cleared them up automatically while making a cup of tea. Then Mark came in, whistling a hymn, his briefcase in his hand and a bag over his shoulder.

"You're home already," he said.

"Where have you been?" Tricia asked.

She guessed at once, because he immediately looked guilty.

"You've been with a woman, haven't you?"

Mark hesitated for a moment, expressions passing over his face—guilt, belligerence, suspicion, and at last his normal arrogance. "Our marriage is a nonsense, it has been for years. You know that. You don't want me and you never have. You'd see that if you looked at it calmly."

"I'm perfectly calm," Tricia said, and she was. The kettle boiled and she poured the water onto the teabag in her cup. "What are you going to do?"

"How do you mean?"

"Are you going to leave us? Do you want a divorce so you can marry this woman?"

"You forget, I'm a Catholic, I can't have a divorce. And we could hardly have this marriage annulled with four children to show for it."

"You're such a hypocrite, Mark," Tricia said, still standing with one hand on the handle of the kettle. "Adultery is all right, betrayal of marriage vows is all right, but divorce, oh no, unthinkable. You write all the time about ethics and virtue and logic, but I think you might apply some of those things to your own behavior."

"You're acting like a child," Mark said, always his accusation. Usually he made her feel like a child, but not tonight.

"I think you should leave. Go back to her, or go somewhere, but leave the house. I don't want to see you here."

"All right, I will." Mark was flushed with anger now. "You don't know anything about making a man happy. You never did. I stayed with you from duty, I supported you all these years."

"Just go away!" Tricia shouted. "Now."

He drew a breath and turned his back and walked down the stairs and out of the front door.

When he had gone she sat down at the kitchen table and stared at the shelves of china against her terracotta walls. When she tried to drink her tea she realized she was shaking when she spilled it all over her hands. She had called him a hypocrite. She had told him to go, and he had gone. Her mother was in hospital. Helen had thought about somebody who wasn't herself and coped just like an adult. She picked up the mug in both hands and carried it to her mouth.

17

Three Is Enough: Pat 1967–1969

The moon landing took Pat by surprise, as it did most people. Of course she'd noticed Sputnik, and Gagarin, but somehow reaching the moon seemed more significant. In the BBC's translation of Leonov's words the Russians claimed the moon for all the peoples of the Earth, but she felt it ominous that they were there, and even more ominous later when they went back and began building a base. She looked up at the full moon from their garden in Harston and felt it brooded over them.

Bee felt completely differently. "It's a triumph for science. Didn't you ever read science fiction? Donald and I used to read *Astounding* whenever we could get it. The moon's the first step. It doesn't matter who got there first. It's part of our future in space. I wonder what they'll do with hydroponics in their moon base. I'd love to work on that."

"They could drop bombs from there," Pat said.

"They can hurl missiles up from Earth just as easily," Bee said, and frowned. "Did you see the cancer cluster figures? I don't think there's any doubt that it's because of Kiev fallout. Children with thyroid cancer, that's appalling. The Americans weren't thinking about us at all when they dropped that bomb. We have our own space agency. I'd like to see some Europeans up there too."

There was an election in the spring of 1968 in which Airey Neave led the Conservatives to victory. He made a speech talking about closer ties with Europe. There was a feeling in Italy too that Europe should become more of a political unit, a third force to stand against both the USA and the USSR. Neave talked about "Neoliberal" economics and monetarist policy. He began a program of returning nationalized industries to private control, while selling shares to the public. This was immensely popular. Pat was astonished to hear Bee's parents when they visited talking about their shares and the money they had made, in addition to their usual sheep-based conversation.

Pat unexpectedly had a letter from Marjorie. They had been on each other's Christmas card lists, but hadn't caught up in person for years. She was getting married to a man she had met in Portugal. Pat, Bee and the children went to the wedding in London. Marjorie had dieted herself gaunt for the occasion, and the white dress was not kind to her complexion, but she was delighted to see all of them. "I hope you enjoy Portugal," Pat said. They gave her a chopping board and a set of good kitchen knives made from the new much touted "space metals."

Ireland wanted to join Europe, just as Europe was talking about political unity and a combined truly independent nuclear deterrent. This led to a renewed wave of Irish terrorist violence in Britain and Ulster, as the IRA feared joining Europe meant being more closely bound to the UK. When Pat and Bee were in Florence that summer they read with horror about a bombing campaign in London.

The weekend after they came home from Italy, they all went to see Pat's mother in Twickenham. She was vaguer than ever, recognizing Pat but uncertain of all the others and seeming overwhelmed by them. Pat talked to the nurse she had been paying to care for her mother and was alarmed. "She's eating like a bird, I can hardly get her to take anything," she said. "Some days she doesn't recognize me. I worry about leaving her at night. She should really be in a home."

"We need to talk about that," Bee said.

Back in the sitting room, her mother was accusing Jinny of having stolen her glasses.

"I haven't seen your stupid glasses!" Jinny said, furious and indignant. "Why would I take them?"

"You've probably put them down somewhere, Helen," the nurse said, soothingly. "Ah, here they are on the windowsill. How did they get there I wonder?"

"She stole them. She's a wicked girl!"

"I did not!" Jinny said, crying now. "I'm not wicked. You shouldn't say so!"

Pat hugged Jinny and looked over her head at Bee.

"Let's all have a cup of tea," Bee said. "Who wants to help me make it? Jinny? Flossie? Let's see if we can find any biscuits."

"We could afford a nice home for her where they'd look after her properly," Pat said, when they were in the car headed home, with all three children asleep in a heap on the back seat.

"She wouldn't know where she was and it would make her worse," Bee said. "We should have her with us."

"Oh Bee, you're so much nicer than I am. I don't know if I could face it. She's never really approved of me, and to have that disapproval around all the time, with the confusion—I don't know. And with the girls about to start school I was looking forward to having more time to work. That's just selfishness. But worst of all, she really upset Jinny, and she'd keep on doing things like that. I don't think it would be good for the children for her to be with us."

"Would you want our children to pack us into homes when we get old?" Bee asked.

Pat thought about it as she negotiated a roundabout and turned onto a new road. "It's so difficult. I think I would, rather than have them disrupt their lives, especially if I was that difficult. She always used to say I was wicked when I'd done anything wrong when I was a child. She used to shut me in the cupboard in the dark when she thought I'd blasphemed. I don't want her saying that the girls are wicked. It's a terrible thing to say. If I was like that—but I don't know. It's easy to say that now, when I'm not helpless. What I'd really want is for them to love us and want us, and I'd really like to love Mum and want to have her to live with us, but I don't. We've never been close."

Bee was quiet for a while. "Old age is terrifying," she said. "And senility is the worst of all, I think."

"Maybe we could find a good home in Cambridge where I could visit her frequently," Pat said.

"Maybe that would be best," Bee said.

They looked at homes, and at last found one in Trumpington, not too far, and clean. It was expensive, but not all that much more than they had been paying for the nurse and the cleaners in Twickenham. Pat drove alone to collect her mother one fine September Saturday. She didn't understand where she was going. As they drove off, with bags packed with what Pat imagined her mother might want, she realized that she was going to have to clear out and sell her mother's house. Pat had been born there, and had been going back there dutifully all her life.

Her mother liked the home at first, she enjoyed being shown around and told Pat how kind the nurses were. She admired the garden and was gracious to the other patients. But when Pat got up to go, congratulating herself on how easy it had been, her mother got up too. "I'll just get my coat, Patsy," she said. "This has been lovely, but I'm tired and I can't say I'll be sorry to be home."

"But you're staying here, Mum, and these people are going to look after you."

"Nonsense! We've just been visiting them, and now it's time to go. I couldn't be expected to stay here!" She wept and raged at last, when nobody would agree that it must be a mistake. Pat was shaking when she got back into the car.

"How did it go?" Bee asked when she arrived home.

"Terrible," Pat said. The girls were planting bulbs along the fence and Philip was asleep on a blanket. "It was all fine until she understood she had to stay, and then she was sure it was a mistake. It must be like a nightmare, being that confused."

Bee put her arms around her. "Would it be better having her here after all?"

"No, I think it's the right thing. But it was so awful."

"We'll all go and see her tomorrow," Bee said. "We won't just abandon her there."

"No," Pat agreed.

"And now I'll put the kettle on. We thought we'd have a picnic tea. The girls have been working hard getting it ready. Come on, wash your hands, girls, it's time for tea."

The girls raced each other indoors. Close in age, they were often taken for twins. Both of them had Michael's dark hair but were otherwise very different. Flossie was long legged and stalky. "A rower, like her mother," Bee said. Jinny was shorter and more solid, with a square face and a turned-up nose like Bee's. They both chattered in Italian as fluently as English, much more fluently than their mothers. Pat had worried about their starting school, about their different surnames and absent fathers. All the children had Michael written down as their father on their birth certificates, as the alternative was to say the father was unknown, which sounded awful. But although they saw Michael for a weekend every month or so and they knew he was their father, it was far from a usual situation. Pat was afraid the presence of two mothers and the absence of a father would be a social embarrassment to them in school. She needn't have worried, at least not immediately, as the girls loved school and nobody seemed to have bothered them about their unusual family.

The girls continued in the village school, and Pat's mother continued in the home in Trumpington. Pat got into the habit of visiting her mother with the whole family on a Sunday afternoon and taking her mother out to lunch in Cambridge on a Thursday. They had two cars now, the big Hillman and a sporty Mini. Her mother often wept and raged when she left, and often asked to go home. She generally recognized Pat, and sometimes the others. She frequently asked Pat where her father was, and even more frequently asked her who was the father of the children.

They went to Italy in the summer of 1969, just after the fuss of the European space launch. "We'll get to the moon yet," Bee said.

"To Italy, Mamma!" Flossie corrected her. To the children Bee was Mamma and Pat was Mum.

"Italy, Italy!" Philip chorused.

On the ferry, as the children ran up and down chasing seagulls and dodging in and out of the legs of other passengers, Bee took Pat's hand. "You're very quiet."

"I keep feeling as if I'm abandoning my mother in the home. I tell myself she won't know the difference, or won't remember, and I want to go so much, even aside from needing to go to write a new book, but I feel guilty."

"She really won't know. Put her behind you for the summer

and enjoy the moment, or you'll just be wracked with guilt and then you'll have left her for nothing."

The sea-wind ruffled through Pat's short hair and blew a strand of Bee's longer hair into her mouth. "You're right," she said. "Let's catch up with the kids before they have to be fished out!"

Her mother did cast a shadow over that summer. Pat kept seeing old Italian women, with wrinkled faces and black clothes. They were old but vital, alive. She had always been aware of them since her first trip to Italy as protectors against predatory men. Now she wondered how old they were and whether they lived with their families. Surely there must be old demented women in homes in Italy, but she didn't see them. She found them in paintings—Saint Elizabeth, and anonymous Renaissance Italian women in crowds. She took the girls to the Uffizi this year and began to talk to them about art and the men who had made the art. Jinny loved the colors and the shapes, and Flossie loved the stories.

Several days were wasted in getting papers allowing her to own the house in Florence she had owned now for more than ten years. "It's just stupid paperwork, there's more and more of it," the official said. "Since you are a European citizen there is no problem, but you need the permit."

Michael came to visit at the beginning of August. She went with him up to Como and Lake Garda, taking photographs for the new book. "Don't you ever get tired of Italy?" he asked.

"No, I never do. Come to that, I never get tired of Florence."

"I was taking photographs for a new guide somebody's doing of Greece. I thought you should have done it, you'd have done it better."

"Greece didn't have a Renaissance," Pat said.

In Florence, when the children were in bed, the three of them discussed whether Pat and Bee wanted more children, and concluded that three was enough. Bee was about to be forty, the age Pat had been when Philip was born, and the oldest age she felt it was safe to have a baby.

"As long as you don't feel—" Pat said.

"I don't. I don't at all. I feel that three is enough," Bee said, firmly. "As for you, it's time you found a nice wife and got married," she said to Michael.

"What would I ever tell her about this?" he asked. "A nice Jewish girl like my parents want me to marry would be shocked. Besides, there's no hurry, and I'm travelling so much at the moment. I keep getting guidebooks, and Sunday supplement travel work. I'm in demand, but only because I can pack up and go anywhere without warning. A wife wouldn't like that."

Reading the English papers, Pat was surprised to find her old pupil Pamela Corey was becoming famous as part of the Second Impressionist movement.

On their return to Cambridge she resumed her routine with her mother, who didn't seem to have missed her or even noticed her absence. "It makes me wonder why I do it," she said to Bee. "She's so often hostile and accusing."

Bee's father died suddenly of a heart attack in November. They all went up to Westmorland for the funeral. They discussed it on the drive up, and Bee offered her mother a home with them if she wanted it. She refused, saying she was comfortable where she was, with Bee's brother Donald and his wife and children close by in the village. Bee's parents had never really approved of Pat, or of the children.

"It's easier, but I always thought I'd end up looking after them," Bee said, as they drove home past the drystone walls and sheep-dotted fells. "It's such a difficult thing."

"You'll miss your father," Pat said.

"I will. He was so proud of me, Cambridge, and the Fellowship and everything. He had a copy of my book on his bedside table—not that he could have made head or tail of plant viruses, but there it was."

"I still miss my father," Pat said. "I wish I could have known him when I was grown up."

"Yes, so do I." Bee glanced from the road to Pat's face. "It's sad you never had that. I had those extra years with my Dad. That's something to be thankful for."

They stopped for the night in Lancaster, staying in the King's Head, an old coaching house hotel on the edge of the city. Pat told Bee about Stan and Flo and the night she had spent in Barrow-in-Furness. "They are the ones who got me started in birding."

"And she was called Flo?"

"Yes, like hundreds of girls of her generation called after Florence Nightingale, I suppose."

"They were so desperate for strong female role models," Bee said. "Were you thinking of her at all when you named Flossie?"

"Not really," Pat confessed. "Neither Nightingale nor Flo in Barrow. Flossie is called after Firenze directly."

The next morning they made an early start and drove out of town early, past the new ugly yellow-brick and plate-glass university, and on south towards home.

18

Divorce: Tricia 1972

She didn't see or hear from Mark for a week. In the end she phoned him at work, which was the suggestion of Barbara from the consciousness raising group. "I'm glad you've finally got rid of him, he sounds like a real slimeball, but you have to get the financial details and everything sorted out. He can't leave you with young children and walk away. Here's my solicitor's number. You need a proper lawyer for a divorce."

At first Tricia's heart sank at the thought of divorce. What had it all been for? And Mark was a Catholic, divorce didn't exist for him. They could get divorced and he'd still regard himself as married to her. But she wouldn't need to. She could be free of Mark. She called the university and asked the switchboard to put her through to Mark.

"Mark Anston," he answered, his voice precise and bored as ever.

"It's Tricia. You probably need some things from the house. And we should talk about what we're going to do."

"This is a bad time," he said. She wondered who was there. Students? Colleagues? Would he have told them?

"Do you want to come around this evening?" she asked.

"Not this evening, I have an engagement. Tomorrow evening, about six?"

"I'll be here," she said, although the next day was Tuesday and she had her Morecambe Preservation meeting after school, which would mean hurrying back afterwards, and no time to visit her mother, still in hospital, until later.

He was late, of course. After thinking about it for most of the previous evening, Tricia had decided not to prepare a meal for him. On Tuesdays after her meeting she usually picked up Chinese take-away for herself and the children, and she did that. They had just finished eating when she heard him let himself in. Helen cleared the boxes and forks off the table without being asked and Tricia went down the stairs to greet him.

"Where are the children?" Mark asked.

"Just finishing their dinner, in the kitchen," Tricia said. Mark walked up the stairs and into the kitchen. Helen looked away from him. George frowned. Only Cathy looked glad to see her father.

"How are you all?" Mark asked.

Tricia could hardly believe how artificial he sounded.

"Fine," Helen answered for all of them. "Where have you been?"

Mark flashed a look of irritation at Tricia, as if he expected her to have dealt with this. "Your mother and I are considering a separation," he said, as if it had been her idea.

"A divorce," Tricia said.

George stood up from the table. "I don't want to listen to this."

"I think it would be best if you all went to your rooms while we talk about it," Mark said. The two younger ones left.

"Do you know Gran fell and I had to get her to hospital?" Helen asked as she followed them towards the door.

"No, I didn't know. Is she all right?"

"She is, no thanks to you," Helen said, stopping and turning in the doorway. "I didn't know where you were. Where were you?"

Mark stood open-mouthed.

"With some floozy, I gather," Helen went on, stressing the word. "Which is rich, considering what you've said to me about my morality. I never went off with anyone and left an old lady alone or somebody else to take care of my responsibilities. That's what I consider immoral. Just so you know." She left, closing the door gently behind her.

Tricia stared after her for a moment before turning to Mark.

"You're turning the children against me!" he stormed.

"I haven't said anything about you to them other than that you had some work to take care of," Tricia said. "Mark, I do think we should be able to discuss this like sensible adults."

"You've never been a sensible adult."

Tricia sat down, everything she had planned to say taken away by that. "What, then?" she asked.

"I need some clothes and some books," he said. "I'm living in an apartment on campus."

"Not with her?"

"Who?"

"Oh come on, you already admitted it! Look, I agree that our marriage is over, but there are some things we need to sort out. Support for George and Cathy until they're eighteen." Barb had told her she would be entitled to money too, but she thought now she was teaching full time she could live on what she earned.

"I thought you could sell the house and buy a smaller one, and the difference would support you all. This house has appreciated quite a bit in the last six years." Mark's tone was even now.

"Sell this house!" Tricia was appalled. "I love this house.

And we couldn't have one that was much smaller—we wouldn't all fit in."

Mark walked over to the door and opened it. "I'm going to get my things, and then I'm going back to campus."

"You'll be hearing from my solicitor," Tricia said.

"Don't be ridiculous. You don't have a solicitor."

"I do now," Tricia said.

She called the solicitor the next morning and made an appointment for after work that day. The solicitor's office was on Castle Hill, and the solicitor herself, L. Montrose, was a woman, well groomed and younger than Tricia. "What are your grounds for a divorce?"

"He has another woman. And he has left me."

"Do you have proof?" Miss Montrose turned a pencil in her fingers. "If he's an unreasonable person it's necessary to have proof of adultery. Otherwise you have to wait for two years' separation, or five if he contests that."

"What would be proof?" Tricia asked, thinking of stained sheets.

"Hotel bills," the solicitor said, surprising Tricia. "Photographs. Private detectives can get that kind of thing, and it might be worth your while using one." She gave Tricia a card. "If that doesn't work then it's desertion, but that's slow, especially if he won't agree. I take it you want money?"

"I have two children under eighteen—they're fifteen and thirteen. I want support for them until they're finished in education. He talked about making me sell the house. I don't want to. But I don't know how much the mortgage is."

"It'll be in his name? I can find out. You've been married how long?"

"Since 1949. Twenty-three years." Almost a quarter century. An immense span of time. "My oldest son is twenty-two." She would have to tell Doug. Her liberation from Mark had come too late for him. "I just want everything settled."

She called the private detective and asked him to follow Mark and send the proof to Miss Montrose. George wanted to know where his father was and why they were separating. Doug, when she told him, wanted to know why she hadn't divorced his father years ago. Helen too was on her mother's side. Cathy was the only one who seemed to miss Mark. The house seemed to breathe more easily without him. She visited her mother every day, and Helen often came with her.

Two weeks later, on a perfect May day when the trees were bursting with new green leaves, she went to see Miss Montrose by appointment.

"I heard from your detective," Miss Montrose said, as if it hadn't been her own idea. She seemed even more sophisticated this time, in a gray suit with lace collar and cuffs. "You may be shocked by these photographs." She slid them across the desk.

At first Tricia wasn't shocked at all. The first was of Mark and a younger man, walking along the sea front in Morecambe. The second was the younger man's hand on Mark's arm. The third was of the two of them going into the Metropole hotel. Then there was a bill, for one double room, in Mark's name.

"Homosexuality is no longer illegal," Miss Montrose said crisply, as Tricia shuffled through the photographs again. "And these alone might not have been enough to secure a conviction when it was. They will, however, will serve adequately as proof of adultery for a divorce court, assuming you want to proceed."

"Why didn't he tell me?" Tricia asked. "He never—all those years! I've always—and he's always been so intolerant. Back at Oxford, even."

"Sometimes men feel they have to repress their urges," Miss Montrose said. "I'm very sympathetic, of course, but moving on, I shall send him a letter asking for a financial declaration preparatory to divorce."

She didn't sound the slightest bit sympathetic. Tricia agreed to the financial declaration and signed what Miss Montrose wanted her to sign.

She walked home through Blade Street and along the canal, pondering the enigma of Mark. He must have known. Why had he married her? Of course, because he wanted children. And because he must have thought, perhaps he still believed, that his natural impulses were evil and wrong. She thought of all those horrible nights with a glass of wine, all that thrusting that seemed so difficult for both of them. Would he apologize to his male friend, afterwards? She felt sorry for him. She hadn't imagined that she could feel that, but she did. She was shocked—not shocked that he had a male partner; she had friends here and in Woking who were homosexual. She was shocked that he had pretended for so long and that she hadn't guessed, and that he hadn't told her even when she confronted him and accused him of having another woman. It was his lack of trust that hurt her the most. The whole thing had been a lie and a sham, even his letters. Twenty-three years of her life gone to a pretense of a marriage.

She stopped by the canal bridge and looked down at the mallards. Most of the ducks were followed by rows of brown-fluffed ducklings. There were the children, of course. She couldn't imagine a world without them. The children were real, were the justification of what she and Mark had done together. But she still felt outrage pushing against her chest. She leaned on the railings and snarled down at the innocent ducklings, bobbing for weed in the water. It was the Pathetic fallacy, of course. How could there be sunshine and ducklings when her whole marriage had been a lie? There should have been torrents of rain, with which Lancaster could generally oblige in any month. She laughed at herself and started to walk again.

She had no idea what she would be able to say to Mark when she saw him. Pity might be worse for him than outrage. And was she going to tell the children? Doug and Helen but not the younger ones? Or should she keep it from all of them forever?

She was forty-six and she had spent half her life in a marriage that was a sham. She looked back at the years since she had married Mark as she walked briskly up the hill and tried to think what had been real. The children, yes. The stillbirths and miscarriages too. The work she had done for CND and her other groups. Her teaching, even the supply teaching. Looking after her mother. Her friends, here and in Woking. It hadn't all been straws in the wind, however it seemed. Her marriage had never been her whole life. Donne was wrong about that as so much else.

She opened the front door and went in. "I'm home!" she called, and heard Cathy and her mother reply from their own corners of the house.

Miss Montrose was efficient, and the divorce moved forward quickly. Mark did not dispute the adultery, and he agreed to everything Miss Montrose suggested financially. "His solicitor probably told him he's lucky we're not asking more," Miss Montrose said, with a tight-lipped smile. Mark never talked to her about the nature of the evidence, though he must have known she knew. She would have liked to talk to him about what he had been thinking, all those years, making everything her fault, but despite that she didn't feel she could torture him that much. Helen had been right to call him a hypocrite, but

Tricia understood that to strip a hypocrite of his hypocrisy can be a real wound.

Tricia's divorce was made absolute in October 1972. In the same month she began teaching an evening class in Feminist Literature in the Workers Education Authority. So many people signed up that it was completely full. She stood up in front of a class of adults, mostly women but with a few men.

She took a deep breath and closed her eyes, her old remedy against nerves. "Some people say women have never achieved anything great," she said, as she opened her eyes. "This class is going to demonstrate that women have achieved great things over and over again, but they've been patronized and ignored whenever they have. Women making art isn't anything new, though there is some wonderful new stuff being done that we're going to get to in due course. I'm going to ask you to read and think, but I'm not going to ask any background knowledge from you, anything beyond what we're bringing to this class. I don't expect you to know it all already. I want us to explore together. And I'm going to begin by reading you a translation of a poem written by Sappho in the Sixth Century before Christ."

19

"I Wish I'd Gone by King's X"
Pat 1970–1971

Everything went on much the same through 1970. The girls were in school, Pat visited her mother weekly, the Como guide book came out, and in Italy in the summer she began working on one for Bologna.

In 1971 Bee began to work on a fungal immunization for elm trees. A new more virulent form of Dutch Elm Disease had come in to Britain from the continent and was killing trees. It could be controlled by lopping infected branches, but something better was needed. "But could you immunize all the trees in the country?" Pat asked when Bee was telling her about it.

"We probably could, but it looks as if we might need to do it every year, which would be a huge job. There's a European agency being set up for crop diseases and improvement, and they might let us have a grant towards paying people to do that, but it's hard to define elm trees as a crop."

"I suppose they sort of are, in a way," Pat said. "I mean, timber?"

"Let's develop the cure before we start worrying about that," Bee said. She was working long hours at it, and teaching and all her other work. She resented needing to take a morning off in April when their turn came to get new identity cards. As they already had passports it was really only a formality. The children were on their mother's passports so Bee and Pat had to produce their birth certificates and have photographs taken. Most difficult was Pat's mother—not only did they have to fill in the forms for her but Pat had to go to Twickenham to find her mother's birth certificate. "We really should do something about putting her house on the market," she said when she came back.

"We should go down one weekend and clear it out," Bee agreed.

The identity card photographs were as unflattering as such pictures always were. Philip was squinting, Flossie was scowling, and Jinny's eyes were screwed up. Bee looked fierce and Pat looked resigned. Only her mother looked natural.

"All this red tape, and for what?" Pat asked, looking through the packet when they arrived. "Just to make us look a pack of fools."

"So the government knows who everybody is all the time," Bee said briskly. "Such nonsense. I'm sure it won't stop the terrorists for a moment."

A few weeks later they were having a picnic lunch in their garden on a warm May Sunday. "Just think, in six weeks we'll be doing this in Florence," Pat said.

"Six weeks!" Jinny said.

"Italy, Italy, Italy!" the children all chorused.

Bee looked serious and put her hand on Pat's knee. "Pat, love—I've been thinking, I don't think I can spend the whole summer in Italy this year. With the fungus and everything. I need to be here to get ahead on work while there isn't any teaching. And there's that conference at ICL at the beginning of August, and they want me to present. I thought I'd come out with you and have a couple of weeks, and come back here on the train. Then I'd come out again at the end of the summer for another couple of weeks."

"Of course, if that's what you need," Pat said.

"It's not what I want. I'd much rather be in Florence with the family. But . . ."

"It's your career," Pat said.

"Not even that, it's the elm trees," Bee said. "I know it's ridiculous, but there it is. I do want to save them if I can."

"I could not love you dear, so much, loved I not elm trees more?"

Bee laughed, then looked guilty, and Pat laughed with her. "It's all right," she said. "I love you loving the elm trees."

So after just over a week in Florence Bee returned to Cambridge, leaving the rest of the family to enjoy their usual summer. Pat missed Bee constantly. They wrote each other long letters, not exactly love letters, but letters full of love and caring. Letters were delivered only erratically in Florence, so Pat collected hers from the post office, a charming building completed only the year before, in the style of the Vasari Corridor.

After she had the mail she would stop with the children at a little gelateria on a nearby corner for a chocolate gelato. They had a game where they could have two gelatos or a gelato and a granita every day if they were absolutely silent while eating the first one, so the three of them sat in a row swinging their legs and solemnly licking their cones while Pat read her letters.

Reading Bee's laconic descriptions and jumbled thoughts she felt as if she could hear her voice:

"The hens are laying well, but they miss the girls collecting the eggs. Saw your mother. She was very gracious, so she clearly didn't know me, but she seemed in good form otherwise. She told me about how she met your father, a sweet story which I expect you have heard. The new fungus seems to be doing well in vitro, still waiting to hear on the vivo test. If it's good I may come to you a week early, because it's hard to be without you so long. I'm going to borrow your old green silk scarf to wear with my suit for the ICL thing if that's all right, it seems to make me look a bit smarter and it smells reassuringly like you. Kiss the children from me, and kiss yourself if you can think of a way to do it. I think of you all every day, and especially when I come home to the empty house. The gooseberries are ripe and I have picked them all. I can't be bothered with making jam so I am putting up a rum pot with the fruit—it will make Christmas presents for everyone we know."

Finishing the letter she would have tears in her eyes, and the girls would hug her. "Mamma sends love to all of you especially," she said, and then told them the bits of news. When she wrote she put in notes and drawings from the children. Flossie wrote letters several pages long about what they had been doing. Jinny drew copies of the shields inside the Bargello, and even Philip drew scribbles that he said were pictures of their garden, or of the Piazza della Signoria, and which Pat labelled. Bee wrote that she was putting them all up in the kitchen.

When she didn't hear for few days she wasn't especially concerned. It was when Bee had been due to go to London for the conference. She did begin to worry when it was five days without anything. When a letter did come, she was surprised how thin it was. She didn't open it until the children were sitting with their gelato.

"Dearest Pat, I seem to have got myself caught up in a silly bomb. I hope you haven't heard and worried. It was in Liverpool Street Station—wish now I'd gone home by King's X! I'm all right, except my legs seem to be pretty much shattered and the docs are talking wheelchairs. Donald came down, and

Michael has been a godsend, actually, but I think—I hate to ask, and I don't even know how you're going to manage it, but I think it would be best if you come home when you can. Love ever, Bee."

She didn't realize she had made a sound until the children were hugging her legs fiercely. "What is it?" Flossie asked in Italian.

"Mamma—Mamma's hurt her legs," Pat said. "We have to go home. We have to go home right now."

The children started to cry, and Pat bent down and hugged them all.

"But we have four Italy weeks left," Jinny said. "And Mamma's coming back for the last two or even three."

"We have to change the plan," Pat said. She was trying to make a new plan as she spoke. Could she drive all that way alone? It would be faster to take the train, but then the car would be here. It was possible to take cars on trains, but could you do that from Italy to England? She had no idea.

"Don't want to go home," Philip said. But even as he spoke he was patting her arm gently. "Mamma come here?"

"Mamma's hurt her legs. Remember when you fell down and cut your knees? Mamma's in hospital in London and she needs us. We have to go and help her get better." Bee wouldn't have said the doctors were talking about wheelchairs if it wasn't serious. Wheelchairs. How were they going to manage? She tried to imagine what could be wrong. Shattered could mean anything—would Bee's legs ever heal?

"Let's go home and pack up," she said, and looked down into three desolate faces. Flossie's lip was quivering as she tried to hold back her tears. "Let's go to Perche No! and have one last gelato and then go home and pack."

In Perche No! she ordered all Bee's favorite flavors, watermelon and white mint and raspberry. The children ordered for themselves, even four-year-old Philip. Eva, the girl at the counter, had known the children for years and spoke to them as old friends. Flossie told them that their Mamma had hurt her legs and they had to go home. "Beatrice?" she said. Pat had always loved the Italian way of pronouncing Bee's full name, but now it was all she could do to stay calm hearing it.

"Give your sister my love," the girl said to Pat, in Italian. "I would send her a gelato if it were possible."

"I'll tell her you thought of her," Pat said. Her sister. It was a misapprehension they never corrected. She looked up at Verrocchio's sad Christ, opening his wound to Thomas, and sent up a prayer for strength and help and healing for Bee.

She picked up an English paper at the little kiosk and found news of the bomb. Six people had been killed and nine injured, three severely. They did not give names, but there was a black and white photograph of the damage to the station. What possible good had it done the cause of a united Ireland to blow up a station in London, to kill six people and smash up Bee's legs? Pat hated the IRA for their casual disregard for other people's lives. Why couldn't they just let Ireland join the rest of Europe and stop making a fuss?

As she walked across the Ponte Vecchio she ran into Sara, one of her oldest friends in Florence. "What's wrong?" Sara asked immediately. The children blurted it out before Pat could speak.

"We have to go back immediately. Bee wouldn't have asked unless it was really important," Pat said.

"How are you going?" Sara asked.

"I think I have to drive, though it will take so long doing it alone. But if we take the train the car will be here, and we'll need it there."

"Why not sell your car here and buy another when you reach England?" Sara asked.

"That's audacious, but I don't think I have time to sell it."

"I will sell it for you," Sara announced. "I'll come with you now and you can give me the papers."

So later that afternoon Pat found herself with three children and a thrown-together set of luggage in a sleeper car on the express train to Paris.

The train proved to be a good idea. None of the children had taken a long train trip before, whereas they were accustomed to the drive. On the drive they would all have missed Bee at every moment. On the train everything was new. They loved their sleepers. The girls had the two top bunks, one on each side, and Pat took Philip in with her underneath Jinny. Besides, it was much faster. With only one driver the drive would have taken days. On the train they did not have to stop for meals or bathroom breaks. "I'm sure we've left half of what we need in Florence," Pat said, putting pajamas on the children.

"Maybe we'll go back soon," Flossie said. "Maybe we'll get Mamma and all go back next week."

"I think it'll take Mamma longer than that to get well," Pat said, and she thought "wheelchairs" and wondered if they would ever be able to go back.

At Dover, the immigration officials gave her a hard time over Jinny. "What is your relationship to this child?"

There wasn't a simple answer. Bee had always been there before. "She's my best friend's daughter. We were all on holiday in Italy. There was a family emergency and she had to come home, and now we're all joining her."

The man looked at Jinny suspiciously, then at her identity card. "She should have a passport."

"She's on her mother's passport," Pat said. "We didn't think." At the Swiss and French borders they had barely glanced at

their papers. Borders within Europe were growing less important. Only Britain still maintained its moat.

"Well, next time think," the man said. "Where's your
mother?" he asked Jinny.

"In London," Jinny said, with a quick glance at Pat.

"All right then. You're lucky you're all British and you've
only been in Europe, or you could be in real trouble."

"Thank you so much, officer," Pat said, and gave the cring-
ing smile she hated giving. She hated getting in because she
was white and had the right kind of voice, too, but she wasn't
going to start any fights. She shepherded the children away.

By the time they reached London it was early evening and
they had been travelling for twenty-four hours without a break.
All of them except Philip were exhausted. Philip had an amazing capacity to sleep in any circumstances, which he had not
lost when he left babyhood. Pat took a taxi to the hospital,
with the children and the luggage. At reception she asked for
Bee, and was told that only relatives could visit and that children were not admitted under any circumstances. She could
have sat down and wept, and perhaps the woman on the desk
recognised her distress. "Her fiancé is with her. I'll send somebody to see if you can speak to him."

"Her fiancé?" Pat blinked.

"Yes."

After a long wait, Michael came out, and Pat understood.
"Oh Pat, thank goodness you're here." The children ran to
him and he bent down and made a fuss of them.

"They won't let me see Bee," Pat said, over their heads.

"Let me talk to them. Wait." Michael went up to the desk
and argued with the receptionist. Pat tried to keep Philip still.
Flossie started to cry. After a while Michael came back. "They'll
let you in for just a minute. I'll stay with the children. You

should have said you were her sister. I told them you were my sister, and she's stretching a point."

"And you told them you're Bee's fiancé?"

"That was Bee's idea. Otherwise they'd only talk to Donald, and he had to go back up to Penrith, the sheep needed him. You have to be a relative, in hospital. Friends aren't anything." He patted her shoulder. "Go in and see her and then I'll talk to you."

Pat followed the directions and found herself in a big ward full of women in beds. All the beds had tight white covers pulled over them. At the end of the room was a television, blasting out a soap opera. Most of the beds had visitors. When Pat saw Bee she couldn't understand how the shape she made under the covers was so small. She was wearing a hospital gown but had Pat's old green silk scarf wound around her neck. She bent down and embraced her. They were both weeping. "Oh Pat," Bee said. "I feel like such a fool."

"I'm just so glad you're alive," Pat said. "I kept thinking how you could have been killed."

"Might have been better," Bee said. "No, I don't mean that. But I've had six operations, and they've given up on trying to save the knees. I'll never walk again. I'm going to be in a wheelchair forever, no two ways about it."

"We'll find ways to cope," Pat said. "I love you so much. I couldn't have managed without you."

"Good to see you too," Bee said, and smiled. "Everyone's looking at us."

"I don't care," Pat said. "Will it hurt you if I sit down on the bed?"

"Yes," Bee said. "Everything hurts me. I'll have to get used to that. And goodness knows how I'm going to manage in the lab."

Pat sat on the chair by the bed and took Bee's hand in hers. "When are they going to let you out of here?"

"It could be a while. But now you're here maybe if you want I can get them to send me to the Addison in Cambridge, which is just as good." Bee bit her lip. "I didn't know if they'd let you in. We told them Michael was—"

"I know. It was a good idea. Michael told them I'm his sister. If you move you to Cambridge we can tell them I'm your sister."

"Hate having to lie," Bee said. "It isn't illegal, for women."

"No, but no point getting into trouble. The children. I had a hard time bringing Jinny into the country. She was very good, she said just the right thing."

"How are they?" Bee asked, and her face crumpled.

"They're wonderful. We came back on the train and they were all three really good. They're longing to see you, but there's no hope of getting them in here."

"You do still—I mean, I'm going to be useless. I don't even know if I'll be able to work. I don't want—"

"Bee, you wouldn't be useless even if you were just a head in a jar," Pat said. "And I still want you. I wish this hadn't happened because it's a horrible thing to happen to you, but I love you as much as ever, more than ever."

"I'll ask about the move to the Addison, then," Bee said. "I think—it could be months before I'm out. And at the moment it's all bedpans, and it might always be bedpans."

"I can cope," Pat said. "If it has to be bedpans, you're worth it."

Then a bell rang for the end of visiting time, and she had to leave.

20

"It'll Change Everything": Trish 1973–1977

George took his O Levels in the summer of 1973 and passed everything with flying colors—seven As and two Bs, far better marks than Doug or Helen had ever brought home. He elected to do sciences at A Level—Maths, Physics and Chemistry. "I want to do space science, Mum," he said. Tricia remembered his enthusiasm for the moon landing and smiled.

"You still want to be an astronaut?"

George blushed. "Not an astronaut. A scientist who works in space. They have Hope Station now, and they're starting to set up the moonbase. That's the most likely way for me to get up there."

"Whatever makes you happy," Tricia said.

Tricia didn't understand her children. She never had. Doug was a minor but significant pop star. Goliath was in the process of breaking up—they kept getting back together and then breaking up again, as Doug's relationship with Sue went through the same process. Doug was working on an album with Peter Gabriel. Helen drifted from casual job to casual job, and from boyfriend to boyfriend. She was nineteen and the beauty she had had as a child had flowered into something so lovely that Tricia was almost afraid for her. Helen's face and figure were perfect, and she knew it. She talked from time to time about modeling or acting, which Tricia encouraged, because it would have been a way for her to become independent, but in the end she always accepted another job waitressing or in a bar. Now George was going into science with a goal of space. Only Cathy seemed like an ordinary adolescent—at nearly fourteen she worried about schoolwork and boys. Cathy always craved approval. Tricia blamed Mark, who had never taken much notice of her, and still did not, even now when she was the only one of the children who seemed to care about him.

Her mother was still at home, still with Marge coming in every day to look after her while Tricia was at work. She was deteriorating visibly—fearful and afraid of anyone new, any change. She forgot even ordinary words and would spit out accusations if anything went wrong. Tricia was horrified how judgemental and unkind her mother could become at those times, though she tried to put herself into her place and understand that really she was afraid. She liked her routine, and slept a great deal of the time.

Tricia was working full time in the Grammar School in Morecambe, which was due to become comprehensive and merge with the local secondary modern school next year. She was also teaching two evening classes, working with the two local preservation societies and with CND, which was contemplating changing its name to the Campaign for Peace, as nuclear disarmament seemed like a won battle. Her life was busy and fulfilling. Her house was always full of friends—the children's friends, her friends from the campaigns or from classes, people she knew who were thinking of starting a whole food co-op and cafe in town, friends from the women's group, and colleagues. People were always popping in for a moment and staying for hours. It sometimes made it difficult for her to get marking done—she started getting up early to do marking before school rather than counting on doing it in the evenings. She didn't miss Mark at all, indeed she felt relieved of a weight since he had left. Although he was still at the university she seldom saw him. He came almost every Sunday to take George and Cathy out for lunch and was punctilious about informing her if he wasn't going to be able to do that.

With all this new bustle and press of things in her life came a new name. It came first from the women's group, where almost all the women used shortened forms of their names as part of their reimagination of themselves. "But Tricia is already a shortening," she said, when Barb said something. "It's Patricia really."

"You should be Trish," Barb said.

Tricia thought about it and decided she liked it, and soon she was Trish to everyone except Mark, who continued to call her Tricia, and her mother, who still called her Patsy when she recognized her.

That summer, 1974, Doug paid for the whole family to have a holiday in Majorca. Trish didn't like the heat or the hotel, which was full of other British holidaymakers. She worried about her mother, who was spending the fortnight in a nursing home in Morecambe. She didn't like the oily food or the flies on the beach, and wished they'd gone to Cornwall instead. To her astonishment, in the second week she ran into Marjorie from Oxford, whom she had not seen since her wedding. Marjorie was married and had twins. They caught up, but found they no longer had much in common, if they ever had. When Doug joined them for a few days at the end she found the reactions of the other holidaymakers to his fame uncomfortable. Marjorie could hardly believe that Trish had a son who was a pop star and became tongue-tied in his presence. Sue wasn't with him, and when Trish asked him he said that they'd broken up permanently this time and Goliath was over.

Just after the New Year of 1975 Helen came in late one night from a night out with a boyfriend while Trish was washing coffee cups after a meeting of the Lancaster Preservation Society.

"Hi Mum," Helen said. "Have a nice evening?"

"Very successful. We think they're going to go ahead with the one-way system and the pedestrianized zone. There won't be any cars in the middle of town except handicapped and emergency vehicles."

"Great," Helen said, sitting down at the kitchen table.

"Shall I put the kettle on?" Trish asked.

"Thanks, Mum." Trish put the kettle on and dried her old brown teapot. "Could we have peppermint?"

"Is your stomach upset?" Trish asked, putting peppermint teabags into the pot.

"A little bit . . . Mum?"

"Yes?" Trish put two mugs on the table.

"How did you know you were pregnant?"

Trish sat down and stared at her daughter. "I knew when I skipped a period. But before that I felt sick, almost from the beginning, and my breasts were tender. That was the sign with all my pregnancies. Why are you asking?"

The kettle shrilled and she automatically turned to pour boiling water into the pot. When she turned back, Helen still hadn't spoken.

"What do you want to do?" Trish asked. "Do you know who the father is?"

"Not for sure," Helen said, looking down at her empty mug. "It could be Martin, or it could be Phil."

"You're not planning to get married then?"

Helen shook her head. "Absolutely not. I thought I was safe because I was on the pill, but then I had those antibiotics for my throat around the time of Cathy's birthday, remember?

And Gaynor says those could have stopped it working. I've missed two periods, and my breasts are sore, and I never feel like eating anything."

"Then you should go to the doctor and find out for sure," Trish said. "It does sound as if you're pregnant though. Do you want to have it?"

"It'll spoil everything," Helen said, and began to cry.

Trish poured out the tea. "Well, babies are people. I didn't understand that for a long time, but it's true. If you have this baby it'll certainly change everything. But you do have a choice." Trish knew all about this from the women's group. "Abortion is legal now. If you go to the doctor and tell her you really can't face going through with it, as a single mother, and you're so young, very likely you'd be able to have a termination at the Infirmary. You'd have to have counseling, but they'd do it. Two periods—eight or ten weeks? It should be quite simple."

"I don't know if I could kill it, though," Helen said, putting both her hands around her mug for warmth. "Babies are people, and if you'd done that we wouldn't be here. I'd like to have a baby. And doesn't having an abortion mess you up so you can't have babies later, when you want to?"

"No," Trish said, firmly, taking a sip of her own tea. "That's a myth."

"Even so. I'd like to have it, but I don't know how I could." Helen looked up at her.

"You can keep on living here and have it, and I'll help as much as I can, but I'm not going to stop working and take charge of it for you so you can keep on living your life the way you do now," Trish said. "I'll help out financially as much as I can, but you know I don't have all that much money. Gran might be prepared to help too—well, you know she won't understand, but I think we could use some of her money to help and she would want to do that if she could understand.

We can probably manage. But it will be a struggle, and your life is going to have to change a lot. Is that really what you want? It's a lot of work having a baby. I found it overwhelming when I had Doug."

"But I won't have to put up with Dad as well," Helen said.

"You'll have to tell your father he's going to be a grandfather, if he is. If you decide to have it. Oh my goodness, I'm going to be a grandmother!" Trish got up and hugged Helen. "I have to say that's a very exciting thought."

"Thank you, Mum," Helen said, then wiped her eyes and blew her nose. "Thank you for being so helpful, and thank you for saying that."

In April, George took the Oxbridge entrance exams, and in June he took his A Levels. He got his three As and was duly accepted into New College Cambridge. "I did think of Oxford because of you and Dad, but this is the best place for what I want to work on," he said.

In mid-August Helen had her baby, a girl. She gave birth easily, in six hours, without any of the complications Trish had gone through. Trish was with her the whole time. She called the baby Tamsin. "Why did you pick that name?" she asked, after they filled out the birth certificate, with the blank for "father" marked defiantly "unknown."

"I thought it was pretty," Helen said.

"It is pretty," Trish agreed. "And so is the baby, she looks just like you."

"I'd rather she was clever like you and George," Helen said. "Pretty doesn't get you anywhere."

Tamsin came home and thrived. Her great-grandmother held her and sang old lullabies to her, though they didn't leave her alone with the baby. Trish, coming home one day after school, heard Helen and Marge laughing downstairs with her mother. The washing machine was spinning down there too, and she thought how much easier it was for Helen being home with Tamsin than it had been for her in Grantham with Doug.

George came home at Christmas and Easter, but spent the summer of 1976 at MIT in Boston on a work/study program. "I think I'll do my Ph.D. there," he said when Trish asked him how he liked it. "Space is American now, whether we like it or not. And we're America's allies, even if they do think we're all pinkos."

"Pinkos!" Trish said. "What an old-fashioned word!"

"I heard people over there using it about the proponents of the new state health system. But it passed, so I don't suppose they meant anything all that bad." George laughed. "After Cambridge where they think my accent's awfully northern it was funny to be in America where they all think it's cute! And they all kept asking me if I'd met Prince Charles and Princess Camilla—for Republicans they're awfully keen on hearing about our royalty!"

One Sunday late that summer Trish had a picnic in the garden with a lot of friends. Tamsin was toddling around from one person to another, holding on to legs indiscriminately. Trish had made a huge salad and Helen had made bread and other people had brought other things to share. She was practically a vegetarian now, as were many of her friends, but one of the younger men from the peace group had brought a cold roast chicken and carved it neatly with Trish's mother's antique carving knife and fork. "I think Gran might like to see that," Cathy said.

"No, she doesn't like new people," Helen replied, before Trish could say anything.

"I'll go and take her some chicken and tell her about it," Cathy said.

When Cathy came back she seemed subdued. "Is Gran all right?" Trish asked.

"Yes," Cathy said. "She's sitting in the sun by the window. She was pretending to read, but she had the book upside down. She liked the chicken. But she said the strangest thing. She said she couldn't remember who I was, but she did remember that she loved me."

"Oh Cathy!" Trish hugged her.

Trish's mother caught a bad chill that autumn and never really recovered. Doug and George both came home at Christmas and saw her for the last time. She didn't know them. By that time she wasn't sure of anyone. Her days of singing with Tamsin were over, she was afraid all the time. She was incontinent and wept at everything, plucking at her blankets and her clothes as if she wanted to tear them off but did not have the strength. She had gone beyond knowing she loved people and was afraid of all of them. It broke Trish's heart when her mother cowered away from her, or fought against her. The doctor suggested that she should go into a hospice, and Trish agreed, but before a place opened up she died, in February of 1977, and was cremated. Doug and George came home for the funeral. But on the day in April it was just the girls and Trish who dug her ashes into the garden. Cathy planted rosebushes over the place.

"Let's try to remember her as she was," Trish said, and then realized that for the children she had always been forgetful. It had been such a long slow decline. She felt exhausted to think how long. Little Tamsin was playing in the dirt, and Trish knew that one day even she, the youngest of them, would die and somebody as yet unborn would mourn. She hoped she wouldn't go through what her great-grandmother had—she hoped none of them would.

That summer Cathy took her A Levels and passed them, doing respectably but not as brilliantly as George. "It seems to me that not having their father at home is better for children's education," Trish said to Barb. Cathy went off to Bristol to study history. Trish drove her down with all her books and clothes filling the Beetle. Helen held two-year-old Tamsin up to wave as they went.

"All the rest of us are making our own way," Cathy said as she settled back into the seat.

"Helen's doing all right," Trish said, stung. "But of course I'm very proud of you, darling."

21

Better to Risk Falling: Pat 1971

Even after the initial shock was over, everything continued to be awful. It wasn't just Bee's injuries, though they were terrible enough. She had lost both legs above the knee—on the left two inches above and on the right four inches. It was the constant grind of lying to be able to see Bee, and coping with all of the children. There were still four weeks of the summer holidays left before the children went back to school, and she had nobody to leave them with even for a moment. Pat was used to being at home with the children, but she was used to Bee coming in and giving her a break. Beyond that she had to cope with trying to see Bee, and the children's constant desire to see Bee. No hospital would allow children to visit. Things were further exacerbated by the fact that either Bee's elderly mother or her brother Donald was her next of kin, and Pat was not allowed to make any decisions for her. Even when Bee was moved to Cambridge it was difficult for Pat to visit. She drafted all her friends to watch the children while she saw Bee.

Once the operations were over she thought Bee would be able to come home, but first the house had to be made ready for her. Everything took forever and cost money. The healthcare itself was still free, thank goodness. The government was talking about privatizing the NHS and replacing it with an insurance based system, but this had not yet happened. There was even a government award to Bee for her injuries and loss of earnings—as she insisted she would be able to work and New College agreed that she would, this was for six months' salary. It paid for the stairlift that was essential for Bee to be able to get upstairs, and for the extra wheelchair that they would have to keep up there for her. Pat had to pay to have the doors widened to wheelchair width, and for a downstairs bathroom big enough for a wheelchair. Having the work done meant workmen constantly underfoot, as well as holes into which Philip fell and the girls poked. Pat sold the Mini and bought a new station wagon, the only car large enough to fit a wheelchair as well as the five of them. At the end of this her finances were considerably depleted, and she began to worry that she had not done the research for the Bologna book.

She had to keep paying the students whom she had hastily retained to look after the garden, the hens, and the bees. Bee had usually done it all herself with help from the children, and Pat didn't know where to start. From feeling comfortably well off, she felt as if money was draining away and she didn't know how it would be replenished.

It was November before Bee came home, delivered by ambulance. A young female social worker had been to inspect the house beforehand. She approved the doorways and the bathroom and the ramp down into the garden and into the garage. She was pleased with the stairlift, but horrified when she saw the double bed in Pat and Bee's bedroom. Too late, Pat realized she should have dissembled. There were four bedrooms—the girls shared one, and she should have pretended that she slept in what was the guest room. She remembered that meeting Marjorie had spoken at so long ago, and the way people would ignore things if not brought to their attention. She decided to brazen it out.

"And your relationship with Miss Dickinson is?" the social worker asked, making a note.

"We're friends," Pat said, blushing.

"I have a note that you are sisters."

"We said that to make visiting easier."

"I see." The social worker made another note. "And whose are the children?"

"Ours," Pat said, drawing herself up. The social worker's eyebrows rose. "That is, Flossie and Philip are mine, and Jinny is Bee's."

"And you're taking care of Jinny while Miss Dickinson is in hospital?"

"Yes," Pat said.

"Can I see the upstairs bathroom now?" the social worker asked, and Pat heaved a sigh of relief.

Now Bee was home, in a wheelchair, but home. They thanked the ambulance driver and Pat wheeled Bee inside. The chair was heavy and not well balanced. Pat had been thinking the girls might be able to push it, but it was immediately clear that they wouldn't.

The children hung back for a moment when they saw Bee, then they flung themselves on her and all of them were crying and hugging, and then the chair tipped and Bee was on the rug with them. Pat saw her wince.

"How are we going to get you up?" Pat asked.

"Don't worry about that for the moment, you come down here," Bee said. Pat pushed the chair back and got down on the floor. She pulled Bee back against her and held her steady as the children again flung themselves on her. Bee winced again, but said nothing.

"Mamma, Mamma," the children said, over and over.

"I loved the cards and pictures you sent me," Bee said. "I'm sorry I couldn't always write back as much as I wanted. But they kept me going in that place, being able to see your drawings. I missed you so much. And you've grown. It's not fair you growing while I couldn't see you!"

They had grown, but not as much as Bee had shrunk. Pat managed to haul Bee up into the old green velvet armchair, which she said she wanted. "I need to get my arms really strong," Bee said. "I've been having physio, and I need to have more. I need to swim, and exercise. I can swing myself from the wheelchair to the toilet—did you get bars put in the toilet?"

"Yes, yes, and we have a new toilet downstairs!" Philip said.

"Two toilets, what would my parents say!" Bee said, smiling over his head at Pat. "Luxury! And then what we need is an electric wheelchair. They're expensive, but it'll be worth it. And I can propel this one myself, if there aren't any steps. Wheel it over here, one of you."

Jinny won the tussle and wheeled the chair over next to the armchair. "A bit more this way, good. Now watch," Bee said, as she swung herself from the chair into the wheelchair.

Pat's heart was in her throat. "Don't fall!" she said.

"I fall a lot," Bee said. "It's better to risk falling than to give in."

"Doesn't it hurt?" Jinny asked.

"Yes, it hurts, but there are worse things. And speaking of hurting, try not to bounce on me quite so much!"

"I love you," Pat said. "I am so glad to have you home."

"No matter how glad you can't be as glad as I am to be out of bloody hospitals!" Bee said. "Now, I'm going to have arms like an orangutan, so I hope that's all right?"

"That's wonderful," Pat said. "Now dinner?"

"Food!" Bee said. "Not that awful hospital pap! How I have been looking forward to some real food!"

"It's pasta with mushrooms and chicken," Flossie confided. "Oh, and Eva in Perche No! wanted to send you some gelato."

"Mum told me about that in hospital," Bee said. "Well, next summer."

Bee was plainly exhausted by the time the girls went to bed. "Let's give them half an hour to fall asleep and go to bed ourselves," Pat said. "We can talk in bed."

"More than talk," Bee said.

"I can see how tired you are," Pat said.

"Not so tired as I am randy." Bee laughed. "Four months in hospital, and I hadn't seen you for weeks before that."

They went up to bed. Bee swung herself onto the stairlift and off again onto the light wheelchair Pat had bought for upstairs. "This one is no good," Bee said. "It can only be pushed."

"I'll push it for now," Pat said. "We'll get another self-propelled one for up here. Or if we get an electric one for downstairs we can haul that one up here."

"That's the best idea," Bee said.

In bed they held each other quietly for a long time before either of them made a move towards making love. Afterwards Bee lay back against the pillows. "Well, that's something I don't need legs for."

Pat laughed, but she was close to tears. "You're wonderful," she said. "Did it hurt you, making love?"

"Well . . . yes. A little. But not enough to stop me." Bee kissed Pat. "What we need to do is get a lawyer and sort out powers of attorney and all of that. Whatever we need to do to become each other's next of kin. I never thought of it until I needed it. And about the children too, to name each other as guardians. I think that's the way to do it, legally. Each other and Michael—if he'll agree, and I think he will. I don't know how I would have coped without Michael when it first happened. He was a tower, he really was. He'd listen to me, when Donald and the doctors wouldn't. And he posted that letter to you. And he put up with all that fuss and the papers and everything."

"Bless him," Pat said. "Yes, we need to do that."

"I'm lucky to be alive, and Jinny's even luckier that I'm alive. If I'd been killed I don't know what would have happened to her, but they might not have let you keep her."

"I don't think they would," Pat said. "I got her into the country on sheer class privilege—she's on your passport and I didn't think. Thank goodness for the identity cards, because she had that. There was a social worker looking at the arrangements for you coming home, and she asked me about the children. We need to set that up for all of them—it might be me something happens to. I was thinking Donald and your mother might have agreed to let me keep Jinny, but they might not. And if something happened to me, who is there? My mother wouldn't be able to make any decisions."

"Michael," Bee said. "We put him on the birth certificates."

"It would really put him on the spot. We need to talk to him. I mean we've decided to live in a certain way, an unconventional way, and the children can't be the ones to suffer by it."

"Well, not any more than is inevitable. They already know not to say they have two mothers. We've talked to them about it."

"Yes, I gave Philip that talk before he started school in September."

Bee sighed. "I'm so sorry to have missed that."

Pat stroked her arm consolingly and then hugged her close. "It really is so wonderful to have you here again. I've missed you so much."

"Me too, you."

Pat rang Michael the next morning after she'd taken the children to school. He agreed to come down at the weekend. She also called Lorna, and asked if she knew any friendly lawyers. Lorna called back later with a name, and Pat called and made an appointment for Monday.

Bee's resolution sometimes faltered and she sometimes grew short-tempered with pain and exhaustion. In general Pat was astounded by how well she dealt with everything. They ordered an electric wheelchair and were told it would be delivered in a few weeks. Michael arrived on Friday evening and disappeared beneath a wave of children. He had brought them cylinders of bubble mixture with wands, a different shaped wand for each child. "Only outside!" Pat said. "Which means not until the morning!"

Michael was very impressed at how Bee swung herself around. "You wait until I have my electric wheelchair," she said.

After the children were in bed it was Michael who opened the subject. "I've been worried about what happens to them if something happens to you."

"That's what we wanted to talk to you about," Pat said. "We're going to make each other the legal guardian of all the children."

"You can't adopt them," Michael said. "I looked into that. Two women . . ."

"We think we can name each other the legal guardian if anything happens. Anyone can be a guardian. But you're down as the father on their birth certificates, you'd be the automatic person they'd ask." Bee looked at him inquiringly.

"Are you asking me to give up my rights in them?" he asked.

"No, only to agree if it came to it that the one of us that was left would keep them all," Pat said.

"What if neither of you were left?"

Pat and Bee looked at each other. "Well in that situation what would you do?"

"I suppose I'd look after them," he said, slowly.

"I know this isn't what we originally said," Pat said. "We hadn't thought about this at all."

"It was all so theoretical," Michael said. "Now they're people, all of them, even little Philip. Yes, all right, if something happens to both of you I'll do it. But what if I did get married the way you're always telling me to do?"

"That would be more complicated," Bee said. "Are you thinking of it?"

"What, jilt you after that photo in the Standard making half of London and my own parents think you're my fiancée? When would I have had time to think about it?"

Bee laughed and then turned serious. "I'm eternally grateful to you for that."

"It was the least I could do." Michael turned his teacup in his hands. "Do you have anything stronger?"

"I think I might have some wine we brought back from Italy last year. I didn't bring any this year because I left in such a hurry," Pat said, getting up.

"She didn't even bring any olive oil or dried porcini," Bee said.

Pat dug up an unopened bottle of red wine and dusted it before taking it through to the sitting room. She gave it to Michael with the corkscrew and went back for two glasses.

"Who opens the wine when you're alone?" Michael asked.

Pat and Bee looked at each other. "Either of us, when we have parties," Pat said. "We don't usually drink wine when it's just us. I mean I don't really drink."

Michael opened the wine and poured a glass for himself

and another for Bee, taking hers over to where she was sitting in the green chair that had become hers in the week since she had been home. He took a sip. "Red Tuscan wine, like we were drinking the night we started this whole thing," he said, turning the stem of the glass.

"I remember that," Bee said. "In Bordino's."

"So I think the sensible thing is if you designate each other guardians and all that. Ideally you'll never need it and everything can go on as it is and the children will grow up with nothing worse to worry about than the European independent nuclear deterrent and the creeping privatization of everything in sight."

Bee raised her glass to that, and Pat raised her teacup.

"But if something does happen to one of you, then the guardian thing, and if that holds up that's all well and good. But if there's a problem then I think the sensible thing is if I marry whichever one of you is left. I am their father, and that's all legal and on their birth certificates and their ID. I'm the natural guardian, and if I'm married to whichever one of you is left, then she'd be the natural stepmother. We wouldn't have to live together or have sex or anything." He drained his glass.

"That's wonderful," Bee said, and there were tears glistening in her eyes. "But it does put an awful burden on you. Philip's not five yet. That means you'd have to stay unmarried for thirteen years. Well, eleven."

"The older they get the less of a problem it is," Michael said. "But I wasn't planning to get married anyway."

"But don't you want children of your own?" Pat asked.

"I have children of my own, isn't that what this is all about?" Michael filled his glass again. "I'm very very fond of both of you, and I love the children. I know it wasn't the plan, it wasn't what we agreed, but I can't help it. I don't know if it's genetic instinct or if they're just so lovable I'd have loved them whoever their father was."

"I have never seen anyone so embarrassed at making a declaration of love," Bee said. "And that includes me and Pat, who were really pretty embarrassed when we first admitted that we loved each other."

They all laughed. "Well, with that settled we can safely go to the lawyers on Monday," Pat said.

Bee looked at Pat with a wicked twinkle in her eyes. "And as far as sex goes, well, there might be sex," she said.

Pat looked back at her and nodded. "If you want to," she said.

"What?" Michael looked from one to the other of them. "I thought you didn't want more children?"

"It might be news to you that there are ways of having sex that do not result in children," Bee said. "Nice ways."

"We do them all the time," Pat said. "We wouldn't have to do *that*."

"So if you want you can come upstairs with us and have lesbian sex," Bee said, leering.

"Oh my God," Michael said. "I don't know whether you're joking."

"We're not joking," Pat said.

22

"Getting Married on the Moon"
Trish 1977–1980

It was Duncan, one of the men in the Lancaster Preservation Society, who suggested that Trish should stand for the local council. At first she was skeptical—she had no qualifications, and why would anyone vote for her? She wasn't even a local, although by now she had been living in Lancaster for more than ten years.

"The council needs people who care, and who have their heads screwed on right about environmental issues. There's so much corruption in the Town Hall," Duncan said, shaking his head. "It's all established interests, and they're all in each other's pockets. They need a shake-up."

"I don't think I have time."

"It's part time. And unpaid, but they get an allowance."

"You stand," Trish said.

"I'm going to, but we need more than one person."

Duncan stood as an independent, and Trish campaigned for him. He was elected, to her surprise, and immediately the profile of the Preservation Society rose. Duncan kept talking to her about what the council did and how it worked and encouraging her to stand next time.

In June of 1978, George graduated from Cambridge with First Class Honors. Trish, Helen, and Tamsin, now almost three, drove down to watch him graduate. Cathy had exams that day and couldn't be there. Mark showed up at the last minute. They sat together to watch him accept his scroll from Princess Camilla. "Now you'll be able to tell them at MIT that you've met her," Helen teased him beforehand. Trish found the ceremony moving, much more so than when she had graduated herself, which she barely remembered. They didn't have this kind of ceremony at St. Hilda's. Even though New College was still new they managed to make the occasion feel special. After all the BA and BSc graduands, those completing Ph.D.s came in, with their bright hoods over their academic gowns. Last a special award was made to a female scientist, Professor Dickinson, who had apparently done something to cure Dutch Elm Disease. Trish clapped with everyone as she walked across the stage, then got up immediately to try to find George in the crush.

Mark insisted that they should all have lunch together in a restaurant he knew. George brought along a girl. "This is Sophie Picton," he said. "She's a biologist. I wanted you to meet her." She had long fair hair neatly wound up in a French twist. Trish liked her smile and the way she listened patiently to Tamsin's chatter. This was especially noticeable as Mark was not patient with Tamsin and kept telling her to be quiet. They ate overcooked food. George, Helen, Mark, and Sophie shared a bottle of white wine, which Mark ordered. Trish noticed that Sophie wrinkled her nose up when she took her first sip.

"So are you still planning to go to America?" Mark asked.

"Yes, I'm going to do my doctorate at MIT, starting in the new academic year," George said.

"You're not expecting me to pay for that?"

"It's fully funded," George said coolly. "As was this. You've only been expected to bring my living expenses up to what you could comfortably afford. I'm sorry if it has left you short."

Trish noticed that Sophie had put her hand surreptitiously on George's elbow, whether to give him support or stop him she didn't know. Mark spluttered and changed the subject—Tamsin had just dropped a piece of chicken onto the table and picked it up and eaten it, which gave him an excuse to fulminate about her table manners.

When they had finished, Mark paid for the meal and left. "I've got a long way to go to get home." He did not seem to realize that the rest of the family also had a long way to go. The rest of them stood outside the restaurant after he had left. "Are you in an awful hurry too, or shall we go down somewhere outside for an hour and enjoy the sunshine?" Sophie suggested.

"Are there any playgrounds where Tamsin could run around for a bit?" Helen asked.

George and Sophie looked at each other blankly. "I can't think of anything like that in Cambridge," George said. "But if we go down by the river she can run around, as long as she doesn't fall into the water."

Trish agreed happily to the river plan. "I used to adore rowing when I was at Oxford. In fact I think I've missed it ever since. I haven't lived anywhere where there was a river."

"You could go out this afternoon," George said. "I had no idea you rowed. Did you get your blue?"

"My college blue," Trish said. "In those days girls couldn't row for Oxford." The young people were suitably horrified. "You've got no idea of the battles we've already won, especially when you're busy looking ahead to the battles we still have to fight."

"That's very true," Sophie said as they sat down on the grass by the river. "Professor Dickinson was talking the other day about how hard it was to be a woman in science when she was starting out, and it made me realize that even though it's hard now it's so much easier than it was twenty years ago."

"And are you enthusiastic about our future in space too?" Helen asked.

"I certainly am," Sophie said, exchanging looks with George. "I've been doing some work on hydroponics that I hope will be useful for the moonbase."

"And are you also going to MIT?" Trish asked.

"Harvard," Sophie said, and blushed.

Trish laughed. "How well you are managing your lives!"

"Dad doesn't think so," George said.

"I think he's jealous," Sophie said, unexpectedly.

"Jealous?" George asked.

"I think Sophie's right," Trish said, remembering. "He got a Third you know, and he was expected to do brilliantly and become a star. It took him a long time to get accepted, to get back into academia. I don't think he has ever really got over that. You're doing what he wanted to do. He's bound to resent it."

"I wish you'd stop making excuses for him," Helen said. She looked at Tamsin, who was running in circles above them on the slope and making plane noises. "You always try to justify him when he's just being a shit."

Trish laughed nervously.

"No, you do, Mum," George said. "Helen's right."

"I suppose I spent so many years doing it to myself that I keep on doing it," Trish said. "I'm sorry. I know I should have been a better mother."

"It's not your fault that Dad's the way he is," George said. "Though I must say that one of the advantages of Boston is putting an entire ocean between me and him."

"Did you get married directly after Oxford?" Sophie asked.

"I taught for two years," Trish said. "Down in Cornwall. Why, are you thinking—"

"Not until we have our doctorates and we're financially in

a better place," George said. "We were thinking of it before Sophie was accepted at Harvard, so she'd be able to come to America, but as things are we don't need to rush it."

"Well, whenever you decide to get married I'll be delighted to have you as a daughter-in-law," Trish said, and shook Sophie's hand enthusiastically. Sophie pulled her into a hug.

"Of course, our dream would be to get married in space," George said, then laughed at Trish's horrified expression. "No, I know you'd want to be there."

"I'll never be an astronaut," Trish said.

That next autumn, after George and Sophie had left for America, Trish stood herself at the council election and was narrowly defeated. "I should have come down to campaign for you," Doug joked when she met him in London. He had released two solo albums since Goliath had broken up, neither of them very successful, but he kept on writing songs and touring. He was also working with other musicians and talked about forming a new group. He always had a new girlfriend but never anyone serious. She told him about George and Sophie and how sweet they were together. "About time old George found somebody," he said. "I think I'll write a song for them and call it 'Getting Married on the Moon.' "

Helen decided to take night classes and catch up on her education. This meant Trish cutting back on some of her own evenings to babysit Tamsin, which she did reluctantly, acknowledging the necessity for Helen to have qualifications. She dropped the Peace Group, and abandoned plans to stand for the city council again.

One day Helen came home with a suggestion. "Why don't we sort out the basement and let it as a flat?"

"I'm not sure I'd want strangers living there," Trish said. "It has its own entrance, but that's the only way into the garden. And the washing machine is down there."

"I wasn't thinking of strangers. You always know a million people, and there would always be someone you know wanting to live there. Right now Bethany and Kevin and Alestra are looking for somewhere."

Bethany and Kevin worked at the whole food co-op. Alestra, their daughter, was a few months younger than Tamsin. "That's an excellent idea," Trish said.

She and Helen spent the next weekend cleaning the basement and painting. They spent the next rearranging furniture. They bought an electric stove and a fridge. Then Helen invited Bethany and Kevin to come and look at it. They moved in the next day.

Although Bethany was Helen's age, she soon became much more Trish's friend. She was passionate about food and often cooked enough for the whole household—vegetable soups, lentil bakes, chili with beans and rice. She played the flute and composed music, and again the house had music rising from the basement as it had when Doug lived at home. Kevin was quiet. "Not much about him," Trish said to Helen, but she put up with him for Bethany's sake. Alestra was neither as pretty nor as lively as Tamsin, to Trish's biased eye, but she was a nice child, and the two of them played well together. Bethany's family paid a low rent, which helped with household expenses, but best of all Bethany and Helen traded babysitting so that Trish was free in the evenings again.

Before Tamsin was born, Trish had made Mark's old study into a nursery, and Helen moved into the room next to it, which had been Doug's. Trish maintained a bedroom for each of her children, though now they were seldom all at home except at Christmas.

That Christmas, Sophie was coming to visit. Trish drafted Kevin to help move beds. There was a double bed in her room, which she wanted put in George's room down the corridor, while George's old single bed would do for her. Lifting her end of the double bed she felt a sharp pain in her chest and left arm and had to sit down. "I think I've strained something," she said, weakly.

"You've gone a funny color," Kevin said. "Should I call the doctor?"

"Just make me a cup of tea," Trish said. He obliged, and after a cup of strong tea she felt much revived. They left the bed in the corridor until Doug arrived and helped Kevin move it into George's room.

"You shouldn't overdo things, Mum," Doug said.

They had a lovely Christmas, with a tree and presents. Bethany cooked a delicious nut roast. On Boxing Day Mark came by for a mince pie and to see the children. Trish noticed how tentative he seemed, how uncomfortable with Sophie and Bethany, how falsely hearty with Kevin. The problem with Mark, she thought, was that he wasn't her husband any more but he couldn't ever be a stranger. He remained hung around her neck like an albatross, father of her children.

After Christmas she saw the doctor and told him about the pain, which had not recurred. He said she should be careful of her heart and told her to exercise more and eat less fat. She looked around for some exercise that didn't bore her and began swimming early every Sunday morning in the Kingsway baths.

That autumn, 1979, Trish stood again for the City Council and was that time elected. She found the work an odd mixture of boring and vitally important. More than anything it was a case of getting to know people and their concerns and organizing them—work she was extremely familiar with from being secretary to so many organizations for so long.

Tamsin started school, and Helen went into full-time adult education. She was learning to program computers, to Trish's complete surprise.

Doug's song "Getting Married on the Moon" was released in the spring of 1980 and went to number three in the British charts and number eight on the US charts, his biggest hit ever. Nobody had yet been married on the moon, though the moonbase generally had a dozen scientists and astronauts on it at any given time. George and Sophie were interviewed by the papers about their dream, and the song was played over and over again on the radio, so that Trish heard it everywhere she went and was tired of being asked about it. "Will your son really get married on the moon?"

"He'd certainly like to," became her standard reply.

23

Orangutan: Pat 1971–1977

The electric wheelchair, built of lightweight space metals, was worth every penny. It was cumbersome and awkward but it gave Bee independence, especially in college. New College tried hard to be accommodating. They built ramps and installed a lift. Every year Bee had to fight the administration to have her classes scheduled in the rooms she could reach, but these were battles she always won. She went on teaching and researching where many people would have given up. "I wasn't about to resign myself to bedpans," she said. She designed long-handled gardening tools she could use from the wheelchair, and taught all the children to help her. She would also lower herself from the chair and work from the ground. She could move around on flat surfaces with her arms. She had first developed this technique on the bed and later extended it to the floors indoors and then at last into the garden. Pat said it was terrible for her clothes, but Bee joked that it cancelled out because of the savings on shoe leather.

They had to give up the bees because there was no way for Bee to lift the hives and nobody else could deal with them without being stung. That was the only sacrifice.

The first year everything was difficult, and money grew tight. "I think we may have to sell the Florentine house," Pat said.

"Never!" Bee said. "It would break the children's hearts."

"I'd be very sad myself," Pat said. "But the property taxes are more every year, and the value has appreciated more than I'd ever have imagined. If we sold it we could live comfortably. And I don't know how you could manage there. You know what the plumbing's like, and the doors are so narrow."

"In the gym where I do my physio they have rings hanging from the ceiling. I was thinking we could put some of those in, and I could get around that way."

"My orangutan," Pat said, fondly. "But even if that worked it would be difficult. Italian workmen? If we sold the house—"

"Are we that short of money?" Bee asked.

"Well, I didn't write the Bologna book. Constable are being very understanding, but they're not going to pay me for a book I haven't turned in. And all the work on this house has been expensive. And keeping my mother in the home. We'll be all right, but it's going to be tight. That money that came in for the French translation got us out of a hole, and the US royalties should come in a few weeks. But we are getting a bit hand-to-mouth."

"We can't sell the Florentine house. It would be crazy." Bee frowned. "You could go to Bologna for a week and do the research and come home and write the book?"

"I can't leave you!"

"I could manage," Bee said.

"I'm sure you could," Pat said, though in fact she was far from sure that Bee could. She couldn't reach the stovetop or the kettle. Remodelling the kitchen was a plan, but they had put it off because of the expense. It was on Pat's list of things they could do if they sold the Florentine house. "But I couldn't manage without you. I'd be utterly miserable, even in Italy. Look what happened the last time I left you! Besides, what if that social worker comes sniffing around again?"

The social worker kept coming back. She wanted to check on Bee's welfare, and on the children's welfare, or so she said. They trod carefully. Pat moved some clothes into the guest room closet and was prepared to say she slept there. The social worker did not go upstairs again, but she questioned the children, which was a worry. It had seemed charming to them for the children to call them Mum and Mamma, but now they worried and tried to train them into calling them by their first names. The girls soon got into the habit, but Philip never did.

"They couldn't really take the children, could they?" Pat asked.

"I don't know," Bee said. "This isn't a situation they'll have space for on their forms."

At last Pat decided to put the family on a more secure financial footing by going back to teaching. Bee was back at work by then, at least part time. Their children were at the village school, an easy walk, and the girls could safely escort Philip. On days when Bee was going in, Pat drove her to New College and then went on to her own work, and at the end of the school day collected Bee and took her home. It worked out relatively smoothly. Pat's old school had no vacancies, but there was an independent day school for girls desperate for somebody to teach English to the fifth and sixth forms. Pat had always enjoyed teaching and she enjoyed taking it up again. In addition to English she taught General Studies— which she turned into a course on Classical and Renaissance art and civilization. The pupils loved it.

She could no longer take her mother out for lunch, but her mother had never seemed to enjoy it much. She continued her weekly visits on Sundays, generally alone as Bee preferred to save her energy for things she enjoyed, and because her mother was generally so savage to the children. Sometimes she recognised Pat, greeting her as Patsy. Other times she was sunk into a world of her own. She would confide that the nurses and the other patients stole her things. She would ask for help in escaping so that she could get home. She often wept and seemed desperate.

Pat tried to sell her mother's house that spring. The money would have been useful to maintain her mother in the home. They all drove down to Twickenham and cleared it out, taking carloads of things to the local charity shops. Then Pat visited an estate agent to get the house put on the market. Everything went smoothly until Pat told them that the house belonged to her mother. "Has she owned the house longer than five years?" the agent asked.

"She's owned it since the 1920s," Pat said. "I think my parents bought it when they married in 1925."

"In that case there will be no certificate of ownership, and she will have to come in and authorize the sale herself," the agent said.

"She's very old, and in a nursing home in Cambridge," Pat explained.

"Then she could fill out these forms and give them to you to bring back," the agent said, producing a thick stack of forms.

"I have the deeds for the house," Pat said.

"Even so, we need these forms," the agent said.

"My mother won't understand them," Pat said.

"Well then you fill them in and just get her to sign."

Getting the forms signed took a struggle that lasted for weeks. Pat's mother was in a suspicious phase and refused to sign anything. When Pat caught her on a happier day, she seemed to have forgotten how to write and sat chewing on the end of the pen. At last she did sign, but she signed them "Love from Gran" in big sprawling writing. Pat visited the solicitor who had seen to the wills she and Bee had made setting up the guardianship of the children and asked what she could do.

The solicitor was unhelpful. "You could set up a power of attorney so that you could do things on her behalf, but you should have done it before, when she was well enough to agree. If this comes before the courts as things are they will appoint somebody to advocate for her who will take control of her estate—a social worker and a financial planner."

"But I've seen her will and she has left everything to me!"

"She's still alive," the solicitor pointed out. "If I were you I'd leave her house alone until it's yours to sell."

"I'm paying out of my own money to keep her in the home," Pat said.

"You could put her somewhere cheaper if you chose." But Pat couldn't bring herself to do it. Her mother couldn't be said to like the home in Trumpington, but she was at least used to it by now, and any change would be worse.

As the summer came they made preparations for Italy. "Should we drive or take the train?" Pat asked in one of their early morning conversations.

"I keep hearing about cars adapted to be driven by hand. Cars with automatic transmissions." Bee devoured everything she could find on assisted technology for the handicapped.

"Here?"

"In the US," Bee admitted.

"Well then, if we drive I have to drive the whole distance, which will mean it will take nearly a week. And our old car is still there. Sara said she'd sell it for us, but she overestimated the demand for right-hand-drive cars in Italy."

"So we could drive back," Bee said.

"We could. The kids loved the train. There was a compartment with four beds, two on each side. I think we could manage."

"What was the bathroom like?"

"Tiny . . . you'd never get the chair in. I could help you."

"I was wondering what chair to take. There's no point taking the powered chair. The power's different in Italy, it wouldn't charge. And it's so heavy to lift up and down onto trains. It might be sensible to take the folding one, which would fit into the car for coming home, and might fit through the doors, except that I can't propel it. This upstairs one is probably best, if it'll fit inside—and then there's the whole issue of getting it home. It's like that puzzle with the fox and the chicken and the sack of grain." Bee laughed.

"We could go both ways on the train. That car's pretty useless to us as it is now. If we need another car it should be an adapted one you can drive, when they start doing them here."

"Or we could fly," Bee said. "It's expensive for all of us, but they know how to deal with wheelchairs and we wouldn't be so tired when we got there."

"I've never flown," Pat said. "I'll look into it. It might be an allowable expense, if I put information about it into the book."

Despite the expense they flew from Gatwick to Rome. Bee had to be carried up the stairs onto the plane, and her chair travelled in the baggage compartment. "Thank goodness it's not a long flight," she said, and refused all drinks.

"Bathrooms in Italy are going to be a real problem," Pat said.

"Oh well, we brought the bedpan if it comes to that," Bee said.

The flight terrified Pat and Jinny, who clung to the arms of their seats at every bump, but the others enjoyed it. The stewardesses were especially solicitous of Bee, and they brought the children so much juice that their mothers feared they would be sick.

"I should have flown back last year," Pat said. "It never crossed my mind."

"It wouldn't have made any difference," Bee said.

From Rome they took the train to Florence. The children got excited as it rushed in and out of tunnels so that hills and medieval towns appeared for a few seconds. "It's so warm," Bee said.

"Italy!" the children chorused, striking up acquaintance with the other passengers on the train in rapid Italian. This was useful when the train stopped in Florence and Pat needed help getting Bee's chair down. A middle-aged man the children had befriended lowered Bee down into it.

"We should have guessed from the way they are with babies and children that they'd be better with disability," Bee said.

"Yes, better in an individual way, but there won't be any proper official recognition. No ramps. All those cobbles. No toilets."

"Stop fretting about toilets," Bee said. "We're in Florence! And Florence makes everything worthwhile!"

Even Bee was a little downcast when she found that the chair would not fit through the front door. She swung herself down and dragged herself in by her arms. Pat put the children to bed straight away, ignoring pleas for just one gelato. She made up a bed for the two of them on the floor in the kitchen. Then she helped Bee in the bathroom. "I'm sorry this puts so much on you," Bee said, dragging herself over to the bed. The chair was parked under the vines by the table where they had eaten so many delicious Italian meals.

Pat was almost too tired to reply. She crawled into the pile of blankets beside Bee and hugged her close. "Of course it would have been better if the bomb had never got you, if you were still well. But it did happen. Random violence is just part of life. The Irish and the Algerians and the Basques and the Red Brigades blow people up, and they don't care who they hurt. We can't help that. It was like being struck by lightning.

And I hate that you were struck by lightning, but I'm just so glad you're alive."

Michael came for two weeks, and while he was in Florence Pat finally managed to get the research done for the Bologna book, and another on Genoa. He helped Pat move the bed downstairs and set it up. "What you need is a slimline wheelchair for this house," he said.

"And a stairlift," Pat said. "Maybe when I've written these books and been paid for them. It's so hard to get that kind of work done in Italy."

"The bathroom first. Rails," Bee said, from outside where she was sitting in her wheelchair.

Their finances gradually recovered. Pat wrote the guidebooks, and if they were not as thorough as the earlier ones nobody complained. Sales continued to be good. She kept on teaching, and Bee stayed on at New College. They often had student volunteers around the house and garden, in the orchard learning to graft or in the conservatory they built on where Bee crossbred plants and did much of her research. They redid the kitchen with low counters accessible from the wheelchair. They eventually managed to make the Florentine house tolerably accessible, widening the doorway, though they never managed to get a stairlift installed.

In 1974 the girls passed the eleven plus and started at Cambridge Girls' Grammar school, where Pat had taught before they were born. Britain was wracked with strikes and reprisals. Violence seemed to be everywhere. The Red Brigades blew up trains and kidnapped politicians in Italy, and the IRA did the same in Britain. Meanwhile Europe moved closer and closer to political unity. Portugal was still embroiled in a vicious colonial war in Goa. The Americans were still fighting in Vietnam, and the French in Algeria. Britain's African colonies were seething with rebellion. In space, the Russian and

European space stations and moon bases glared at each other, and America tried belatedly to catch up and build their own space station. The Soviets crushed dissent in Poland as they had earlier in Hungary and Czechoslovakia.

In 1975 Michael became the art director of the *Observer* newspaper. In 1976 Bee finally managed to get a car she could drive. The social worker kept calling twice a year. Bee and Pat tried to treat it as routine, but it always unnerved them. The threat of losing the children was always with them. The children grew up clever and confident, with Bee's practicality and Pat's love of words and Michael's aesthetic sense. They continued to be bilingual in Italian, which delighted all their parents.

Pat's mother deteriorated still more. She almost never knew Pat and was almost always afraid and savage. In the spring of 1977, she caught a chill and died. She was buried in Twickenham, next to Pat's father and Oswald. It was a bitterly cold day with an east wind biting through their coats.

"Don't put me here," Pat said to Bee and the children as they walked back to the car. Flossie was pushing Bee's chair. "I don't care what you do with me, but not here."

"That's a really morbid thought, Mum," Philip said.

24

Full Life: Trish 1980–1981

Trish taught full time, served as a councillor, taught two evening classes, was secretary of the two preservation societies, and attended her women's group. Her calendar was always full and when anyone suggested anything she had to pull out a diary. Bethany took over most of the cooking and Helen did most of the cleaning. Sometimes the house had a neglected air, but Trish didn't care. She usually took Tamsin and Alestra to school and Bethany, whose hours at the food co-op were flexible, picked them up. Cathy graduated in the autumn of 1980 and took a job at once in London, working at a merchant bank.

"What do you actually do?" Trish asked.

"You wouldn't understand," Cathy said. Cathy had had a girlfriend at university, worrying Trish and almost giving Mark apoplexy. Now she had a boyfriend, Richard, an accountant. They took a flat together in Kentish Town and played charmingly at domesticity.

"Your generation does much better at this kind of thing than mine did," Trish said to Helen as they went home on the train after visiting Cathy and Richard.

"I don't know," Helen said. "I think it'll be up to Tamsin's generation to get it right. Look at Doug."

Doug's love life was a disaster, even as his career seemed to be rising again, despite the new punk trend. Trish grimaced. "Even so."

"And I'm not doing so well," Helen said. Men continued to be attracted to Helen's undiminished beauty, but never anyone she could respect. "I sometimes wonder if it's because I'm called Helen. If the name had an effect."

"I don't see how it could. We called you after Gran, and Gran wasn't a beauty."

"Well, much good it's done me. Anyway, you shouldn't give up on your generation because of Dad. You're not too old to find somebody else."

Trish laughed.

Helen worked hard on her computer course, and graduated to a computer degree at the university. "I saw Dad today," she said one evening. "He was surrounded by students and pretended not to see me."

"You were always his favorite," Trish said, sadly.

The Saturday before Christmas they had a tree-decorating party, before the family arrived for the season. Lots of Tamsin's friends from school came, and a surprisingly large number of the people Trish had randomly invited over the course of the week before. They ate Bethany's mince pies, helped out by some from Marks and Spencer, and drank tea, Ribena, and a wine punch Helen made. When the tree was decorated and the children were in bed the last survivors of the party sat around in the kitchen drinking peppermint tea and eating bread and cheese. Kevin was missing, he had been spending a lot of time away from home recently in a way Trish tried not to see as ominous. The lingerers were Bethany, Helen, Duncan, Barb, Barb's new partner Jack, and one of Helen's tutors, a visiting American who had been introduced as Doctor Lin.

Trish found herself talking to Doctor Lin, who was about her own age. "I'm spending a year here as part of a faculty exchange program," he said. "And before you ask, yes, this is my first time in Europe, and I like it very much."

"Where do you usually teach?" she asked.

"Berkeley, near San Francisco," he said.

"My son is at MIT."

"I did my Ph.D. at MIT."

Trish confessed that she had never been to America and would like to visit. "George keeps suggesting it, but it's so far, and so expensive. I've never flown. There's so much I've never done."

"That's sad," he said. "I'm very much enjoying having new experiences."

"Are you enjoying British food?" she asked.

He laughed. "I think the mince pies are wonderful. They remind me of Chinese food, sweet but not sweet, and spiced."

"Chinese food is something else I've never had, except for takeaways. Are you Chinese?" she asked.

"I was born in New York. But my parents came from Hong Kong."

In the New Year of 1981 Doctor Lin telephoned Trish and invited her to eat Chinese food with him at the Jade Garden restaurant which he thought the most authentic of the local possibilities. She recognized his voice at once. She pulled out her diary and arranged to do it on her next free evening.

"A date!" Bethany said, when Trish mentioned it.

"He's a lonely American far from home, and he's just being kind and friendly," Trish said. Then she paused and looked at Bethany. "What should I wear, do you think?"

Bethany laughed. "When did you last go on a date?"

"I'm not sure I ever did in the sense you mean. Certainly no more recently than 1949."

"Let's look through your wardrobe."

"I've got clothes that look like a schoolteacher and clothes that look like a town councillor and clothes that are only good for gardening and housework," Trish said.

In the end she wore a skirt and a blouse that Bethany said went well together, with some jet beads that had belonged to her mother and now belonged to Helen. She was nervous waiting for him to arrive, but not at all nervous when he was there. He was shorter than she was, which was subtly reassuring. They didn't run out of things to talk about, which had been one fear, nor did he talk endlessly about computers. The Chinese food was delicious, though it didn't remind Trish at all of mince pies—it was much like the Chinese takeaways she had bought when the children had been teenagers and she had been too busy to cook. He showed her how to use chopsticks and asked her to call him David.

"Is that your real name?"

"It's the English form of my name."

"What is it really?"

"Da Wei," he said. "Lin Da Wei. Chinese people put the surname first. But David is what I'm used to being called, so please call me that."

The next week he took her to a concert at the university, and the week after that she invited him to Sunday lunch, a meal cooked by Bethany and attended by all of Trish's household. Afterwards she and David went for a walk alone down the canal as far as the aqueduct. It was a brisk walk, because the air was cold.

"Is it much warmer than this in America?" Trish asked, looking at how he kept his hands in his pockets.

"In California it is," he replied. "In New York where I grew up it's much colder in winter. But this is a damp cold. It gets inside you."

He admired the views from the aqueduct, which took the canal over the Lune river far below.

"When the spring comes we must go for some walks up to Silverdale, on the limestone. It's a different landscape. And also you should see the Lake District before you go. It's the most beautiful part of England. It would be a shame to come and only see Lancaster."

"I don't like driving on the wrong side of the road, so I haven't been to many places."

"I can drive you there," she said.

Two weeks later he invited her to Manchester to see the celebrations of Chinese New Year. She had to miss a meeting of the peace group to make it. Manchester was about an hour away down the motorway. Trish drove. It was the year of the Rooster, and there were big pictures of brightly colored roosters displayed in Manchester's Chinatown. Trish liked the dancing dragons and thoroughly enjoyed the food and the friendliness everyone showed. "We should have brought Tamsin, she'd have loved this," she said.

On her next free evening they had dinner at Jade Garden again and when they were finishing David put his hand on hers. He had not touched her before, except to position her fingers on her chopsticks. "I like you very much, and I think that although your life is so busy there are ways you're lonely. It's the same for me. At the end of June I will be going back to San Francisco. My life is there, and so are my wife and family. But between now and then you and I could have fun together."

Trish moved her hand away. "I don't think—"

"Try something new," he said.

"Your wife . . ."

"We have an agreement. She doesn't mind what I do when I'm away. It doesn't hurt anything between me and her. I won't tell her anything except that I have found a friend—and I have told her that already. What you and I do before I go home to her can't hurt her, and she can't hurt you."

So they became lovers, and it was a revelation. Trish had thought she would put up with the sex for the sake of his company, which she did enjoy. Instead for the first time in her life her body opened up to pleasure. Nothing could be more different from Mark. For one thing, David expected to stay in bed all night and cuddle, which was in itself very pleasant. They moved the double bed back to her room. For another he liked the light on when they made love. "I want to see you," he insisted.

"I never was much to look at," Trish protested, "And now I'm old, past menopause. I'm a grandmother."

"And I'm a grandfather," he said. "How old are you?"

"Fifty-five," Trish admitted.

"I'm only fifty-two, old woman."

He made love slowly, caressing her body. He taught her new acts and positions, some of them delightful. "Is this how Americans make love?" she asked.

"It's how I do," he said. Unlike Mark, he liked conversation in bed, he liked her to tell him what she was feeling and what she liked and what she wanted him to do.

"Even after four children and all those stillbirths I feel as if I might as well have been a virgin until I met you," she said.

They continued to go out, for meals, to concerts, and as the weather improved driving up to the Lake District for picnics and walks. He was good with the whole family. Everyone liked him. She teased him that he'd have to give Helen good grades, and he said that there was no need, she was getting good grades on her own. Trish continued to do all her work, though more and more often she skipped the peace group and the women's group, which seemed less relevant than they had. David wasn't like the men they talked about.

He didn't move in. He kept his room on campus and spent three or four nights a week with Trish. Time seemed to go very fast. When it was time for him to go back to the States she drove him to Manchester airport. "Will I ever see you again?" she asked.

"It doesn't seem likely," he replied. "I'm sorry, Trish. It's been wonderful. But I don't expect I'll come back here, and if you came to San Francisco my wife wouldn't like it."

"How about Boston, when George graduates?"

"If you're going to be in Boston write to me. I'm not there often, but it's not impossible. I might be able to find an excuse. I can't promise. We shouldn't spoil what we've had. You always knew it was going to end now." Trish kissed him for the last time when she dropped him off outside the airport. She drove home, tears running down her face.

Helen tried to cheer her up. "Well now you know there are men who aren't like Dad, maybe you can find another."

"How on Earth do women tell?" Trish asked.

Helen laughed and shook her head.

"I wish I'd never met him," Trish said to Bethany, down in the basement later. "I was happy being busy. I liked my life. I made room for him in it, and now he's gone and I have this huge hole where he was."

"I think Kevin has done the same," Bethany said.

"I did notice that he hasn't been around very much," Trish said. "Has he really left you?"

"He's left town, as best I can tell. He hasn't told me anything. He's just kind of oozed away, and now I don't know where he is. I don't know how I'm going to afford to pay rent on my own."

"Never mind paying rent, we can manage," Trish said, putting her arms around Bethany. "I should pay you for doing so much cooking. But how could he just leave that way?"

"When you're not married you can just walk away," Bethany said. "I might be able to make him pay something for Ally, if I could catch him and take him to court. But he doesn't have anything—he'd consider it bourgeois to have enough money to pay for her—so probably that's it. I'm sorry to drop this on you when you're upset about David."

"Troubles come not in single spies but in battalions," Trish said.

Bethany blinked. "I'm sure that's something very erudite?"

"*Hamlet*. It just felt appropriate. If Helen had just lost a man as well I'd think it was something in the stars over the house."

"Helen has found a man, I think," Bethany said. "But I'll let her tell you about it."

Trish wept alone for David and tried to put a good face on it before the world. She kept his business card on her bedside table. It said "David Lin" and underneath that his name in Chinese characters, and then his address in San Francisco. She looked up how much it cost to fly to Boston.

It took Helen a long time to tell her mother that she had a new boyfriend. "Boyfriend" didn't feel like the right word, as it hadn't for David. Helen's new partner, Don, was divorced, and thirty-six. Helen was twenty-seven. "He's serious, Mum," Helen said. "Not like the others. Not just seeing my looks." He was another mature student taking the same degree Helen was. "But he's doing it part time. He has his own business, importing computers and selling them. He says he wants to know how they work so he can be better at that."

"Computers and space," Trish said. "My children are so futuristic."

"And a pop star and a banker," Helen reminded her.

"I could never have imagined any of that," Trish said.

25

Different News: Pat 1978

When she was fourteen, Flossie announced that she wished to be known as Firenza in Italian and Flora in English. Her mothers did their best to comply. She also took to doing her hair like the statue of the goddess Flora and to being more enthusiastic about flower gardening than vegetable gardening. Bee found this amusing and encouraged the flower growing, with the result that the garden was a mass of blooms that year. Jinny, meanwhile, was getting top marks in school and affected to care nothing about her appearance. Philip had just passed his eleven plus and was learning to play the oboe. He sang in the church choir. The girls played popular music as many teenagers did, enjoying Italian pop and the new "Volga beat" songs that everyone seemed to be dancing to. Philip turned up his nose at all of that and played Vivaldi and Stravinsky when it was his turn to use the music center.

"Are we driving to Italy this year or what?" Jinny asked one June Sunday as they were just finishing lunch.

Pat and Bee looked at each other. "Driving, I think," Pat said. "They've been bombing trains again, and now we can take turns driving it's cheaper and more practical again."

"Can we stop in Menton and see the gardens?" Flora asked.

"It depends on whether it makes sense, but I should think

we can go that way and stop there," Bee said. "I'd like to see them too. They have the oldest olive trees in Europe."

"They have water hyacinths," Flora said.

Pat looked at Jinny, whose turn it was to clear the table. Jinny obediently began to gather up plates. Pat got up to fetch dessert—a strawberry cake she had made. In the kitchen she automatically switched on the radio. "Not known yet whether the blast was nuclear," the announcer was saying.

Jinny put the plates down with a clatter. "Nuclear?" she said.

"There has as yet been no official Pakistani response. United Europe has asked China for clarification."

"What's happening?" Bee called.

Pat took the cake through into the dining room. "It looks as if China has intervened in the Indo-Pak war. They don't know if it's nuclear."

"What are we doing?" Bee asked.

"Asking for clarification, apparently." Pat switched the television on.

"Geiger counters as far away as Tehran are confirming that the strike on Delhi was definitely nuclear," it said as the tubes warmed up.

"What should we do?" Flora asked.

"It's just like before you were born, the Cuban Missile Exchange," Bee said. "It doesn't mean it's the end of the world and that everyone will push the buttons just because somebody has."

"They could, though," Philip said. "It could be the end of the world."

The phone rang, and they all jumped. Bee wheeled over to answer it. Pat switched off the television and everyone listened. "Yes, we're all here, yes, we're all safe, yes, we have heard the news. It doesn't seem as if there's anything we can do about it, so we're going to have some cake. I'm glad you're safe. Well don't go any nearer! In fact, come home if you can. I understand that. Well, stay safe. We'll see you in Florence. We love you." She put the receiver down. "Michael. He's in Jerusalem."

"Does he think it'll be the end of the world?" Philip asked.

"No," Bee said crisply. "If he thought that he'd have asked to speak to all of you. He just wanted to make sure we knew what was happening."

"Is Jerusalem a target?" Flora asked.

"It might be, if the whole Middle East goes up. But they seem to prefer suicide bombs and assassinations to all-out war these days," Pat said.

"That's a comfort!" Bee said.

Pat switched the television on again. They ate the cake without tasting it and later drank a pot of tea without tasting that. Jinny kept switching the channel. "Do you think you'll get different news on ITV?" Flora sniped.

"I wish we could just switch channels and have different news," Bee said.

"I wish we had any news and not just the same thing repeated over and over and people speculating about what it means," Philip said. "I'm going to go upstairs and practice. If it's going to be Armageddon that's what I want to be doing, and if not I'll need to be in practice for the concert next week."

"That's a really good way of looking at it. We're not doing any good sitting here," Pat said. She got up and went into the kitchen to wash the dishes, but she switched the radio on and kept listening to people saying nothing about the nuclear exchange.

When she went back in to the dining room the television was on but only Jinny was there. "Bee and Flora decided that if it was the end of the world they wanted to be grafting geraniums in the conservatory," Jinny explained.

"What do you want to do?" Pat asked.

"I don't know yet." Jinny started to cry. "I'm only fourteen. I don't want to die. I haven't found my passion yet."

"I didn't find mine until I went to Florence when I was—" Pat counted on her fingers. "Twenty-four. I loved English literature too. I always have loved it."

"But Florence was your passion?"

Pat sat down next to Jinny. The television was still on, interviewing people in India and Pakistan and giving no new information. She turned it down so the voices were a quiet background but loud enough for them to hear and turn it up again if there was anything new. "Florence, the Renaissance, yes."

"I don't know what mine will be!"

"You've got plenty of time to find out," Pat said. "Sometimes it's harder for people who are very intelligent and talented in lots of directions. I've noticed that with girls in school. It takes longer to see what's important."

"Unless they blow the world up before I can find out," Jinny said. "Or the IRA get me, or a car crossing the road."

Pat hugged Jinny to her and rocked her. "Those things could happen, but we have to live as if they won't. Or if they do we have to find ways to cope and follow our passion anyway, like Bee has."

"I wish I knew already, like Flora and Philip," Jinny gulped.

"They may not know. They're so young. They may be wrong." Pat gave Jinny a tissue. "Blow your nose."

Jinny did. "I want to do something to make the world a better place."

"It's so hard to know whether you have," Pat said. "I mean, I write my guide books, and people use them, but it's a very little thing."

"If the Chinese were going to nuke Florence now, would you want to be there?" Jinny asked.

"Yes," Pat said immediately, and then directly afterwards contradicted herself. "No. What good would it do? I wish I were there right now so that I could go and stare at the Botticellis the way Philip's playing his oboe and Bee's grafting. But if it has to die what good would it do me to die with it? It would be better to live on and tell people how it used to be."

"Now it's my turn to tell you to blow your nose," Jinny said.

"I'm sorry—wait."

The television had cut back to the announcer, who was looking grave. They froze, but it was only news about the fallout from the Delhi bomb.

"Numbers that big become meaningless. They'd do better to show us one child who will die," Pat said. "Look, it's not doing us any good to watch this."

"But there might be some news," Jinny protested. "At any minute, there might."

"I know." Pat smiled through her tears. "But we can listen to the radio in the kitchen. Let's make dinner. If we were going to eat one last thing, what would you want it to be."

"Gelato!" wailed Jinny, choking on the word.

"Well, if the world's still here we'll be in Florence in three weeks," Pat said. "Meanwhile I think it's time to get out the pasta maker. I have one tin of truffle butter that I was saving, but I think we could have it today. Come and help."

Pat called the others for supper at six o'clock. "Come and eat. Italian dinner tonight. We have homemade pasta with herbs from the garden and truffle butter, followed by gammon and eggs, then fresh raspberries and cream."

"You picked the raspberries?" Bee asked.

"Jinny picked them," Pat said.

"Well, I suppose we might as well," Bee said. She wheeled out of the conservatory. "You've made a feast!"

There were flowers on the table, Bee's grandmother's lace tablecloth and Pat's mother's best china plates. "It seemed appropriate," Pat said.

Philip came down and was appropriately enthusiastic about dinner. "I was wondering if I could go to choir school," he said, as he came back from clearing the pasta plates. "I might be able to get a scholarship. A boy from choir did."

"If it's what you really want," Bee said.

"I really think it is." Philip hesitated. "What I'd really like would be to go to choir school in Italy."

"Do they even have choir schools in Italy?" Pat asked.

"There's one in Rome and one in Milan," he said. "Or there's Wells. Wells is the best one in England, everyone says."

"There's King's College right here in Cambridge," Pat said. "Going away to school costs a lot of money, and also we'd miss you."

"I'd miss you too," Philip admitted.

After dinner they switched the television on again, and were rewarded with some actual news. It was announced that in a joint communication from Moscow and Brussels that the USSR and United Europe had informed the governments of India, Pakistan and China that no more nuclear strikes would be tolerated.

"Does that mean it's over?" Flora asked.

"I have no idea," Pat said. "It might. Or it might mean that if those countries won't listen, then we—or the Russians—would hit them from the moon. That could mean the end of everything."

"What are the Americans doing?" Jinny asked.

"Splendid isolation," Bee said. "Always their default policy. It's what they do best."

They went to bed and woke the next morning to a world that, as after the Cuban Exchange, seemed determined to carry on as if nothing had happened. The millions dead in China and India, the millions more predicted to suffer radiation and cancer deaths, were not exactly forgotten but swept under the carpet. The mood was that of having dodged a bullet. The girls in Pat's classes the next day seemed on the edge of hysteria, needing very little to tip them into either laughter or tears. It was almost exam time, and she read poetry to them, couching it in terms of revision.

Three weeks later the family were in Florence. Pat went alone into the Duomo and quietly gave thanks to God for the world still being there. She went with the children to the Sunday morning service and prayed for the preservation of Florence.

On Monday morning Michael joined them. The children were off with their friends, and the three adults bought gelato in Perche No! and went to sit in the piazza to watch the sky darken behind the Palazzo Vecchio. Pat kept dissolving into tears. "We have to do something to stop this all being on a knife edge," she said.

"What can we do?" Bee asked.

"Your books help people appreciate what they're looking at when they see it," Michael said.

"I was wondering whether I could use the semi-demi-fame I have from the books to start a movement to say that some places just shouldn't be harmed. But I'm sure everyone would agree and then not take any notice."

"Maybe we could start an organization," Michael said. "Get the paper behind us."

"Maybe. But it would need to be international to do any good." Pat stared out across the square where Florentines and tourists were mingling on the ancient cobblestones in the twilight. "And why would China care about Florence? And the US left the United Nations, they don't care about anything, but they have all those nukes."

"The problem is that we say using nukes at all is barbarous and unthinkable and nobody should do it, and then we do it. If we said there were certain places that were sacrosanct then it would be tantamount to admitting that using them was acceptable," Bee said.

Pat leaned down and put her hand on Bee's shoulder. "But people are using them. The Americans and the Russians, and now the Indians and the Chinese. People will carry on using them to end arguments. And it's all very well if the Russians will act with Europe, the way they did this time, but what if it's us against them next time? In space and on Earth? All those bombs in orbit and on the moon?"

"There might not even be plants left," Bee said. "But that doesn't mean we can condone using them at all in any circumstances."

"You sound like CND."

"Maybe we should join CND," Bee said. "We used to go on peace marches, not that it did any good."

"We just live our lives and hope history doesn't notice us," Michael said. "But we could try to start up a list of places so precious they shouldn't be harmed. An international list. The Great Wall of China. Angkor Wat. Machu Picchu. Florence."

"The seven wonders of the world," Bee said.

26

In Sickness and in Health
Trish 1982–1988

Trish flew to Boston to see George get his Ph.D. "We're going to the moon, Mum," he said, when he met her at Logan airport.

"Because of the song?" she asked.

"Well, it probably helped, and we are going to be the first people to get married there, but really it's because of our work."

"That's wonderful," she said.

"When we come back we'll have another wedding on Earth. We don't want you to miss it, or Sophie's parents either. But it does seem like a wonderful opportunity."

"How long will you be on the moon?" she asked. "On the moon. Amazing to think of it."

"A year or two, maybe more," George said.

She stayed with George and Sophie for a few days. She watched George's ceremony, and she visited MIT and Harvard and the Mary Baker Eddy Library with its stained glass globe big enough for a group to walk inside. Then she spent a blissful weekend in a hotel with David Lin. They all had dinner together in a Japanese restaurant where the food was so beautifully presented it was the most Trish could do to eat it.

Back at home, both of her daughters had news. Helen was moving in with Don, which of course meant that Tamsin was also going. This made a huge difference to Trish's daily life, even though they only lived in Scotforth, between Lancaster and the university. She saw them often, but they were no longer part of her everyday life. Cathy surprised her even more. She came home for a weekend, alone.

"I wanted to tell you that I'm having a baby," she said. They were in the kitchen, and by chance Cathy was sitting in the same chair Helen had sat in years before when she had asked Trish how she had known she was pregnant.

"Are you and Richard getting married then?" Trish asked, feeling déjà vu.

"No. In fact, we've broken up. He doesn't want children, and we had a huge fight about it." Cathy stared out of the window as she spoke. "I thought—well, never mind. But he accused me of trying to trap him, and so of course we couldn't possibly keep on being friends after that. What actually happened was that we were on holiday in Hungary and his contraceptive shot had worn off and then we ran out of condoms and he said that hundreds of times nothing happens. But of course it did."

"Is he going to support the baby?"

Cathy turned back to her in surprise. "I can support the baby perfectly well myself."

"Are you going to move back home? There's plenty of room, and we managed with Tamsin so—"

Cathy laughed, an uncomfortable laugh that sounded on the edge of tears. "Why would I move home? What would I do in Lancaster? I'm not Helen, Mum. I'm not a teenager. I'm almost twenty-three. I have a good job in London."

"Twenty-three is still very young to be on your own with a baby. I'll do anything you want me to to help, whatever you want."

"I'll get a nanny," Cathy said.

Cathy's baby, James Marcus Anston, was born in April 1983 in London. Trish was there for the birth, she had been there for the whole Easter holiday. He was born by caesarean, as the doctors felt it might be dangerous for Cathy to try to deliver him. Trish bit her tongue on her own stories of giving birth so many times. She admired Jamie, and admired too Cathy's organization. She took only the statutory eight weeks fully paid maternity leave, and thereafter had two nannies, one for day and one for night.

Helen and Don opened a shop in the middle of Lancaster to sell computers to businesses and individuals. They sold Trish a word processor with a green screen, which she used for making notes for her classes. She found it much easier than the typewriter because she could go back to correct errors.

George and Sophie went to the moon, and were married there. It was international news, and the song got revived and played everywhere again. Doug's career was in a down phase again, but the publicity sent his records soaring up the charts. He came home for a few months to detox. "I have to get off the smack, Mum," he said. "Heroin is terrible stuff."

"Anything I can do to help."

"I'll just stay here and work on writing new songs and go cold turkey."

It wasn't that easy, of course. He did manage to give up the heroin, but he kept on smoking and drinking. He filled the house with musicians and instruments and mess. Bethany, who had long since stopped even pretending to pay rent, but who took care of the house instead, protested at the mess, the noise, and the cigarette butts. He countered by mocking at Bethany's flute music, and she grew furious with him. "It's not your kind of music and you know nothing about it," she said. Trish tried to mediate, but found it very difficult when Doug was so clearly in the wrong. Eventually he moved out in anger in the spring of 1984.

George and Sophie stayed on the moon. Trish heard about them on the news from time to time and had a three-minute phone call from George once a month. Whenever she looked up at the moon she had a thrill of wonder thinking that George was there. She missed him, and found the phone calls unsatisfying. But she would walk along the canal and look up at the silver disk and shake her head and marvel.

A few weeks after Doug moved out, Trish was summoned out of a council meeting with an urgent message. "Your husband is in the Infirmary and needs you."

She finished the meeting and then went to the Infirmary. Mark had suffered a stroke. "He's only fifty-four," she said.

He was paralyzed down one side and could not speak. "People do sometimes make a good recovery from this kind of stroke," the doctor said. "But there may be another clot, and while we're doing what we can, it doesn't look good."

She called the children, pushing ten pences into the pay phone in the hospital corridor. Helen said she'd be there in half an hour. "Don's setting up a big system in Torrisholme so he's not here. I'll drop Tamsin with Bethany if that's all right."

"You do that. She's at home with Alestra tonight. And tell her where I am and that I may be late and she shouldn't worry."

Doug was in London, working on a new album. He refused to come. "Dad and I have always hated each other. There's no point pretending anything different, Mum."

"I know you've always had a difficult relationship, but that might be a reason to try to reconcile now before it's too late."

Doug blew a raspberry down the phone. "I'm sorry, Mum, but there's no point, and I'm not buying into all that hypocrisy."

She left a message for George to be relayed to the moon-base when possible. "I know you won't be able to come, and your father can't speak, but if you send a message I'll make sure to read it to him," she said, after she had explained the situation.

Cathy was out. Trish left a message with the nanny and said that she would call again later.

Helen arrived as she was on her way back to the ward where Mark was. She was hugely pregnant and her walk was a waddle. "I could hardly fit behind the wheel of the car," she said. "Tell me it's not the same ward where they had Gran that time? I couldn't stand the irony."

"It's a men's ward, but it's very similar," Trish admitted.

Mark glared at them from the bed when they went in. Helen went over and took his good hand. "Are you all right, Dad?"

Trish did not ask how he could possibly be considered to be all right. She saw the body in the bed as the shell of the man she had loved and hated and finally pitied. She pitied him even more now. She was trying to think what she was going to do if he did not die. If he recovered that was all well and good, but what if he continued to live in a state of paralysis, as so many people did after strokes? She did not want to have him at home, she shrank from the thought, but what else was there? She couldn't cast the burden onto the children. He bellowed suddenly, making both of them jump and bringing in a nurse.

"What does he want?" Helen asked the nurse.

"No telling when they're in this state," the nurse said.

Trish went to try Cathy again and this time caught her. "I can come, but it's going to be very complicated," Cathy said. "Should I bring Jamie? Dad's only seen him once."

"Do whatever is easiest," Trish said. "This might be a false alarm. He has had a stroke, but he could live for years."

"Or he could die tonight," Cathy said. "But it's so late now. I'll come first thing in the morning, I should be there by lunch time."

Trish went back in. "Cathy's coming tomorrow," she said.

"Good," Helen said.

Mark grimaced, or perhaps it was supposed to be a smile. A nurse came in and took his blood pressure and adjusted the drip in his arm. "I think I should go and collect Tamsin and get her home to bed," Helen said. "It's getting late."

"Yes, go and come back tomorrow," the nurse said. "He'll probably sleep now."

So Trish went home. Helen took Tamsin and went home, and she and Bethany sat in the kitchen and drank chamomile tea. "How is he really?" Bethany asked.

Trish explained concisely. "Sometimes people live for years and years in that condition. He could die at any minute, and I think it would be a blessing if he did. What am I going to do if he doesn't?"

"It's not your responsibility," Bethany said. "You're divorced. They shouldn't even have called you really."

"I feel so sorry for him seeing him so helpless like that," Trish said. "And I did say 'in sickness and in health'."

"That doesn't count after divorce," Bethany said. "It gets cancelled out."

"It's not as simple as that," Trish sighed.

"Go to bed. And don't feel responsible for him."

Trish went to bed, and was roused by the telephone in the small hours. She thought it must mean that Mark had died, but it was Don. "Helen wanted me to tell you that she has gone into labor. She's gone to the Infirmary in the ambulance. I'm going to bring Tamsin to your place and then join her there."

"I'll see you soon," Trish said. She dressed and made tea

and ate a handful of nuts and raisins. She wrote a quick note for Bethany: "Helen in labor. Tamsin will be asleep in her room. Please give her breakfast and take her to school! When Cathy comes if I am not back send her to the Infirmary to see Mark. Thanks, T."

Don arrived with a sleepy Tamsin. "Hi Gran. I might as well have gone to bed here earlier!"

Trish hugged her. "Isn't this exciting! You go up to bed. Bethany's downstairs, and I've left her a note to wake you in the morning. This reminds me of that night nine years ago when you were born."

She pulled her coat on and hurried out into the night with Don. As they walked down the hill she thought what a strange world it was—Mark possibly dying while Helen's new baby was being born. She couldn't say that to Don, she didn't know him well enough.

"Have you thought about names?" she asked instead.

Helen's labor went easily, as it had with Tamsin. Don stayed in the room the whole time, which was the first time Trish had ever heard of a man being present at a birth. The baby was another girl. "Donna Rose," Helen said, looking down at the red-faced bundle.

"She's perfect," Don said, sounding awed.

Trish went to look in on Mark. He was asleep, snoring. He looked helpless and diminished in size under the hospital covers.

By the time Cathy arrived Trish was exhausted to the point where she could barely keep her eyes open. "We think your father's going to pull through," the doctor said to Cathy.

Trish went home and slept. She was woken by the telephone again—this time George, calling from the moon to find out how Mark was. "They think he's going to survive. But he's paralyzed and he can't speak," she said.

"What are you going to do?" George asked, his voice strange and full of echoes.

"When he's well enough to come out of hospital I think I'll put him in his study."

"It shouldn't all fall on you, Mum," George said.

"Who else is there?" Trish asked. She didn't want Mark, but she felt she couldn't just abandon him.

Mark was released from hospital in October, by which time Trish had his study ready for an invalid. He still couldn't speak, but he could make noises and call out. Doug, home for Christmas as usual, took one look at Mark and turned his back. "He's like an animal."

"You'd feel sorry for him if he was an animal," Trish said. As she had done with her mother, she found a woman to come in and take care of Mark while she was at work. This one was called Carol. She had been a nurse and stopped when she had children, and now did private nursing.

Trish's life settled into a routine again. She continued to teach at the school, and to teach her evening classes. Mark—paralyzed, incontinent, bellowing—was a burden she had to deal with. She tried not to let it grind her down. She didn't know if he was alert and angry inside his head, or how much the stroke had wiped away. Was he trapped in inarticulacy, did he long to be sarcastic and unkind as he had always been? Or was he really the animal he seemed? She sat and read to him sometimes on evenings when she was at home, trying to convince herself he was quieter when she did that. She fed him and cleaned him up, like a huge baby.

"I don't understand why you're doing this," Bethany said.

"I couldn't expect the children to do it. And those nursing homes are terrible places. I go sometimes to visit my old headmistress. The smell—disinfectant over stale urine. I couldn't send him there. And a private home would be so expensive."

"He has his pension from the university. Or Doug could pay it without noticing. And George and Cathy are doing well." Bethany shook her head. "You're too nice."

"Maybe I want to have him in my power," Trish joked, and then she wondered if it was true. But she didn't feel as if the thing in the bed was really Mark; more that it was a shell Mark had left behind, a shell that needed tending. "He's just another baby, but one who won't grow up."

Bethany stayed downstairs, a tower of strength. On Trish's suggestion she stood for the council, and won, which now gave the Preservationist Independents a bloc of six, which as they tended to caucus with the Greens gave them a reasonable say in what got done. The days when Trish could overhear the mayor saying that global warming meant it was a waste to put money into Morecambe were over. She found the work was often frustrating when established interests refused to consider things that she thought were good sense. There was a huge battle that year over moving the market. It had been on its present site since 1660, not long enough for it to be considered traditional, according to some of the council who wanted to sell the land for a mall. The Preservationists resisted them fiercely and won. The market was revamped and made fireproof and given ramps, but stayed where it was.

Helen had another baby, a boy, Anthony, in September 1986. Cathy continued to be a banker and a single mother, but in 1986 she began dating another woman in her bank, Caroline. By winter they had moved in together and she brought her home for Christmas. Trish did not take to Caroline, who treated her as if she knew nothing about feminism and needed to be educated. She tried not to be relieved when she and Cathy broke up before the next Christmas.

George and Sophie came home from the moon, and had a party to celebrate their wedding with their Earth friends in

Sophie's family home in Aberystwyth. Trish couldn't make it because of Mark, so she held another party for them in Lancaster. They settled down in Cambridge and had twins, Rhodri and Bronwen, born in February 1988. "We didn't want to risk having babies on the moon," Sophie said. George went back into space soon after, to the big international space station, Hope. He was there for several months at a time, then back in Cambridge for a few months. Sophie was working in Cambridge on the Mars terraforming project and on hydroponics for the planned domes.

"Will you go to Mars?" Trish asked, apprehensively.

"Not on the first mission," George said. "But maybe eventually. When the twins are big enough. Mars will be a proper home one day."

27

Time's Wingéd Chariot: Pat 1978–1985

Philip went to the King's College and worked seriously on his music. Pat and Michael began the Seven Wonders Foundation, which eventually grew entirely out of their control. Soon they had lists of seven wonders on each continent, though Pat never felt that any of the American ones could possibly really count. "New York's skyline, indeed," she muttered to Bee. "I'm glad to have anything protected, but how can that be considered artistic or historical?"

"They'll be moving all their weapons in there," Bee warned.

All the countries of United Europe and the USA and the USSR signed the Seven Wonders Pledge, along with Israel and Egypt and China and India, which made Pakistan the only nuclear power holding out, and Michael felt confident that the Shah of Iran would help put pressure on them.

When they came home from Italy in the autumn of 1980 it was to terrible news from Lorna. "Thyroid cancer," she said.

They visited Lorna in hospital where she was starkly bald from chemotherapy and so thin her bones showed. "If only it did some good," she said.

"She's only fifty-two," Bee said, afterwards as she wheeled herself back to the car. "My age."

"Is it radiation?" Pat asked.

"Maybe. It could just be one of those things. There have always been cancers. But thyroid—could be. Could well be. Not likely Delhi, but it could be Kiev. That was such a thoughtlessly placed bomb. Poor Lorna."

"She was the first lesbian I knew well," Pat said.

"Me too. The first lesbian I ever knowingly met. At one of your parties in that flat on Mill Road." Bee levered herself into the driving seat.

"She was the person I asked what women do together, when I first realized I was falling for you." Pat wiped her eyes and heaved the wheelchair into the car.

"Really? I never knew that. I didn't ask anyone. I just sort of went on instinct." Bee shook her head as Pat sat down and did up her seatbelt.

"Poor Lorna. Well, she may pull through."

"No," Bee said. "Not with anaplastic thyroid cancer. Don't get your hopes up. We can cure AIDS and leukemia, but not this kind of cancer."

Lorna died before Christmas. They went to her funeral on a bitterly cold day. Although they hadn't belonged to a choir in years, Lorna's partner Sue asked Pat and Bee to sing "Gaudete." "Lorna used to talk about you singing that at a party years ago," Sue said. Pat sang it, and remembered the party, before Suez or the Cuban Exchange, before the children, when she and Bee had only just met. Bee's voice was as powerful and true as ever. "We really did know Lorna for a long time," she said to Bee on their way home.

Bee's mother also died that winter, at a great age. They all went up to Penrith for the funeral. There was a bit of trouble as Bee's brother Donald tried to put Bee and Jinny in the first car and the rest of the family in their own car. Pat would have let it be, but Bee insisted fiercely that her family were staying together. In the end they drove their own car and left immediately from the graveside. "Why did he have to be like that?" Bee asked. "I hate it when people won't acknowledge my family as real. All of us."

The girls took their A Levels that summer, 1981. Flora did well but not spectacularly and took up a place at Lancaster. She had grown out of the flower goddess phase and chose to study computer science. Jinny did brilliantly. She was accepted at Pat's old college, St. Hilda's, to read English, but in Italy that summer she changed her mind. "I want to study here," she said. "My student loans are good for anywhere in Europe, aren't they?"

"They are," Pat said. "But are you sure?"

"What could be more blissful than studying sculpture in Florence?" Jinny asked. "Can I live in the house?"

"There will be some students living here, but there should be room for you as well. Is sculpture your passion then, Jinny-Pat?"

On the day of the Indo-Pak crisis Jinny had been a plump teenager with long black hair, and now she was a willowy girl with a short crop that curled over her ears, but the look she gave Pat was exactly the same. "I still don't know. But it's closer."

"We might all fly out for Christmas," Bee said when they told her. "I've always wanted to do Christmas in Florence."

They did that, and discovered the lack of insulation in their house. "It was built to catch drafts," Jinny said. "Thank you for bringing all my warm clothes!"

In Italy, instead of presents being brought by St. Nicholas at Christmas they are brought by La Befana, the Epiphany witch. "More like Halloween than Christmas!" Philip said.

Bee was enchanted with the tiny objects on sale for nativity sets. "Baskets of mushrooms!" she said. "Prosciutto!"

"You're buying all the toy food, and we don't actually have a Nativity set," Jinny said.

"I'm going to give them to Flora," Bee said. "Look, a tiny salami! And a wild boar!"

Flora arrived on Christmas Eve and was enchanted with the miniature food. "They'd be wonderful for a doll's house," she said.

"I knew you'd like them," Bee said.

"But it's freezing! I had no idea it was cold in Italy in the winter!"

"It's one of Italy's best-kept secrets," Jinny said. "I suggest you sleep with two hot water bottles."

Michael, being Jewish, did not celebrate Christmas. When he visited in the middle of January he was delighted to eat Pat's truffle pasta with the wild boar salami they had brought home. Philip at fifteen, the only child still at home, ate three helpings.

"You're looking tired," Bee said to Michael when they had finished dessert. "Have you been working too hard?"

"I've been feeling a bit run down. And I keep falling asleep. And I've had a sore throat that doesn't seem to go away. I may see the doctor about it."

"You do that!" Pat said.

Two weeks later when Pat came home from school she found Bee crying into her geraniums in the greenhouse. Pat crouched before the chair and put her arms around Bee. "What's wrong?"

"Michael has it."

"What?" Pat asked.

"Thyroid cancer. Anaplastic, just the same as poor Lorna. There's no point him trying the chemo. I told him so. It works for breast cancers and liver cancers, but not for that. Do you think he should come here to die?"

"Yes," Pat said. "Or we should all go to Florence, perhaps? But what about Philip? He has O Levels this year. How long has Michael got?"

"Months," Bee said. "Probably not a year. I think he should come here. Philip's O Levels aren't all that important to him. He's already taken Grade 8 in music in all his instruments, and music is clearly what's going to be his thing."

"His passion," Pat said. "You're right. Yes, call Michael and tell him we'll take care of him."

"A lot of it will fall on you," Bee said.

"The bedpans," Pat said, and rolled her eyes. "How easily it all comes down to bedpans. You know I don't mind."

"Michael's ten years younger than me and twelve years younger than you. We were all together on the morning of Kiev," Bee said.

"You said then that the radioactivity wouldn't get here for days," Pat said, who remembered that with a burning clarity. "Days later we were here and he was in London, or who knows where, taking pictures."

"I'm a biologist, why would you think I know anything about radioactivity or fallout?"

"But—" Pat stared open mouthed. "You're a scientist. You sounded so confident. You were standing right there when you told me."

"You were pregnant and panicking," Bee said. "Everything I know about radioactivity is on a cellular level."

Michael drove down the next day. "You remember we wanted to start our own Renaissance? We're not going to have one," he said to Pat.

"We got the Seven Wonders going," she said. "That's something. And you have taken some wonderful pictures."

A burst of Albioni came through the open window of Philip's room above the front door. "And there are the children," Michael said. "Maybe they'll do better with the world than we have."

In the sitting room Bee was talking to one of her old students, Sophie Picton, who was briefly visiting Cambridge, and indeed Earth, from Galileo, the European space station. She had brought Bee some cuttings from space, and was taking some of Bee's plants back up with her. "These should make the air smell a lot better," she said.

"I'll keep working on it," Bee said.

"You should come up and work on it," Sophie said. "In zero gravity you'd be able to move about as well as anyone else. Better, because your arms are strong."

"Oh, that's a tempting thought," Bee said. "But I have my responsibilities here."

Pat brought everybody some fruitcake and tea and Philip came down to join them and they chatted until Sophie left. Then they settled Michael into Jinny's old room at the front of the house. Most of Jinny's things were in Florence, and Pat moved the rest into the spare room.

"What we need to think is not that you're here to die but that you're here to celebrate while you can," Bee said.

"Champagne every night?" Philip asked.

"Good things while we can have them anyway," Pat said. "Flora's going to come down at the weekend."

"I want to take a series of pictures of you two and the children and the house and garden," Michael said. "Nothing posed, just the way you go about your routine."

"All right," Pat said, exchanging looks with Bee. "My favorite picture of yours is still the one you took of Bee in Florence when the girls were babies."

"Though your second favorite is St. Mark's Square taken from ground level," he said.

"It was the way you didn't care at all if you completely ruined your clothes," Pat said.

They put the news on after dinner, but after a few minutes Bee switched it off. "Nothing but violence and explosions and men posturing," she said.

"Do you really want to go to space?" Pat asked Bee the next morning when she was dressing for work.

"No," Bee said. "Well, yes. I always have loved science fiction and I'd love to go to space. But the way it is now with nobody sharing what they're doing it's anti-science. I'd be happy to give cuttings to the Americans and the Russians, but that's not the way we do things any more. I hate that. Working on what I work on it's not so bad, but if I were to really go into the space stuff it would stifle me not to be able to share freely." Bee stopped. "Besides, we have to make choices. I used to think we had time to do anything we wanted, but we can only do some of the things in any one lifetime."

"But at my back I always hear time's wingéd chariot hurrying near. And yonder all before us lie deserts of vast eternity," Pat said.

"Deserts of vast eternity," Bee echoed. "What's that from?"

"Marvell's 'To His Coy Mistress,'" Pat said. "It often comes into my mind. It's about doing things while you can."

"A good sentiment," Bee said, wheeling herself towards the stairlift.

It took Michael eight months to die, and so he died in Florence at the end of August.

He had taken his series of photographs of them—of Bee swinging between the wheelchair and her green chair, and hauling herself up off the bed; of Pat cooking, and pushing her hair back impatiently as she typed; of Jinny pulling on her boots, and laughing with her head thrown back, looking exactly like Bee; of Philip playing the oboe, and clearing plates from the table; of Flora arranging flowers, looking like a goddess, and scrunching up her face at the thought of asparagus.

He had kept photographing them right up to the end, the last of them were still in his camera. He had not been able to speak for the last two weeks, the growth in his throat was too much. He had written down detailed instructions for how the photographs were to be processed.

When they had driven down to Florence in late June, as soon as Philip's exams were over, they had discussed Michael's funeral. "There's a Jewish cemetery in Florence," Michael said. His voice was hoarse already.

"It's some kind of ancient monument," Pat said. "I don't think it's still used."

"What kind of a guidebook writer are you?" Michael teased. "There's a modern Jewish cemetery to the north of the city just out of town. I'll talk to the rabbi and sort it out."

"You don't speak Italian," Bee said.

"The rabbi speaks Hebrew."

"Do you speak Hebrew?" Philip asked in astonishment.

"Of course I speak it," Michael said. "I'm Jewish. And I spent a year in Israel after university. I've met the rabbi of Florence. I've been to the synagogue."

"I've seen it, I've never been inside," Pat said. "They built it in the nineteenth century in the thought that they'd make something Jewish but worthy of Florence. Certainly the outside does that."

"The inside is lovely too. It had more treasures, but the Nazis destroyed them," Michael said. "They used it as a garage and tried to blow it up when they left, but the Florentines defused the bombs."

"Good for them. The Florentines also refused to blow up the Ponte Vecchio or Michelangelo's bridge," Pat said.

"I think it was the German in charge who refused to blow up the historical bridges," Michael said.

"Am I half Jewish?" Philip asked suddenly.

"No," Michael said. "Nobody is half Jewish. You're either Jewish or you're not, and you're not, because it goes by the mother. But you're Jewish enough by the Law of Return that you could have an Israeli passport if you wanted one."

"You're not—I mean you eat pork," Philip said.

"I may be a bad Jew, but I'm a Jew. The rabbi in Florence will bury me, don't worry."

When he died, it was by suffocation—the tumor in his throat grown too big for him to breathe around. "If they operated to remove it, it would just drag the process out and be more agonizing," Bee said. Until the last two weeks of silence and pain the process had not been too bad. He had drunk granita even when he could swallow nothing else. All three children were in Florence—Flora had come down alone by train to join the rest of them at the end of her term. But only Bee and Pat were with him when he breathed his last.

"We never meant to be a family when we invited him to be a sperm donor," Bee said as Pat closed Michael's eyes. "Isn't it funny how things happen?"

"There's no word for what he was to us," Pat said, weeping. "He was the father of our children, and our intermittent lover, and most of all he was our very good friend."

He was buried in the Jewish cemetery with Jewish rites. It was the first Jewish ceremony Pat had ever seen, and she found it much more moving than the other funerals she had attended.

Two years later, in 1984, Philip went to music college and Flora graduated from Lancaster. Jinny still had another year of her four-year course to go. Flora had met a young man in her first weeks in Lancaster and they both moved on to take the PGCE, the qualification necessary now to teach. When they graduated from that they announced that they were getting married.

"She's so young!" Bee said.

"Well, Mohammed seems nice enough," Pat said.

"I'm not sure I'll ever get used to his name," Bee said.

"Turkey's in Europe now," Pat reminded her. "I know it hasn't been in Europe since the Roman Empire, but now it's back. They're going there on honeymoon, and stopping to see us in Florence on the way back."

They had the wedding reception in their garden. Flora carried roses and geraniums she had planted herself and looked radiant. Philip gave her away, looking very grown up in his suit, and afterwards played a composition of his own as she and Mohammed walked through the guests to be photographed. "I wish Michael could have photographed her now," Bee said.

"Does Mohammed know that Michael was Jewish?" Jinny asked.

"Does Mohammed know Michael was Flora's father?" Pat asked in return. "Does Mohammed know that Flora has two mothers? We don't know and we haven't asked. He seems nice, but such a conventional young man, not to mention from a culture we don't know much about."

"I'm glad she's keeping her own name," Jinny said.

"You're not planning on getting married then?" Bee asked. "No beautiful Italian men?"

"Plenty of beautiful Italian men, but I'm not planning on getting married any time soon. But I do have an exciting offer of sharing a studio. Not making copies of classical works, doing our own thing."

"Henry Moore? Neo-Impressionism? What is your own thing?" Pat asked.

"Neo-Renaissance? That's what you'd like." Jinny laughed. "You'll have to wait and see. Also, I'm taking a course in museum work, so that I can earn some money while I wait to be discovered."

"Sensible and practical," approved Bee.

"Flora's the practical one, she's got a job teaching already," Jinny said.

"And Philip has got really good," Bee said. "I hadn't noticed, because he's always been good at playing, but his composing has improved no end. That was like real music today."

"They're all growing up," Pat said. "It seems like yesterday that they were babies, and now—"

"I can't believe you said that!" Jinny said. "That's such a cliché! I can't believe those words actually came out of your mouth! Flora! Pat said it seems like yesterday that we were babies!"

Flora came over and kissed them, carefully, so as not to mess her dress. "I love you," she said. "Thank you for giving me this wedding, and thank you for giving me my childhood."

"It's old cliché week in the garden," sighed Jinny.

28

Getting Old Is a Terrible Thing
Trish 1989–1993

Trish didn't remember the heart attack or collapsing in the classroom, just the struggle to breathe afterwards. From the time she woke in the Infirmary and was reassured that it had been a small heart attack and she was going to be fine, it never felt as if she had enough air. Helen was there, and Cathy came, and George was in space and sent a message—in many ways it felt like an action replay of Mark's stroke, except that Doug came and brought huge bouquets of lilac and sat blubbering at her bedside. She thought it excessive, considering that they'd told her she was going to be fine. They let her out with prescriptions, diet sheets and an exercise program.

It was March of 1989. She was sixty-three. She took early retirement from teaching—it felt early to her, though standard retirement age was sixty and many people retired at fifty-five. Trish didn't feel ready to stop teaching. Fortunately, she still had her adult education work, which she expanded. She also retired from the council, because her doctor said she should avoid stress, and she could not deny that the council was stressful. It didn't help much with stress, as Bethany was still on the council and talked about it at home so Trish's blood still boiled regularly.

She swam every morning, and walked down to the Kingsway

and home again, close to a mile. She resolutely ate low fat foods. She took her pills. She read to Mark. She helped Alestra and Tamsin, now fourteen, study for their O Levels. She babysat for Donna and Tony. She saw her other grandchildren when she either visited them or they visited her.

In June, peaceful protests in China led to a shooting in Tiananmen Square. An unarmed girl was shot by a soldier—images went around the world, immediately iconic. The world reacted in horror. World leaders contacted the Chinese immediately—President Frank of the US was first to deplore the violence, followed by President Jahn of Germany and then by the leaders of every other country, and the United Nations. The Russian Premier, Gorbachev, happened to be in London discussing the open frontier project, so he was interviewed on the BBC. Trish was watching in Mark's room, as she often did. Television tended to quiet him, and she felt sharing it with him was companionable. Listening to Gorbachev saying how unthinkable it was for the state to condone violence in that way and China should apologize, she spoke aloud to Mark.

"Do you remember when the Russians were the big enemy and we were all afraid of them? First they were our friends, in the war, Uncle Joe, and then in the Fifties they were built up as the villain, the Iron Curtain and all that nonsense. It was nonsense. There's no difference between Eastern Europe and Western Europe, really, we all care about the same things, a social safety net, individual liberty, prosperity."

Mark bellowed, and Trish patted his hand. "Are you trying to say Stalin purged people in the Thirties?" she asked. "That was a long time ago. Look at Germany. They were even more evil in the Thirties, and they're reunited now, and everything is all right."

The Chinese apologized and extended the freedoms the students had been protesting for, and everyone relaxed.

In September Mark died. It was another stroke which came in his sleep. Trish found him in the morning breathing heavily and impossible to rouse. She called the doctor, and he died in the Infirmary a couple of hours later. Trish went home and sat in his empty room, still full of the clutter of his last years—bedpans, pajamas, the television, his tablets, the hospital bed. It was hard to believe he was really gone.

"Nobody else would have taken him in like that," Bethany said when she came home.

They cremated him and scattered his ashes with Trish's mother's in the garden. All the children and grandchildren came to the funeral, even Doug. Elizabeth and Clifford Burchell came, and Elizabeth spoke about the importance of Mark's work. Their son Paul was with them because Mark had been his godfather. He was a doctor, and looked very dignified. Trish remembered putting him to her breast when he was a baby.

Trish did not speak. She found it hard to know what she felt. She was relieved, but also much sadder than she would have imagined.

"What are you going to do with those rooms now?" Bethany asked.

"Well, I need them when the children are all home," Trish said.

"We could make it into a little flat and let it," Bethany said. "There are always students looking for places."

"I don't want to live with strangers," Trish said.

"Alestra and I could move up there and we could let the basement, which is almost self-contained."

Trish shook her head. She redecorated the room as a library.

The whole family came for Christmas, as usual. Doug wasn't looking well. His happiness was clearly faked. He had bought expensive presents for all the children, but watching them opening presents he almost cried. On Boxing Day as Trish bundled up to go out for her walk he grabbed his jacket and said he would come too.

They walked along the canal bank in silence for a while. "What's wrong?" Trish asked.

"I'm not sure whether I should tell you."

"You should definitely tell me," Trish said. "Whatever it is. I'm your mother."

"I have AIDS," Doug said. "It's so unfair. I was clean. I got off the smack, you know I did, I came here to do it. But sometime back then, sharing needles . . ." he trailed off.

Trish could hardly take it in. "I thought it was a gay plague," she said, and thought at once of Mark. She had never told any of the children about that. It felt like an invasion of Mark's privacy.

"It's passed through blood, apparently, and if you share needles you can get it that way." Doug stared out over the gray water. A brightly painted canal barge passed them, moving slowly north. A little white terrier on the deck barked at them.

"Are you sick?"

"I'm on drugs that are supposed to help, but they just seem to make me sicker. It's an immune deficiency, which means that if I catch anything at all it could just kill me, like that." He snapped his fingers.

"Oh Doug!" Trish opened her arms and hugged him. "What a horrible thing. What are you going to do? Do you want to come home?"

"I want to write songs for AIDS awareness, and raise money for helping people who have it, and for a cure," he said. "If I have time. While I can. If I—when I get sick, I'd like to come home."

"How long will it be?" Trish asked.

"Impossible to tell." Doug ground his teeth. "I'll let you know when I know. And I'm going to tell the others too, even though Helen will fuss and Cathy will have a fit. There's a lot of stigma about AIDS that there shouldn't be, and I'm going to be public about it, so they'll know anyway. But I wanted to tell them myself."

"I'm proud of you," Trish said. "You're being so brave and responsible."

"You're crying, Mum," Doug pointed out.

"Shouldn't I be crying, hearing that my son has an incurable illness?"

That evening when the children were in bed, Doug told the others. Helen and Don had gone home, so he had to break it to her separately the next day.

It took him three years to die. For the first two of those years he was constantly in the public eye, writing and performing for AIDS charities. Then, in August 1992 he got sick and came home. It was like being under siege, reporters constantly camped on the doorstep. Alestra was just about to leave for university, and hated being photographed and seeing her picture in the tabloids.

"It's my fault," Doug said. "I made myself news, and I can't turn that off because I don't like it. I'll have to go into hiding."

"I'll come with you," Trish said.

"It'll mean giving up your classes and everything."

"Not for long. And you're more important."

They didn't go far. Doug went into a hospice in Grange-over-Sands. It was run by Buddhists, but after she got used to the oddity of seeing nurses in orange robes that didn't seem strange. Trish stayed nearby in a guest house. The hospice had a central courtyard with sand neatly raked around stones in a

Zen pattern. All the rooms opened onto a cloister that ran around this courtyard. The cloister was full of benches. The courtyard had a glass roof. "I expect in a warm place it would be open to the sky, but they made concessions to the weather," Trish said.

They could also sit on benches in front of the hospice, where they could see Morecambe and the nuclear power station over the water—often they could see Lancaster's microclimate and a sharp-edge of rain that was falling there while in Grange the sun shone. Doug was taking painkillers and the pain came through all the same. He played the guitar until he was too weak. They walked slowly into the village and watched ducks in the duck pond, some of them ridiculous colors. Trish went home sometimes to collect things they needed and see Bethany; Doug stayed where he was.

In those strange months in Grange, Trish noticed that she was becoming forgetful. She would lose words—she'd be in the middle of saying something and forget how she had meant to end her sentence. She'd forget what something was called, or the name of an author. Once she forgot the word "Korea" and had to say "That peninsula near China, where there was a war in the Fifties." She remembered her mother and felt a cold dread.

She talked to Doug about it. "I wish I had the chance to live long enough to get senile like Gran," he said.

"Maybe I'll have another heart attack before I get that bad," Trish said, optimistically. "Getting old is a terrible thing."

"It's better than the alternative," Doug said, grinning.

"I don't know. Maybe you're lucky to miss it. They say those the gods love die young."

"It's just that there's so much I would have wanted to do. I always thought there was time to have kids later, time to write the serious music I wanted to write, time to see the parts of the world I haven't seen. Most of what I have seen has been touring, you know how it is, everywhere seems the same. Japan, Paris, I always said I'd go back when I had more time. Now I never will. And all the songs I meant to write. All the songs I did write, the ones I sweated blood over, and what will I be remembered for? That little bit of nonsense about George and Sophie getting married on the moon that I wrote in five minutes in the back of a taxi."

"That's a wonderful song, and it was a wonderful thing you did for your brother. Don't undervalue it because it came easily."

George and Sophie and the twins visited. Rhodri and Bronwen were four now. They loved the ducks on the pond. Sophie and Trish took them for a walk up Hampsfell while George and Doug had a long conversation. From Hampsfell it was possible to see all the way to the Lake District, where Trish had been so often with the children when they were younger and then with David. She could also see far out over the bay below them. Up there she could almost get enough air.

All the food at the hospice was vegetarian and macrobiotic. Trish, who rarely ate meat anyway, enjoyed it. "I wonder how far we'd have to go to get a burger?" Doug asked one day when he was very weak.

"Carnforth?" Trish wondered aloud. "There's certainly nothing in the village. Do you want to try?"

"I was joking, but actually yes, I'd love to. Let's do it. One last crazy expedition!"

They got into Trish's car—a sober and fairly new Fiesta, not the Beetle Doug had bought her long before. Doug could hardly keep himself upright in the passenger seat. He wound down the window. "It's great to feel the speed," he said, though they were barely going at thirty on the winding road. They went south to Ulverston, where they found a Burger King.

Trish ate onion rings. "I hope you know these are terrible for my heart," she said.

Doug could only manage half his burger. "That was delicious," he said. "All that ketchup and mustard, not to mention dead cow. I expect I've set myself back several cycles on the wheel of resurrection with that."

"Do you believe in that?" Trish asked.

"Not even a bit. I picked this place because it was near and they'd give me privacy."

Doug slumped asleep on the drive back and Trish had to call for help to get him into bed. The next day he winked at her as he ate his seed porridge for breakfast. "Thanks for indulging me yesterday, Mum. Thanks for being here."

Trish blinked away tears. "I'm glad I can be here. I'm glad there's something I can do for you."

Doug died in November. Trish was at his side. He was asleep, breathing with difficulty, and then his breathing just stopped. The nurse went over and opened a window. "So his soul can leave," she said.

"Is that a Buddhist belief?" Trish asked.

"It's an Irish one," the nurse said.

"This is the third death I've watched. First my mother, then my ex-husband, and now my son."

"It never gets easier," the nurse said.

All the papers had been signed and all the arrangements made, except for the death certificate. Trish walked out into the dawn and wished she still believed in God. The sea was still lapping on the shore, the last stars were vanishing as the sky brightened. But the sky was empty of comfort. There was no loving God waiting, no heaven where Doug could find happiness. Just the cold contingent universe where things happened for random reasons nobody could understand. Nevertheless, while she was torn apart with grief for Doug she also felt at peace. His struggle was over. There was no more pain. And she had been with him and helped him. She had seen his whole life, from his birth to his death. "Everyone is born," she said to the empty sky. "Everyone dies."

It was cold comfort as time went on and she began to understand what missing him meant.

Doug's funeral was held in Lancaster cathedral, which was packed for the occasion. There were pop stars and punk stars and actors, friends of Doug's and reporters and fans. The family sat alone at the front, packing into two pews. Trish tried to sit still. There were musical tributes and people talking about how Doug would be remembered. George talked about what the song had meant to him. Afterwards, the body was quietly cremated. Trish sprinkled the ashes on the roses with her mother and Mark. "Put me here too," she said to Helen.

"Mum! Morbid!" Helen said.

"I'm sixty-six, I have to think about it."

"No you don't!"

Trish took up her evening classes again, but more and more she found herself using her notes for a kind of reassurance she had never needed—a furious checking on names and titles. She started to make endless lists so that she wouldn't forget things, and if she didn't put things on her lists she often did forget. She confided in Bethany but not in her children. "They keep telling me that this house is too big and I should buy something smaller," she said. "If they knew about this, they'd have me in sheltered accommodation before you can say Jack Robinson."

Bethany shook her head. "Maybe it's the heart tablets. Maybe they're making it worse. I read something about that."

Trish went to the doctor and changed the prescription of

the beta blockers, and her memory did seem to improve. She heaved a sigh of relief and tried to get on with her life. The family gathered for Christmas and the absence of Doug was like an ache that even the youngest of them seemed to feel.

29

Retirement: Pat 1986–1990

Pat retired from teaching in 1986 when she was sixty. Sixty was still the official European retirement age for women, though they were talking about raising it to be sixty-five, the same as for men. Flora also stopped teaching that year to have a baby, Samantha Deniz, born in May. Pat and Bee went up to Lancaster as soon as they had the news that little Sammy had been born. They held her on her first day of life. "She looks exactly like you did when you were born, exactly," Pat told Flora.

"All babies look alike," Flora laughed. The birth had been difficult and she was exhausted but triumphant.

Philip came from Manchester, where he was studying music. "How disconcerting to suddenly be an uncle," he said. "You should have warned me, Flo."

"How could I have warned you?" Flora asked.

"I'll compose a piece of music for her," he said.

Bee and Pat drove Philip back to Manchester. "So I want to explain to you about my living situation," he said from the back seat.

"You're living with someone?" Bee asked.

"I'm living with two people."

"We know that, you told us when you took the flat. But is one of them . . . significant?" Pat asked.

Philip laughed. "They're both significant. That's what I wanted to tell you."

"He's had to work hard to find a way to shock his lesbian mothers," Pat said to Bee. "I mean we didn't make it easy for him, poor boy. He couldn't just be gay like any normal young man."

"Why would it shock you, it's what you two were doing with Michael all my life!"

"I was teasing," Pat said. "Sorry."

"You're seriously romantically involved with two people?" Bee asked.

"Fairly seriously, yes," Philip said. "Sanchia's Dutch, she's three years older than me, she's an organist, making a living giving piano lessons. Ragnar's Norwegian, he's my age, he's a flautist with the Symphony, and he also works part time in a bar."

"Wow," Pat said, trying to make up for her earlier joke. "They sound amazing. I can't wait to meet them."

"Do you have any other surprises?" Bee asked.

"Well, they call me Marsilio," Philip said. "So if you wouldn't mind? I'm going to use it professionally. So many people are called Philip. Marsilio—"

"Just you and Ficino," Pat said. "So are you bringing them to Florence?"

"If there's room. But just for a week or two, because I have an engagement for August, playing oboe for somebody who's going to be on maternity leave. Babies seem to be breaking out all over."

"We'd be delighted to have them in Florence," Pat said. "Flora's not going to be able to make it this year."

Sanchia and Ragnar spoke perfect English, which was a relief. Ragnar looked like a Viking, huge with a curling beard and long hair. Sanchia was stunning, but she didn't look Dutch.

"My mother was from Indonesia," she explained when Bee asked.

Driving back to Cambridge Pat and Bee discussed them. "Not many people get into a long-term relationship when they're in college," Pat said.

"No, but Philip is just the person to do it," Bee said. "I liked them, especially her."

"They all three seemed so comfortable together," Pat said. "He seems happy with them. That's what matters."

"I don't know if I'll ever be comfortable calling him Marsilio," Bee confessed. "I'm so used to him as Philip."

Jinny came over from Italy the next week to see her new niece. She spent a day and a night in Cambridge while she was there. "I'm thinking I want to take a course in architecture next year," she said.

"In Florence?" Pat asked.

"Oh yes. Because it's in Florence I want to work. People keep building new houses around about. Suburbs. And they're like the suburbs here. Between here and London it's all suburbs. And you've seen Flora's house. Somebody needs to be designing small houses for ordinary people to live in that are beautiful. I have the aesthetics, but I don't have the technical qualifications. This is what I want to do."

"You've found your passion at last," Pat said, looking at Jinny's face.

"I really do think I have," Jinny said.

"Can you still get student loans or will you need some money?" Bee asked.

"I'm going to need some money. But I'll pay you back."

"Pay it forward," Bee said. "Pay for your own children to follow their passion. Or for other friends you know who may need help."

Pat was working on a guide to Trieste that summer. She

missed Michael acutely whenever she worked with a different photographer and had to explain exactly what she wanted. She was also updating her Florentine guide and refused to change any of the photographs. "None of those things have changed," she insisted to her editor.

"What about this gelateria?" he asked, pointing to a picture of Perche No! "Is that still there?"

"Exactly the same," Pat assured him. "Just as wonderful as ever. The best gelato in the world, just as it says in the book."

She took Ragnar and Sanchia around and was delighted to see them fall under the enchantment of Florence.

"They did this," Ragnar said. "As well as the music. All this at the same time."

"It's possible," Sanchia said, leaning back against Philip as she ate a gelato and stared at Orsanmichele, as Pat had done on her first visit to Florence. "I have to come back."

"I'm so glad you see it this way," Pat said. "Not everyone does. My daughter Flora's husband just said how pretty it was. And some Italians just take it for granted."

The next year, 1987, Bee retired. "I'll keep on with my own research at home, but I'll have done with all the going in to college and keeping office hours and marking," she said. They had a ceremony for her retirement and gave her a specially designed electric wheelchair with tractor treads for use in the garden. "So much nicer than a gold watch," she said.

Flora had another baby in March 1988, Cenk Michael. "It's pronounced Jenk," she said. "It was Mohammed's father's name."

"It's lovely," Pat said, diplomatically. "So easy to say."

Philip had composed a piece of music for baby Sammy, and he composed another for Cenk. He graduated and began a life of standing in for people in orchestras while working on his compositions. He and Sanchia and Ragnar continued to live together as best they could with their careers, and to come to Florence for at least part of every summer.

Jinny qualified as an architect. Her senior year project for a small but beautiful house won a European design award. She immediately became a junior partner in a firm in Florence. Her designs went into use almost at once. "Ginevra could make a lot of money if she went into designing for our richer clients," a senior partner told Pat at a party.

"It's not what she wants," Pat said, proudly. Jinny now lived at the Florentine house permanently and paid the property taxes on it. Pat and Bee still came out every summer, and Philip and his household for part of every summer. Flora and Mohammed had only been there once since their wedding.

"We should make a new will and give Jinny the Florentine house," Pat said. "We haven't made wills since they were tiny and we were worried about social workers."

"And dear old Michael promised to marry whichever of us was left," Bee said, smiling.

They made new wills. "We want to leave the Florentine house to Jinny and the Harston house and the remainder of our estates to the other two equally," Pat said.

"That's not possible," the solicitor explained. "You own these properties between you, and that makes it more complicated."

They eventually decided to give Jinny the Florentine house now and leave the Cambridge house to whichever of them survived the other, and then divided between the other children. "Are you sure that's fair?" Bee asked.

"They'll sell our Harston house and use the money. Jinny will live in the Florentine house," Pat said. "That makes it fair, even if it is worth more."

"There will be death duties," the solicitor said. "There wouldn't be if you were married, but as things are."

"It makes my blood boil," Bee said.

They also filled out powers of attorney in case of incapacity, naming each other, remembering how they couldn't sell Pat's mother's house. "These wouldn't necessarily hold up," the solicitor said. "Not if anyone challenged them."

"Does *anyone* in that sentence mean our children or the government?" Bee asked. "Our children wouldn't, but the government is another thing."

"It certainly wouldn't hold up under a government challenge. But it's better than nothing."

On their way back home from the solicitor's Bee started to laugh. "I was just thinking how grown up all that made me feel," she said. "I'm sixty-one!"

The next March Pat had a heart attack in the early hours of the morning. She knew at once what it was, a pain in her left arm and chest. She managed to waken Bee before she passed out, and Bee called an ambulance. She woke up in the Addison, alone.

She struggled to press the button to ring for the nurse. "Is my friend waiting?" she asked.

"Try to relax," the nurse said, taking her pulse professionally. "Don't worry about anything."

"I'll worry myself into another heart attack this minute if you don't let my friend in. She's in a wheelchair."

Bee was waiting, and they let her in. "They wouldn't tell me how you were," she said, wheeling herself right up to the bed and taking Pat's hand.

"I had to threaten to have another heart attack to get you in," Pat said. "You wouldn't believe how much good it's doing my heart to see you."

"I called the kids, and Philip's on his way. Flora said she'd come first thing in the morning, and I told her Philip was coming and we'd get in touch if it was really serious."

"Having grown-up children who know what we want as next of kin is such a relief," Pat said.

"He should be here any minute. He was in Glasgow."

"Of course, it would help if they weren't so far away."

The Addison assured Pat that it was a minor heart attack. They gave her stacks of pills, a diet sheet that didn't allow her to eat anything she liked, and instructions to exercise. "I get loads of exercise," she complained.

"Get more," Bee said, unsympathetically. "I can't have your heart packing in on us."

"Do you think I should ask them if the prohibition on ice cream includes gelato?"

"No," Philip said. "Because you're going to eat it anyway, so you might as well not ask. All this low-fat stuff is going to be hard. You love fat. You never cook anything that doesn't have half a bottle of olive oil in it."

"Except when I've run out of olive oil, and then it has half a pound of butter," Pat said. "Though I have noticed that Sainsbury's do a very decent olive oil these days."

She took the pills regularly and tried to walk more. "I used to love rowing, but I haven't done it since we moved out here. I'll walk in Italy."

"You'll walk now. You can push me if you like, that'll be good exercise."

"Slavedriver," Pat said.

The news was terrible, as usual. There was a massacre in China, repression in the Soviet countries, and yet another assassination of the president in the US. The war between Uruguay and Brazil threatened to go nuclear, and the Americans said that they'd regard any intervention from Russia or Europe as a hostile act against their hemisphere. "Well, keep peace in your hemisphere, then," Bee snarled at the television. "No more nukes!"

That summer in Italy Pat found that she couldn't remember Italian words she knew perfectly well. She'd launch herself into a sentence and come to a dead stop when the words weren't there. She'd never had that experience before and it confounded her. "Do you think it might be your tablets?" Jinny asked.

Back in Cambridge she asked her doctor and had her prescription changed. She couldn't tell if it had helped, she wasn't speaking Italian. The next summer things didn't seem to be any better. Pat noticed that she was sometimes forgetting words in English too.

"I'm afraid I'm going like my mother," she confessed to Bee in the dark.

"You're only sixty-four," Bee said, holding her tight. "Don't cry now, Pat love. Hush. You'll be all right."

30

Twins: Trish 1994–1999

George rang up one morning in the spring of 1994. "I was wondering if I could ask you to do me a big favor," he said.

"Yes, of course, what?" Trish answered, looking frantically for her glasses, her notebook and her pen so that she could note down whatever the favor was before she forgot.

"They want us back on the moon, and it would be for a year," George said, as she found the notebook on the counter and her glasses on their beaded chain around her neck. Tamsin had given her the chain for Christmas. "At least a year, maybe two. It's really important for Sophie that she go."

"But what about the twins?" Trish asked. "You can't take them, can you?"

"Medical opinion thinks it wouldn't be good for growing bones to be in gravity that low. That's the favor. We wondered if you could take them. There's room, and they always love visiting you. We could ask Sophie's parents, but they're getting old. Well, they're younger than you are, but they're somehow resigned to being old and sort of mummifying in it, not like you. I always feel I have to tiptoe in their house—whereas your house is always lively."

"Of course I will," Trish said, sitting down at the kitchen

table and fumbling with the notepad. "When would you have to go?"

"Sophie would go almost immediately, but I'd stay here until the end of the school year. Then they could come to you for the summer and start school up there in September."

"You seem to have it all sorted out," Trish said. "I should really check with Bethany before disrupting her this way."

"I thought they could go to my old school," George said, disregarding this. "That's another plus to them being in Lancaster. The schools in Aberystwyth are very dull. But Lancaster has great schools, it always has had. I know the Grammar School has gone comprehensive, but from what I hear everyone's getting an excellent education up there."

"The schools are doing fine. And so is the university. We saved the market. And we're even keeping the old swimming pool open instead of opening a stupid new one in the middle of nowhere," Trish said, well briefed on local issues by Bethany. "But why are you talking about the grammar school? How old are the twins now, exactly?"

"They were six in February," George said. "Too young for the grammar school for a while yet!"

After she had put the phone down she found her pen and wrote firmly TWINS, JUNE and put it on the fridge. Then she wrote it down on all her other lists.

Bethany helped her get rooms ready for Rhodri and Bronwen. They got a man to come and help move beds and paint, and they bought new duvets—one with dolphins and one with dinosaurs. "That wouldn't have been my top choice to say boy or girl," Bethany said, shaking the covers on.

"They're very pink dinosaurs, and the alternative was yachts or houses," Trish said. "Boy and girl stuff doesn't matter the way it used to anyway. Things are much less gendered than they were when my kids were small, or even when Tamsin and Alestra were."

"It's great really," Bethany said. "Huge strides for women. Dinosaurs!"

George arrived with the twins on a rainy Sunday morning. "We've brought masses of books and toys and clothes," he said, proceeding to unload the car and dash inside with armfuls of things. "But buy them whatever they need. I've opened an account for you to draw on." He handed her a checkbook and a bank card. "The pin number is the year of your birth, change it when you get the chance."

Trish wrote the number down on her pad. "I'll change it," she said.

"Would you really forget it?" George asked.

"Things fall out of my head like water sometimes," she admitted. "And I never know which things."

"You won't forget to collect the children from school?" he asked anxiously.

"Bethany's here to help," Trish said.

"That's a relief!"

The children had vanished into the house. "Helen's coming over later with her kids so they can all play," Trish said. "How long are you staying?"

"Just tonight I'm afraid. Tomorrow morning I'm flying from Manchester to Miami and from there to Kennedy. I'll be on the moon before next Sunday."

"Amazing," Trish said.

"Thanks for doing this, Mum. It makes all the difference knowing they'll be looked after properly."

Rhodri and Bronwen ended up staying for two years on that visit. Trish enjoyed having children around again. She cut down her evening classes to one a week, for which Helen babysat. She taught two adult education classes in the afternoons, which she did not enjoy as much—they were basic literacy classes. At her evening classes she had the fun of seeing people who had never had the chance to appreciate literature learning how to do it. Here she was teaching adults to read, which she admitted was necessary, but more of a slog.

She spent more time with Helen than she had for years. Helen worked while her children were at school. She did some programming for businesses where Don sold systems, and some time working in the shop selling computers and games and other programs. She stopped work every day at three and collected the children from school. Often now she collected all four children and brought them back to Trish's house for a few hours.

"It reminds me of when Tamsin and Alestra were young," Trish said, listening to the children chase each other around the garden.

Tamsin was in the third year of a professional nursing program in Manchester. Alestra was about to graduate from university.

"Not when all of us were young?" Helen asked.

"I was exhausted all the time when all of you were young," Trish said. "It was no fun at all. I don't know how I kept my head above water. And your father—and I was pregnant all the time."

"You never found anyone else, after David Lin," Helen said.

"I never had the opportunity," Trish said. "You're still happy with Don?"

"Yes, except that he's so totally predictable. I know what he'll say about everything all the time. He never surprises me. He's very dependable, and I think that's what I wanted when I first met him. But that's all he is."

"He's a good man and he loves you," Trish said.

"I know." Helen put her tea mug down. "I'm not going to do anything stupid. It's probably just working together as well as being married."

One day in the winter of 1995 Bethany came home very excited. "I have a recording contract!" she said. "I can't believe it. At my age! I've finally been discovered!"

Trish was thrilled and asked all about it.

The next day when Bethany mentioned it she had forgotten all about it. "A recording contract! How wonderful. Why didn't you tell me?"

"I did tell you," Bethany said, looking devastated.

"I'm sorry!"

"Not your fault, and it's not important. I'll tell you about it again. But I am worried about your memory."

"So am I," Trish said.

"We sell a kind of tea called ginkgo that's supposed to help with memory."

Trish bought some and drank it every day, even though it tasted disgusting. She couldn't see any improvement.

George and Sophie came back from the moon in June 1996 and the twins went home with them. "This may happen again," Sophie said when they came to collect them. "I'm going to be in Cambridge for a year, but after that would you be prepared to have them again?"

"Of course," Trish said. She had got used to them and felt bereft without them. She was seventy that year and her family made a big fuss, with a cake and a party. She would have preferred to ignore the occasion. She didn't like to think of herself as old, still less old and senile.

When the twins came back in the summer of 1998 they were nine, nearly ten. They were both wonderful with computers. Rhodri persuaded Trish to buy a new computer, from Don and Helen of course, a Mac. It was expensive, but Trish had enough money. Doug had left half his money to AIDS charities, but the half he had left to Trish made her more comfortable than she had ever been. She bought a new car every few years and could afford the Mac without asking herself how much money she had.

Rhodri showed her how to use it. All she had used her old computer for was making notes for her classes, like a glorified typewriter. This one was different. It could go online, and once it did it had Google. Google was what Trish had wanted for years, the ability to search for something she had forgotten. "If only Google would tell me where I'd left my glasses!" she said. But it told her the lost word "samurai" when she searched for "Japanese warrior" and the author of *Sonnets from the Portuguese*. It helped her fill in the blanks. The Mac also let the children email to and fro with their parents on the moon and their cousins and friends across town. "What a wonderful machine."

The twins noticed that she was forgetful. "I told you that already, Gran!" Bronwen said when Trish forgot something.

Rhodri was good at thinking of ways to help. The computer had a "to do" function that reminded her to take her pills and collect the children from school and teach her classes. It beeped in a friendly way to remind her when she had to do something, and when she checked it told her what. She used it for her lists and notes. She wrote them down on a notepad that she carried with her and then transferred them into the computer at night. Doing that she was sometimes distressed at how many times she had written down the same thing.

Cathy, coming up for a weekend with fifteen-year-old Jamie, was skeptical of the computer, and of the twins when she caught Bronwen reminding Trish to take her pills. "Are you looking after those children or are they looking after you?"

"A bit of both," Trish said, honestly.

Cathy's son Jamie was sullen and spoilt in Trish's estimation. He attended an exclusive private school where he seemed to learn less than Trish's other grandchildren did in the state system. They went on a picnic to Windermere and Jamie found fault with everything from the food to the lake. What worried Trish was the way Cathy agreed with him and appeased him, as if she were afraid of upsetting him. Jamie reminded Trish of Mark, and of Doug as a child, enjoying bullying. She didn't understand how he could be like Mark. He had only been a year old when Mark died. Surely a tendency to like bullying couldn't be genetic?

The next year, when he was sixteen, Helen told Trish that Cathy was going to buy Jamie a moped. "A moped, in London! I'd never let Donna or Tony," Helen said. "And they're going to be on at me again now that Jamie has one. Cathy has no sense with that boy."

"No, she doesn't," Trish said. "And it's not being a single mother, because look at you with Tamsin, or Bethany with Alestra for that matter."

"I was never on my own with Tamsin the way Cathy has been with Jamie. You were there, and Gran, and then Bethany too. Cathy had nannies and au pairs, but they were employees. She's got too much money, that's what it is. Did you know she boasts about being in the sixty percent tax band?"

Trish couldn't remember. "Are you short of money?"

"We're doing fine. Computers are the big thing. I'd rather do more programming and less selling, but that's not the way things are these days. My only problem is that I'm bored with Don. He doesn't want to do anything different, ever. I suggested we have a holiday in Greece or Italy, but he only wants to go to Spain like always."

About a month later, in early December, Trish got an anguished call from Cathy very early one morning. "Mum!"

"What's wrong?"

"He hasn't come home!"

"Jamie?" Trish rubbed her eyes and looked at the clock: 06.17.

"He wasn't home and I went to bed, and he still isn't home." Cathy was screeching into the phone.

"Call the police," Trish said. "He's only sixteen. They'll have to do something."

She made a note to herself "Jamie missing." She didn't think she'd forget, but these days she never knew what might go out of her head.

"Wouldn't they have called me if they knew something?" Cathy asked, sounding a little more collected.

"If they knew something, probably, which means he probably isn't in a hospital or anything like that. But if he's gone off somewhere they can try to find him." Trish calmed Cathy down and got her to agree to call the police.

She got up and had a hot bath and a cup of tea to get her mind working. Then she got the twins up for school. They were old enough to go by themselves now, but she made Rhodri porridge and Bronwen toasted cheese. "The strongest correlation to doing well in school—" she began when Rhodri protested.

"—is eating protein in the morning, yes, I know," Rhodri said.

"And your father always ate breakfast and none of my other children did, and look at him now."

"I can't, the moon has set," Rhodri said.

"Smartass," Bronwen said.

They went to school and Trish called Cathy back. "Any news?"

"Nothing," Cathy said.

That afternoon the telephone shrilled, but it was Helen, calling to tell Trish that Donna had won a County Art Prize. Trish wrote it down before she forgot. "Did you speak to Cathy?" she asked.

"No?"

"Jamie didn't come home last night."

"That doesn't sound good," Helen said. "Oh no. I hope it's not something terrible."

"Coming off the road on that machine would be terrible enough. There was ice last night." Trish shuddered.

She called Cathy again and had no answer. She left a message. The twins came home from school, and Bethany came home from the food co-op and made dinner. She had a council meeting that night and was in a rush so Trish didn't take her aside to tell her about Jamie.

Cathy called just after ten. She was hysterical. Trish caught "pond" and "dead" and "body."

"What has happened?" she asked. "Shall I come? Where are you, Cathy?"

Cathy was at the police station in Twickenham. "Twickenham! That's where Gran lived and I grew up."

As it turned out, it was also where Jamie had died, skidding on an icy road and coming off his moped and going into a pond, where he had drowned. Trish went cold hearing about it.

"Shall I come?" she asked again, calculating how she would ask Helen and Bethany to cover for her with the twins.

"What good would it do, Mum?" Cathy asked.

After that she went to bed. She had thought it bad to outlive a son; now she had outlived a grandson.

She remembered it in the morning. She knew she had, because she had told Helen when she called in to the shop and spoke to her. Helen had been shocked that Cathy hadn't called her, and that Cathy hadn't wanted Trish to go. "Does she want me?" Helen asked. "Should I call and ask? She shouldn't be on her own."

"You can try," Trish said.

But by the weekend when Cathy called again she had forgotten. It had all drained out of her mind as if it had never happened. She heard Cathy's voice and answered "How are you, darling? How's Jamie?" She remembered almost at once, as soon as she heard the tone of Cathy's voice change, but by then it was too late. She deserved everything Cathy called her, unkind as it was. She should never have forgotten. She wouldn't have believed it was possible that she could, except that somehow she had.

She went downstairs to Bethany. "I'm going senile. I'm going like my mother was."

"What have you done now?" Bethany asked.

"Have I said that before?" Trish asked, appalled.

"Only hundreds of times," Bethany said. "What is it?"

Trish told her about Jamie, and about forgetting. "I didn't say anything at home because of the twins. They'll have to know, but I didn't know how to tell them, and then I just—it went out of my mind."

"Cathy will never forgive that," Bethany said. "But it's not your fault, Trish, you know it isn't. It's no more your fault than if you had Parkinson's and you dropped a cup and it broke. It's a medical symptom."

"I do blame myself. And you're right that she'll never forgive me. She's always been the most difficult of them, and now she'll be sure I'm a senile old fool and not fit to have charge of myself never mind the twins."

"I'm here for the twins if it comes to that," Bethany said. "And Helen and Don. You're not in sole charge. And you're not dangerously forgetful anyway. You do forget things, but you're all right."

"The Mac helps a lot," Trish said. "It's a godsend. And so are you, Bethany. I don't know how I'd manage without you."

"Well, I'm here," Bethany said.

31

I Hope I Forget: Pat 1992–1999

Philip took a course and trained as a carer for disabled people. "There were very few places, and I'm sure I got into it entirely by explaining that my mother was a double amputee who had been in a wheelchair since I was four years old," he said.

Bee laughed. "Why do you want to do it?" she asked. "Couldn't you teach, like Sanchia, or do casual work like Ragnar?"

"I could, but I'd rather help people," Philip said. "I need something to bring in money, and this is good money and odd hours, just what I want. Casual work is boring and pointless, and teaching is soul-destroying. And once I have the qualification I can do this anywhere in Europe. If I happen to have three days free in Heidelberg or Venice I can pick up some caring work there."

"Teaching can actually be rewarding," Bee pointed out.

Philip blushed. "Your kind of teaching, of course, or even Mum's, but teaching music to beginners is what I meant. I've seen it grinding Sanchia down."

Things went on as they were. Pat grew more forgetful and started relying on lists again as she had when the children were young. She stopped driving because she felt she wasn't safe, and she stopped writing and updating her guidebooks after the final update of the Rome books in 1994. She handed on all her materials to a young writer Constable recommended who would keep them going. "They're an institution," her editor said. The new girl seemed impossibly young, but she was older than Pat had been when she had written the first Florence book. "And she loves Italy. That's her real qualification," Pat told Bee.

In 1998 Jinny announced that she was getting married to a contractor called Francesco. Pat and Bee rushed off to Florence at Easter to meet him and his family. He was younger than Jinny and had typical Italian good looks. "I'd like to sculpt him," she confided. "If I did, would you mind if I put it in the courtyard?"

"Better ask him. It's your house now," Pat said.

"A contractor, eh?" Bee said. "Maybe we can finally get a stairlift put in. And a recharger so I could bring the electric wheelchair to Italy, maybe?"

The wedding was arranged for July, when they would be in Florence as usual.

Pat was reading the new Margaret Drabble when Philip called with news of his own. "Sanchia's pregnant," he said.

"Whose is it?" she asked.

"We don't know and we don't care," Philip said.

"Of course. Well, congratulations."

"I'm a little overwhelmed. Remember how surprised I was to find I was an uncle? Finding I'm going to be a father is even more overwhelming. Oh, and write this down right now, Mum! I don't want you forgetting to tell Mamma! Where is she anyway?"

"She went somewhere, I forget," Pat said. "Maybe physio? Is it Wednesday?"

"It's Thursday," Philip said. "Have you written it down?"

"Yes," Pat said, writing it down carefully. "I'll tell her the second she comes in. Will you all come to Italy for Jinny's wedding?"

"I will absolutely come, and I think I can speak for the other two in saying they will want to be there and will come unless there's something that absolutely prevents them—I know Ragnar has a performance in Helsinki sometime this summer but I can't remember when."

Pat sat and waited for Bee to come home, her notebook on her lap. As soon as she heard the car she got up and went out. "Sanchia's pregnant!" she called, as soon as Bee was out of the car. The new car allowed Bee to drive it in her chair.

"Who's the father, or don't they care?" Bee asked.

"I think they said they don't care. And Philip said he'd come to Jinny's wedding," Pat said.

Then as she came close enough, Pat saw Bee's face. "What's wrong?"

"I did think about not telling you, because this isn't something I want to tell you over and over, love. But it's fucking anaplastic thyroid cancer, the same as Michael had, and Lorna."

"Oh Bee, no." Pat found she was sitting on the ground on the drive with no idea how she had got there. "How are we going to manage?"

"You forgot where I was going, didn't you?"

"I did." Pat looked up at Bee. "Have they developed any better treatment?"

"Nope. Six to nine months if we do nothing, six to nine months if we mess about with surgeries and chemo."

"It's March . . ."

"It's April," Bee said. "Get up from there and make me some dinner. I'll make Jinny's wedding, that's one thing. I'll be glad to see her settled. I thought she never would be, over thirty and nobody serious."

"Bee, you're talking as if—"

"Well, how do you want me to talk? Like a tragedy? There's nothing I can do about it. If you like I'll say we're totally doomed—I'm dying and you're going senile, and I think I have the best of it. But what good does that do? Might as well live while we can. Dinner while I can still eat. Sex while we can still enjoy it. Music. Let's sing together after supper. Graft a few plants and see if I can make some new ones that produce more oxygen for the Mars mission. See Jinny married, maybe see Sanchia's baby if I'm very lucky."

"Oh Bee," Pat said, getting up carefully. "What am I going to do without you?"

"I have no idea. So let's enjoy the time we have left."

"Do you want to go to Florence?"

"I want to go in the summer when we always go. For Jinny's wedding, for the summer. Then I want to come home when we always do, and be here where I have the conservatory all set up to work in. I want to go on as normal as best we can—but Pat? Please try to remember this, because if you forget and I have to tell you again and again it's going to drive me mad." Bee's chair hummed off indoors and Pat followed.

"I'll try to remember," Pat said. "I don't see how I could forget, as it's the worst news I've ever had, but there seems to be no control over what I forget and what I remember."

"I do know you can't help it," Bee said. "I'm not angry with you. I'm angry with the cancer, with the stupid Americans who just had to retaliate with an H-bomb and no thought about the winds and who they were hurting, with the equally stupid Russians who thought they could get respect by taking out Miami, and with the Indians and the Chinese. This could be from that just as easily. We've only got one habitable planet and it's so fragile, and we keep on screwing it up. Dropping nukes and burning oil. That's what makes me angry, not your infirmity."

"I don't want to be like my mother," Pat said.

"You're going to be seventy next year, and you're a million times better than she was at that age," Bee said.

Jinny's wedding took place in Santa Maria Novella, a wonderful Renaissance church near the railway station in Florence. Jinny had gone through the forms of conversion to Catholicism especially so that she could get married there. ("Though I don't mind promising to bring the children up in the faith if it means they can be baptized in the Baptistery," she had said quietly to her mothers the night before.) She piled her dark hair up on top of her head, which made her look very like Bee. Jinny had the same plain square friendly face. Francesco was bringing all the beauty, Pat thought, and hoped Jinny wasn't bringing absolutely all the brains. Philip gave Jinny away as he had given Flora away. Sanchia, visibly pregnant, and Ragnar were there. Sammy, twelve years old now, was a bridesmaid, along with three of Francesco's nieces. Flora was matron of honor. Mohammed looked proud of her. It was the first time either of them had been in Florence since their honeymoon.

Pat prayed for Jinny and Francesco, and for Flora and Mohammed, and for Philip and Sanchia and Ragnar, and for all her grandchildren born and unborn. She thanked God for them and for Bee, and prayed that Bee might be cured by a miracle. Looking up at Botticelli's nativity scene, anything seemed possible. "Come on, God, you can do it," Pat prayed. "St. Zenobius, patron of Florence, you healed a dead elm tree, and Bee loves elm trees. You could heal her, couldn't you?"

They had the reception in the garden of their house, though it was a crush with all of Jinny's Florentine friends. She had built houses for half of them, it seemed. They were going to honeymoon on the Adriatic coast.

"This will probably be the last time the whole family will be together," Bee said, hoarsely, when she made her toast. Pat remembered how wonderful Bee's singing voice had been. "It's not the whole family, of course, without Michael, but he's buried here so that's as close as we can come. I'd like to propose a toast to our family, while we still can."

Pat had never forgotten that Bee was dying. She wished she could forget it. Instead she woke in the night remembering it, overcome by a sense of dread.

Jinny and Francesco departed for their honeymoon. The rest of them stayed on in the Florentine house for a few weeks.

Pat walked around Florence with Sammy and Cenk, telling them stories and showing them things. She fed them gelatos and granitas. She took them to the Uffizi, which had finally installed a lift. Bee could see the Botticellis again. "You're the one who cares about them," Bee muttered, but she did not turn down the opportunity to go up and see them.

She told Sammy and Cenk about Cellini as they looked at his statue of Ganymede in the Bargello. She told them that the torso was Roman and he had made the rest of it, the head and arms and legs and the eagle, and how it was a microcosm of the Renaissance, taking the Roman core and building on the rest in their own imagination. "How can she remember all this when she can't remember where to meet us for lunch?" Flora asked Bee.

"She's known all this forever," Bee rasped.

Sammy and Cenk took to Florence as the children always had. Before long they were begging Flora to let them stay longer and for just one more gelato. "They can stay for the summer with us, if you like," Pat offered.

"If there's room for me to stay as well," Flora said. Mohammed went home, and Ragnar went off to his engagement in Finland, but the rest of them stayed. Jinny and Francesco came home, and Flora took the children back to England for the new school term. Philip and Sanchia left, and eventually one evening as they sat on the patio alone after Jinny had gone to bed Bee told Pat that it was time for them to be going.

"I want to die at home. I've only been lingering because I just can't bear the thought that it's the last time you'll ever see Florence. I tried to get Flora and Philip to promise to bring you but they wouldn't. You can forget that if you like. In fact it's better if you do. If you think you'll be back next year like always."

"I could come back," Pat said. "Unless I forgot about changing trains somewhere."

"Somebody would need to go with you," Bee said. Her voice was very hoarse now. "Look, I know you'll probably forget, but I do want you to know this even if you can't hold on to it. I've arranged for what's going to happen to you after I die. You're going to go into a home in Lancaster, near Flora. I tried to get something here but you won't believe the prices in Italy. And you've forgotten Italian and the nurses wouldn't speak English, so England is probably better."

"Near Flora," Pat said. "Not so far from Philip too. It won't be so bad."

"Jinny has promised to come over and help you move," Bee said. She scrubbed away a tear. "I could keep on looking after you at home and bringing you here every summer forever if it wasn't for this stupid stupid cancer. It's the worst thing about dying. I've had a good life, with you and the children and my work. It would have been better if I'd kept my legs, but I've managed without. I made the serum for the elm trees. I made plants that are being used in space."

"You've done a lot, accomplished really important things," Pat said. "And we've been so happy." She reached across and took Bee's hand, Bee gripped it firmly.

"We have been happy," Bee said.

"And I know you'd have kept on looking after me," Pat said. "Couldn't we just . . . drive the car off a cliff somewhere on the way home? Wouldn't it make more sense? For both of us?"

"I wish we could," Bee said. "But we flew, remember? And Cambridge is rather lacking in cliffs."

"But I could linger on for years," said Pat, appalled.

"I know. I'm sorry. Look, tomorrow is our last day. You should do all your special Florence things. We both should. For the last time."

"Yes, we must, all our special things," Pat said. Then she was quiet for a while, though she kept her grip on Bee's hand. "Bee? I hope I forget."

32

Google: Trish 1998–2015

The next time George and Sophie came home from the moon they took the twins back permanently. The twins were eleven, ready to start secondary school. She had hoped they might go to the excellent local schools in Lancaster, but George had heard from Cathy and didn't regard her as really capable of looking after the twins any more. "I've found schools for them in Cambridge where they can go in as day pupils when we're home and board when we're not. They can come here, or to Helen's, for holidays." George was being brisk with her and the children. He was probably right that she wasn't capable. "I know it's been a lot to ask of you, Mum," meant that. She was being punished for forgetting about Jamie by losing the twins. Or maybe she was imagining it, maybe this would have happened anyway.

"They will come to see me?" she asked, hearing herself sounding pathetic and cutting herself off.

"Of course, Mum, we'll all come to see you."

"How will you manage, Gran?" Rhodri asked as his father was taking an armload of bags to the car.

"I've got the Mac all set up," she said. "And Bethany will be here. Your dad's right, you shouldn't really be helping me."

"We liked it," Rhodri said.

With that she had to be content. She wrote it down in the diary program on the Mac so she could remember it, or at least look at it and see it again. She emailed Rhodri and Bronwen, and they emailed her—at first frequently and then less often as they settled into their new schools and got used to living with their parents again.

The Mac and Bethany mostly kept her on track, but she got caught out now and then. She'd be told something, write it down, and forget to transfer it to the computer. Then she'd forget all about it. Helen was used to her, but Cathy and George only visited occasionally and were shocked.

They might have let her carry on living at home if it hadn't been for the university expansion. The government were funding extra places at all universities, and Lancaster was taking advantage of that to build new libraries and lecture theaters and halls. Bethany was planning officer of the new Green-dominated council, and she told Trish all about it, sometimes several times. The problem was that the university didn't have enough space in the halls of residence for all the new students. They hadn't even had enough room for all the students they'd had before. Students had always lived in town, and in Morecambe, and in the countryside around. But now there was a new influx, and housing was in demand. House prices rocketed. Trish's house, which they had bought in 1968, had been fully paid off since 1988. It had always been too big for most people, but it was now worth a fortune to the developers.

"Have you thought of moving somewhere smaller, Mum?" Helen asked.

"Where would I put my teapots?" Trish asked, looking at her mother's china on the open shelves.

Cathy came up and tried. "This house has appreciated a great deal. You could move somewhere small and comfortable and free up a great deal of capital."

"Anyone would know you were a banker," Trish said.

"So how about it?"

"I like this house."

Eventually the three children ganged up on her. They all sat around the kitchen table and proposed it again. "But where will Bethany go?" she protested.

"That's Bethany's problem," Cathy said.

"Bethany is part of this family too. She's been looking after me all this time. She helped bring up Tamsin and the twins."

"We're very grateful to Bethany," George said. "But she's not part of this family, and if she's hoping to gain any financial benefit beyond all the years she's been living here rent-free—"

"That's not what I meant at all," Trish said. "You twist me around."

"You sold Gran's house in Twickenham without even really asking her," Helen said. "I remember when we went down there."

"I do too," Trish said. She looked at Helen. When had she stopped being beautiful? It wasn't anything she did. She was just effortlessly lovely, all the time, until one day she just wasn't. She was the same person with the same face, but no longer a beauty. It was 2004, and Helen, her oldest surviving child, was fifty.

"You should be in a home," Cathy said.

She managed to put them off until the next weekend, and talked to Bethany. "They want to sell this house and throw you out. Is it too late for me to give it to you?"

Bethany laughed bitterly. "They'd easily find doctors to say you weren't in your right mind if you did. In fact, it would be quite hard to find anyone to say you were!"

"They don't need the money. Cathy's rich, and George is very well paid, and Helen is all right."

"Helen could do with the money. You've forgotten that Don's divorcing her." Bethany poured Trish more tea. "Remember? He found out she was having an affair with that customer in Quernmore?"

Trish didn't remember. "At her age?"

"I'm the same age as she is," Bethany said. "And you were older when you got involved with that Chinese American, what was his name?"

"Lin Da Wei," Trish said. "But we called him David. He still sends me Christmas cards, lovely American ones. He was such a nice man. Wonderful in bed."

Bethany smiled. "Good. I'm glad somebody was."

"Did I tell you about Mark?"

"You did. Please don't tell me again, I just ate."

Trish laughed. "Will you be all right?"

"I've got the money from the record, remember? It's not much, but it's my little savings. You know the food co-op only pays peanuts and the council only pays grifters. I could pay rent somewhere. There are lots of co-op houses that I'd fit into, or even communes. We don't all have to be as bourgeois as your children."

"I could give you some money without them knowing. You deserve it. I'd really give you the house if I could, so we could stay here as we have been."

Bethany looked uncomfortable. "Helen says your mother got incontinent at the end, and also terrified and aggressive."

"She did. But it was only right at the end. Oh God, I don't want to end up like that!" Trish wailed.

"You're nothing like that," Bethany said. "I don't want them to shove you in a home, but there's nothing I can do about it. You're not my mother—and my own mother I wouldn't cross the road to shake hands with. She threw me out when I was pregnant with Alestra."

"I hate to ask, considering what they're doing to you, but will you come and visit me in the place they're making me go?" Trish asked.

"I'll come as long as you keep recognizing me," Bethany said.

"That will be a long time."

Trish walked slowly and carefully down to the bank the next day and drew out a thousand pounds, the maximum withdrawal. She put it in an envelope and pushed it under Bethany's door. She did the same on each of the next six days, writing "ATM" on her lists so she wouldn't forget. When Cathy asked her the next weekend what she had done with the money she said that she couldn't remember. It was the first time she had ever used her forgetfulness as an excuse. Usually she tried to cover it up if she had forgotten. Now she knew perfectly well what she had done but Cathy had no way to know that.

The worst thing about going into the home was that they wouldn't let her take the Mac. "I need it. I need it more than anything else," she said.

Cathy wouldn't listen. "Nonsense, Mum, what do you want with that old thing?"

"I send email to Rhodri and Bronwen."

"You can send them cards when it's their birthdays."

"It helps me remember things," she begged. "My pills. I'll never remember my blood pressure pills without the Mac."

"The nurses will remind you," Cathy said.

She let her take books and clothes. Trish kept pleading for the computer. She called Helen, who she hoped might understand. Helen listened to her for a while then asked to speak to Cathy. Trish waited in anxious hope, but Cathy snapped the phone shut and tossed it down on the counter when she had finished.

"If Helen wants, she can get you a new computer. A laptop. This one with the big monitor is bigger than they'll let you have."

"But I won't know how to use the new computer," Trish said. "I understand this one."

"Helen will set it up for you," Cathy said. "Lot of nonsense anyway. I wish I could do without mine. I hate the things. Do you want to take your china?"

"Am I allowed?"

"They said small ornaments, and I think that would count," Cathy said.

Trish packed her mother's china carefully. She also took the gold disk Doug had been awarded for "Getting Married on the Moon" and photographs of all her children and grandchildren. Then Cathy helped her on with her coat—entirely unnecessary help.

The home was up on the Moor with a fine view down over Lancaster. Trish remembered when she first came to the city and learned to drive. As a supply teacher she had driven to schools in all kinds of funny places. She had looked down at the town, and the sea shining in the distance, from this very place.

When she stepped inside the home it felt like prison doors closing behind her. But they were kind, very polite. "Oh, the healthy heart diet," the nutritionist said. Trish wished fiercely that she had eaten all the things she wasn't allowed and burst her heart before she had given up her house and turned poor Bethany out.

Her room faced the back, with trees behind. It had a pale green blind and a hospital bed. There was a shelf for her knick-knacks, and a little bookshelf and an armchair. She arranged the china carefully.

"This is it, then?" she said to Cathy.

"Yes, I'm sure you'll be very comfortable. The bathroom is just outside, to the right."

"I saw it," she lied.

Helen came to see her the next day, bringing a laptop. "Cathy was right that the Mac would be too big. This is a MacTop, it's the same thing only smaller."

"Oh bless you, darling. Thank you for bringing it so quickly." It was small and folded, but it had the familiar Apple logo on it, and the aesthetics of it reminded her of her beloved Mac.

"Well, you sounded as if you really desperately wanted it. And I can still get a discount in the shop," Helen said.

"What's wrong in the shop?" Trish asked.

"Oh Mum, I've told you a million times that Don and I are getting a divorce," Helen snapped.

"Sorry," Trish said. "I'm sorry. My silly brain. I forget these unforgiveable things. I keep doing it. But the computer will help. Rhodri put all my programs on the Mac. Can you put them on here?"

"What programs?"

"My to-do list, which beeps to remind me to do things. And the diary program so I can write down things I want to re-member. Of course, all that will be on the Mac so I'll have to start again. And Safari for Google, and email."

"You won't have net access here," Helen said, then seeing the incomprehension in Trish's face. "You won't be able to go online. You won't be able to use Google or email. What did you use Google for, anyway?"

"To remember things," Trish said with all the dignity she could manage, though she was starting to cry. "You can look anything up on it, even things you didn't ever know."

"Yes, it's—I use it all the time," Helen said. "I had no idea. You were using the Mac to make up for not being able to re-member? Using Google to fill the holes?"

"Yes," Trish said. "Rhodri showed me how."

"He's a smart kid," Helen said. "That's how you stayed so functional so long. I'm impressed. They ought to write programs especially for old people. And as we get older and we already know computers, there'll be more and more use for them."

"Do you think you'd be able to set it up on here for me?" Trish asked.

"No. I'm sorry. The to-do list and the diary, yes, no problem. I might even be able to get your old diary off the Mac and transfer it for you—is there a password on it?"

"Moonday. With two Os," Trish said. "Rhodri put it on."

"Well unless Cathy has thrown it out already I'll get the diary off it and load it on here for you so you'll have what you saved," Helen said. "And I won't read it, don't worry."

"It's nothing you couldn't see. Just things I wanted to remember," Trish said. "But Google?"

"Well, as far as the internet goes, you have to be connected, and you have to pay for that. You have to dial-up to connect. There has to be a phone line. You had that at home, but there isn't any here, and I can't see how I could get them to set it up. You don't even have your own phone line. It's just not possible." Helen opened the MacTop. It played exactly the same little song on boot up as her old Mac had. Helen juggled icons and brought up the same "to-do" and diary programs that she knew.

"That's something at least," Trish said, taking it. "Thank you so much."

Helen managed to save her old diary too, and brought it in a few days later and added it to the MacTop, which meant she had that to look at when she wanted to check things.

The only problem with the MacTop, apart from the persistent lack of Google, was that there was no desk in her room, so she had to use it in the armchair, and she kept forgetting to plug it in to charge so it was often out of batteries when she wanted it.

Bethany visited her often, and so did Helen. Donna and Tony came sometimes. Tamsin came when she was at home, and Alestra called in occasionally. George and Sophie brought the twins a couple of times every year. Time passed, every day like the last. Trish grew frailer and more easily confused.

33

The Last Gelato: Pat 1998–2015

They had their last day, on which they ate so much granita and gelato that Pat was almost sick. They went to the Uffizi and stared at the Botticellis and the Raphaels. They watched the sky fade from the Piazza della Signoria, and looked up at Machiavelli's office window and the shape the Palazzo Vecchio made against the sky. Pat said goodbye to Cellini's Perseus and to the copy of Michelangelo's David. They ate dinner at Bordino's with Jinny and Francesco, and told Francesco, who was nonplussed by the story, how they had decided to conceive Jinny right there. She said goodbye to the Duomo, and at Giotto's tower Pat couldn't hold back the tears any longer. They had one very last gelato on the way back.

The next day Jinny drove them to the airport and they flew home.

A week later Philip and Sanchia got married in a registry office in Cambridge, very quietly. "Did I know this was going to happen?" Pat asked Bee.

"No, this is new," Bee reassured her.

"Stupid regulations," Philip said. "Sanchia wouldn't be entitled to any maternity leave or any benefits having a baby unless she's married."

"How did you decide which of you she was going to marry?" Bee asked.

"We did a DNA test to see who was the father, and it was Ragnar, so she's marrying me," Philip said. "That way we are all the parents."

"This was difficult for us too," Pat remembered. "Michael was wonderful."

"I don't think it's any of the government's business. All this regulation all the time. Cameras everywhere. Caring what goes on in people's bedrooms. All this talk about vice."

"The cameras are just trying to catch suicide bombers," Sanchia said.

"And when they do catch them they execute them on TV," Bee said, scratchily. "It makes me sick."

"On TV?" Pat asked. "That's awful. When did they start doing that?"

"That's your memory being merciful," Philip said.

Pat and Bee were the witnesses and the only people to attend the wedding. Afterwards the bride and groom went back to Manchester, where Sanchia had lessons to give and antenatal classes to attend. "I would stay and look after you, but the baby's due so soon, and I want to be there," Philip said.

"I understand," Bee rasped.

Bee was in too much pain from the cancer now for Pat to sleep in the same bed. Pat's small movements in the night shook the bed and woke Bee, and then she would lie sleepless for hours. So they developed a routine where Pat would cuddle Bee until she fell asleep, then she would get up and sleep in Jinny's old room. Pat managed the bedpans, under Bee's direction. "Life always comes down to bedpans," Pat said. "But it doesn't matter when there's love as well."

"Love and bedpans and Florence, that's you," Bee croaked. "Give me one of my really strong painkillers now. That's the right bottle, yes, the brown one, give it here. Plenty of them, more than enough to last."

The doctor, an old friend, stopped in regularly to check up on them. When Bee stopped being able to eat the doctor insisted that she go into a hospice.

"You need to be properly looked after," he said. "And a feeding tube. Don't tell me Pat could manage that."

"Call Jinny," Bee said to Pat as soon as he had gone.

"Flora?" Pat suggested. "She's so much nearer."

"It has to be Jinny." Jinny was Bee's natural daughter, of course, her next of kin, the only one who could make decisions for her.

Pat called Jinny in Florence, and Jinny flew home right away. Bee went into the hospice, but Jinny and Pat visited her every day. She stopped being able to speak, but her eyes were alive. She squeezed Pat's hand and Pat sat there talking to her, not knowing what she was saying really but knowing Bee was there, was listening.

Then Bee died, choking for breath, with both of them at her bedside. Pat's own chest felt tight hearing it and her heart beat faster. Now would be a good time to have another heart attack, she thought at it, encouragingly, but her heart took no notice and kept on beating.

Jinny drove Pat home, and Pat went to bed. She couldn't forget that Bee was dead, much as she would like to. She knew Bee had made a plan for what would happen next, though she couldn't remember what it was. She stared into the dark. She had cried so much that her eyes burned but no more tears came. She got up, knocking into the little table they had brought in here when Bee had been sickest. She put the light on and fumbled about for her pills. She had her blood pressure pills, and there were also some of Bee's strong painkillers left. She thought Bee might have been saving them for her, for now, making sure she knew which ones they were. She went downstairs and poured water into one of Bee's wineglasses. She swallowed all of Bee's pills and then all of hers. She sat down in Bee's green armchair and waited, trying to think of the time she had sat in the Palazzo Vecchio watching the sky darken and realizing that she loved Bee. She took down the photograph Michael had taken of Bee and the babies. She wanted that to be the last thing she saw. She crashed into the mantelpiece and fell on the rug. The pills must be taking effect, she thought. Good.

Then Jinny came in, rumpled with sleep. "What are you doing banging about down here?" Then she saw her. "No. Oh no. Not you too."

Pat tried to speak and say it was what she wanted, but Jinny took no notice. She was calling for an ambulance. Then it was hospital and a stomach pump.

When Pat woke, Philip and Jinny were arguing. "I can't believe you did that," Philip said. "It can't have been easy for her, and it was so clearly what she wanted."

"I didn't know what had happened! I thought she needed help!"

For a moment she didn't remember what had happened, and then she did. Bee was dead, and she had botched joining her. Thank you for nothing, St. Zenobius, she thought. She didn't want to open her eyes, didn't want to be alive.

"I couldn't lose them both like that," Jinny said.

Pat opened her eyes and tried to smile.

They packed efficiently for her move to the home. "It's near Flora," Jinny said.

"I think I remember that," Pat said.

"You broke the glass in this picture of Mamma and the girls," Philip said. "I'll have it mended."

"Thank you."

She took the album of pictures of all of them that Michael had taken when he was dying, and copies of her guide books. She took all her art books and boxes of English literature. She took her Life List and her birding books. She took the old green silk scarf, hardly more than a rag, that Mark had given her for Christmas in 1948, and which Bee had clung to in hospital after the accident. She let Jinny pack clothes and her mother's china. She picked up her binoculars.

"You won't want those, Mum," Philip said. "What will you do with them in a home?"

"Watch birds," Pat said.

"Oh, let her," Jinny said. "She might as well bring them if she wants them."

They drove north towards Lancaster. She told them about that time in the war when she had been held up in Lancaster and gone to Barrow-in-Furness. "Did I tell you this before?" she asked.

"Maybe when I was a little girl," Jinny said.

"I don't remember ever hearing about it," Philip said. "It's fascinating."

"I can still remember that kind of thing. I just forget new things."

"I know," he said. "Look, it won't be so bad. I'll come and see you regularly. I'll bring you anything you need. I'll bring the baby to show you."

"Has it been born yet?" she asked.

"Not quite yet," Philip said. "Any day now. That's why you're giving me a ride to Manchester, so I can be home with Sanchia while it's born."

The home stood on the moor overlooking the town and the bay beyond. It seemed clean and the nurses were friendly. Flora met them there. Pat had a room to herself, with navy blue curtains, a hospital bed, an armchair, and a little bookshelf.

Jinny arranged the books on the bookshelf and Pat arranged her mother's china on the little knickknack shelf on the wall. "I want Michael's photo of Bee there," she said.

"It's broken, remember? Philip's mending it for you."

"Oh yes." Pat had forgotten. "I keep forgetting things."

"We know," Flora said.

"It's all right," Jinny said, and Pat dissolved in tears because Jinny sounded so much like Bee saying that.

"Put my little *Madonna of the Magnificat* on that shelf," she said, when she had recovered.

"You didn't bring it, Mum," Jinny said. "But it's in the book, isn't it?"

Jinny found it in the Uffizi book and Pat looked at it, hardly able to see. How had she forgotten to bring the print?

"We're going to sell the Cambridge house," Flora said.

"Yes, and divide the money between you and Philip," Pat said, absently. That was what they had agreed.

"Well, the money may go to keep you in here. This isn't cheap," Flora said. "There used to be state homes for old people, but not any more."

"Bee's insurance will help," Jinny said. "I'll put it into an account for this."

"We're grateful," Flora said, stiffly, her back to Jinny. "It's very good of you."

"Don't be ridiculous," Jinny said. "Of course I want to help as much as I can."

Jinny went over to Pat then and hugged her. "Now Pat, you remember where the bathroom is? Just outside here to the left."

When they left Pat alone at last she sat down and wept. She couldn't remember if there had been a funeral for Bee, but she couldn't forget that she was dead. Maybe she could forget? Maybe she could pretend that she was here temporarily, that

Bee would come and rescue her? But she knew that was dangerous, because it wasn't true, and she was so unclear on what she remembered now that if she started to pretend things that weren't true she could entirely lose her grip on reality. She found her notebook and her pen. She should make a list.

"*Madonna of the Magnificat,*" she wrote. "Photo of Bee. Philip will bring."

She settled into the routine of the home. There were meals at regular times. She could see trees outside the window, and sometimes there were birds, when she could find her glasses and the binoculars at the same time. She read the chart on the end of the bed to see how confused they thought she was. She read her books, and books Flora brought her from the library. She made friends with the other residents, as best she could. She remembered her mother and tried hard not to be like that, not to attack people, not to scare them.

She became deaf and needed hearing aids, which were one more barrier to communication and one more thing for her to constantly lose. "You were lucky to be spared this," she told the photograph of Bee.

Flora visited every week, occasionally bringing Mohammed and the children. Flora also took her out sometimes—to the park, or down to the shore, and at Christmas to Flora's house. Sammy sometimes came alone, and Pat tried to be interesting when she did, telling her about Florence, showing her pictures and reminding her. Flora's family went to Turkey most summers to see Mohammed's family, but they never went back to Florence. She tried to encourage Sammy and Cenk to remember it, but she never knew how successful she was.

Sanchia's baby was a boy, Karl Ragnar. The next baby, two years later, she thought might be Philip's, but she didn't ask. That was a girl, Anna Louise. She wrote the names down and tried hard to remember them. Philip brought her mended photograph back, and she put it in the center of the shelf. He came to visit every few months but he seldom brought the rest of the family. His career as a composer seemed to be taking off, but she found it hard to keep track. She had given up on the news entirely now, especially after the nuclear exchange in the Middle East.

"They got Tel Aviv and the Assam Dam, but they didn't take out any of the Seven Wonders," Sammy told her. "Mummy said that's because of you and our grandfather."

"Bee used to say using them at all was unconscionable," Pat said. "And all the fallout."

"Well, people have them, they're going to use them," Sammy said, shrugging. She showed Pat a photograph on her phone of a boy she liked at school. "Isn't he smooth?"

Jinny had two children, a boy and a girl, Domenic Michael and Beatrice Patricia. She sent photographs of them, which Pat stuck in the back of her album with their names written on the back. It meant a lot to her that Bee had genetic descendants, however much they both had truly believed that all the children were all of theirs. Bee had been so interested in genetics—mostly plant genetics, true, but human genetics too. Jinny visited only very occasionally, because she had small children and Florence was a long way. She wrote often, and Pat treasured her letters. Jinny wrote that an elm tree had been planted in a dome on Mars in memory of Bee by one of her old pupils. Pat wrote that on all her lists so that she wouldn't forget. She did forget, but she kept finding it again. ("Was that the best you could do, St. Zenobius? Well, I suppose it was better than nothing.") Jinny sent her postcards of Florence, which she kept on her bedside table and looked at until they became crumpled and the nurses threw them away.

Sometimes she dreamed that Bee was dead and woke with

a sense of relief that it had been a dream, and then remembered that it was true. She forgot that she had tried to kill herself and wondered why she had not. She beat her head on the pillow and bit her lips, and sometimes she called out for Bee, although she knew she would not come.

34

Choices: Patricia 2015

"Very Confused Today" her notes read.

She lay face down on the bed, her eyes buried by the pillow. If she sat up and looked around she might see something to anchor her in one life or the other, her MacTop, or her photograph album, Doug's gold disk or her framed picture of Bee with the babies. Lying like this she could hold herself between them, hold all the memories, both lives, both worlds. The life where she had married Mark and the life where she had lived happily with Bee for forty years. The life where she had been Tricia and then Trish, and the life where she had been Pat. It occurred to her as she lay there that in the world where she had been Trish she could have married Bee, there had been marriage equality there from the early Eighties onwards. That was so deeply and bitterly unfair that she could hardly bear to think of it.

In the world where she married Mark, she could have married Bee. If she had ever met Bee in that world. She couldn't make it make sense. Bee had been in both worlds, though she hadn't realized it. Sophie had worked with her in both worlds. Bee's work on plants for space had been the same—but in one world it had been for an international space station and moonbase, and in the other it had been for a European one, hostile to the Russians and the Americans. She could remember both things at the same time, as if both things were true, but they couldn't be. How could it be possible?

Could Bee still be alive, in Trish's world? A Bee who had never known Pat, a Bee who still had her legs? There hadn't been a Kiev bomb so there wouldn't be any thyroid cancer. She was two years younger than Pat. But even if she was there, and alive, and if there was a way to contact her, she wouldn't know who Trish was. And she knew there was no way somebody as wonderful as Bee wouldn't have found another partner.

A nurse came in and disturbed her, giving her medication—the same medication in both worlds, the stuff that kept her traitor heart beating evenly. She took her glasses off and put them on the bedside table. That way she couldn't see anything that would tip her into one world or the other. "Lie down and try to sleep now," the nurse said.

She lay down obediently. The nurse switched off the light as she left, leaving only the little nightlight by the door, enough for her to see if she needed to go to the bathroom. Was it to the left or the right? She was perpetually confused about that.

She had been so happy as Pat. Even with everything, her life had been so good. Despite the nuclear wars and the violence and the tyranny. As well as having Bee in her life, she had had Florence. Though of course Florence must have existed in the other world as well, except that she hadn't known except in the most abstract terms. In the one world she had known Italy well, written books about it, even spoken Italian, and driven regularly through France and Switzerland. In the other she had only been out of Britain twice, once to Majorca and the other time to Boston. There was no comparison, when it came to the richness of her own life. She had no desire to be Trish, when she could be Pat. Pat and Trish both had Donne and Eliot and Marvell, but Pat had Bee and Botticelli as well.

Then she thought about her children. Which were her real children? Poor Doug and dear Helen and brilliant George and troubled Cathy? Or sensible Flora and wonderful Jinny and talented Philip? Was Sammy or Rhodri her favorite grandchild? Only one set of them could possibly be real, but which? She loved them all, and there was no real difference in the quality of her love for them. She remembered Helen nursing Tamsin and Philip asking Michael whether he was half Jewish. She loved them all and worried about them all. If she had favorites, and what mother didn't, then she had favorites in both sets.

It was when she thought about the world that she wept. Trish's world was so much better than Pat's. Trish's world was peaceful. Eastern and Western Europe had open frontiers. There had been no nuclear bombs dropped after Hiroshima, no clusters of thyroid cancer. There had been very little terrorism. The world had become quietly socialist, quietly less racist, less homophobic. In Pat's world it had all gone the other way.

She tried to imagine why. She couldn't imagine that anything she had done had changed anything. In Pat's world she had started Seven Wonders, but in Trish's world, which still had the United Nations, they had their own program like that. She had marched for peace in both worlds. She had written more letters as Trish, but surely that couldn't have achieved anything? She hadn't been important, in either world, she hadn't been somebody whose choices could have changed worlds.

But what if she had been?

What if everyone was?

She remembered years ago when George had been a boy reading science fiction, he had talked about tiny events having huge effects. A butterfly flapping its wings in Lancaster could cause a hurricane in China. He had flapped his wings like a butterfly and she had sent him out into the garden. What if her actions had been like that butterfly's wings? What if by marrying Mark she had tipped the world into peace and prosperity? Perhaps the price of the happiness of the world was her own happiness?

She groped to her feet and went over to the window. She could see the moon through the branches. Which moon was it? Were George and Sophie there, happily working on science together? Or was it the other moon, the one with the deadly cargo of rockets ready to rain down on the planet? She rested her forehead against the cold glass and tried to think. She knew she was confused. She wanted to ask somebody for help, but she knew that even the most sympathetic listener would assume she was crazy. She couldn't be sure she wasn't crazy, except that what she remembered was so completely contradictory. She remembered the United Nations calming everyone down over Suez, and she remembered the Suez war coming almost to the nuclear brink. Those things couldn't both be true. And she did get confused and she did forget things, but she didn't remember extra things.

She was just an old woman with memory problems. Or maybe two old women with memory problems. She laughed to herself. She was herself, whether she was Pat or Trish. They knew different things and cared about different people, but she was the same person she had always been. She was the girl who had stood before the sea in Weymouth and in Barrow-in-Furness, the woman who had stood before Botticelli and before hostile council meetings. It didn't matter what they called her, Patricia or Patsy or Trish or Pat. She was herself. She had loved Bee, and Florence, and all her children.

Could she slide the worlds closer together? Get rid of the wars? Or would one world end and the other go on? Would Pat's world end in fire and she would forget it and go on as Trish? Would she forget Bee and Flora and Jinny and Philip and the sky over the Palazzo Vecchio and the taste of gelato? She wondered who owned her house in Florence in Trish's world, and whether they loved it as much as she and Bee had. The door wouldn't have been widened for the wheelchair, and there wouldn't be rails in the bathroom. For that matter, who owned her Lancaster house in Pat's world? It wouldn't have her mother's ashes in the garden, or Doug's or Mark's. She felt herself drifting. She leaned harder against the cold glass to hold herself there.

As Trish she had lost all faith in God. As Pat she had gone on believing. Now she didn't know what she thought. She didn't believe in Providence, in a loving God who did what was best for everyone. That wasn't compatible with the facts. But she did remember both worlds. Maybe God, or something, wanted her to choose between them, make one of them real.

She had made a choice already, one choice that counted among the myriad choices of her life. She had made it not knowing where it led. Could she made it again, knowing?

She sat down carefully on the edge of the bed and looked up at the blur that was one moon or the other. How many worlds were there? One? Two? An infinite number? Was there a world where she could have both happiness and peace?

All those deaths, all that destruction, all those cancers, and also that slide to the right, that selfish dangerous pattern. Or the open world, the world with hope and possibilities and Google.

Mark. Those letters. How had she been so young, so naive? How had she been taken in by him? Mark or Bee. No choice, except that she wasn't choosing only for herself. And whichever way she chose she'd break her heart to lose her children. All of them were her real children.

But she took a breath and smelled again that corridor in The Pines, the smell of summer sweat, of chalk, of hot dust and iodine disinfectant. She saw the late evening sun coming in through the little window at the end and catching all the dust in its beam. She felt her strong young body that she had never appreciated when she had it, constantly worrying that she didn't meet standards of beauty and not understanding how standards of health were so much more important. She bounced a little on her strongly arched young feet. She felt again the Bakelite of the receiver in her hand and heard Mark's voice in her ear. "Now or never!"

Now or never, Trish or Pat, peace or war, loneliness or love?

She wouldn't have been the person her life had made her if she could have made any other answer.

Acknowledgments

First I must thank my husband Emmet O'Brien for love and support and putting up with me when I am writing. My aunt Mary Lace read the book as it was being written and was helpful and encouraging. I had useful conversations as it was being written with Rene Walling and Alison Sinclair. I also had a great deal of help on all sorts of odd questions from my Livejournal correspondents—papersky.livejournal.com, where I post wordcount and queries as I am going along. I really appreciate this help—there are still some things you just can't Google, and having a community to ask has meant that I have been able to come much closer to answers. Thank you.

I especially want to thank Ada Palmer for Florence, and also for being supportive and perceptive about this book both in progress and in revision.

After the book was done it was read by Caroline-Isabelle Carron, Maya Chhabri, Pamela Dean, David Dyer-Bennet, Ruthanna and Sarah Emrys, David Goldfarb, Steven Halter, S. Kayam, Madeleine Kelly, Naomi Kritzer, Marissa Lingen, Elise Matthesen, Lydia Nickerson, Emmet O'Brien, Doug Palmer, Alison Sinclair, and Tili Sokolov.

Ruthanna Emrys and Lila Garrott helped me write more confidently about sexuality. Doug Palmer was immensely helpful on matters relating to amputation. Maya Chhabri was a godsend when it came to Italian affairs. Lesley Hall was terrific on many things medical and sexual. Marissa Lingen gave me wonderful help with tech, and not the kind people usually mean when they say that.

I'd like to thank the Evans Library at Texas A&M for allowing me to do my copyedit in their space.

Patrick Nielsen Hayden and everyone at Tor have been supportive and worked hard on this book, as always. I really value that and try not to take it for granted.

Turn the page for an excerpt
from Jo Walton's next novel

Available now from Tor Books

1

APOLLO

She turned into a tree. It was a Mystery. It must have been. Nothing else made sense, because I didn't understand it. I hate not understanding something. I put myself through all of this because I didn't understand why she turned into a tree—why she chose to turn into a tree. Her name was Daphne, and so is the tree she became, my sacred laurel with which poets and victors crown themselves.

I asked my sister Artemis first. "Why did you turn Daphne into a tree?" She just looked at me with her eyes full of moonlight. She's my full-blooded sister, which you'd think would count for something, but we couldn't be more different. She was ice-cold, with one arched brow, reclining on a chilly silver moonscape.

"She implored me. She wanted it so much. And you were right there. I had to do something drastic."

"Her son would have been a hero, or even a god."

"You *really* don't understand about virginity," she said, uncurling and extending an ice-cold leg. Virginity is one of Artemis's big things, along with bows, hunting and the moon.

"She hadn't made a vow of virginity. She hadn't dedicated herself to you. She wasn't a priestess. I would never—"

"You really are missing something. It might be Hera you

should be talking to," Artemis said, looking at me over her shoulder.

"Hera hates me! She hates both of us."

"I know." Artemis was poised now, ready to be off. "But what you don't understand falls within her domain. Ask Athene." And she was off, like an arrow from a bow or a white deer from a covert, bounding across the dusty plains of the moon and swooping down somewhere in the only slightly less dusty plains of Scythia. She hasn't forgiven me for the moon missions being called the Apollo Program when they should have been called after her.

My domain is wide, both in power and knowledge. I am patron of inspiration, creativity, poetry and music. I am also in charge of the sun, and light. And I am lord of healing, mice, dolphins, and sundry other specialties I've gathered up, some of which I've devolved to sons and others, but all of which I continue to keep half an eye on. But one of my most important aspects, to myself anyway, has always been knowledge. And that's where I overlap with owl-carrying Athene, who is goddess of wisdom and knowledge and learning. If I am intuition, the leap of logic, she is the plodding slog that fills in all the steps along the way. When it comes to knowledge, together we're a great team. I am, like my sister Artemis, a hunter. It's the chase that thrills me, the chase after knowledge as much as the chase after an animal or a nymph. (*Why* had she preferred becoming a tree?) For Athene it's different. She loves the afternoon in the library searching through footnotes and linking up two tiny pieces of inference. I am all about the "Eureka" and she is all about displacing and measuring actual weights of gold and silver.

I admire her. I really do. She's a half-sister. All of us Olympians are pretty much related. She's another virgin goddess, but unlike Artemis she doesn't make a fetish of her virginity. I always thought she was just too busy working on wisdom to get involved with all that love and sex stuff. Maybe she'd get around to it in a few millennia, if it seemed interesting at that point. Or maybe she wouldn't. She's very self-contained. Artemis is always bathing naked in forest pools and then punishing hunters who happen to see her. Athene isn't like that at all. I'm not sure she's ever been naked, or even thought about it. And nobody would think about it when they're around her. When you're around Athene what you think about is new ways of thinking about fascinating bits of knowledge you happen to have, and how you might be able to fit them together to make exciting new knowledge. And that's so interesting that the whole sex thing seems like a bit of relatively insignificant trivia. So there were a whole host of reasons I was reluctant to bring up the Daphne incident with her.

But I really was burning with the need to know why Daphne turned into a tree in preference to mating with me.

I went to see Athene, who was exactly where I expected her to be and doing exactly what I expected her to be doing. She fights when she needs to, of course, and she's absolutely deadly when she does—she has the spear and the gorgon shield and she knows everything about strategy. But most of the time she's in libraries, either mortal libraries or Olympian ones. She lives in a library. It looks like the Parthenon in Athens on the outside, and on the inside it looks like . . . a giant book cave. That's the only way to describe it.

There's one short stumpy pillar just inside, where the owl sits napping with its head curled around under its wing. Generally the spear and shield and helmet are leaning against that pillar. There's also a desk, where she sits, which is absolutely covered with scrolls and codices and keyboards and wires and screens. There's exactly one beam of sunlight that comes in between two of the outside pillars and falls in exactly the right place on the desk to illuminate whatever she's using at the moment. The rest of the room is just books. There are bookcases around the walls, and there are piles of books on the floor, and there are nets of scrolls hanging from the ceiling. The worst of it is that everything is organized—alphabetized, filed, sorted, even labelled, but nothing is squared off and it all looks like the most awful mess. I never go in there without wanting to straighten it all out. It bothers me. If I'm going to see her, often I ask her to meet somewhere comfortable to both of us, like the Great Library, or the Laurentian Library, or Widener.

As I said, we make a good team—but we generally make a team as equals. I don't tend to go to her as a suppliant. I don't tend to go to anyone as a suppliant, except Father when it's absolutely unavoidable. It's rare for me to need to. And with Athene, on this particular subject, it made me deeply uncomfortable.

Nevertheless I went to her library-home and stood in the beam of light until she realized it had widened to the whole desk and looked up.

"Joy to you, Far-Shooter," she said when she saw me. "News?"

"A question," I said, sitting down on the marble steps outside, so I wouldn't have to either hover in the air or risk treading on a book.

"A question?" she asked, coming out to join me. She lowered herself to the step, and we sat side by side looking out over Greece spread out before us—the hills, the plains, the well-built cities, the islands floating on the wine-dark sea, the triremes plying between them. We couldn't actually see the triremes from this distance unless we focused, but I assure you they were there. We can go wherever we want, whenever we want, but why would we stray far from the classical world, when the classical world is so splendid?

"There was a nymph—" I began.

Athene turned up her nose. "If this is all, I'm going back in to work."

"No, please. This is something I don't understand."

She looked at me. "Please?" she said. "Well, go on."

As I said, I don't often come in supplication, but that doesn't mean I don't know the words. "Her name was Daphne. I pursued her. And just as I caught her and was about to mate with her, she turned into a tree."

"She turned into a tree? Are you sure she wasn't a dryad all along?"

"Perfectly sure. She was a nymph, a nereid if you want to be technical about it. Her father was a river. She prayed to Artemis, and Artemis turned her into a tree. I asked Artemis why, and she said it was because Daphne wanted it so desperately. Why did she want to become a tree to avoid me? How could she care that much? She hadn't made a vow of virginity. Artemis told me to ask Hera and then said maybe you would know."

Grey-eyed Athene looked at me keenly as I mentioned Hera. "I thought I didn't know, but if she mentioned Hera then maybe I do. What's at the core of what Hera cares about?"

"Father," I said.

Athene snorted. "And?"

"Marriage, obviously," I said. I hate those Socratic dialogues where everything gets drawn out at the pace of an excessively logical snail.

"I think the issue you may be missing with Daphne, with all of this, is to do with consensuality. She hadn't vowed virginity, she might have chosen to give her virginity up one day. But she hadn't made that choice."

"I'd chosen her."

"But she hadn't chosen you in return. It wasn't mutual. You decided to pursue her. You didn't ask, and she certainly didn't agree. It wasn't consensual. And, as it happens, she didn't want you. So she turned into a tree." Athene shrugged.

"But it's a game," I said. I knew she wouldn't understand. "The nymphs run away and we chase after."

"It may be a game not everyone wants to play," Athene suggested.

I stared out over the distant islands, rising like a pod of dolphins from the waves. I could name them all, and name their ports, but I chose for the moment to see them as nothing but blue on blue cloud shapes. "Volition," I said, slowly, thinking it through.

"Exactly."

"Equal significance?" I asked.

"Mm-hmm."

"Interesting. I didn't know that."

"Well then, that's what you learned from Daphne." Athene started to get up.

"I'm thinking about becoming a mortal for a while," I said, as the implications began to sink in.

She sat down again. "Really? You know it would make you very vulnerable."

"I know. But there are things I could learn much more quickly by doing that. Interesting things. Things about equal significance and volition."

"Have you thought about when?" she asked.

"Now. Oh, you mean *when*? When in time? No, I hadn't really thought about that." It was an exciting thought. "Some time with good art and plenty of sunshine, it would drive me crazy otherwise. Periclean Athens? Cicero's Rome? Lorenzo di Medici's Florence?"

Athene laughed. "You're so predictable sometimes. You might as well have said 'anywhere with pillars.'"

I laughed too, surprised. "Yes, that about covers it. Why, do you have a suggestion?"

"Yes. I have the perfect place. Honestly. Perfect."

"Where?" I was suspicious.

"You don't know it. It's . . . new. It's an experiment. But it has pillars, and it has art—well, it has very Apollonian art, all light and no darkness."

"Puh-lease." (That wasn't supplication, it was sarcasm. The last time I used the word it was supplication, so I thought I'd better clarify. But this was sarcasm, with which I am more familiar.) "Look, if you're about to suggest I go to some high-tech hellhole where they've never heard of me because it'll be a 'learning experience,' forget it. That's not what I want at all. I am Apollo. I *am* important." I pouted. "Besides, if they think the gods are forgotten, why are they writing about us? Have you read those books? There's nothing more clichéd. Nothing."

"I haven't read them and they sound awful, and the only thing I want to get from high-tech societies is their robots," she said.

"Robots?" I asked, surprised.

"Would you rather have slaves?"

"Point," I said. Athene and I have always felt deeply uneasy about slaves. Always. "So what do you want them for?"

Athene settled back on her elbows. "Well, some people are trying to set up Plato's Republic."

"No!" I stared down at her. She looked smug.

"They prayed to me. I'm helping."

"Where are they doing it?"

"Kallisti." She gestured towards where Thera was at the moment we were sitting in. "Thera before it erupted."

"They're doing it before the *Republic* was written?"

"I said I was helping."

"Does Father know?"

"He knows everything. But I haven't exactly drawn it to his attention. And of course, that side of Kallisti all fell into the sea when it erupted, so there won't be anything to show long-term." She grinned.

"Clever," I acknowledged. "Also, doing Plato's Republic on Atlantis is . . . recursive. In a way that's very like you."

She preened. "Like I said, it's an experiment."

"It's supposed to be a *thought* experiment. Who are these people that are doing it?" I was intrigued.

"Well, one of them is Krito, you know, Sokrates's friend. And another is Sokrates himself, whom Krito and I dragged out of Athens just before his execution. If Sokrates can't make it work, who can? And then there are some later philosophers— Platonists, Plotinus and so on, and some from Rome, like Cicero and Boethius, and from the Renaissance, Ficino and Pico . . . and some from even later, actually."

I was suspicious, and a little jealous. "And all of these random people in different times decided to pray to you for help setting up Plato's Republic?"

"Yes!" she sounded wounded that I doubted her. "They absolutely did. Every single one of them."

"I have to go there," I said. I wanted to try being a mortal. And this was so fascinating, the most interesting thing I'd heard about in aeons. Plato's *Republic* had been discussed over centuries, but it had never actually been tried. "Where are you getting the children?"

"Orphans, slaves, abandoned children. And volunteers," she said, looking at me. "I almost envy you."

"Come too?" I suggested. "Once you have it set up, what would stop you?"

"I'm tempted," she said, looking tempted, the expression she has when she has a new book she very much wants to read right now instead of fulfilling some duty.

"Oh do. It'll be so interesting. Think what we could learn! And it wouldn't take long. A century or so, that's all. And it'll have libraries. You'll feel right at home."

"It'll certainly have libraries. What will be in them is another question. There's some dispute about that at the moment." She stared off at the clouds and the islands. "Being a mortal makes you vulnerable. Open. Love. Fear. I'm not sure about that."

"I thought you wanted to know everything?"

"Yes," she said, still staring out.

We didn't have the least idea in the world what we were letting ourselves in for.

About the Author

Jo WALTON won the Hugo and Nebula Awards in 2012 for her novel *Among Others*. Before that, her novel *Tooth and Claw* won the World Fantasy Award in 2004. The novels of her Small Change sequence—*Farthing, Ha'penny,* and *Half a Crown*—have won widespread acclaim. A native of Wales, Walton lives in Montreal.

A tale of gods and humans, and the surprising
things they have to learn from one another

THE
PHILOSOPHER
KINGS

HUGO AND NEBULA AWARD—WINNING
AUTHOR OF *AMONG OTHERS*

JO WALTON

978-0-7653-3267-7 • HARDCOVER AND E-BOOK

Twenty years have elapsed
since the events of *The Just City*. The City
has now split into five cities, and low-
level armed conflict between them is not
unheard-of.

The god Apollo, known as "Pythias" in
the City, is now married and the father of
several children. But a tragic loss causes
him to become unhinged with grief and
consumed with the desire for revenge.

Along with his daughter, several of his
sons, and a boatload of other volunteers,
Apollo goes sailing into the mysterious
Eastern Mediterranean of pre-antiquity to
see what they can find. What Apollo, his
daughter, and the rest of the expedition
will discover…will change everything.

Praise for *The Just City*

★ "The award-winning Walton has
written a remarkable novel of
ideas that demands—and repays—
careful reading. The plot is always
accessible and the world-building
and characterization are superb. In
the end, the novel more than does
justice to the idea of the Just City."
—*Booklist* (starred review)

"Nobody writes like Walton.
The Just City manages to both
sympathize with social engineering
at the same time as it demolishes
paternalistic solutions to human
problems. In so doing, this book
about philosophy, history, gender,
and freedom also manages to be a
spectacular coming-of-age tale."
—Cory Doctorow, *Boing Boing*

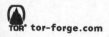

TOR® tor-forge.com